THE BOOKBINDER OF JERICHO

The Dictionary of Lost Words
One Italian Summer: Across the World and
Back in Search of the Good Life

The Bookbinder of Jericho

PIP WILLIAMS

Chatto & Windus

LONDON

1 3 5 7 9 10 8 6 4 2

Chatto & Windus, an imprint of Vintage, is part of the Penguin Random House group
of companies whose addresses can be found at global.penguinrandomhouse.com

First published in Australia by Affirm Press in 2023
First published in the UK by Chatto & Windus in 2023

penguin.co.uk/vintage

A CIP catalogue record for this book is available from the British Library

Map and map illustrations by Mike Hall

HB ISBN 9781784745189
TPB ISBN 9781784745196

Printed and bound in Great Britain by Clays Ltd, Elcograf S.p.A.

The authorised representative in the EEA is Penguin Random House Ireland,
Morrison Chambers, 32 Nassau Street, Dublin D02 YH68

Penguin Random House is committed to a sustainable future
for our business, our readers and our planet. This book is made
from Forest Stewardship Council® certified paper.

MIX
Paper | Supporting
responsible forestry
FSC
www.fsc.org
FSC® C018179

For my sister,
Nicola

~

'Now goddess, child of Zeus, tell the old story for our modern times. Find the beginning.'

Homer, *The Odyssey*, translated by Emily Wilson

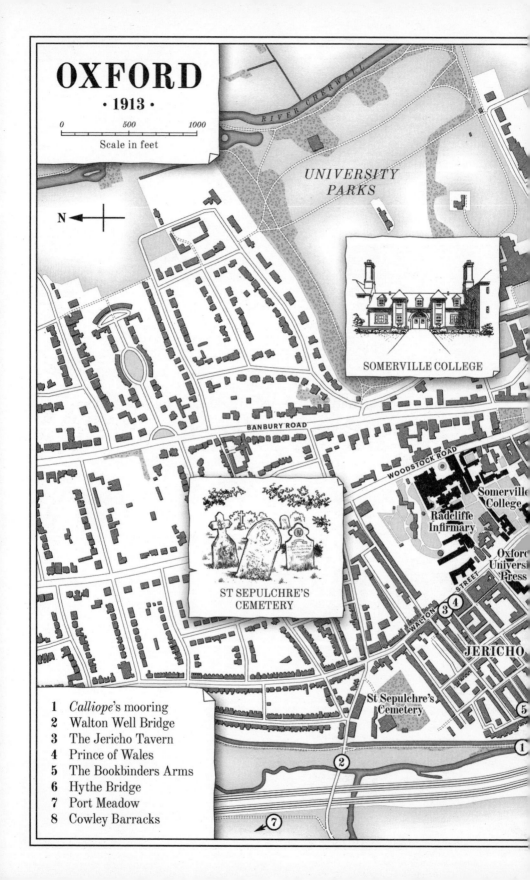

OXFORD
· 1913 ·

0   500   1000
Scale in feet

N

UNIVERSITY PARKS

RIVER CHERWELL

SOMERVILLE COLLEGE

BANBURY ROAD

WOODSTOCK ROAD

ST SEPULCHRE'S CEMETERY

Somerville College

Radcliffe Infirmary

Oxford University Press

WALTON STREET

JERICHO

St Sepulchre's Cemetery

1 *Calliope*'s mooring
2 Walton Well Bridge
3 The Jericho Tavern
4 Prince of Wales
5 The Bookbinders Arms
6 Hythe Bridge
7 Port Meadow
8 Cowley Barracks

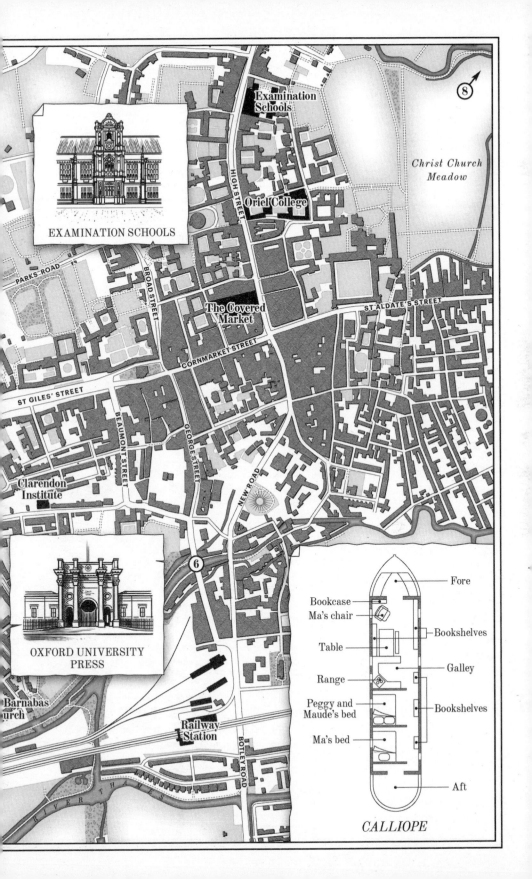

EXAMINATION SCHOOLS

OXFORD UNIVERSITY
PRESS

Examination
Schools

Oriel College

Christ Church
Meadow

PARKS ROAD

BROAD STREET

The Covered
Market

ST ALDATE'S STREET

CORNMARKET STREET

ST GILES' STREET

BEAUMONT STREET

GEORGE STREET

NEW ROAD

HIGH STREET

Clarendon
Institute

Barnabas
urch

Railway
Station

BOTLEY ROAD

RIVER THAMES

8

6

Fore

Bookcase

Ma's chair

Bookshelves

Table

Galley

Range

Peggy and
Maude's bed

Bookshelves

Ma's bed

Aft

CALLIOPE

Before

Scraps. That's all I got. Fragments that made no sense without the words before or the words after.

We were folding *The Complete Works of William Shakespeare* and I'd scanned the first page of the editor's preface a hundred times. The last line on the page rang in my mind, incomplete and teasing. *I have only ventured to deviate where it seemed to me that …*

Ventured to deviate. My eye caught the phrase each time I folded a section.

Where it seemed to me that …

That what? I thought. Then I'd start on another sheet.

First fold: *The Complete Works of William Shakespeare.* Second fold: *Edited by WJ Craig.* Third fold: *ventured to* bloody *deviate.*

My hand hovered as I read that last line and tried to guess at the rest.

WJ Craig changed Shakespeare, I thought. Where it seemed to him that …

I grew desperate to know.

I glanced around the bindery, along the folding bench piled with quires of sheets and folded sections. I looked at Maude.

She couldn't care less about the words on the page. I could hear her humming a little tune, each fold marking time like the second hand of a clock. Folding was her favourite job, and she could fold better than anyone, but that didn't stop mistakes. *Folding tangents*, Ma used to call them. Folds of her own design and purpose. From the corner of my eye, I'd sense a change in rhythm. It was easy enough to reach over, stay her hand. She understood. She wasn't simple, despite what people thought. And if I missed the signs? Well, a section ruined. It could happen to any of us with the slip of a bonefolder. But we'd notice. We'd put the damaged section aside. My sister never did. And so I had to.

Keep an eye.

Watch over.

Deep breath.

Dear Maude. I love you, I really do. But sometimes … This is how my mind ran.

Already I could see a folded section in Maude's pile that didn't sit square. I'd remove it later. She wouldn't know, and neither would Mrs Hogg. There'd be no need for tutting.

The only thing that could upset the applecart at that moment was me.

If I didn't find out why WJ Craig had changed Shakespeare, I thought I might scream. I raised my hand.

'Yes, Miss Jones?'

'Lavatory, Mrs Hogg.'

She nodded.

I finished the fold I'd started and waited for Mrs Hogg to drift away. *Mrs Hogg, the freckly frog.* Maude had said it out loud once and I'd never been forgiven. She had no trouble telling us apart, but as far as Mrs Hogg was concerned, Maude and I were one and the same.

'Back in a mo, Maudie.'

'Back in a mo,' she said.

Lou was folding the second section. As I passed behind her chair, I leant over her shoulder. 'Can you stop for a second?' I said.

'I thought you were desperate for the lav.'

'Of course not. I just need to know what it says.'

She paused long enough for me to read the end of the sentence. I added it to what I knew and whispered it to myself: '*I have only ventured to deviate where it seemed to me that the carelessness of either copyist or printer deprived a word or sentence wholly of meaning.*'

'Can I keep folding now, Peggy?' Lou asked.

'Yes, you can, Louise,' said Mrs Hogg.

Lou blushed and gave me a look.

'Miss *Jones* ...'

Mrs Hogg had been at school with Ma and she'd known me since Maude and I were newborns. Still, Miss *Jones*. The emphasis on Ma's maiden name, just in case anyone in the bindery had forgotten her disgrace.

'Your job is to bind the books, not read them ...'

She kept talking but I stopped listening. I'd heard it a hundred times. The sheets were there to be folded not read, the sections gathered not read, the text blocks sewn not read – and for the hundredth time I thought that reading the pages was the only thing that made the rest tolerable. *I have only ventured to deviate where it seemed to me that the carelessness of either copyist or printer deprived a word or sentence wholly of meaning.*

Mrs Hogg raised her finger, and I wondered what response I had failed to give. She was going red in the face, the way she invariably did. Then our forewoman interrupted.

'Peggy, as you are up, I wonder if you could run an errand for me?' Mrs Stoddard turned a smile on the floor supervisor. 'I'm sure you can spare her for ten minutes, Mrs Hogg?'

Freckly frog nodded and continued down the line of girls without another glance at me. I looked towards my sister.

'Maude will be fine,' said Mrs Stoddard.

We walked the length of the bindery, and Mrs Stoddard stopped occasionally to encourage one of the younger girls or to advise on posture if she saw someone slouching. When we got to her office, she picked up a book, newly bound, lettered in gold so shiny it looked wet.

The Oxford Book of English Verse, 1250–1900. We printed it almost every year.

'Has no one written a poem since 1900?' I asked.

Mrs Stoddard suppressed a smile. 'The Controller will want to see how the latest print run has turned out.' She handed me the book. 'The walk to his office should relieve your boredom.'

I held the book to my nose: clean leather and the fading scent of ink and glue. I never tired of it. It was the freshly minted smell of a new idea, an old story, a disturbing rhyme. I knew it would be gone from that book within a month, so I inhaled, as if I might absorb whatever was printed on the pages within.

I walked back slowly between two long rows of benches piled with flat printed sheets and folded sections. Women and girls were bent to the task of transforming one to the other, and I had been given a moment's reprieve. I started to open the book when a freckly hand covered mine and pushed the book shut.

'It won't do to have the spine creased,' said Mrs Hogg. 'Not by the likes of you, Miss *Jones*.'

∽

I took my time walking through the corridors of the Clarendon Press.

Mr Hart had a visitor: her words were escaping the privacy of their conversation. She was young, well spoken, with a faint hint of the

Midlands. I lightened my tread so as not to scare the words into silence.

'And what does your father think?' asked Mr Hart.

I paused just outside the office door. It was half-open and I could see her fashionable shoes and slim ankles below a straight lilac skirt. A long matching jacket.

'He was reluctant but eventually persuaded.'

'He's a businessman. Practical. He didn't need a degree to make a success of milling paper. He probably can't see the point for a young woman.'

'No, he can't,' she said, and I felt her frustration. 'So I must show him the point by making it worthwhile.'

'And when will you come up to Oxford?'

'September. Just before Michaelmas term. I'm coming up to Somerville, so we'll be neighbours.'

Somerville. Every morning, I imagined leaving Maude at the entrance to the Press and walking across the road and into the porter's lodge of Somerville College. I imagined the quad and the library and a desk in one of the rooms that overlooked Walton Street. I imagined spending my days reading books instead of binding them. I imagined, for a moment, that there was no need for me to earn an income and that Maude could fend for herself.

'And what will you read?'

There was an answer on the tip of my tongue, but the young woman stole it.

'English. I want to be a writer.'

'Well, perhaps one day we will have the privilege of printing your work.'

'Perhaps you will, Mr Hart. I look forward to seeing my name among your first editions.'

There was a hush, not uncomfortable, and I knew they were looking at the Controller's bookshelf, at all the first editions with their pristine leather spines and gold-leaf lettering. The book in my hand asserted itself. I'd almost forgotten why I was there.

'Give my regards to your father, Miss Brittain.'

'I will, Mr Hart.'

The door swung open and I had no time to step back, so for a moment we stood eye to eye. Miss Brittain might have been nineteen or twenty, twenty-one perhaps, the same age as me. She was my height and just as slender, and she was pretty, despite her mousy hair. Lilac suited her well, I thought, and I wondered what she might think of me. Pretty, no doubt; everyone said so. Hair as dark as the canal at night and eyes to match, like Ma's. Though my nose was different: a little too big. I might not have been so conscious of it except I saw it in profile when I looked at Maude.

It was just a moment, but sometimes that's all it takes – I could see there was something steely in Miss Brittain's expression: a determination. We could be friends, I thought.

She seemed to know better. She was not rude, but there were protocols. She saw the apron of a bindery girl over a plain brown cotton-drill skirt and a wash-worn blouse, sleeves rolled up to the elbows. She smiled and nodded, then walked away along the corridor.

I knocked on the open door and Mr Hart looked up from his desk. I'd been nine years at the Press and never seen him smile, but one now lingered around the corners of his mouth. When he realised I was not Miss Brittain returned, it retreated. He motioned for me to come in but returned his attention to the ledger on his desk.

My ten minutes had run down, but it was not my place to interrupt. I looked beyond Mr Hart and out the window. There she was, Miss Brittain, crossing Walton Street. She stopped on the pavement and looked up at the windows of Somerville College. She stayed there for some time, and people were forced to walk around her. In that moment, I felt her excitement. She was wondering if one of those windows would be hers. She was imagining the desk overlooking the street and all the books she would read.

And then there was a tightness in my chest. A familiar resentment. Perhaps Mrs Hogg knew the truth of things and I had no right to read the books I bound, or imagine myself anywhere but Jericho, or contemplate for one moment that I could ever have a life beyond Maude. The book started to feel heavy in my hands, and I was surprised I'd been entrusted with it at all.

And then I was angry.

I opened *The Oxford Book of English Verse* and heard the spine crack. I turned the pages – John Barbour, Geoffrey Chaucer, Robert Henryson, William Dunbar, Anonymous, Anonymous. If they had names, might they be Anna or Mary or Lucy or Peg? I looked up and saw the Controller staring at me.

For a moment I thought he might ask what I thought. But he simply held out his hand for the book. I hesitated and he raised his eyebrows. It was enough. I put the book in his hand. He nodded and looked down at his ledger.

Without a word, I was dismissed.

PART ONE

Shakespeare's England

August 1914 to October 1914

Chapter One

The paperboys shouted the news all over Jericho; our walk to work was noisy with it. 'Defend Belgian neutrality,' Maude repeated. 'Support France.' She said it all, just as the paperboys did, over and over.

When we stopped at Turner's Newsagency to collect our post, the counter was crowded with people buying newspapers.

'Nothing this morning, Miss Jones,' Mr Turner said when he finally saw me. I picked up a copy of the *Daily Mail* and handed over a halfpenny. Mr Turner raised his eyebrows; I'd never bought the paper before. *Waste of a halfpenny*, Ma used to say. There were always papers lying around at the Press.

Maude scanned the front page as we walked along Walton Street. '*Great Britain declares war on Germany*?' It was a headline and a question – she was confused by the celebrating of young men and the worry she saw on the brows of their mothers. But was she asking what war would mean for England or what it might mean for us?

'We'll be all right, Maudie.' I squeezed her hand. 'But some things may change.' I hoped they would and felt a little guilty, but not a lot. Maude continued to scan the newsprint.

'*Practical hats at popular prices*,' she read aloud. It was her habit, ever since she'd learnt to read. It was a skill hard earned, and although she didn't care to read a book, she loved headlines and cartoons – words already arranged and ready to use.

We joined the mass of men and women, boys and girls, flowing through the stone arch of the Clarendon Press. We walked through the quad, past well-tended garden beds, the copper beech and grand pond, into the south wing of the building – the Bible side, we called it, though Bibles were now printed in London. Once inside, all the vestiges of an Oxford college gave way to the sounds and smells and textures of industry. We stored our bags and hats in the cloakroom in the bindery, took clean aprons from their hooks and made our way through the girls' side. The tables were piled high with text blocks in need of sewing, and the gathering bench was arranged with sections ready to be collated into books.

The folding benches were arranged in three long rows with room for twelve women along each. They faced tall, undressed windows, and morning light spilled over quires of flat printed sheets and piles of folded sections from the day before. Lou and Aggie were already in their places at one end of the bench directly under the windows. Maude and I sat between them.

'What have they given us today?' I said to Aggie.

'Something old,' she said. She never cared what.

'You've got bits and pieces from *Shakespeare's England*,' said Lou. 'Proof pages. They'll take you five minutes. Then there's his complete works to keep you going for the rest of the day.'

'The Craig edition, still?'

She nodded.

'Surely everyone in England has a copy of that by now.'

I pulled the first proof sheet in front of me and picked up Ma's bonefolder. No one else liked folding proof pages – there were never enough to get into a rhythm – but I loved them. And I especially loved them when they kept coming back. I'd look for the changes that had been made to the text and congratulate myself if I'd anticipated them. It was a small achievement that kept the monotony of the day from sending me mad. Mrs Stoddard made a point of giving me the proofs, and everyone was grateful.

I cast an eye over the printed sheets from *Shakespeare's England: An Account of the Life & Manners of His Age*. They were chapter proofs and likely full of errors. One I'd seen before – an essay about booksellers, printers and stationers. I'd been caught reading it the last time it came through – 'Your job, Miss Jones …' – but it was worth the reprimand. It was about us, what we did here at the Press and how in Shakespeare's day it had been dangerous to print a book considered obnoxious to the Queen or the Archbishop of Canterbury. Off with their heads, I'd thought at the time. The other proof chapters were new: 'Ballads and Broadsides', 'The Playhouse', 'The Home'. There were fewer than there should have been. If *Shakespeare's England* was to be ready for the three hundredth anniversary of the Bard's death, all the proof pages needed to be coming through now.

The last printed sheet was the first proper draft of the preface. I looked to see where Mrs Hogg was hovering. She was by the gathering bench, checking that the trays of sections were in the correct order. I brought the preface to the top of the stack of sheets and read a few lines: *Those who want to know what Shakespeare thinks must not neglect what his fools say.*

It was enough to keep me going. I took up the right edge of the sheet and brought it to the left, lining up the printer's marks just so. I ran Ma's bonefolder along the crease to make it sharp.

First fold. Folio.

I turned it. Took up the right edge and brought it to the left. It was double the thickness and there was a slight increase in resistance.

I adjusted the pressure on Ma's bonefolder – instinct, not thought. I made the crease sharp.

Second fold. Quarto.

Ma's bonefolder. I still called it that despite its being mine for the past three years. It was nothing more than a flat bit of cow bone, rounded at one end and with a point at the other. But it was silken smooth from decades of use, and it still held the shape of her hand. It was subtle, but bonefolders, like wooden spoons and axe handles, wear the character of their owner's grasp. I'd taken up Ma's bonefolder before Maude could claim it. I'd wrestled with the way it felt in my hand the same way I'd wrestled with Ma's absence. Stubbornly. Refusing to yield.

Eventually, I'd stopped trying to hold it my way, and I'd let the bonefolder settle into my palm as it had once settled into Ma's. I'd felt the gentle curve of the bone where her fingers had lain. And I'd sobbed.

Mrs Stoddard rang her bell and I let the memory go.

'There's to be a parade,' she said. 'A farewell for the Press men who are in the Territorial Army and others who've managed to volunteer since the announcement was made.'

The *announcement*. She couldn't get her tongue around *war*, not yet.

There were more than fifty of us bindery girls – the youngest twelve, the oldest beyond sixty – and all of us followed Mrs Stoddard through the corridors of the Press as if we were schoolgirls on an excursion. When our chatter became too much, our forewoman stopped, turned and held a finger to her lips. Like schoolgirls, we obeyed, and only then did I understand what this war might mean for us: the print house was utterly silent. The presses had been stopped. I'd never known it to be quiet and was suddenly unnerved. We all felt it, I think, because our chatter didn't resume until we came into the quadrangle. Six hundred men and boys were already gathered there. Mrs Stoddard ushered us forward, and I realised that almost every family in Jericho was represented.

There were machine minders and compositors, foundry men, mechanics and readers. Apprentices, journeymen and foremen alike. They were gathered in groups according to their occupation; the state of their aprons and hands made it easy to recognise them. They filled the spaces between the Bible side and the Learned side, around the pond, between the garden beds and all the way back towards the house where Mr and Mrs Hart lived. We'd never gathered like this, and I was impressed by our number; then I realised that at least half the men were of fighting age, or soon would be. I studied the crowd.

Older men passed the time in quiet conversation; younger men were more animated, some congratulating friends, others boasting that the Kaiser didn't stand a chance.

'It's bound to last more than a year,' I heard one lad say.

'I hope so,' said his friend.

They were barely sixteen.

Two foremen, dressed in the uniform of the Territorial Army instead of their Press aprons, tried to bring the younger recruits into line, but the lads were bursting with details of the night before. Those who'd been outside Buckingham Palace held court. They told of the crowd and the crush, the countdown to midnight, the cheers when it was clear the Kaiser would not retreat from Belgium and that England would go to war. 'It's our duty to defend Belgium,' said one, 'so we sang "God Save the King" at the top of our lungs.'

'God save us all,' said a gravelly voice behind me. I turned and saw old Ned shaking his head. He removed his cap and held it to his chest, his gnarled and ink-stained fingers worrying the fabric. When he dropped his head, I thought it was in prayer.

Then a voice, clear and familiar. Maude singing 'God Save the King' at the top of her lungs.

'That's it, Miss Maude,' shouted Jack Rowntree.

Jack was our neighbour on the canal, an apprenticed compositor. He'd be a journeyman in three years if nothing changed. He stood in the centre of the quad with all the others who'd joined the Territorial Army over the past few months in anticipation. I thought about the picnic we'd had just a few days before. A cake for his eighteenth birthday, a game of charades.

'Don't encourage her, Jack,' I shouted, but he held his hands up as if he had no choice and began to conduct. Maude kept singing and the lads took up the verse. There was the assured voice of a tenor, then a baritone. Soon the rest of the Press choir joined in, and the quad resounded like a concert hall. The foremen gave up their efforts to have the recruits fall into line. They folded their arms until the anthem had been sung to the end. The last notes hung in the cool air for a full minute, undisturbed.

Then one of the foremen shouted to the men to form two lines. His voice was more commanding in the hush, and the men did as they were asked. But it was not as soldiers might. There was quiet jostling and adjusting, and a couple of lads swapped places to be near their mates. Before they'd settled, Mrs Stoddard directed us bindery girls to arrange ourselves on either side of the parade. 'It's a pretty face they want to see when they march out of here,' she said, 'so be sure to keep smiling.'

Lou was the first to sob. Other girls sought out their beaus in the line and blew kisses. Some brought out handkerchiefs to wave or wipe their eyes. The apprentices stood taller. One or two suddenly looked pale. Jack caught my eye and I expected some smart comment, but it didn't come. He just nodded and smiled a little. Then he turned his face forward.

I counted sixty-five recruits. Some were grey at their temples, their faces lined with life. But most were young, and too many were yet to fill out. Mr Hart strode across the quad with Mr Cannan, the Press Secretary, the master of us all. We rarely saw him among the paper and the ink and the presses, but there he was, scanning the rows of men, calculating, perhaps, what the war might cost the business of the Press. He saw a man he knew and stepped towards him, shook his hand.

'His assistant,' whispered Aggie. 'He'll have to write his own letters now.'

Cannan stepped back as Mr Hart spoke to one of his foremen. Two puny youngsters were pulled from the parade. They tried to protest, but there was no point. I wondered what adventure they thought they'd miss out on. Then the Controller stood on a box and said something fitting – I can't recall what. There'd been rain overnight and it clung, here and there, to leaves and stone. It darkened the gravel beneath our feet. I wondered who would make us laugh if Jack went away, who would lug our water and seal our leaks. I wondered who would take over his work in the composing room. If all these men left, *Shakespeare's England* might never be finished.

The morning sun reflected in a puddle. An old boot splashed it away. I looked up. The men were marching out through the stone archway into Walton Street. Everyone was clapping, calling after them.

'Come home safe, Angus McDonald,' a bindery girl shouted, her face wet with emotion.

'Come home safe, Angus McDonald,' repeated Maude. Angus McDonald blew her a kiss and Maude blew one back. His sweetheart scowled at my sister, but there was no need. From then on, Maude blew kisses to them all.

When the last of the men had disappeared into the street, we fell quiet. We formed awkward groups around the quad, and one or two foremen looked at their pocket watches, anticipating a late finish. The Controller and the Secretary were talking in low voices, both frowning. Mr Hart looked towards the archway and shook his head.

Mrs Stoddard was the first to mobilise. She clapped her hands. 'Back to work, ladies,' she said. Mrs Hogg led the way.

The foremen followed suit, and all the remaining men returned to their jobs: to the machine rooms and type foundry, the composing room and paper store, the reading rooms, depot and the men's side of the bindery. Not one was spared the loss of a well-trained man.

Only the girls' side of the bindery would be fully staffed from now on, I thought. I fell back to walk with Mrs Stoddard. 'Who's going to fill all the vacancies?' I asked.

'Bright young women, if those in charge have any sense and the unions allow it.' She glanced sideways. 'There are no restrictions on women working in administration, Peggy. You could consider applying for something.'

I shook my head.

'Why not?' Mrs Stoddard said.

I looked to Maude.

'Why not?' Maude said.

Because you need me, I thought. 'Because you'll miss me,' I said.

Mrs Stoddard stopped walking and looked me in the eye. 'The door will not stay open for long, Peggy. You must try to slip in while you can.'

∼

I tried to slip in during my afternoon tea break.

The presses had resumed, but the noise faded as I moved along the corridors. Then the smells of machine oil and gas lamps, and the low-tide fishy smell of glue, were replaced by wood polish and a hint of vinegar. I took the letter I'd written from the pocket of my apron and read it. It was neat and without error, a convincing application. But my hand shook as I knocked on Mr Cannan's door.

It was answered by a young woman.

'Can I help you?'

She had the same nose as her father, the same cultured speech. I'd heard she was a poet. She held a bundle of papers in her hand and I realised she had come to assist. Of course she had. She had the right education and all the time in the world. It made perfect sense.

'Is that for Father?' She nodded at my application letter.

I shook my head and backed out. 'I'm in the wrong place,' I mumbled as I closed the door.

I ripped my letter in half, turned it, ripped a second time, turned it, ripped a third time. Then I walked back towards the low-tide fishy smell of the bindery.

Chapter Two

The sense of celebration was still there as we walked home through the streets of Jericho.

'God save the King,' someone said as they passed us.

'God save the King,' Maude said in return.

We crossed Walton Well Bridge and came down onto the towpath, overgrown and chattering with the buzz and chirp of summer. For a moment I could smell the canal, the cloying stench of waste – human, animal, industrial – but I was used to it and it seemed to fade as we walked towards home, though I could see its rainbow shimmer on the surface of the water. Maude slowed to pick some colour – meadowsweet, willowherb and butterfly bush. 'A posy for Rosie,' she said.

There were only two narrowboats moored within sight of the St Barnabas belltower: *Staying Put* and *Calliope*. *Staying Put* was like a carnival, painted with flowers and castles and flourishes of all kinds. Rosie Rowntree kept it clean and bright, and she surrounded it with live blooms throughout the spring and summer. She had geraniums in pots on the roof and she'd planted a verge garden with flowers and vegetables. It extended two boat-lengths along the towpath and was a welcome mooring for her husband, Oberon, when he was able to stop with his working boat and spend the night.

'God save the King,' said Maude as we approached.

'Good to see you home,' said Old Mrs Rowntree, Rosie's mother-in-law. She was sitting among pots of lettuce and sweet pea, the *Oxford Chronicle* in her lap, the page trembling as she turned it. 'There'll be carousing tonight. Best you're out of it.'

Rosie was tending a trellis of runner beans that leant against the hull of *Staying Put*. Her son had marched off to war, and when she turned I saw all the emotion of the day in her face. Her voice tried to contradict it.

'Over by Christmas, they say.' She was nodding. Encouraging agreement. Maude held out her posy, untied and leggy, and Rosie took it as a mourner might. I didn't know what to say.

'It is what they say,' said Old Mrs Rowntree.

It was a relief to look upon *Calliope*. She was dark blue with gold lettering, like the binding of an Oxford World's Classic. She was practically touching *Staying Put*, and the closeness had always felt like a comfort. I held open the hatch for Maude and stepped in after her.

Calliope smelled a little sweet after having been shut up all day. A little earthy. The hatch swung closed behind me and I breathed it in. *It's the smell of books*, Ma used to tell people when they asked. *It's the paper decomposing.* They'd screw up their noses and Ma would laugh and say, *I've come to love it.*

Ma had brought two books with her when she first moved onto *Calliope*: translations of *The Odyssey* and *The Tragedies of Euripides, Volume II*. They'd belonged to her own mother and were worn from reading. Her collecting had only started after we were born. She picked up books at curiosity shops and fêtes, and sometimes she bought them new – Everyman's Library editions for a shilling each. Most, though, were from the Press. They were bound but they had defects. Whenever

I asked if she'd been given permission to bring one home, she'd never quite answer. *It's waste*, she'd say. *Not good enough to sell*. Then she'd hand it to me. *But good enough to read, don't you think?* I always said yes, though when I was small I could barely understand a word of them.

Ma stored her books on a row of narrow shelving that ran between the windows, bow to stern. When those shelves were full, Oberon Rowntree built her another row. Soon after that, he built another. When we were ten years old, he told her a fourth row of shelves could not be accommodated, so Ma bought a small bookcase from the bric-a-brac woman at the Covered Market. It had been dragged from the river at low tide and looked worthless, but Ma cleaned it, then sanded it, then oiled it. She placed it beside her armchair, just inside the hatch, then she filled it with her favourite novels and all her Greek myths. *Why do we have so many books?* I liked to ask. *To expand your world*, she would always say.

When she died, my world shrank.

That was when my own collecting began. Unbound manuscripts, parts of books, single sections. Pages with no clue as to the title or author. In three years our shelves had lost their order. *Calliope* became messy with fragmented ideas and parts of stories. There were beginnings with no endings and endings with no beginnings, and I stored them wherever they would fit and in plenty of places they didn't. They were tucked between bound volumes and piled under the table. A few sewn manuscripts with no boards rested in the plate rack above the galley bench.

Finally, there were pages I didn't care for. We cut them square and stored them in an old biscuit tin that we kept on the table. While I cooked, Maude folded them into all manner of shapes. Folding, for her, was like breathing, and she'd been doing it since she was little. For as long as I could remember, her creations had been strung around *Calliope* like bunting.

I removed my hat and put it on the hook by the hatch door. Then I took the few steps to the table where Maude was already sitting, already folding. I removed her hat too.

She was making a fan.

'Good idea,' I said. It was warm.

She nodded.

I hung her hat beside mine, then went to the galley and unwrapped the kippers we'd bought on the way home. I revived the coals in the range and, when the plate was hot enough, placed the frying pan on top. I began to sweat.

'Can I have that fan when you've finished?' I said to Maude.

She passed it across the counter that separated the table from the galley. Everything in *Calliope* was within arm's reach, and it took no more than a few steps to go from sitting room to galley to our bedroom and then Ma's. We called them rooms, but they were just spaces defined by their function. I fanned my face.

'Come home safe, Angus McDonald,' Maude said.

'Do you even know who Angus McDonald is?'

She shook her head.

'Open the hatch,' I said.

'Let in some air,' she finished.

From the galley, I watched her fasten one door open, then pick up *A History of Chess* to hold the other door in place. I waited for her usual comment.

'Needs fixing,' she said.

The hatch had needed fixing for a while, but *A History of Chess* seemed more than adequate. And there was something about picking it up, placing it, then removing it when we closed ourselves in. The weight of its nine hundred pages. Knowing Ma had folded some and that we had folded others. That Ma had sewn the text block together and her friend Ebenezer had knocked it back and cased it and covered it in leather – blue, like *Calliope* – with *A History of Chess* embossed in gold leaf. *It didn't pass inspection,* Ebenezer had said when he handed it to me. I'd thought he might cry, so I'd looked at the book instead. There was nothing wrong with it as far as I could see. Ma had been dead a month.

I opened the galley window and air moved through *Calliope*. A paper bird fluttered. It was Tilda's, the one with the broken wing.

Tilda was Ma's dearest friend. When Ma had died, Tilda stayed – just long enough for me to start crying and Maude to start talking again. She'd made that first Christmas bearable, and that first New Year. She'd left us to cope on our own for the first few months of 1912, then turned up for Easter. A few months later she'd got us through Ma's birthday, and when we'd turned nineteen she'd arrived with a cake. On the anniversary of Ma's death, Tilda had brought soda water and Stone's Original Green Ginger Wine. *Your Ma had a taste for it,* she'd said, then poured us each a glass of soda and added a good splash of the ginger wine. We'd drunk it like it was lemonade. *They're over,* she'd said, filling our glasses a second time – not bothering with the soda. *All the firsts. The first Christmas, Easter, birthday. The first anniversary of her death.* She'd clinked her glass against ours and drunk. *There'll be no more and you can start living without her.* It wasn't entirely true, but I was glad she'd said it. It felt like permission.

Tilda was an actress and a suffragette. She came and went as she pleased or needed, and the last time we'd seen her was last spring, a few days after we'd turned twenty. She hadn't mentioned our birthday, but she'd sat with Maude all evening, folding pages, then she'd hung their paper sculptures from the curtain rail above the galley bench as if she were decorating for a party.

I put my hand to Tilda's bird. Rag paper. Strong. Despite the wing, she'll fly for a while yet, I thought, and I was glad of it.

Maude sat back down to her folding and picked up the conversation where she'd left off.

'Come home safe,' she said. 'Come home safe.'

'Come home safe, Jack Rowntree,' I finished.

'Jack Rowntree.' She nodded. 'Come home safe.'

I took napkins and cutlery from the drawer and put them on the table. Two glasses and the jug. Nearly empty, but enough for the two of us. I'd fill it later. The rain overnight would have topped up the barrel. Maude put her papers aside and fingered the lace around the edge of her napkin. It was stained yellow with age. She laid it flat on the table and folded it in half.

'Granny's napkins,' she said, folding it again, then bringing one corner towards another.

'A wedding present,' I said.

She liked this conversation, and I had stopped resisting it. *Pretend you're on the stage*, Tilda had once said. *Deliver your lines each night with the same enthusiasm. Your audience will be putty in your hands.*

'From old aunt whatshername,' said Maude, folding the napkin this way and that until it was something else.

'A book would have been more useful,' I said.

'Can't blow your nose on a book.'

Ma used to say the last line; now it was Maude's. She picked up a knife and fork and placed them inside the pouch she'd just made. Then she started on the other napkin.

I drained the kippers and fried cold mash left over from the night before.

'Jack Rowntree, come home safe?' she said.

A question I didn't know how to answer. But if I didn't answer, she might repeat it over and over.

'He'll be safe enough while he's training,' I said.

'I'll miss your singing.'

'Did he tell you that?'

She nodded.

'Maybe when you think of Jack you can sing one of his favourite songs,' I said, and immediately regretted it.

'*After the ball is over, after the break of morn ...*'

I lifted the fried potato from the pan to our plates and wondered if Tilda had been in London for the countdown to war. I took the plates to the table.

'Nothing green,' said Maude.

I'd meant to boil beans. 'We'll live,' I said.

'Not as long.' Ma's refrain.

~

8 August 1914

Hello Pegs,

What a time! Of course I was in London. It was quite a party, though I'm still not sure why. Some men hardly need an excuse to behave badly and as far as excuses go, war is a good one. I was grabbed by no fewer than six men and three managed to plant a kiss, more or less successfully. They were all young and ready to sign up (which I suppose is why I let the better-looking lads have their way). They were gathering ladies' favours, like knights of old.

I think it was inevitable that we'd get involved — we're obliged, after all, and the news from Belgium has been awful — but I couldn't quite imagine what it would feel like. I'm going to be honest, Pegs, it feels bloody exciting. I'm weary, you see, of our other war. On that front we seem as far from victory as ever. Asquith has become immovable on votes for women and morale is low among the ranks of the WSPU.

But now we have a distraction. Mrs Pankhurst thinks the war could be our Trojan horse and she's already mobilising her troops. She was furious when Millicent Fawcett declared the suffragists would suspend all political activity for the duration. Panky knows our tactics won't find many supporters while a real war is raging, but she can't abide just giving it up. And it's not in her nature to follow the NUWSS into a polite peace. You wait, Pegs, she'll find a way to keep us in the papers.

Tell Maude I've been practising my folds and am close to perfecting the swan. I have enclosed my latest attempt and though I am proud of it I expect she will be scathing.

Tilda x

Chapter Three

Over the next few days, Jericho lost the air of celebration but not the anticipation. Small groups gathered outside shops and on street corners, their outrage and fervour echoed in the paperboys' chants. The words fell like snowflakes onto Maude's tongue. *Invasion, barbarians, our duty,* she said. *Poor bloody Belgians,* she said. They stuck for a moment, then were gone. More than one conversation agreed with Rosie Rowntree: *Over by Christmas,* most were saying. *Over by Christmas,* Maude repeated.

On Saturday afternoon we took the motorbus out to Cowley – it would go past the barracks, and I was curious. The motorbus was full of young men, fathers with grown sons, a few couples. I recognised four printers' apprentices as they bounded up the stairs to the top deck. The motor growled as we climbed the hill to Temple Cowley, then it turned onto Hollow Way and slowed.

'Litter, litter everywhere,' Maude said, and I looked out at what she saw.

Not litter. Men. *Kitchener's army,* the papers called them. They were everywhere they shouldn't be. They stood along the verges smoking and talking. Some sat with their heads resting between their knees.

Some slept beneath the hedge. Two were brawling, then a third joined in. The top deck erupted in cheers and encouragements. The closer we got to Cowley Barracks the more littered the road became. It was as if some great wind had swept across Oxfordshire and collected men from fields and factories and high streets, then let them fall like leaves around the keep of the barracks.

We stopped, and the motorbus bounced as the young men from the top deck flew down the stairs. The apprentices passed by our window. They blew kisses to Maude, and Maude blew kisses back. An echo, that's all. Nothing in it. We watched them join the queue of men waiting to enlist. So many were underfed, undersized. They had sallow faces and missing teeth. How could they win a war? I thought. And for the first time, I was anxious.

The motorbus continued on Hollow Way and we saw tents beyond the hedgerow, a man shaving, another with his shirt off, washing.

'They've been here for days,' I said.

'For days,' said Maude.

'But why?'

'Remember Belgium.' A poster she'd seen.

'Half of them have no idea where Belgium is.'

'An adventure,' she said. 'A chance to do something important. My ticket out of this place.' Things she'd heard.

$\sim$

On Monday morning, Maude and I ran late, and by the time we arrived at the bindery, most of the girls were at their stations. I looked around for the freckly frog and braced for a dressing-down. But it was Mrs Stoddard who raised her brows and looked at the large clock that marked the passing of our days. I relaxed.

'Mrs Hogg has gone with Mr Hogg to Cowley Barracks,' she said. 'She'll be back before morning tea. In the meantime, you're gathering

Shakespeare with Louise and Agatha.' Then she turned to my sister with a gentle smile, conspiratorial. 'Don't let her get distracted, Maude.'

Maude straightened. 'Gather, not read,' she said.

A frown troubled Mrs Stoddard's brow. 'Did you speak to Mr Cannan, Peggy? About the vacancy?'

'I tried,' I said, 'but that door had already closed.'

$\sim$

After lunch I stood on one side of the gathering bench, opposite Aggie. Piles of sections stretched along both sides, along an upper and a lower tier, waiting to be gathered into *The Complete Works of William Shakespeare*. It was an enormous book, made up of eighty-five sections, give or take, each folded thrice to make sixteen pages.

I fingered the section that brushed my thigh. The front pages. It would be the last I gathered but the first to be read. It included the title page, a list of illustrations and the contents – *The Tempest, The Two Gentlemen of Verona, The Merry Wives of Windsor* – the rest of the plays and all the poems. I swiped a section from the top tier onto my left forearm, took a step to the left and swept up the next section, then the next. It took a few moments to get my rhythm – for my body to remember the dance. Then I was moving along the length of the long bench, my legs crossing one in front of the other, my hand a blur as it passed over the piles of sections. The click of my heels and the swish of paper created the music I moved to. The hubbub of the bindery fell away, and if my hips moved more than necessary, well, who could say for sure that the movement didn't increase my speed?

I swept the front pages onto the pile in my arm – I had half of a single book – and gave the pile to Maude. She tapped each edge against the table, then married my sections to those being gathered by Aggie on the other side.

I looked to my partner across the gathering bench – the slightest of nods – then off we went for another turn of the dance floor.

Every title section signalled a complete block of text, and Maude piled one atop the other. There were fifteen before I paused to check that she had not been diverted from her task – my sister's hands also had a habit of dancing, but to a tune all their own. The text blocks were all perfectly neat and tidy, and if nothing interrupted Maude, they would continue to be.

Mrs Hogg had returned and she rang the bell for the first shift to take their tea. We were in the second shift and my rhythm barely faltered. Then she barked a warning for any girl who dared return late. It sounded sharper than usual, and I assumed the army had accepted Mr Hogg, despite his wife's protests.

I finished my lap and put the pile of sections in front of Maude. I removed my cardigan.

'It's warm,' I said. 'All this dancing.'

'Warm.' She nodded as she tapped the edges. The text blocks were beginning to overwhelm her workspace.

'Stop for a minute, Maudie,' I said. I looked for Lou and saw her returning from the sewing machines with an empty trolley.

'Do you have another load for me, Maude?' Lou asked.

Maude held up a fan. She'd unfolded the last section I'd gathered – once, twice – then let her fingers dance around until the section was something useful.

'It's warm,' she said, handing Lou the fan.

'Maudie —' I began.

'Just what I need,' said Lou. She took the fan and moved it in front of her face – enough so we all felt the breeze. Then she passed the fan to me. 'Sometimes I think you put her up to it, Peg.' She smiled.

Lou began her check of each new text block – an expert flick through the section. If they were in the correct order and the right way up, she'd initial the last page and pop it on the trolley headed for the machine sewers.

I looked around the bindery. Mrs Hogg was instructing one of the newer girls, and Mrs Stoddard was in her office.

'Lavatory break, Aggie. If anyone asks.' I picked up the text block that belonged to Maude's fan and walked towards the cloakroom. In truth, I could have taken just the ruined section – the rest of the block was perfect – but what use did I have for just the title and contents?

I put Shakespeare in my bag.

When it was our turn for tea, I went to find Eb in the book repair room on the men's side of the bindery.

Ebenezer was a quiet man, short-sighted and kind. Too kind, it was often said, and most called him Scrooge on account of it. His quiet generosity had spared almost all his co-workers some inconvenience at one time or another – to their pride or to their pocket. He noticed errors before the foreman: just a nod and a word and no one would know. His apprentices were the most competent, and two had risen to be his foreman. Mr Hart had stopped asking Eb to apply for more responsibility. *It's not in my nature to take charge,* I'd heard him say to Ma. When I'd asked her later if that was why they'd never married, she shook her head. *He's asked three times,* she said, *but I don't love him in the right way.* She'd had the courage to say no, but she liked him enough to let him keep loving her.

'Waste,' I said, handing the text block to Eb. 'Could you trim it?'

'Waste, indeed,' he said as he made the text block square on his small guillotine and trimmed away the folds.

~

Butterflies slowed our pace along the towpath – meadow browns and common blues busy among the tall grass and nettles, the folds of their wings irresistible to Maude. Then I saw a painted lady, her black and orange markings like an exotic mosaic. We'd had a warm summer and so here she was. She. The painted lady always reminded me of Tilda.

Rosie and Old Mrs Rowntree were sitting on deckchairs in Rosie's verge garden.

'Welcome home, girls,' Rosie said. 'We've been waiting for you.' She pointed to two empty chairs and held up a pot of tea.

Maude stepped between flowerpots and hugged Rosie. She bent to kiss the cheek of Old Mrs Rowntree. Two shaky hands held Maude's face.

'Yours is a smile to chase away woe, Miss Maude.' Then Old Mrs Rowntree patted the chair beside her. 'Tell me about your day.'

Maude offered up fragments of conversation and Old Mrs Rowntree nodded and exclaimed in all the right places.

'I'll join you in a bit,' I said to Rosie.

'Take your time,' she said.

Back on *Calliope*, I took the text block from my bag and went to sit on our bed. I fanned through the pages.

We already had Shakespeare – sonnets, plays – individually and as collections. But we didn't have the complete works. There'd never been the money, or the opportunity. Still, it was so big I needed to inspect it before deciding if it was worth sewing and giving a berth.

I liked the introduction, and when I turned to the sonnets, something about the typeface drew my eye along. I read a few and decided I'd keep the lot. I left the text block beside my sewing frame on the table, grabbed two shawls and went to join the others.

'I lost myself in the fine words of Mr Shakespeare,' I said, to account for the time I'd taken. I put a shawl across Maude's shoulders and sat in the empty chair.

'Which words, Peg?' asked Old Mrs Rowntree.

'The sonnets.'

'I like the sonnets,' she said. 'More than the plays.'

'Do you have a favourite, Ma?' asked Rosie.

'*Weary with toil, I haste me to my bed, but then begins a journey in my head.*' She frowned, shook her head. 'I used to know it by heart.'

'You would have had cause to recite it when you were younger, Ma.'

'It wasn't really about hard work,' said Old Mrs Rowntree. 'It was about missing someone you love. About how their face comes to you in the dark and quiet of night and starts you thinking.'

She looked down at the blanket on her knees and tried to adjust it, but her right hand began its violent shake. Maude put her own hand on top of the old woman's and smiled when the shaking stopped. Then Old Mrs Rowntree placed her left hand on top of Maude's, and Maude accepted the invitation to play. Rosie and I watched as their hands slipped from bottom to top, getting faster and faster until Old Mrs Rowntree declared Maude the winner.

~

Night took its time to fall, and Maude refused to go to bed while she could still see what was beyond the windows of our narrowboat. I set up my sewing frame, positioning it so I had one arm on either side, like a harpist might sit with her harp. While Maude folded butterflies, I bound one section after another to the cords.

When I reached *The Taming of the Shrew* I put down my needle and palm shield and massaged the muscle between my thumb and forefinger.

'I'm weary with toil,' I said.

'Haste me to my bed,' Maude said, not looking up from her folding.

I watched her hands sculpt the paper into a butterfly with wings that slid over each other, as in life.

You are my toil, I thought as I rose from the table. I pulled a section from the pile I had not yet bound, then kissed Maude's crown and whispered, 'Haste us to our bed, the world has gone dark.'

Later, when Maude's breath had lengthened into sleep, I took up the loose section of *The Complete Works*. There was light left in the candle, so I read Old Mrs Rowntree's sonnet. Number twenty-seven. The old woman had remembered it right – if not the whole verse, at least the sentiment. And I wondered how many nights the Rowntrees would have to journey in their heads before this war was fought and Jack was home.

The candle guttered and I snuffed it.

Chapter Four

Summer mornings had no manners; they slipped beneath our curtains and roused a winged chorus, and I was awake long before I wanted to be. But Maude slept on, the trill and coo, the caw and quack no match for the depths of her slumber.

I retrieved the section of sonnets I'd been reading the previous night, but I only read one before I felt the wash of the canal against *Calliope*'s hull. It felt like we were being rocked in a cradle.

'Oberon,' I whispered into Maude's ear.

'Caressing *Calliope*,' she said, without opening her eyes. It's what Ma would say when our boat undulated with the tide.

We lay there until the undulations stopped and it was easier to walk around. There was more movement than usual, and I made a mental note to tighten *Calliope*'s ropes.

It would take the Rowntrees a little while to encourage *Rosie's Return* into her mooring, but when it was done there'd be coal for our coal bin and bacon for breakfast. While Maude emptied our chamber-pots, I made the bed. Then I set the kettle on the hot plate and measured enough coffee for five into a muslin bag. Maude returned with the pots and put them beside our bed.

'Wash your hands, Maudie' – I nodded at the wash basin – 'and your face, and anything else that needs it.' We were twenty-one and she still needed reminding.

I poured boiled water over the muslin bag and set the pot on the hob to keep warm. By the time I was dressed, the coffee was brewed and Oberon was knocking on our hull – two quick raps, no more than needed. *Sums him up,* Ma once said, and Rosie had added that he was no taller or fatter than he needed to be, and economical with both words and bad tempers: *No one better to share a small space with,* she'd said, and they'd laughed.

I opened the hatch and Oberon gave me a nod. Then he passed me a pail full of coal. I emptied it into the coal bin under the stairs leading to the foredeck. It was barely half-full.

'Can you spare another?' I asked as I handed the pail back.

'Spare another,' said Maude.

'I can,' he said.

'You can always refuse,' I said.

He smiled and cocked his head towards *Staying Put*. 'Not worth her wrath.' Then he looked up to the heavens. 'Or hers.'

Maude returned to the galley and came back with a mug of coffee. She handed it to Oberon just as Rosie appeared on the towpath, wearing her heavy pleated skirt, high-laced boots and a boatwoman's black bonnet. It's what she'd worn when she and Oberon had worked the waterways together. It's what her mother had worn and her grandmother.

She missed the waterways, she'd told me. She missed Oberon. He was the son of a bindery girl and a paper mill worker; he hadn't been born to a life on the waterways, like Rosie had, but he'd die working them, she was sure of that. Rosie would have too, if she'd had the choice. But their first baby had been sickly. It had made sense for Rosie to stay put. *Just for a while,* she'd told Oberon, and he'd painted

37

Just for a While on the hull of their butty boat. He converted it from cargo to a full cabin, anticipating a brood of babes, and Rosie made it a home. Then he sold their horse and put an engine in their lead boat so it could fly along the Grand Union Canal, day and night. After the baby died, Rosie wanted to join Oberon again, but Old Mrs Rowntree's hands had begun to shake too much to fold sections, and she couldn't hold a kettle without scalding herself. Rosie refused to move to land so Old Mrs Rowntree moved on board. When Rosie had Jack, she asked Oberon to rename their narrowboat *Staying Put*.

Now Oberon delivered coal and bricks for Pickfords. His relentless schedule meant he could only sleep on *Staying Put* one night a month, a little longer if his boat needed repairs. But he stopped for breakfast once a week, usually on Sundays.

'Give me that,' said Rosie, holding her hand out for the empty pail. She took it along to *Rosie's Return*, lifted the tarpaulin and skimmed more coal.

When the business of the coal was done, Rosie led Oberon back towards *Staying Put*. A tub of hot water was waiting, and a clean shirt and corduroys had been laid out. She wouldn't give him breakfast until the working week had been scrubbed from his skin. There was always enough bacon for Maude and me.

After breakfast we sat in Rosie's verge garden, and Oberon read out the headlines from the *Oxford Chronicle*: '*Germans sack Louvain, Oxford to take refugees, Fashion and Foibles, Country Notes, Health and Home.*'

'Fashion and foibles,' Old Mrs Rowntree suggested. 'What's the topic this week?'

'Secrecy,' Oberon said.

I expected something about local gossip.

'*War is always a stern God,*' Oberon began, '*but he never offered such a face of steel – especially to you women – as he does today. Your men leave you – you know not where – you may hear from them but their* letters contain no postmark and they do not contain a word of what you would most like to know ...'

'Health and home,' Rosie interrupted, her hands waving away the words, stopping Oberon mid-sentence. She stood and gathered up our mugs. Mine was half-full but I let her take it.

Oberon moved his attention to the topics in the Health and Home column. '*Nerves, Need for economy* or *More rules*?' he asked.

Rosie smiled down at him. 'Nerves, obviously.'

Oberon read: '*Women and weaklings are the only folks who receive sympathy for the ailments lumped under the label "nerves".*'

Rosie scoffed and Oberon paused. She gave a slight nod and he continued.

'*When the strong man's nervous system gives way, he is generally reckoned a bit of a humbug. Yet if a motorcar develops a flaw ...*'

Rosie retreated into *Staying Put* and Oberon paused again.

'Go on,' said Old Mrs Rowntree.

We listened to the end, and Oberon moved on to local news, correspondence, advertisements for specials on groceries – it was all about the war, even when it wasn't.

When it was time for Oberon to leave, Rosie joined him on *Rosie's Return*. She stood proud at the stern, her hand on the tiller, and they moved slowly along the canal towards Wolvercote. We all knew the routine – it hadn't changed for twenty years. After a mile or two he'd let her off and she'd walk back along the towpath.

We sat with Old Mrs Rowntree in the verge garden, waiting for Rosie's bonneted silhouette to come towards us. She never looked so confident as she did on those mornings. But on this morning, she faltered. Her face softened, and she sped up. I looked in the other direction and saw Jack – long strides, an unmistakable smile. He'd been at Cowley Barracks for just a few weeks, but we greeted him like he'd just returned from Mons.

We didn't realise how much we'd missed him, and we each tried to make up for his absence. Rosie fed him too much and Old Mrs Rowntree kept him close, her shaking hand stroking his, like it was a cat. I talked too much about changes at the Press: who else had signed up, who'd tried and failed. Life on the girls' side of the bindery was exactly the same, I told him.

Only Maude was herself, and when he was left alone for a few moments, Jack found her on *Calliope* and they sat quietly – her folding, him watching. He set up the chessboard and they had a game, barely a word.

He took his leave after supper and I think he was relieved to return to Cowley – our attention and constant handling seemed to have frayed his edges. We stood on the towpath and watched him walk back towards Oxford. He grew taller with each step, unbending himself after the smallness of *Staying Put*.

~

13 September 1914

Hello Pegs,

When I told your ma I would stay in touch with you girls, I was thinking Christmas cards, the odd postcard. I was not thinking letters and I would never have guessed I'd write two in as many months. This is a record for me. I don't even write to my brother as often. I'm selfish, you see. Your ma knew it, my brother knows it, all my friends know it. Deep down, you know it.

Now, to the point of this letter (my hand is already cramping). You haven't met my brother, but you can trust me when I say Bill is the kindest of men and the idea of going off to Belgium or France to shoot Germans does not appeal to him at all. Anyway, some silly girls in the WSPU pinned a white feather on the lapel of his jacket while he was waiting for a tram. He removed it but enough people saw. Someone actually spat on him.

I have objected to this new activism and been put in my place. It's part of a deal Mrs Pankhurst has made with the government — in exchange for the release of all the suffragettes currently in gaol, the WSPU will actively support the war and help boost recruitment. Feathers, it seems, are to be part of the arsenal that will be fired at pacifists, the indifferent and the scared. I like Mrs P less and less but can't help admiring her. It's been an effective strategy — Bill signed up the next day. His wife was delighted. I was not. I have left the WSPU.

Regrets? Of course. I am still a foot soldier to the cause (the original cause, the one where you and Maude and I get the vote). Do you know, the first time I met you was at a WSPU meeting in Jericho? Helen brought you along. It was you and Maude I noticed first, of course. Peas in a pod. Fifteen or sixteen, I can't remember, but you'd not been long at the bindery. When I asked Helen why she'd come, she looked at you, then she looked at Maude. When she looked back at me her eyes were full of grief. Grief, Peg. I'll never forget it.

Anyway. Seems it is indulgent to grieve for our marginalisation now there is a war on. I tried going back to the stage but the only parts I was offered were 'Nanny' and 'Old whore'. I might have taken the part of 'Old whore', but when I asked the director how old the whore actually was, he said, 'Thirty-five, but she's had a hard life. You could pull it off.'

I walked straight from the theatre to the office of the Red Cross and put my name down to join the Voluntary Aid Detachment. (I took five years off my age and said I was thirty-three. The clerk didn't bat an eyelid.) I'm doing my VAD training at St Bartholomew's in London. I have to pass first aid, home nursing and hygiene before they can sign me up, but it's all a bit of a doddle. Your ma thought I'd make a good nurse. Excellent bedside manner and a strong stomach, she said. I did love nursing her, Peg. It was the least selfish thing I've ever done. And now look at me — writing letters when I could be out at a party.

I'll come and stay before I start my training. Not sure exactly when but you'll know when I turn up.

Tilda x

P.S. My note to Maude includes a request for a paper heart. It's for Bill. I intend to pin it to the lapel of his uniform when he gets leave from training. Remind her, will you?

I remembered that WSPU meeting. After it was over, Ma had invited Tilda back to ours for supper. She'd called out to Rosie to join them and while they settled in Rosie's verge garden I made tea and buttered bread. I heard them talking, like old friends, and wondered what made them laugh. As the kettle heated, I stood by our open hatch and listened. Tilda was doing impersonations of men saying awful things about women. *Empty-headed. Emotional. Temperamental. Ignorant. They would weaken Great Britain if allowed to vote.* She used different voices, and I was convinced there were other people out there. 'Put simply,' Tilda said, her voice deep, her accent as posh as that of a Gown from Balliol, 'women have smaller brains. It would be unfair to tax them with the rigours of voting.'

'But not unfair to *actually* tax them,' Ma said, and Tilda laughed and Ma joined in and there was something musical about it.

When I took out the tray, Ma was laughing so hard she was barely able to pick up the teapot. Tilda insisted she sit down. Then she insisted I sit down. She took up the pot and poured three cups. She handed one to Rosie, then one to Ma, then one to me. When I said I'd get another cup, she waved the suggestion away and took a small flask from a bag that held all the pamphlets she hadn't managed to give away after the meeting.

'Tea does not agree,' she said, smiling. She drank from the flask then offered it to Ma, who held out her cup. Tilda poured the liquor into Ma's tea, then Rosie's.

I held out my cup. 'Just a drop,' I said. 'I have to work in the morning.'

And then it was *me* making *her* laugh. She looked at Ma, who nodded, then she poured the whiskey into my tea. Maude was on *Calliope*, folding, but if she'd been there, Tilda would not have offered. If she had offered, Ma would have shaken her head. I sat with them till the tea went cold and Tilda's flask was empty.

'Maudie,' I said. 'Tilda wants you to make her a love heart.'

Maude nodded. Her note from Tilda was open and already read, and the square of red paper Tilda had included was half-folded in front of her. I sat and watched her hands moving in ways I hardly understood.

'For Bill,' she said. 'The kindest of men.'

~

In bed, I read Tilda's letter again. A VAD. A volunteer nurse. A new life, decided on a whim. *Remind her, will you,* Tilda had written, and my jaw clenched. Remind her to fold a heart, brush her teeth, wear a hat, put on a coat when the weather turned cold. *She'll need someone,* Ma had said between painful breaths. So don't go, my mind had screamed.

A new life, I thought. 'I'm not going anywhere,' I said, to the indifferent night.

Chapter Five

Maude and I were taking our tea break in the quad, making the most of a weak autumn sun. All around us the trolleys trundled; reams of paper went in one direction, boxes of books in another. A boy with limbs like twigs dragged his load as if it were a stubborn mule. Two older lads teased him as they passed, their own loads delivered. For a moment I could imagine that the Kaiser hadn't invaded Belgium and that Britain had no obligation to go to war, that the Press was at full capacity and nothing had changed.

But the quad was not quite as busy as it had been just months before, and the boys seemed younger, the men older. It seemed a long time since we'd seen Jack striding between the pond and garden beds for a quick hello.

Someone else was striding towards us, though. Jack's foreman. A good sort, Jack liked to say. He stopped a few feet from where we sat and looked from me to Maude, then back again. My sister and I were identical in almost every way, but our gaze betrayed the difference. Maude's gave the impression she was daydreaming or disinterested, even if she looked you in the eye. Mine was suspicious and there were lines between my brows that did not exist on Maude's face.

Most people took less than a second to work out who was who.

'It's Peggy, isn't it?' said the compositor.

'It is, Mr Owen.' I took a bite of my biscuit.

He turned to Maude, who was looking just beyond him. 'And you must be Maude. I'm Gareth. I work with your neighbour, Jack.'

She met his eye. 'Over by Christmas,' she said, then she watched his mouth for a response.

'I hope so,' he said.

'I'll miss your singing,' she said. If I had to guess, I'd say she was focusing on his beard, noticing the grey woven through the black. Listening to every word.

I watched the compositor's face, curious how he would interpret my sister's expression.

He didn't miss a beat. 'He *will* miss your singing. He told me so himself.'

Maude nodded as if it were natural that she should be a topic of conversation between Jack and his foreman.

Mr Owen turned back to me. He hesitated. I was intrigued.

'Maude,' I said, 'do you think Mr Simms will let you pick a posy for Rosie?'

'A posy for Rosie,' Maude said with a nod, as I knew she would. She went over to where the gardener was clipping a hedge.

It would have been easy enough to ask Mr Owen to sit, invite him to speak, but I just took another bite of my biscuit.

He lifted his cap and swept a hand over mostly black hair. Long fingers, quite beautiful but marred by the bulbous thumb of a seasoned compositor. He replaced the cap. Glanced around. I made no effort to put him at ease.

'Do you mind if I sit?'

I shifted along the bench. We sat at either end.

'Jack said you might be willing to help with a project of mine.'

'Did he?' I took a sip of my tea. It was cold. I took another sip, as if it wasn't.

'He said you have a fondness for the books we churn out.'

Bloody Jack, I thought.

'He thought you might be interested in a book I'm typesetting.' Again, the hand through the hair. This time he kept the cap off. Held it against him like a man asking for pennies. 'It's a book of words.'

'They usually are.'

He laughed, put on his cap. 'Women's words. A friend has been collecting them, writing them down. Giving them meanings.' He was smiling, despite himself.

'Sounds like a dictionary.'

'That's exactly what it is.'

My veneer of disinterest cracked a little.

'But the words won't be in the New English Dictionary,' he said.

'I thought every word was going to be in the New English Dictionary?'

'I thought so too, but Esme ...' Did he blush? 'That's to say, Miss Nicoll, works in the Scriptorium where the words are defined. She says that some will be left out.'

He paused and searched my face. There was something about his account that was familiar. Tilda had a friend – 'my wordy friend' she called her. I tried not to let my interest show.

'It will be a gift,' he said.

'A gift?' And there it was, curiosity, in my voice and the widening of my eyes. I tried to tame it, Maudify it, but he'd already noticed. His smile broadened.

'She doesn't know about it.'

A secret, of course, and a declaration of love. He wanted to win her over with this gift, shore up their relationship. Everyone was doing it in one way or another: lovers were proposing, fathers were passing on pocket watches and sage advice, mothers were knitting thick socks and vests (they might not be able to protect their boys from the Hun, but they sure as hell could protect them from the cold). They were battening down the hatches the way we did on *Calliope* when we knew a storm was coming.

'I can typeset it,' he said, 'and print it, but Jack suggested …'

'What did Jack suggest?' It was sharper than I intended; Jack knew about the pages I brought home from the bindery. The thought he might have told his foreman made me furious.

Mr Owen leant back a little. Weighed his words. 'Jack's been helping me. Double-checking the type. And Ned has set up a small letterpress so I can print the pages. It's all happening after hours.'

'By which you mean … ?'

'The Controller doesn't know about it.'

I felt my pulse quicken, as it so often did when I read a page I wanted to keep – desire and risk. I looked around the quad. The gardener was tying string around Maude's posy.

'Go on,' I said.

'Well, once it's printed, I'll need to fold the sheets, gather them, sew them. I'll have one set of pages, so I want to do it right. Jack said you might like to help.'

'He did, did he? Mr Hart would have my wages if I got caught.'

'I reckon you might be right, but Jack's exact words were: "Peggy'll throttle me if she's not part of this".'

'Women's words, you say?'

Mr Owen smiled.

'What's so funny?'

'That's the hook, Jack said. "She won't be able to resist."'

Dear Jack, I thought. How I missed him.

'What do you say?' he said.

'I'll have to find a way around Mrs Stoddard.'

Maude came back with her posy. Mr Owen stood up to let her sit down.

'Thanks, Peggy,' he said.

'I can't promise anything, Mr Owen.'

'Call me Gareth.'

I nodded, but I wouldn't.

~

Dictionary fascicles came through the bindery on a regular basis. I looked forward to them, and Mrs Stoddard rostered Maude and me onto folding whenever they came through. Folding allowed my eye to linger for a moment, and as the pages piled up I could memorise a word and its meaning. By the end of a shift I could tell you when it was first written down and recite the sentence it was used in. Maude enjoyed my attempts at Chaucer. 'Gibberish,' she would say. She never asked what it meant.

I was working on *Sorrow to Speech*, proof pages that needed folding and cutting but would never be bound or covered. I wondered what errors the readers might find, what words the editors would take out, what additions they might make. The final pages would likely come through in a few weeks, and if I was tasked with folding them again, I'd test my memory.

I chose a word. *Spalt*. There were a few senses, but the one I liked meant a silly or foolish person. I read the quotation: *I can no wayes excuse those Gossips ... who are rapt in the companie of certaine Spalts*. It was obsolete, according to the proof, but I could think of more than one in the bindery who'd fit the description. I folded once, twice – quarto. Then I slid the next sheet of pages in front of me.

It had been a week since I'd spoken to Mr Owen, and I'd been thinking of the best way to help him. I could do most of the work at home, but I doubted Mr Owen would let the pages out of his sight, and it wouldn't be right inviting him to *Calliope*. If Mrs Stoddard turned a blind eye, we could easily fold, gather and hand-sew the sections on the girls' side. But to trim and cover we'd need to use the men's side.

I decided to ask Ebenezer.

Our day ended an hour earlier than the men's – a concession to the work that awaited most of us when we got home. I left Maude to help Mrs Stoddard close shutters and turn down lamps. Then I went to find Eb.

The men's side sounded different, smelled different. The whispering of paper and the constant hum of sewing machines were replaced with the irregular rhythm of guillotines and the mechanical construction of boards. The smells of oil and glue filled the air: the low-tide fishy smell. In the moments it took to adjust, I imagined one of the books that was just then being trimmed, or glued or knocked back, being read. Reading was such a quiet activity, and the reader in their parlour or leaning against the trunk of a tree would never imagine all the hands their book had been through, all the folding and cutting and beating it had endured. They would never guess how noisy and smelly the life of that book had been before it was put in their hands. I loved that I knew this. That they didn't.

The door to the book repair room was open, and I could see Eb leaning into his task. I waited, not wanting to cause a slip. The room was small, no machines. He did everything the way it had been done for centuries. There was space for two, and sometimes an apprentice would stand alongside him, or I would be called in from the girls' side to resew an old book by hand, like Ma used to do. Eb could sew as well as any of us, but it was considered women's work by the unions, and by most of the men. Today, he was alone.

The bench was littered with the tools of his trade. Bonefolders of various shapes for page folding and leatherwork, brushes for glue and glaire and gilt, tools for decorating leather and cloth, a gilding cushion, linen, tape and shears. My sewing box was where I'd left it the last time I'd been there. It held needles, thread and cord, a leather thimble and palm shield. Ma had made them for me when I'd begun to sew.

There were three books on Eb's bench – likely from a college library or a country home. Two were in a state of undress, their new casings and red Morocco leather laid neatly beside them. The other was dressed, and Eb was in the process of finishing.

I stood at the open door and watched him wipe a swatch of old leather over his hair, then use it to pick up a leaf of gold. It fluttered as it was lifted by the static, but it kept its shape. He laid it on the newly tooled leather covering the book in front of him, and I wondered what the title was. He brushed off the excess, then he lifted his thick glasses off his nose and bent close to the book to check for errors.

I moved into the room.

'Will it live to be read another day?'

He looked up and replaced his glasses. Then he smiled the way he always did when he saw Maude or me.

'It will,' he said.

I held out my hand and he placed the book in it. A thin volume. *Othello: The Moor of Venice.*

'It's beautiful, Eb. Like new.'

He ignored the compliment. 'It's a hundred and eighty years old.'

'What was the last binding like?'

He found the scraps of it beside his bench and held them up – crumbling board beneath faded, torn cloth. 'Not the original,' he said. 'That would have been calf or sheepskin. But this lasted about eighty years – not a bad innings; it was well read.'

'And this will last a hundred, at least,' I said. 'We'll be dust.'

He nodded. 'Don't mind the thought.'

'Being dust?' I smiled.

'Someone from the future holding my work.'

'I like it too, Eb. But I doubt anyone thinks about the people who've bound their books.'

He shrugged. 'I don't need them to know who I am.'

'I do,' I said. It just came out and I didn't really understand what it meant.

Eb was about to respond so I quickly offered back *Othello*. 'You better take this, or I might put it in my pocket.'

He took the book and placed it back on his bench.

'Can I ask a favour, Eb?'

He nodded. He always nodded.

'I'm helping someone bind a book. A dictionary, of sorts. But it's not Press work.'

His glasses slipped; he pushed them up his nose. 'What kind of work is it?'

I lowered my voice. 'A work of love.'

He blinked, and I knew I was taking advantage.

Chapter Six

The girls' side had emptied for the day and Mr Owen stood on the threshold. Like all the men, even Mr Hart, he waited to be invited in.

Mrs Stoddard came out of her office.

'Shutters and lights when you're done, Peggy.' She attached her hat and walked towards the door.

'You're in good hands, Gareth,' I heard her say.

'I appreciate this, Vanessa.'

She waved her hand. 'You appreciate nothing, I'm completely ignorant.'

She left, and he came towards me. 'It's hard to keep a secret in this place.'

'Depends who you want to keep it from,' I said. 'No one would tell the Controller.'

He smiled. 'Thanks for this, Peggy. I've been at the Press twenty years and the girls' side of the bindery is still a mystery.'

'It's not so hard, what we do in here.'

He looked to where Maude was still sitting, folding.

'Takes its own skill,' he said.

'It takes us seven hours to learn the folds and how to gather sections.

Seven days to become a competent sewer,' I said. 'Not quite the same as a seven-year apprenticeship.'

'A book would be worthless if its pages were misaligned, or it was sewn poorly.'

I shrugged. Not worthless.

'Where do we start?' he said.

I pointed to the roll cradled in his arm. 'Are they the printed sheets?'

'They are.'

He'd wrapped them in brown paper, which was tucked neatly at the ends, and his free hand reached across and stroked them – the gesture was protective, the look on his face unsure. I wondered how his gift would be received, how I'd receive it if I were her. I led him to the folding bench and pushed aside a small pile of sections.

'What have you been folding?' he asked.

'Proof pages for *Shakespeare's England*,' I said. 'An essay about scoundrels and vagabonds.'

He nodded. 'We've had a few draft chapters come through the composing room. Not enough, though. Hart's already grumbling about what that will mean for the printing house if all the copy comes in late.'

'Plenty of overtime, I'd have thought.'

'And no men to do it,' he said.

The compositor placed his roll in the space I'd made on the bench. He untucked the brown paper from each end and let the sheets unfurl.

Octavo. Eight pages each side, sixteen pages a sheet, each the size of a New English Dictionary page. There were two columns instead of three, and the entries were well spread out. I leafed through the sheets to count them. Twelve. Ninety-six pages in total. A lot of words.

'And none of these will be in Dr Murray's dictionary?'

'Some will be,' he said. He turned the edges of a few sheets and one word caught my eye.

'*Sisters*,' I said. 'Surely that's in Murray's dictionary?'

'It will be, though it's years away, but Esme says the examples they've collected leave this sense out.' He lifted the sheet so I could see the full entry.

SISTERS

Women (known or unknown) bonded by shared experience, a shared political goal, a shared desire for change.
1906 TILDA TAYLOR: Sisters, thank you for joining the fight.
1908 LIZZIE LESTER: You don't have to be flesh and blood to be sisterly, you just have to want good for each other.
1913 BETTY ANGRAVE: Let's not forget our sisters who work for their living, who own no property, who have no means for education.

I stroked Tilda's name, her words. She'd said them at every meeting Ma had taken us to. *Sisters*, Tilda called the women who turned up, most of whom she'd never met. It was a word I'd sometimes hated for the way it became singular when applied to Maude and me. *The sisters, the twins, the girls.* We were indistinguishable, and the effort to define us separately was too much for most people. It was a word of convenience that made me disappear, but when Tilda used it at those meetings it felt deliberate and strong. It felt subversive and I wanted to *be* one of those sisters.

'She's captured something, don't you think?' His voice brought me back to the bindery.

I read the other quotations, re-read the definition. *Women (known or unknown) bonded by shared experience.* It wasn't the words that drew me to Mr Owen's sweetheart, it was the image I had of her pockets full of slips and her head full of longing to be more than she was allowed to be. *A shared desire for change.*

'She has,' I said. 'It makes perfect sense.'

'It could have come straight from the New English Dictionary.'

'But you've used a different typeface,' I said. 'What is it?'

'Baskerville,' he said.

'Why?'

A pause, like the white space between paragraphs. He was thinking of her.

'For its clarity and beauty.'

He let the sheets fall back into a neat pile. 'I wouldn't know where to start with the folding – the pages are all out of order.'

I made a show of turning the pile so it was properly oriented. 'If you don't place your sheets correctly at the start, you'll muck up the whole section.' I glanced to where my sister sat. 'Won't you, Maudie?'

She nodded but didn't look up. 'The whole section, maybe the whole book.'

He smiled and noted the orientation of the sheets. 'First page face-down and to the left. Got it.'

I placed the first sheet, held the right edge and brought it over to lie against the left. 'These printer's marks need to line up. If they don't, your pages will be out of register.' I adjusted the alignment, then used Ma's bonefolder to make the crease. 'Fold one,' I said. 'Now turn it so the crease is near your belly and do it again. Fold two.' I turned it a final time. 'You have eight pages each side, that's called an octavo, so you need three folds.'

'Let me guess,' he said. 'Right side over left, register, crease.'

'Yes, but you'll need to use the bonefolder to keep your crease neat from inside the fold – at this stage the thickness of the section can result in wrinkles.'

I finished the third fold and handed the section to Mr Owen.

He tried to leaf through it.

'It'll need trimming before you can properly turn the pages.'

'When does that happen?'

'Once all the sections are folded and gathered, sewn and nipped.'

'Nipped?'

'All the air squeezed out of the text block.'

He nodded. 'Can I have a go?'

I moved away from the bench and let the compositor sit in my chair. He took the next sheet but Maude leant across and put her hand on the paper so he couldn't proceed.

'Practise,' she said, frowning up at me.

'Good idea.' I found some spare sheets and put them in front of our student. Maude and I stood on either side as the compositor took the top sheet and slowly went through the steps I'd shown him. I held my finger to my lips to stop Maude from coaching.

'Rubbish,' she said when he held up his first section, the edges misaligned.

'I forgot about the printer's marks.'

'And you didn't orient the sheet properly,' I said. 'The pages are out of order.'

'I assumed they were already the right way round.'

'Never assume,' said Maude.

Mr Owen folded five more practice sheets before he remembered all the steps. Another five before he completed a section without the paper slipping and ruining his registration.

'Do you think he's ready, Maude?'

'Ready,' she said.

I removed the practice sheets and Maude slid the women's words back along the bench.

The compositor readied himself. I think he was waiting for me to say he could start. But I didn't, immediately. I looked at the words his sweetheart had collected and felt a shiver of excitement. It had something to do with the names against the quotations and the way she'd captured their speech. I imagined some of the women wouldn't be able to read the words they'd uttered, yet here they were, in print. Their names now part of the record. But my hesitation also had something to do with the man who sat ready to fold them – the way he'd straightened.

I told him to start.

It was a strange pleasure to watch the women's words twist and turn in this man's hands. Eventually, twelve sections sat one on top of the other to the left of the compositor. He turned to Maude, then to me. He was like a boy seeking praise, though he must have been nearing forty.

'Good,' I said. 'And already gathered into the right order.'

Maude flicked through the sections – a final check. She took up a pencil and initialled the last page: *MJ*. Mr Owen frowned.

'Quality control,' I said. 'Every text block gets the same treatment, but don't worry, it won't be seen. The end papers will cover it.'

He took the gathered sections from Maude, then wrapped them in the brown paper and tied the parcel with string. When I offered to keep them in the bindery until next time, he declined.

∾

A few days later, Mr Owen was once again on the threshold of the girls' side. Mrs Stoddard manufactured some overtime folding for Maude, and I led the compositor through the men's side of the bindery. The machines were quiet. Stacks of gathered sections sat beside guillotines, newly trimmed. Mr Owen stopped at one and picked a section from the top.

'*Sorrow to Speech*,' he said, fanning through it.

'The next Dictionary fascicle,' I said. 'It came through the girls' side earlier this week.' I'd checked for *spalt* and was glad it had escaped the editor's pen.

He laughed. 'I only corrected the formes last week,' he said. 'Typesetting goes at a snail's pace compared with every other part of the process.'

'Do you always work on the Dictionary?'

'Most compositors have a speciality. Mine is dictionaries.'

'How long have you been setting type for the New English Dictionary?'

'Since my first year as an apprentice. Dictionaries were my mentor's speciality, so they became mine.'

'You must have a good vocabulary.' I was joking, but his answer was serious.

'Better than it would have been,' he said. 'You can't help learning a thing or two working here.'

'But isn't it all back to front for you?'

'I learnt to read the mirror image – just like you must have learnt to read upside down and sideways.'

'What makes you think I read what I fold?'

He replaced the pages from *Sorrow to Speech*.

'Don't you?'

The answer flushed my cheeks. I turned towards the repair room.

Eb was leaning over a finishing press and removing glue from the spine of an old book. He looked up when we came in. Pushed his glasses up his nose.

'Thanks for this, Ebenezer,' said Mr Owen.

Eb shook his head, always shy in front of gratitude. From his satchel, Mr Owen took out the parcel and put it on the bench. Eb pulled on the string and the brown paper fell away to reveal the sections. For a moment he said nothing, did nothing, but he couldn't take his eyes off them. The sections contained the least valuable words in the English language but it was as if he'd just unwrapped Shakespeare's first folio.

We got to work.

Eb trimmed the pages while I strung five linen cords between the top and bottom of the sewing frame. I invited the compositor to sit beside me at the bench.

'We'll sew the sections to these,' I said, and I placed the first section on the frame, its centre fold against the cords. 'By the time we're finished, all the sections will be stitched onto these cords in a way that will make them act a bit like springs – letting you open and close the book without it losing shape.'

'Strength and flexibility,' Eb said. 'A book needs both.'

I angled the frame to suit me and sewed the first section to demonstrate, but my hands knew each movement without my having to think, and Mr Owen was quickly bewildered.

I remembered the pain and frustration of my own first lesson. *Your stitching is what will hold the story together*, Ma had said, just when I wanted to give up trying.

It took me two days to sew a single book when others could sew eight in the same time. When it was done, the tension was uneven and the sections were poorly aligned. It was not good enough for casing-in, so Mrs Stoddard let me take it home. It was *On the Origin of Species by Means of Natural Selection*; Ma had chosen it on purpose. She knew my clumsy fingers would ensure it ended up on one of her shelves. Eb had cased it in and given it a plain cloth cover.

I added the next section of *Women's Words* and slowed my actions down.

'If you bind the sections well enough,' I said, 'your work will be invisible.'

I moved over and let the compositor sit in front of the frame. The next few sections were slow going. His hands moved awkwardly, and the stitching was too loose and too tight by turns. But then he found his rhythm. I watched him push the needle through the centre of the section and loop it around the first cord, the second, the third. His stitches lined up as they should and by the fifth cord the section sat comfortably on top of its sisters. Eb and I were silent as the compositor placed the next section. Then the next. He placed the ninth section and I saw him pause.

There is satisfaction in sewing the parts of a book together. Binding one idea to the next, one word to another, reuniting sentences with their beginnings and ends. The process of stitching can become an act of reverence, and when there are more sections on the frame than on the bench, you begin to anticipate the moment the parts become a whole.

There were three sections left, and Mr Owen had noticed. He lost his rhythm. He pushed too hard and the needle found the tip of his finger, drawing blood. I winced. He sat back and put pressure on the small wound. Eb handed him a clean cloth.

'We have to wait now,' I said, nodding at his finger, 'or you'll stain the pages.'

'What happens to a book that's poorly sewn?' he asked.

'The text block will lose its shape and that will undermine the casing.'

'Peg's quite fond of poorly sewn books,' said Eb.

I shot him a look. The compositor smiled.

'Don't worry, Peggy, I already know about your collection of misfits.'

Jack. I tried to look annoyed but it was hard. I liked the idea of being talked about. I turned towards the sewing frame.

I loved books at this stage of the dressing, and it was true that *Calliope* was full of them. Books that had been sewn and then damaged somehow. Pages torn or glue spilled or something less obvious – some fault in the rounding or knocking back of the spine, a weakness that could have been hidden by a good cloth casing but wasn't. I ran my finger over the naked spine of *Women's Words*. The backs of the sections were like vertebrae, the cord they were being sewn to like the stays of a corset.

I wanted the binding of the women's words to go on and on, but there were only ninety-six pages, and there was only one volume. I anticipated its absence, as I sometimes did with books I grew attached to through the folding and gathering, and especially the sewing. But there'd be no waste with this one. No opportunity for even a small part of *Women's Words* to end up on *Calliope*.

'Did you ever think to print more copies?' I asked.

The compositor shook his head. 'Just the one. I didn't realise all the ways I could ruin it.'

I laughed. 'Eb won't let you ruin it, and neither will I. But I think others might be interested in this dictionary.'

He frowned, just slightly, and I was suddenly impatient. All this effort might have been nothing more than a gesture, like putting a frame around a lady's needlepoint just so it can hang in the parlour. I realised he might not see these words as I saw them: as a new idea, an argument of some kind, a redress or correction. My mind ran along like a train. The myriad ways our words had failed to be bound. And here they were, finally. And there was only one bloody copy.

'I kept the formes,' he said.

The train slowed.

'I'll print more. But this needed to be unique. Singular. Hers shouldn't be a copy.'

The train stopped. My frustration ebbed.

'Do you understand?' he said, as if he needed me to.

I understood completely. 'One of a kind,' I said. 'At least for a moment.'

He took the cloth from his finger. The bleeding had stopped. He sewed in the next section.

Chapter Seven

Someone was chatting with Rosie in her verge garden. A long red coat with black trim. A painted lady, I thought. Maude ran ahead, scattering the ducks that had gathered on the towpath. Tilda wrapped both arms around her and when I caught up, she kept one arm around Maude and placed the other around me. Statuesque, Ma had called Tilda once. We'd grown as much as we would and only just came to her shoulders.

'They suit me, don't you think?' she asked Rosie, kissing Maude's head, then mine.

'They're not baubles you hang from your ears,' said Rosie.

'If I could, I would. Then I could take them everywhere with me.'

If only you would, I thought. 'What makes you think we'd want to come?'

'Oh, you'd want to come, Peg. This one, though …' She held Maude a little tighter. 'I reckon she's quite happy where she is.'

'Happy where she is,' Maude said.

We had a picnic on the verge. Tilda had brought a wedge of Stilton, a jar of pickled onions and a large white loaf. She'd also brought enough anecdotes to keep us laughing and mildly shocked until the light faded and Old Mrs Rowntree was shivering. We retreated to our narrowboats.

Inside, I made hot chocolate and poured Maude a mug. Tilda declined.

'When does nursing training start?' I asked, sitting down at the table.

Tilda poured herself a dram of whiskey. 'Day after tomorrow.'

Just two days. My mug stopped halfway to my mouth.

'Oh, I know. You want me to stay forever.'

I took a sip.

'Not forever,' I said.

Tilda talked and we listened and the night fell inky beyond *Calliope*. I made the lamplight brighter and we soaked up the life she'd been living since we'd last seen her, the drama and comic turns. Then she suddenly stopped talking.

'Enough about me,' she said, looking around as if she'd just realised where she was. 'What have you two been doing with yourselves?'

In answer, Maude held up a paper butterfly. 'Enough about me,' she said.

Tilda laughed. Her great guffaw. 'Touché,' she said. 'But don't pretend you're not interested in my comings and goings, Maudie. You hang on my every word.'

'Every word.' Maude nodded.

'What about you, Pegs? What's changed?'

Tilda was like a storm. She blew in and churned things up and exposed what I tried to keep submerged.

'Nothing's changed,' I said. 'I fold, I gather, I sew. When I saw your letter, I thought about joining the VAD. But I realised I can't.'

'There's Maude,' said Maude.

'It's not like that, Maudie,' I said.

'Of course it's not,' said Tilda. 'Only women of means *and* no obligations can join the VAD. Peg's just feeling a bit useless.'

'I *am* a bit useless.'

'Early days,' she said. 'Oxford is about to be inundated with the bruised and the broken – something is bound to present itself.' She poured herself another whiskey and leant back in her chair. 'So, tell me what books you've been folding – anything you'd like to bring home?'

'Yes, actually.' And I began to tell her about the women's words.

Tilda sipped her drink and became unusually attentive. A strange smile played on her lips.

'That would be Esme,' she said.

'I wondered if you knew her. I saw your name.'

'More than once, I hope. I've introduced Esme to a whole world of words.'

'She's your wordy friend?' I said.

'She is.'

'Why haven't you introduced us?'

'Helen met her once, at one of our suffrage meetings.'

'That isn't an answer.' I folded my arms. Waited.

She poured another whiskey. 'I don't want to share you,' she said. 'Any of you. I'm selfish, remember?' She picked up the glass and downed it in one. 'I don't want to explain Helen to anyone, Peg. Not even Esme.' Then she laughed. 'Especially not Esme.'

'What's so funny?'

'I'm just imagining her putting Helen's name at the top of one of her slips of paper and trying to define her.' The smile left her face and for a while we were quiet. Maude's hands had slowed.

Then Tilda looked up from her empty glass. 'It's impossible, don't you think?'

~

Two days later, we waved Tilda off at the station. It was noisy with tearful farewells – young men in uniforms with sharp creases and shiny buttons, their faces full of an imagined adventure. The platform echoed with their promises to stay safe. Every one of them thought he had what it would take to stay alive. I thought of Jack – he was sure of it.

Tilda stood at the open window near her seat.

'Write to us,' I shouted.

'If I have time,' she shouted back.

～

Mrs Hogg rang the bell and we joined the flow of women leaving the bindery for the day.

'Hello, Peggy.'

He was standing just beyond the door, trying to keep out of the way and failing.

'Mr Owen,' I said, conscious of turning heads. The ripple of a disturbance caused by a man so near the girls' side.

'Hello, Gareth,' said Maude, without a thought to the turning heads.

'Hello, Maude,' he said, then more quietly, 'I thought you and Peggy might like to join me for the final touches.'

'*Women's Words*,' she said, not quietly at all.

He nodded.

Eb had everything ready. His bench had been cleared of official jobs and in the centre was a thin volume, the size and shape of a Dictionary fascicle, beautifully bound in green leather. Mr Owen stood aside so Maude and I could move in close.

Already, there was a simple design impressed around the edge of the cover, and the title had been tooled on the front and spine. *Women's Words and Their Meanings*. It was a whisper of what it would become once the gilt was added.

Beside the volume was a sheet of graph paper with the border design drawn on it and evidence of tooling. I picked up one of the small metal stamps Mr Owen had used and pressed the pattern into the palm of my hand. It was a simple shell, and the indentation was gone in a moment, but the tool still held traces of paper and graphite and leather, all bound by heat. The pattern would stay on my skin until I washed it off.

I put my hand on the volume. 'May I?' I asked Mr Owen.

'I think so,' he said, looking to Eb.

Eb nodded and I opened the cover, turned to the first printed pages.

Women's Words and Their Meanings
Edited by Esme Nicoll

A flush of feeling, warm and prickling. Envy, and something else. A whisper in my ear. *Why not?*

'Ready to go?' asked Eb.

I looked up and saw they were all looking at me.

'What do you think, Peggy? Shall we finish it off?' asked Mr Owen.

His gift had become important to me, and he knew it. I wondered for a moment if he resented sharing the experience. I decided he didn't. I stepped away from the bench and gestured for him to take my place.

Eb secured the volume in a finishing press so the spine could be worked on first. Then he explained the process of gilding.

'Glaire, grease, gold,' he said, putting all three within easy reach of the compositor.

'Glaire, grease, gold,' echoed Maude.

'What's glaire?' I asked. Bindery girls didn't learn to gild.

'Egg white, essentially,' said Eb. 'It helps prepare the leather to take the gilt.' He took a small brush and dipped it in the glaire, applied it to the embellishment impressed on the leather at the top of the spine and then offered the brush to Mr Owen. 'You do the rest. It won't harm the leather, but try not to paint it on too thick. We need two dry coats before we apply the grease.'

'Like putting an egg wash on pastry,' I said to Maude.

When the grease had been applied, Eb showed us how to handle the gilt.

He fanned a narrow spatula at the edge of the gold leaves to breathe air between them. The top leaf lifted and he caught it on the blade. He transferred it to a small rubber mat, then used the same tool to cut the leaf into various-sized strips. 'It's easily disturbed,' he continued. 'You have to learn how to move the air around it.'

He positioned the blade at the bottom edge of a small strip and blew gently to lift it. Then, with extraordinary swiftness and delicacy, he caught it, carried it to the leather spine and laid it down. The gold relaxed into the valleys of the impression, as if relieved to be home. Eb brushed away the excess. The pattern shone. He offered me the spatula. 'Why don't you do the spine?'

'Good luck,' said Maude.

My hand shook, and the gold sheets folded in on themselves: once, twice, three times. 'It seems folding is all I'm good at,' I said after ruining a third.

Eb intervened. Handed me the blade with a strip of gold leaf and nodded towards the spine of the book. 'It's big enough to lay on "Women's",' he said.

I laid the leaf of gold over the word and felt the static attraction that drew it towards the text. I brushed away the excess leaf, then laid another, and another. Finally, the whole title was illuminated.

Eb removed the book from the finishing press so Mr Owen could work on the front. The compositor hesitated. It was the last task, I realised. When it was done, the gift would be ready.

'I've been practising,' he said. He pointed to a swatch of leather covered in gilded patterns and random letters. He lifted the first gold sheet. He didn't have the swiftness or delicacy of our mentor, but he managed to gild the words without assistance.

And then he was finished, and no one spoke.

'Thank you,' he finally said. He offered his hand to me, then Maude.

'Thank you,' said Maude, and it might have been an echo, but I think she meant it.

'Thank *her*,' I said. 'Miss Nicoll.' For the words, I might have said; for collecting them, understanding them, giving them the time of day. I turned quickly and left.

~

9 October 1914

Hello Pegs,

If it's any consolation, it's not the adventure I was hoping for — all we do is tidy lockers, clean bedpans and roll bandages. Our chief duty, though, is to 'wear the uniform with pride'.

The debutantes at St Bart's take this very seriously and are forever ironing and polishing shoes. It's new to most of them (having grown up with staff, poor things) and they treat it like a game of role-play. I care a lot less and am forever being reprimanded for creases and scuffs and general disobedience. Sister has suggested I might be better suited to something else. She has a point, which is very irritating, so out of spite, I've signed up for the duration. Only illness, death or marriage will release me.

Tilda x

P.S. How's your French? Papers say there's a trainload of Belgians coming your way — might give you something to do.

Chapter Eight

Maude was dressed in her best, her hands busy folding a loose page from a book that had nothing interesting to say. I left the coffee to steep on the range and went into the bedroom to check my hair, my face. I pinched my cheeks and took a lipstick from the cupboard above our bed. It had been Tilda's. I used it sparingly. I rubbed my lips together and watched the colour spread and fade from deep red to something more respectable. I wanted to add more, but it wasn't a dance we were going to. I put the lipstick down, then looked up, quickly, trying to catch my reflection unawares.

I did this sometimes, hoping the face that looked back would be mine. But it was almost always Maude's, and I would feel the discomfort of not knowing who I was. *Read the mirror image*, I thought, remembering the compositor's words. I looked away, looked back.

The rouged lips helped, the pinched cheeks. Maybe it was the eyes, a deeper blue against the smudge of kohl, but there I was. Peggy Jones. Pretty Peggy Jones. I picked up the lipstick and added more colour.

The smell of brewed coffee brought me back to the narrowboat, to Maude in her best dress, to the train making its way into Oxford.

I returned to the range and filled two flasks with coffee. I put them in the basket with two packets of biscuits.

Rosie called from the towpath.

'It's time to go, Maudie,' I said, holding her coat out to receive her arms. She complied. I handed her the basket and she added a small pile of folded gifts: fans, bookmarks, birds with flapping wings.

Rosie was in her second-best dress, her church hat pinned firmly to her salt-and-pepper curls – this wasn't an occasion for a boatwoman. We looked at each other approvingly.

'You're a picture,' Rosie said, and I waited for her to repeat the compliment for Maude. When she didn't, I was grateful.

Maude peered beneath the cloth covering Rosie's basket.

'Sweet buns,' she declared.

'You can have one now or later, Maude,' said Rosie. 'But not now *and* later; they're for the refugees.'

'Now *and* later,' said Maude.

Rosie pulled the basket away. 'Now *or* later,' she said.

'Now,' Maude said, and Rosie lifted the cloth on the basket.

Maude took her time, selected the biggest, then took a bite. A ribbon of heat drifted into the autumn air.

'They do smell good,' I said, and Rosie held the basket towards me. I broke my bun down the middle and let the steam rise to my nose. Apple, and a mix of spices that made everything Rosie cooked a little more delicious than anyone else's.

We walked along the towpath to the Hythe Bridge, then joined a small caravan of people heading towards the station. We were mostly women, dressed for Sunday despite it being Wednesday. We carried all manner of baskets and bags. We might have been going to a fair.

We were early, of course. The train wouldn't arrive for another half-hour, but we wanted to be ready. The Belgians had been travelling a long time. They'd be tired, hungry, frightened. They'd be traumatised.

The Rape of Belgium is what the papers were calling the German invasion. Homes sacked and burnt, towns destroyed, ordinary people beaten and shot, even when they didn't hold a gun, even if they were women or children. Some had survived for weeks in basements, others had run and been killed by electrified fences. The rumours of what they did to women were worse than nightmares. We wanted them to feel safe, welcome. We wanted them to know we were better than the Germans.

Mrs Stoddard was already there, setting up a trestle laid with white cloth. Another woman was unfolding a banner with *Oxford War Refugees' Committee* inexpertly painted along its length. She secured it to the table with tins of beans.

Maude saw Mrs Stoddard and waved. Mrs Stoddard beamed. This was her doing. She had arranged with Mr Hart for Maude and me to be at the station when the refugees arrived.

Rosie and I added our buns and biscuits and flasks of coffee to the table. As other women arrived, I helped Mrs Stoddard arrange their plates of food and flasks of hot drinks in a way that would ensure an efficient flow of people from one end of the table to the other. I imagined each Belgian as a section of a book and wondered what story they would tell if they were all sewn together.

The spread of food was irresistible to Maude. I watched her reach for another of Rosie's buns, but I was too far away to stop her. One or two women scowled and made a show of slapping the hands of their children who thought to follow suit. Maude noticed none of it. I noticed every gesture.

I moved towards my sister, but Mrs Stoddard intervened. 'Maude,' she said, in exactly the voice she used when giving Maude a special task in the bindery. 'Did I see gifts for our visitors in your basket?'

Maude looked up from the plate of buns and nodded. Then she looked to me. 'Gifts?'

I took the basket from under the trestle – a trove of folded treasures and half an apple-and-spice bun. I took out the bun and handed Maude the basket just as the chug of an engine was heard. Before I could stop her, she strode towards the edge of the platform along with a dozen children. I joined the mothers calling for them to stay well back.

The whistle sang, loud and cheerful. Then the platform filled with steam, and the smell of coal smoke replaced the spice of Rosie's buns. Mrs Stoddard handed me a bowl of apples. 'Take these and offer them to people as they get off.'

I wove through the crowd of women and children who jostled for a view of our visitors. Maude was at the front holding a folded gift, ready to give it to the first person out of the carriage. One or two local children were looking in her basket, asking if they could have a paper bird. 'No,' she said, and the children retreated, obedient.

I smiled. It was impossible to misunderstand Maude when she said yes or no. Her face, her hands, her whole body concurred with the word that came out of her mouth and people rarely needed further explanation. Children, especially, seemed to know that no argument would be successful.

The guard walked the length of the train, asking people to stand aside, give the passengers room. The crowd stepped back, stepped forward. Like water in his wake.

I looked to where Mrs Stoddard stood ready behind the trestle, with Rosie and three others from the refugee committee. She was straightening her hat. Rosie was standing on tip-toe to see over the crowd.

What were we expecting? I suddenly wondered.

There were four carriages. Their doors opened.

A woman stood on the top step of the second carriage, where the welcome was thick with children and mothers and noise. She wore layers of clothes: the hems of two skirts and the collars of two blouses were visible beneath a cardigan and heavy coat. There was a small trunk in her hand – too small, I thought, to hold a life. She made no move to step down onto the platform, and the look on her face had me betting she would turn and push her way back into the carriage. (Refuge, I thought, from the eagerness of the refuge-givers.) A beautiful face. Her skin smudged with the grime of travel, pale hair escaping its pins, pale-blue eyes, bewildered.

I looked around. She'd arrived at a celebration. I thought of what she might have been fleeing and I was ashamed. Of my best dress, the colour on my lips. I shifted the bowl of apples to my hip and took the hanky from under the cuff of my sleeve. I wiped my mouth clean.

Then Maude was there, at the door of the second carriage, with her basket of gifts. She held up a paper fan, and the pale woman looked as if she had no idea what it was. As if she had no idea what was going on. My sister waited. Offered no explanations – she never did. After a few moments, Maude opened the fan as a Spanish lady might: one hand, one movement, the folds opening out like a peacock's tail. It was one of the fans she'd embellished along the edge with blue roses. 'Why blue?' I'd asked when she'd been colouring them. She'd shrugged.

Maude raised the fan towards the woman's face and I watched as the breeze it created shifted loose strands of hair, gossamer threads. I watched the woman step down from the train, watched as her trunk dropped and toppled. It's hardly possible that the platform went silent, but that is how it seemed to me. It looked like a reunion, and I watched, as a stranger might, wondering at the relationship between these two women. I had a moment of separation from my sister, a rare sense that she was unfamiliar, as the stranger wrapped her arms around Maude and sobbed.

But sobbed isn't quite the right word. It was more than that. Something wrenched itself from the woman. Something that had been anchored to the depths of her. Maybe we did fall silent. Her distress was confronting. Embarrassing. Nothing we understood. The crowd stepped back from it. People turned their faces, tentative now, to others stepping from the train. I saw their relief when they were met with smiles. Saw them rush to take the luggage of the best-dressed Belgians. The least traumatised. Usher them to the trestle, pour them tea or coffee, give their children sweets.

Only Maude was comfortable with the woman's pain. She stood her ground and returned the embrace. The woman was tall, and her pale face bent to the dark crown of my sister's head. She held her tighter than a stranger should, like a mother would hold a child who had wandered off and now was found. I expected Maude to pull away, her tolerance for a stranger's touch stretched to its limit. But this woman needed someone to hold and my sister had decided it could be her.

I made my way towards the small space that surrounded their embrace. They parted before I could get there, and the woman took a step back, disoriented. She looked Maude in the eye, as if my sister might explain something. Maude just nodded and held her gaze, as Ma had always told her to do.

It seemed enough.

I stepped closer and Maude turned. The woman turned. She did what everyone did and looked from me to Maude, then back to me. For once I was glad of it. Her face had composed itself into something I recognised.

'Twins,' I said.

'That is obvious.' She spoke English.

'My name is Peggy, and this is Maude.'

Maude held up the fan and the woman took it. She opened it like a Spanish lady might. She closed her eyes and fanned her face. 'Thank you,' she breathed.

'Thank you,' repeated Maude. Same accent, her voice breathy. Oh, Maude, I thought, not now.

The woman opened her eyes and looked directly at my sister. Maude looked directly back.

~

Mrs Stoddard was flushed and smiling. The trestle was almost empty, the platform too. The majority of the Belgians had been taken to Ruskin College, empty of students since most had joined up. It would be their home until something more permanent could be arranged. But a few had stayed behind with their billets, to help pack up. They were women, on their own. They stacked mugs and plates into baskets and folded the soiled cloth that had covered the trestle. The tall, pale woman was among them, her distress now barely visible as she scraped plates free of crumbs and half-eaten oat cakes.

Since they arrived, most of these women had had the look of someone just woken. I'd noticed one or two look back at the train, as if they'd left something on board. A husband, I thought. A lover, a brother, a favourite hat. They accepted mugs of coffee with dirty hands. They took biscuits and buns and ate too quickly. Whenever it was required, a smile would spread across their exhausted faces, but it would quickly fade. Only now, as they busied themselves with the debris of their arrival, did they look comfortable.

Mrs Stoddard handed me a tea towel bulging with leftovers.

'Your reward for staying to clean up,' she said.

I nestled it into our basket. Oatcakes and apples for tea, I thought.

'But before you go, come and meet the others.' Mrs Stoddard ushered us over to where the committee ladies stood, removing their aprons. We were introduced.

Miss Bruce was in charge. 'Miss *Pamela* Bruce,' Mrs Stoddard stressed. 'Her sister is Miss *Alice* Bruce, vice-principal at Somerville.'

Miss Pamela Bruce was solid and straight, with steel-grey hair piled high on her head, making her seem taller than she was. She held out her hand, a gesture I wasn't used to, but I shook it. Then she offered it to Maude, who didn't.

'Peggy loves Somerville,' Maude said.

I would have pinched her if there'd been no witnesses. 'The building,' I said quickly, 'that looks over Walton Street.'

Miss Bruce considered my sister, noted her guileless expression and gave her a gentle smile of acknowledgement, then she turned to me.

'The building is quite ordinary, as far as colleges go.'

'And this,' Mrs Stoddard said, placing a hand on the arm of the woman with the pale eyes, the pale hair, 'is Lotte Goossens.'

She must have introduced the other Belgians, the other members of the refugee committee, but the only name I seem to have heard was Lotte's.

'Lotte will be staying with me,' Mrs Stoddard said. 'When she's ready, she will start working in the bindery.'

PART TWO

The Oxford Pamphlets

October 1914 to June 1915

Chapter Nine

It was a clear morning, October crisp.

'Blood, mud, rain,' Maude said, as we entered Turner's Newsagency to pick up our post. 'Race to the sea. Allies dig in at Ypres,' she said. 'Training to start at Port Meadow,' she said.

'You could sell papers, Miss Jones, if you grew tired of the Press,' Mr Turner told her.

I thought of the Belgians at the station, what they'd escaped. Then I tried to think of all the Press men who might be in Flanders. There were too many.

When we arrived at work, only half the benches were piled with printed sections.

'The machine room is still adjusting,' said Mrs Hogg. 'Until they do, Mrs Stoddard insists your hands stay busy.' She handed me a pair of knitting needles and a ball of wool.

'What am I supposed to do with these?' I asked.

'Not so bright after all, are you, Miss Jones?'

'Mufflers,' said Lou when I sat among the others she was instructing. I wasn't the only one who'd forgotten what we'd been taught as schoolgirls.

'I hope the Belgian women can knit,' I said.

'Mrs Stoddard says there'll be plenty to do by the time they start.'

I looked over at Maude. She was not expected to knit, and so there was a pile of printed sheets on her bench. I leant over to see what she was folding.

Poetry. A small volume – one section, sixteen pages. Twelve sonnets plus front and back pages. The pile indicated around forty copies. We printed more of these every week. Outpourings of grief or glory by women and men who could afford the rising costs of printing. Paper was becoming expensive, but there was no end to these little volumes. We loved to mock them, but we were grateful. Without them we would have less to do and Mr Hart would have fewer reasons to pay us. I read a few lines out loud.

'*Dawn breaks red across an English sky*
Morning bird songs falter.
Dawn knows well my midnight cry
My sorrow it can't alter.'

Sweetheart? Brother? Friend? I wondered who she'd lost.

Then, before I could quash it: 'If only she'd taken up knitting instead of poetry. Everyone would be better off.'

'Be kind, Peg,' said Maude. Ma had said it, once or twice.

'Damn.' I dropped a stitch.

'Language, Miss Jones.'

'Sorry, Mrs Stoddard,' I said. 'I was never very good at this. Pity the poor fellow who gets' – I held up my muffler – 'whatever this is.'

'Tension is your main problem. It's inconsistent.' She took the knitting from my hand and pulled at it. She looked at Lou, who shrugged. 'Lucky for you we've just had a delivery of sheets.'

'What are they?'

'Does it matter? It gets you out of knitting.' But she knew it did, and she smiled. 'An Oxford Pamphlet. *Might Is Right* by Sir Walter Raleigh.'

One fold.

It is a very dangerous doctrine when it becomes the creed of a stupid people …

Two folds.

A nation of men who mistake violence for strength, and cunning for wisdom …

Three folds.

England may be proud to die; but surely her time is not yet.

Chapter Ten

Mr Hart started to welcome Belgians into the Press a week later. If their English was good enough, the men were given positions in the paper store and type foundry. If not, they were sent to the wetting cellar, drying rooms and the warehouse. They might have been grown men, but they were treated like apprentices of fourteen. The women came to the bindery.

Lotte and two other Belgians arrived on the girls' side after lunch on a Monday. As Mrs Stoddard showed them what was being done at the various benches, the gossiping hum quietened. We slowed our folding, paused in the dance of gathering. New girls were starting all the time, but they were Jericho girls, neighbours or relations, and we hardly paused to welcome them. These women were strangers.

Mrs Stoddard rang her bell, though she hardly needed to; we were all paying attention.

'As you know, Oxford has welcomed two hundred Belgians, and I am very pleased to introduce you to three of them.' She looked to the women beside her. Only Lotte looked back. The other two hung their heads like they were being admonished by the headmistress, and I realised they were much younger than Lotte, probably younger than me. Seventeen or eighteen, no more. Mrs Stoddard put her hand on the shoulder of each as she said her name.

'This is Lotte, this is Gudrun and this is Veronique.'

Lotte nodded at the mention of her name. Gudrun looked up and blushed crimson. Veronique tried to smile, then burst into tears. Lou was beside her in a second, her arm around her shoulders, dabbing the girl's face with a hanky.

'Thank you, Louise,' Mrs Stoddard said. Then she addressed us all. 'As you can imagine, ladies, this is a very emotional time for our guests. Please be kind and help them settle in. I expect you all to be supportive.'

There was general enthusiasm for the idea, and a number of women offered to help train the newcomers. But Mrs Stoddard had already decided who she would allocate that task to, and spaces were arranged beside our chairs.

Lou led Veronique to the space beside her. Lotte sat between Maude and me. Gudrun sat on the other side of Aggie. We were folding an Oxford World's Classic – *Lorna Doone* – and we sat in a row along our bench. Lou, Aggie, Maude and I had been in the same class at St Barnabas and joined the bindery together when we were twelve. We couldn't remember a time before we were friends. That was part of Mrs Stoddard's plan. 'They can become part of your group. You can help them with English, and they can help each other when language is an issue. Lotte is the most fluent, and she's older. The younger girls are here with their families.' She'd gone silent then, like there was more to say but she wasn't sure if she should. 'I think it best to keep them together.'

It was a privilege to be asked, to be trusted, and we all thanked Mrs Stoddard for her confidence in us. But as Lotte sat down between Maude and me, I suddenly resented having to share her.

Veronique was still crying, so Lou just sat with her arm around her, gently moving the printing away from where her tears might fall.

Aggie was already explaining the folds to Gudrun, her words keeping pace with the swift movement of her hands. Gudrun just stared as the paper shrank to the size of a single page in a matter of seconds.

'Slow it down, Aggie,' I said.

Aggie looked at Gudrun. 'You understand, don't you?' Gudrun said nothing, so Aggie said it louder. 'Understand?'

Gudrun shook her head.

'It's quite simple; let's start again.' Aggie pulled another sheet in front of her and made the folds, no slower than the last time. 'See. Simple. You have a go.' She slid a sheet over to Gudrun, who looked mystified and made no attempt to start. Aggie slid it back and made the folds again, as swift and efficient as ever.

I watched this routine through three more cycles, fascinated. Aggie's optimism never faltered, her speed never slowed. Gudrun's attention became more concentrated, and on her fifth attempt she got it. Aggie embraced her. Gudrun beamed.

When Veronique finally stopped weeping, Lou took a different approach. She placed a sheet between them and put her hand over Veronique's. She helped her find the printer's marks and match the edges of the paper, then she placed the bonefolder and encouraged Veronique to press the paper into a crease. They folded five sheets this way before Lou sat back and let Veronique do her own. When she was done, Lou made a simple correction, watched her again, then placed a quire of sheets beside her charge. She checked occasionally that the folds were straight, but Veronique folded all twenty-four sheets without error.

I'd been so absorbed in watching Aggie and Lou that I'd neglected Lotte. I shifted my focus to her station and saw a small pile of neatly folded sections. Maude was folding slowly; Lotte was copying. Every now and then, Maude looked at Lotte's work. If there were no errors, she'd nod. If something was not right, she'd say 'no', but she wouldn't make the correction. Lotte had quickly learnt to wait until Maude reached the relevant fold in her next sheet, then she'd copy her and wait for my sister's nod of approval. It was how Tilda had learnt to fold Christmas stars, though Lotte seemed to have an accuracy that Tilda lacked. Her finished folds sat one on top of the other in perfect alignment.

There was nothing I could contribute. I looked at the quire of sheets in front of me and folded them, as I would have if the Belgians had not been there. When I finished one quire I raised my hand for the sections to be collected, then began on another. I was halfway through when I heard Maude say, 'That's one for the home library.'

I looked over and noticed Lotte's bonefolder had slipped and made a small tear. Lotte turned to me for the first time since we'd sat down to work.

'Home library?'

'Sometimes I take home ruined sheets,' I said.

'They allow it?'

'No one has said I can't. Not exactly. And it will just go to waste.'

She passed me the torn section, the beginning of chapter sixteen: *Lorna Growing Formidable.* I secreted it beneath my quire of unfolded sheets.

Mrs Hogg rang the bell for the first shift to take their tea break.

'Freckly frog,' Maude said, when Lotte turned to the sound.

'Mrs Hogg,' I corrected.

'That's us,' said Aggie. She sped through her last fold and turned to Gudrun. 'What do you like to drink, strong tea or weak coffee?'

Gudrun looked mystified, again.

'The tea is always strong and the coffee is always weak: which would you like?' Aggie said, louder.

'She isn't deaf, Aggie. Slow down and use fewer words,' I said.

'Slow down? I'm not sure I can, Peg.' She smiled and stood up. Gudrun followed suit. Then Aggie took her by the arm and they started walking out of the bindery. 'If you want to get on, you're going to have to learn more English. And if we're going to be pals you need a nickname. Can I call you Goodie? Of course I can. I'll have you speaking English in no time, Goodie.'

The rest of us waited for Veronique to finish the sheet she was working on. Maude looked at Lotte's folds. She nodded.

'Thank you, Maude,' said Lotte.

∽

The Belgians improved by degrees. Lotte was by far the quickest learner, but perhaps she had the best teacher. Maude didn't rush like Aggie. Nor was she distracted by the circumstances that had brought her apprentice to England. Lou began every day with questions about how Veronique was settling in. No matter how Lou phrased it, Veronique began to weep.

'Just stop asking, Lou,' I finally said. 'You're killing her with kindness.'

Lou was mortified and stopped asking immediately. But she replaced words with gestures. A hand on the girl's arm, a meaningful look, a hug when she made an error. I considered telling Mrs Stoddard that Veronique could do with a dose of Aggie, and Goodie could do with a dose of Lou.

As for Lotte and Maude, they were perfectly suited. They spoke about folding and little else. It drove me mad. All I had to offer was conversation, and it was rarely welcome.

'What part of Belgium are you from, Lotte?' I asked, after we'd been working alongside each other for two days.

She hesitated, her bonefolder hovering. Then she made a second fold and I knew I must wait for her reply.

I was working on Dictionary pages – the first proofs for *Speech to Spring*. In the silence I read the last three words of the page facing me.

Speechification; speechifier; speechify: To make or deliver a speech; to harangue or hold forth. Tilda liked to *hold forth*, I thought, as Lotte completed the section.

'Louvain,' she said.

The name was familiar.

'What is it like?' asked Aggie, one ear always tuned to other people's conversations.

Lotte drew in a slow breath. 'It was like Oxford. Now it is like hell.'

'Oh,' said Aggie, chastened.

Louvain. What had I read?

Maude stretched to put her hand on top of Lotte's tall pile of sections. 'Enough,' she said. 'We all fall down.'

I was going to explain what Maude meant, but Lotte stood and picked up the pile.

'Just raise your hand,' I said. 'The trolley girl will collect them.'

She heard me, but she neither sat nor raised her hand. She just walked away with the sections.

Louvain. I racked my brain. Something in the *Oxford Chronicle*. Mrs Stoddard rang her bell and I lost the thread of memory.

~

On their fourth day in the bindery, we instructed the Belgians on the gathering of sections.

Aggie, like me, loved to dance them into piles, and Goodie soon picked up her steps. Goodie was talking more, though she rarely made sense, and every now and then the two of them would laugh out loud at some misunderstanding.

Maude did not gather, as a rule, so I instructed Lotte. I dragged it out, wanting an excuse to be close, to look into her face and try to understand her, to have her look at me the way she looked at Maude.

She cut me off.

'I understand. Thank you, Peggy.'

We took our places either side of the long gathering bench, Lotte's side a perfect mirror of mine. I swept the first section onto my arm. Lotte did the same. Then the second, the third. Lotte didn't dance but after a few rounds she'd found a rhythm.

She's too smart for this work, I thought, and I wanted to ask what she'd done in Belgium. Who she'd been. I glanced up to look at her pale face. The lines and tension that were always there seemed to fall away as she became more proficient in her gathering. She had a look of Maude about her; there was comfort in the repetition – it was crowding out the noise and distraction. Silencing thought. Dulling memory, perhaps.

Veronique was with Lou and Maude at the end of the gathering bench. Maude tidied the text blocks as we delivered them. Lou checked them, made her mark on the back section, then passed them to Veronique, whose only job was to put them on a trolley.

Mrs Stoddard rang her bell for stretches. She was a firm believer that movement was good for our bodies and minds, and had devised two-minute routines to break the monotony of bindery tasks. Every hour she would ring her bell, and girls across the bindery would stop their work to bend and stretch and twist, our movements particular to whatever task we were on.

Lotte and I finished our sweep of the book we were gathering and began the routine. I moved my head from side to side and Lotte followed. I looked to the ceiling and then to the floor. I held both arms straight in the air and used my left hand to stretch my right side, then my right hand to stretch the left. Lotte mirrored my every move, and when I was done, we stood facing each other. She smiled.

'I like this custom,' she said.

I smiled back. We resumed our gathering and, while Lotte still did not dance along the line, she seemed looser.

Veronique, on the other hand, looked tense. Lou was showing her how to check that the gathered sections were in the correct order and the right way up.

'I'm not sure she can read it, Lou,' I said when I placed my next text block in front of Maude. 'She might struggle to see up from down.'

'Oh, Peg, you're right. Poor girl. I can't imagine.' Lou took Veronique's hand and patted it. By the time I'd gathered my next bundle of sections, Veronique was doing Maude's job of tapping and tidying, and Maude was playing with the edges of a section, part of a text block already checked and on the trolley.

'Maude,' I said.

She looked up and I shook my head just slightly. She removed her hands from the text block and let her arms fall to her sides. Her fingers began manipulating her skirt into an accordion of folds.

~

By the time we returned to the folding bench the next day, Goodie and Veronique had grown used to Aggie and Lou, and Lotte continued to turn to Maude for any instruction she needed. I had no business at all sitting among them. Not even Maude seemed to need my monitoring, and my vigilance waned.

Then I noticed Lotte pause before finishing a section. Her body was still but her head turned to watch my sister. I looked beyond Lotte and recognised the shift in Maude's posture: a forward lean, and the gentle nod of her head that accompanied the movement of her hands as they manipulated the paper to her own design.

Her name was on the tip of my tongue. If I caught her early, it was all I needed, but there was a point at which she could not be stopped. She had to complete what had been started, as if it were a breath. *It's like asking you to close a book halfway through a paragraph*, Ma had said, before I'd finally understood.

But her name never left my tongue. Lotte reached out and placed her hand over Maude's. A wordless gesture. I watched for signs of Maude's discomfort: her teeth against her bottom lip, the rhythmic rocking. Her fingers were moving beneath Lotte's, and I waited to see if her hand would escape. But they weren't restrained, just shadowed. Lotte moved her fingers too, the movements in sync but slowing, diminishing. Stopping.

Lotte moved her hand away then, very slowly. She straightened the flaps that Maude had made in the corners of the sheet. Between each movement, Lotte paused. Remained still. She was waiting, as I was, for a sign that she had gone too far. When it didn't come, she continued.

Lotte took up Maude's bonefolder. Paused. She handed it to her. Maude took it. Made the first fold, the second fold. Lotte turned back to her own pages.

I felt more redundant than ever.

∽

22 October 1914

Hello Pegs,

You don't really want to be a VAD, you just want to DO something. Don't get me wrong, I think you'd be a terrific VAD but you don't quite fit the bill. The truth is, most of us have nothing better to do.

I have finally found my place among the young ladies with means. It was touch and go for a while, on account of my advanced age and 'interesting background'. The debutantes hate using the term 'working class'; 'actress' makes them blush and half of them whisper 'suffragette' like it's a dirty word (and they never say dirty words). But I have turned all these things to my advantage and am plying a trade in black market advice. Make-up and hair, mostly. Sometimes contraception. (According to Matron, the best contraception is a professional manner and a face free of make-up. Needless to say, I also get the occasional debutante asking me what to do when the professional manner and clean face have been ineffective.)

The subtext, of course, is that I'm here if you need advice about any of the above.

Tilda x

P.S. You'll find French letters in a black velvet purse in the box I've left in Helen's wardrobe.

P.P.S. If you really do want to do something, why not volunteer at one of the military hospitals setting up in Oxford? The carnage at Ypres has filled every bed at St Bart's. I'm sure Oxford will start getting ambulance trains full of wounded and there just aren't enough hands to do everything that needs doing.

Chapter Eleven

Why not volunteer? Tilda had said.

I walked along High Street, more nervous than I wanted to be. When I got to the Examination Schools, I hesitated. They were being used as a hospital, but for the longest time, I'd dreamed of entering in a black gown, of sitting down with other students and writing what I knew on one of the examination papers. Those papers were printed at the Press. I'd folded them, collated them. I'd been told the consequences of sharing the questions that were on them, though few of us who worked with the papers would have the opportunity. We were Town, the students were Gown. Oil and water, usually. Sometimes a student would try to bribe one of the printing apprentices. They'd stand at the bar of the Jericho Tavern or the Prince of Wales, waiting to strike up a conversation when the apprentices came in for a pint. The apprentices would string them along, drink the beer they'd been bought, have a laugh. But they wouldn't take the money. It wasn't just the Controller they'd have to face if they got caught. It was their brothers, their uncles and fathers. Letting down the Press was like letting down your family. The Gowns would skulk out as ignorant as when they'd skulked in, only a few bob poorer.

They might have had better luck with a bindery girl. We spent more time with the pages and had more opportunity to read what was on them. I could think of a dozen who might have been swayed by flattery, though few of them had the motivation to commit a question to memory. And memory was all we had, because the process of binding examination papers was strictly monitored.

I made a game of memorising questions. I was drawn to English, History and Classics – I could make neither head nor tail of Ancient Greek, but I liked the stories. Ma had loved reading them, retelling them, and *Calliope* held tight to her favourites. But there was so much we didn't have. If an examination question suggested the names of gods I did not know, I'd walk with Maude to the Clarendon Institute and spend an hour in the 'Stute library searching for their stories. I might make sense of the question, but my answer, I knew, was never better than the library I had access to.

The High Street entrance to the Examination Schools was grand, like all the University buildings on the High. If I didn't walk beneath the admiral arch of the Press every day, I might have turned and gone home, too intimidated to walk past the stone columns and through the heavy ornate doors. The Press was part of the University; I'd always known this. I felt it as I walked through the quad each morning; between the Bible side and Learned side, past garden beds, the pond with its water lilies, the swathe of bicycles beneath ivy-covered stone. Any visitor could be fooled into thinking it was a college, but our quad was mostly gravel, not lawn, and if they stepped into the building, they would smell ink and glue and oil. Their ears would ring with the presses. As soon as I put on my apron and sat at my bench, I knew it was the building and the books that the University valued. It wasn't me or Maude or Mrs Stoddard. It wasn't even Mr Hart. We were just part of the machinery that printed their ideas and stocked their libraries.

I stood on the footpath, watching the heavy doors of the

Examination Schools open and close as men went in and came out. They wore military uniforms mostly. A few wore the white coat of a doctor. Only a couple wore the gown of a scholar. A reflex made me look down to check I wasn't wearing the apron of a bindery girl.

I moved to enter and was stopped by a uniform.

'Looking to volunteer?' He was tall, well built. Well spoken. It was an officer's uniform.

I nodded.

'You'll find the registration desk round the corner, in Merton Street.'

The trades' entrance. 'Thank you,' I said.

'Thank *you*, miss,' he said, smiling. 'Can't tell you how grateful those lads will be.'

Did I straighten a little? I think I did.

~

If the Examination Schools had a trades' entrance, this wasn't it. I walked between two stone pillars into a quad as well kept as any college but busy with men in uniform instead of men in gowns. There was another woman, looking lost, and when she was pointed in the direction of a doorway, I followed.

There was nothing utilitarian about the Examination Schools. The walls were oak-panelled and the ceiling was pressed metal. The floor was flagged in coloured tile. Signs directed us up a wide stone staircase to the first floor. The woman took the stairs without pausing to look around. She was used to this, I thought, even though her clothes seemed plain. I looked more closely at her skirt – a finely woven wool; at the cuff of her sleeve, a simple unfrayed lace. She'd dressed down. I'd worn my Sunday best.

She didn't hesitate to open the door to the registration office. Despite the sign telling us to *Enter*, I would have knocked. When she held the door for me, I had the impression of a schoolmistress. She was taller than me, like most people, but not by much. She added height through her bearing and the pompadour style of her hair. I wondered how long it had taken to achieve. I nodded my thanks and forced myself to walk ahead of her into the room.

The clerk looked up, his eyes comically large behind thick lenses. 'Here to volunteer?'

'That is an excellent assumption,' my companion said, her tone teasing a smile from the clerk.

'And what is it you'd like to do?' he asked.

'That all depends on what needs doing,' she said.

He appraised her for a moment, his huge eyes taking in the lace at her cuff. 'We need readers and letter writers,' he said. 'There's plenty who've volunteered without the disposition for either, so we have more than enough women to roll bandages and hold hands.'

'That's settled then,' she said.

'Right.' He took a form from a tray on his right. 'Full name?'

'Guinevere Hertha Artemisia Jane Lumley.'

He raised his eyebrows.

'I know,' she said. 'Take it up with my mother.'

Then he looked at me. 'And you?'

'Margaret Jones.'

'Oh, you fortunate thing,' said Guinevere Hertha Artemisia Jane Lumley.

While the clerk completed the paperwork, the door behind us opened. Three more women came in. No lace at their cuffs. Their skirts, like mine, a sturdy serge.

The clerk handed Miss Lumley the form. 'Give this to the matron on the ground floor, general ward.'

'It will be my pleasure,' she said.

He looked beyond her and waved the other women forward. I took a step back, not quite sure what I should do.

'You're with me, it seems.' Miss Lumley held out her hand. 'Lovely to meet you, Margaret Jones. I'm Gwen.'

'I've never answered to Margaret,' I said, taking her hand and holding it firmly. 'So you'd better call me Peggy.'

~

Matron asked us to come every Saturday afternoon to read and write and generally keep the men company.

'We have about three hundred and fifty beds and more than half are already occupied. I expect it will be full before Christmas and we will need all the help we can get,' Matron told us.

'I am at your beck and call, Matron,' Gwen said.

'Beck and call won't be necessary,' Matron replied.

'That's a relief,' I said, before I could stop the thought leaving my mouth.

Gwen laughed, not unkindly, while Matron took me in. Clean, tidy, signs of wear, I thought.

'You work, Miss Jones?'

I nodded. She nodded back, then she turned to Gwen. Took in the lace at her cuff. The quality of her skirt.

'How do you fill *your* days, Miss Lumley?'

'I've just come up to Somerville, so I should fill them with reading.'

'Should?'

'Yes, well. It's so easy not to, isn't it?'

Matron didn't respond.

'And you, Miss Jones, where do you work?'

'The Press,' I said. 'In Jericho. I work in the book bindery.'

'Oh, how wonderful,' said Gwen. 'What are you binding this week?'

'We've just finished *Lorna Doone* and have moved on to Oxford Pamphlets and the New English Dictionary.'

'Really?' She looked impressed. 'Daddy's collecting it as it's published; where are they up to?'

'Subterranean,' I said.

'Below ground,' she said.

'Existing or working out of sight,' I said. 'An alternative sense.'

The matron cleared her throat. 'May I interrupt?'

'Of course, Matron,' said Gwen, as if Matron might like to offer a third definition of *subterranean*.

Matron took a deep breath. 'I will put you down for Saturday afternoons, initially. Be here at two o'clock. When the wards start to fill, you may like to add a shift during the week.' She looked at me. 'After work is ideal. Twilight makes some of them restless. A boy who seems perfectly settled and sane can suddenly start asking where he is, where his pals are. It's not unusual. But keeping them calm can take up more time than we are likely to have.'

'So, we're a team?' asked Gwen.

'Yes, you are a team,' said Matron. 'If you haven't been on a hospital ward before, you may find it a little confronting at first. I think it helps to have a friend nearby.'

'We are to be friends, Peggy. What do you think of that?' said Gwen.

I thought it unlikely. 'I'm sure we'll get on famously,' I said.

Chapter Twelve

Rosie and I stood talking on the towpath. It was almost dark, and beneath her coat she was dressed for bed. Her arms were folded across her chest as she listened.

'She's attached herself to Maude like a stray dog to the butcher's boy,' I said. 'It's odd.'

'What's odd about it?'

'Once they realise what Maude's like, people usually find me easier to talk to,' I said. 'But Lotte's different. The harder I try, the closer she gets to Maude. I might as well not be there.'

Rosie laughed. 'Peggy Jones, I reckon you're jealous.'

'I just don't think she needs me.'

'Who doesn't need you?'

'Lotte, of course.'

She raised her eyebrows. 'Of course.'

'I just feel in the way.'

'So you've volunteered.'

'I need to do *something*.'

'And Maude agrees with this, does she? Sitting beside you while you read to those boys? What if she suddenly decides she doesn't want to be there? Will you just leave the poor lad mid-sentence and bring Maude home?'

I knew where this conversation would end, which was why I'd started it. 'Maude doesn't know yet,' I said.

Rosie unfolded her arms. 'Tell her she'll be spending Saturday afternoons with Old Mrs Rowntree and me.'

I smiled. 'Thanks, Rosie.'

'Well, I need to do *something*,' she said, teasing. 'I'm sure we'll both end up with medals for our sacrifices.'

I hugged her tight and returned to *Calliope*. Maude was laying out the remaining squares of coloured paper that Tilda had sent. She did this sometimes, instead of folding, and I imagined her considering their potential. Planning her next move, like a general. She looked up as I came in.

'Need to do *something*.'

'Were you eavesdropping?'

'Yes.'

'Do you mind spending Saturday afternoons with Rosie?'

'No.'

'What shall I read to the soldiers?'

She looked around *Calliope*, at the shelves of books and piles of unbound manuscripts crowding the floor. She focused on Ma's bookcase. '*Jane Eyre*,' she said. Then she looked back to her papers as if the decision had been made.

Jane Eyre. My first grown-up book. *You'll wear out the words*, Ma had said, when I'd read the last page and returned immediately to the first.

~

I met Gwen in Merton Street, as we'd planned. I was a little early; Gwen was a little late.

'Ready?' she said, as she approached.

'I think so.'

'I'm a little nervous, I must confess. I've heard some awful stories about missing limbs.' She looked towards the building. 'I hope I don't stare when I shouldn't.'

'I hope I don't look away,' I said.

Gwen took my arm. It surprised me, but I didn't show it. We walked together into the Examination Schools.

We were escorted to a general ward.

'Most will be here for a week or two,' the clerk said. 'They'll spend a few more weeks recovering at home, then they'll be sent back to their platoons.' He held the door open. 'Some poor fellows will be here for months, maybe longer.' He adjusted his glasses. 'They won't be sent back.'

There were about forty beds, only two-thirds occupied. A few men were getting around on crutches, and there was a hubbub of noise as the tea trolley went from patient to patient and the men carried on conversations across the room. The clerk caught the eye of the sister.

'Two volunteers for you, Sister. Readers.'

'We've been expecting you,' she said. 'They're a rabble, I'm afraid.' She looked down the ward and smiled. 'Half of them are ready for discharge; it's hard to keep them quiet in the afternoon. There are a few who can barely read, and two who've lost their sight, temporarily, we hope. They both need their letters read and assistance in responding.'

Gwen laughed. 'I think I put a little too much thought into my role as a reader.' She opened her bag and revealed a collection of leather-bound books.

Sister nodded at two beds close to the nurses' desk. 'Private Dawes and Second Lieutenant Shaw-Smith,' she said. 'The specialist wanted them kept together – easier for his rounds. Of course, we couldn't put a private in with the officers, so the young lieutenant is with us for the duration.'

Of course, I thought.

They were both sitting up, steaming cups of tea on the lockers beside their beds, identical bandages covering their eyes. They each had dark hair and cleanly shaven faces. One had a large nose and strong chin. The other, a few spots along his jawline. They were both slender beneath their covers and the large nose seemed a little older than the spotty chin, but I would have been surprised if either was much older than me.

We approached them, and their heads moved in small increments in the direction of the sound of our shoes on the stone floor. They were like sparrows, I thought. Alert, ready to fly.

'Gentlemen,' said Sister. The men moved their heads in unison, their bodies leant towards her voice. 'I'd like to introduce you to Miss Lumley and Miss Jones. They have volunteered to help you with your correspondence.'

Their heads turned a little this way, a little that.

'Nice to meet you,' I said. The heads settled, facing me. 'I'm Peggy, Peggy Jones.'

'Oh, yes, lovely to meet you,' said Gwen, a little loudly. The heads jerked towards her.

The boy with the spots held out his hand. It hung in midair for a moment before Gwen took it. 'The pleasure is ours, I'm sure,' he said.

He spoke with the well-rounded vowels of a well-rounded gentleman. Though it was hard to reconcile with the adolescent skin. I assumed from the accent that he was Second Lieutenant Shaw-Smith. I moved to the side of the other lad's bed.

'You must be Private Dawes,' I said.

'That's right, Miss Jones. But I reckon you can call me Will.'

'And you can call me Peggy.'

'You can all call me Gwen,' said Gwen, still a little loud. 'And what shall we call you, Lieutenant?'

'Harold.'

'I have a brother named Harold.'

'I hope he fares better than me, Miss Lumley.'

'Oh, he will. His asthma will keep him behind a desk in the War Office – he's very embarrassed about it.'

It was all silence and knitted brows for a moment. Then Gwen took Harold's hand.

'What would you like me to read?'

We read their letters and penned replies. After an hour, Sister came to tell us it was time to leave them to rest.

'I think that went very well,' she said. 'The clamour in here can be quite disorientating for them. A nurse dropped a bedpan yesterday and Private Dawes thought he was back in France, poor boy. I think having a single voice to focus on, a woman's voice especially, might reassure him that he isn't.'

I could see it myself. Their heads no longer flicked this way and that.

'I know you're just rostered on Saturdays, but it would do them the world of good if you could come every other day or so. They'll be discharged soon, so it won't be for long.'

'Of course,' said Gwen. 'What do you say, Peggy?'

I hesitated. They waited.

'I can't see why not,' I said, though I knew full well why not.

'Matron mentioned that you work at the Press in Jericho. Is that right?' asked Sister.

'I do.'

'After work, then. Would six o'clock suit you?'

Of course not, I thought. I'd barely have time to get home and sort out Maude.

'It'll suit me just fine,' I said.

~

A few days later, I hurried Maude home through the streets of Jericho. *Calliope* was as cold as a block of ice when we came aboard and I cursed myself for not stoking the range that morning. Maude took off her hat but left on her coat. Then she sat at the table and took up the folding she'd been doing that morning.

'I bought a treat for you, Maudie,' I said.

She looked up and I took an Eccles cake from my bag.

'I have to go out,' I said. 'I'm reading to the soldiers again.'

She put out her hand, but I held on to the cake.

'After you've folded a few hearts.' I went to the galley and put the Eccles cake on a saucer. Then I opened the range and poked around, hoping for something to kindle. By the time I got it going, it was almost six o'clock.

'I'll be back by half-seven.' I'd never left her alone for so long.

On the table was a patchwork of coloured paper. A quick calculation. I counted out twelve squares and arranged them in a pile.

'Twelve hearts,' I said, putting them at her elbow. Maude was like a metronome, once she was set in motion she would go until someone stayed her hand. I relied on it. 'I'll cook tea when I get home,' I said.

~

Gwen was scribbling a letter for Harold when I arrived at the Examination Schools.

'Yours sincerely, Lieutenant Harold Shaw-Smith,' he said.

Gwen didn't write it down. 'Is Felicity your sweetheart, Harold?'

'Well, yes. It's not official. But yes.'

'She may not be aware of that fact if you end your letters with your rank and full name. Let alone *Yours sincerely*. What does she call you?'

'Harold,' he said.

'No pet name, no endearment?'

He hesitated.

'You're blushing, Harold. Which means she does have a pet name for you. This is very good news.' Gwen leant forward, lowered her voice. 'Do you mind if I give you a little advice?'

He shook his head.

'Your Felicity has been checking the post every day since you left for France. When this letter arrives, she will read it where she stands, scanning it for news of your health and a sign of your affection. If she gets to the end and sees that her letter has come from "Yours sincerely, Lieutenant Harold Shaw-Smith", she will carefully fold the pages, return them to their envelope and leave them on the side table in the hall until it is time to read them to the family after dinner. *But* if the letter, dull as it may be, is signed by the man she is in love with, then she will take it to her bedroom and read it over and over, looking for other signs of affection within the reportage of your weeks in France and the boredom of your temporary blindness. She will hold it to her breast and no doubt shed a tear or two.' Gwen paused to let her words sink in. 'Which scenario do you prefer, Harold?'

He swallowed. 'The second, Miss Lumley.'

'Of course you do,' she said. 'So, how would you really like to sign this letter?'

'Yours, affectionately, Lieutenant Harold.'

Gwen frowned. '*Lieutenant*. Really?'

'Yes, Miss Lumley.' He cleared his throat. 'That's what Flick calls me when …' He failed to finish and bent his bandaged head to the bedsheet, an attempt, perhaps, to hide a private smile. He was completely unsuccessful, as Gwen simply adjusted her own posture so as not to miss a single expression.

'Oh, I *see*,' she said. '*Lieutenant* Harold it is, then.' Gwen signed the letter, her own smile broad. 'Now, is there anything you'd like to say to Flick that it would be unwise for her to read aloud in the parlour after dinner? We can insert it as a separate page.'

Gwen took out a clean sheet of writing paper and leant in even closer. Harold lowered his voice and recited until the page was full and his face was burning.

'Do you have a sweetheart, Will?' I asked.

'Nah, not yet, miss. Why, are you interested?'

'Don't be cheeky,' I said, smiling.

Will motioned for me to come in closer. 'You can call me *Private* Will, if you like.'

I snorted and it made Will laugh. It took a few minutes for us to settle to the task of a polite reply to his aunt Lyn.

~

'It feels good, doesn't it?' said Gwen as we left the Examination Schools and walked along the High.

'It depends. Are you talking about this damned drizzle' – I looked to the grey sky – 'or are you talking about reading letters to Will and *Lieutenant* Harold?'

Gwen laughed, opened up her umbrella and held it over both our heads. 'The latter, obviously. But I suspect it is the assistance we can give with their *replies* to letters that might do the *most* good.'

We turned into Cornmarket. 'I think *Lieutenant* Harold might still be blushing. What on earth did he ask you to write?'

'Let's just say that when Flick receives the letter, she too will have cause to blush.'

'And when it dawns on her that another woman is privy to her lieutenant's thoughts?'

Gwen stopped, suddenly. 'Oh. I didn't think of that.' She shrugged and we walked on. 'I suppose Flick will get an extra thrill from the thought or she will chastise him. Either way, their relationship will develop in the appropriate direction.'

We reached the Martyrs' Memorial and turned down Beaumont Street. Not the most direct route home, but that route was the towpath via the Hythe Bridge. Since Oxford had filled with soldiers it had become unsavoury, according to Mrs Stoddard, so I avoided it at night.

'It does feel good,' I said, and in my head I was already composing a letter to Tilda about how I was finally doing something useful.

I turned with Gwen up Walton Street. When we reached Somerville, she took my hand and squeezed it. 'Better run, I'm late for Hall. Roast chicken for dinner, usually edible. I'll see you soon?'

Dinner. I'd lost track of time. 'Yes,' I said. 'Day after tomorrow.' I should have rushed off, but I didn't. I stood on the footpath as she walked into the porter's lodge. The ease of her entry made me hate her, just a little.

~

It hit me as soon as I opened the hatch. An acrid, burnt smell. My guts were in my throat before my eyes could register that there was no damage.

And no Maude, though the lamp was still burning.

I raced back onto the towpath and jumped down onto Rosie's foredeck. I banged on the hatch door.

'Rosie! Rosie!'

It opened, and Rosie put her hand on my arm. 'Calm yourself, Peg. No real harm done,' she said. 'Just a burnt pot and the waste of an egg.' She looked behind her and I followed her gaze. Maude was sitting with Old Mrs Rowntree, playing chess.

I slumped against the frame of the hatch and watched Maude take Old Mrs Rowntree's bishop. It was just a burnt pot, but it might have been more. I thought of all the paper on *Calliope* and felt ill. I wouldn't be able to make it work, I decided, and immediately I began to miss Will, *Lieutenant* Harold, even Gwen – such an unlikely friend.

Maude's knight took Old Mrs Rowntree's queen.

'Check,' she said.

Chapter Thirteen

The next morning we walked along Walton Street in silence. Maude had no compulsion to fill it. She took my arm as if nothing had happened and I tried not to resent her. I imagined another woman sitting by Will's bedside, writing his letters. She'd be young and pretty and have plenty of time and no reason to run late or leave early. She'd be well spoken, well educated. A student at St Hugh's or a friend of Gwen's from Somerville. 'I love you, Maudie,' I said. Because right then, I didn't.

~

We were folding the pages for *Dot and the Kangaroo*. Octavo. Three folds. The same pages, over and over.

'Kangaroo,' Maude said, trying the word out. 'Kangaroo,' she said again.

Lou and Aggie chatted to their charges. Lou still spoke softly to Veronique. Aggie still made no adjustments for Goodie, but the young Belgians were both improving. They were smiling more. The same could not be said for Lotte. She understood everything but avoided the conversations that floated around her. I had learnt not to ask questions about her life in Belgium, but I managed to glean fragments when she responded to Maude. My sister was the only person Lotte cared to speak to.

'Aggie talks like a locomotive,' Maude said, matter of fact. I'd explained the simile, and she was fond of repeating it. Aggie had forgiven me long ago.

'But Gudrun's English improves,' said Lotte.

'Yours is better,' said Maude.

It wasn't a question, just a fact, but Lotte explained.

'I studied English.'

'At university?' I asked.

Lotte looked at me and I saw her discomfort.

'Yes.'

'Why English?'

'So I could work at the university library,' she said. Very quiet.

'Read the books,' said Maude, just as quietly.

'Yes. Read the books, the English books. Study them.' Barely a whisper.

'Like Peggy,' Maude said.

And for a moment, Lotte was curious. I saw it in the quick glance she sent my way, but then it faded.

Mrs Hogg rang the bell for the end of the day and we finished our folds. Aggie began talking a mile a minute and Goodie cocked an ear to the gibberish. She broke into a smile every time a word or phrase made itself understood. They led the way out of the bindery.

Mrs Stoddard came into the cloakroom as we were pinning on our hats. 'I'll be another ten minutes, Lotte,' she said. 'If you don't mind waiting, we could walk home together.'

'I will wait,' said Lotte.

'How are you enjoying your volunteering at the Examination Schools, Peggy?' Mrs Stoddard asked.

'I don't think it will work out,' I said.

'I thought you enjoyed it.'

I did enjoy it. I enjoyed being useful, I enjoyed talking to Gwen, I enjoyed walking along the High and pretending I was the only woman in Oxford who looked like me. 'It wasn't what I expected,' I said.

Mrs Stoddard frowned.

'Burnt pot,' said Maude. 'Waste of an egg.'

Mrs Stoddard's face slackened into pity.

People didn't realise that pity made you feel worse. It was easier when they changed the subject.

'It's just a pot,' I said. Then I took Maude's coat from the hook. 'Let's go, Maudie.'

We walked across the quad and under the arch. On Walton Street, we paused. Somerville was lighting up. The students coming back to their rooms after a day of classes, meetings with their tutors, a long afternoon in the Bodleian reading about history, philosophy, chemistry. I took Maude's hand, breathed deep to stop my fingernails from digging into her skin. We turned to walk home.

'Peggy!'

Lotte was walking at a pace, trying to catch up. We stopped.

'I would like to …' She searched for the right words, then looked to Maude, her face relaxing into a rare smile. 'Maude, I would like a walking companion. Will you join me on Saturday?'

Maude was rarely asked to do something without me, and I expected her to turn to me for the answer, but she didn't. She just looked at Lotte until she'd worked out the answer herself.

'Saturday,' she said. 'Yes.'

'I will be grateful,' said Lotte.

~

On Saturday Gwen was already sitting beside Lieutenant Harold when I arrived, late and out of breath.

'You can stop fretting, Will. Peggy's here now.' She turned to me. 'We weren't sure you were coming. Instead of replying to letters, we've spent our time trying to guess what had become of you. I thought that perhaps you had been asked to bind the complete works of William Shakespeare single-handed ...'

Almost, I thought, smiling. My sewing frame was heavy with the plays, just the sonnets to go.

'Harold suggested you had been recruited as a spy, and Will insisted you were meeting a beau and had forgotten all about us. I do believe he was a little jealous.'

'That's not true, miss,' said Will. 'You're too old for me.'

'And how old *are* you, Will Dawes?'

'Twenty-one.'

'Snap.'

He blushed then. 'Obviously, it's not your looks I'm going on, you just sound so ...'

'Wise?' said Gwen.

He laughed. 'Yeah. Wise, that's it.'

Gwen winked at me. I sat in the chair beside Will. Took a deep breath. Thought of Lotte and Maude and how they were getting on.

'Have you had any letters, Will?'

'Plenty.' His hand searched for the handle to the drawer of his locker. He fumbled with the envelopes and I resisted the urge to help. *They have to learn to manage*, Sister had said. *Just in case.*

∾

'Was everything all right?' Gwen asked as we walked away from the Examination Schools.

'It was my sister,' I said. 'I thought I could leave her alone. It seems I can't.'

'I didn't know you had a sister. How old is she?'

'We're twins. She's … well, she's different. It's hard to explain.'

Gwen didn't ask me to try. 'Who's with her now?'

I told her about Lotte. 'Her English is better than the others, but she speaks half as much, and mostly only to Maude.'

'Do you know where she's from?'

'Louvain. She worked at the Catholic university, in the library.'

Gwen took in a sharp breath. 'Oh. Poor woman.' She linked her arm with mine. 'It doesn't bear imagining.'

'What doesn't bear imagining?'

'It was destroyed. Burnt. All those books. It would have gone up like a bonfire.'

~

I hurried along the towpath, sniffing the air for any sign of mishap. There was none. When I reached *Calliope* I peered in through the galley window. Lotte was sitting across from Maude, folding. It could have been Tilda, and I realised there was something similar in the way they sat with Maude – their long spines, normally so straight and a little rigid, were supple; their movements were unguarded, as if no one was paying them any attention. Maude managed to quiet something in both women.

Lotte looked up as I came in. Stiffened a little. But she smiled, a small smile, and I believed it.

'Maude is teaching me her folding craft.' She held up a swan. 'She is very talented.' More words than she'd volunteered the whole time she'd been in the bindery.

Maude looked at the swan, then at me. 'Better than Tilda,' she said.

Lotte looked confused.

'Tilda is a friend,' I said, 'with very little talent for folding.'

'A talent for life,' said Maude. It was one of Ma's refrains.

'She was close to our ma,' I explained.

'Ma is dead,' said Maude, and I flinched.

'I will go now,' said Lotte.

~

A week later, Will's bandages were removed. I sat with him while he tried to focus on people, then objects, then words on a page. It took days, but eventually he could read his own post.

'A month or two at home should have me right as rain,' he told me. 'Then it's back to France.' He said it so casually, but his lip quivered and his eyes filled. 'Still not used to how bright everything is,' he said, dabbing them with his sleeve. 'It's bloody irritating.'

The day Will was sent home, Sister told us that Harold was being transferred to another ward. He'd developed an infection. There was little hope he'd see again.

'He won't be returning to France,' she said.

Gwen was silent. Shaken.

'What can we do?' I asked.

Sister sighed. 'Get used to it.'

Chapter Fourteen

It was Saturday, and we woke and dressed for work as normal, but I insisted we wear our good hats, and took extra care rolling Maude's hair into a tight bun. I kept my own bun loose. We stepped onto the towpath.

It was a good day. The kind of day when our world seemed twice as big, twice as bright and colourful. No breeze or boats disturbed the canal and everything was reflected. Maude moved beyond *Calliope's* stern and I watched her head tilt. She was examining the reflection, comparing it to the original. She liked to do this on perfect days. *There is beauty in symmetry,* Ma would say. *We can't help but notice it.*

I joined her and saw what she saw. The surface of the canal held a palette of autumn colour and the belltower of St Barnabas had a twin. *Calliope* herself was also reflected, her blue hull and gold lettering: the script a mirror image but easy to read. I imagined everything that was inside had a watery double. Then the wind came up and the water shivered. Everything was singular again.

We walked through Jericho, and Maude bounced along as if Christmas was around the corner. Instead of tinsel and fir trees, windows were adorned with red, yellow and black. The colours flew from the branches of trees and rosettes hung on every second door. It was still early, but as we came along Walton Street, we saw a young woman standing in front of the Prince of Wales selling small rosettes and coloured favours. Men, young and old, insisted they be pinned to their lapels, bringing the girl in close. The sense of occasion brought smiles instead of reprimands from Jericho's mothers and aunts. They were waiting their turn to add coins to her collection box.

The Mayor of Oxford had declared 7 November to be Belgian Day, and the rosettes and favours were being sold to raise money for the refugees. On either side of the arch into the Press, a woman stood with her tray of favours. Printers, compositors, errand boys and foundry men mingled as they lined up to buy them.

'Help those whose lives have been ruined,' shouted the young woman closest to us. 'Buy a favour. Buy two!'

Maude walked ahead and joined the queue.

We'd stayed late at work the night before, with Lou and Aggie and a few others, to decorate the girls' side of the bindery. Mrs Stoddard had supplied the crepe and we'd wrapped it around pillars and hung it from the ends of benches. When we arrived, there were few women without the colours of Belgium pinned to their collar. We hurried in with others who'd been caught up buying favours. There was no reprimand from Mrs Stoddard, but the ire of some was not lost on me. Their unadorned collars made it clear what they thought, and a few had removed the coloured crepe from their benches.

I took my place between Lotte and Aggie.

'Why is Martha Burton so sour?' I asked Aggie.

She leant in close. 'Her nephew was at Ypres. Her sister got a telegram yesterday.'

'We did not ask for this,' said Lotte, not looking up from her folds. I thought she was talking about Belgian Day, but she might have been talking about the war. Perhaps she was talking about both.

Aggie grimaced, mouthed *sorry* and turned to Goodie, who was enjoying the increased attention that Belgian Day had afforded her. Instead of folding, she was chatting to girls further along the bench about leaving a wardrobe full of dresses and good hats when she'd fled.

'Did you leave behind any brothers?' one girl asked.

'No, dresses only,' Gudrun replied. 'But now just one small wardrobe, so a good thing, yes.'

I turned to my own pages but could not help looking sideways at Lotte. Her jaw was clenched. Her breath was deep. Maude was looking at her too. A question furrowed her brow.

If I could have reached across and put my hand over Maude's mouth, I would have. *Leave Lotte be,* I would have whispered.

'Lives have been ruined,' Maude said.

Lotte stopped folding. I stopped folding. I readied myself to intervene, to explain away my sister's words. Just an echo. But they were only echoes if you didn't know the code. Instead of stiffening, Lotte's body relaxed. She looked at Maude and spoke very quietly.

'It feels that way.'

Maude nodded. She didn't need more.

At midday, Mrs Stoddard rang her bell and encouraged us to go out and enjoy the festivities. 'Every penny you spend will go towards the refugees.'

'A good excuse for a treat,' Aggie said, when we were taking off our aprons and pinning on our hats.

'Save your pennies, Agatha,' said Martha Burton. 'Isn't it enough that our boys are dying for them, now they want our money too? Half of them are better off than we are.' She looked sideways at Goodie.

Aggie gaped. Lotte stood motionless, her back to Martha, her hand resting on the hook where she'd just hung her apron.

'Better off than we are,' Maude echoed.

'For once a bit of sense from you, Maude Jones.'

Maude searched for more words. 'Ruined,' was all she managed.

It was Martha who snapped. Martha whose eyes brimmed as she began to shout. 'You're right about that too. *Ruined.* Yes. Can't argue. My sister's life is *ruined*, no doubt about it. And what for?' She stared at Lotte's back and I noticed Lotte's hand was still on the hook, her knuckles white from rage or fear, or perhaps just hanging on.

∾

There was a crowd on Walton Street. Hundreds of Press workers leaving for the afternoon mingled with men in khaki or in hospital blues and dressing-gowns. They were patients from the Radcliffe Infirmary. Some had been brought out in wheeled chairs, others on crutches or on the arm of a visitor. All of them had favours pinned to their collars.

'Peggy!'

I looked around. There were women still posted on either side of the Press entry, their trays almost depleted. One of them was waving.

I told Aggie and the others that we'd catch up with them near the town hall. They turned towards Oxford, and I turned to Gwen. Then I hesitated.

'Why don't you wait here, Maudie. I won't be a minute.'

She shook her head and put her arm in mine.

'Stick like glue,' she said. A childhood instruction.

'Good God!' said Gwen, as we approached. 'You never said you were identical.' She peered at Maude and then at me. 'My goodness, how do people tell you apart?'

'Kind eyes,' said Maude, looking at Gwen.

Gwen was amused and made a show of examining our eyes. 'It's true, your eyes are kind, Maude, but your sister's eyes are not *un*kind.' She turned to me then and held my gaze, teasing. 'Peggy's eyes are …' She paused, as if thinking. 'Curious. Is she curious, Maude?'

'Like a cat,' my sister said.

'Like a cat,' repeated Gwen.

I looked away.

'We should get going, Maudie,' I said. 'Catch up with Aggie and Lou.'

'I'll come with you,' said Gwen. 'I've made a small fortune today, it's time to play.'

'Time to play,' Maude agreed.

'I'll just return this to Somerville. Come with me.'

It wasn't a question, and she was crossing Walton Street before I could object.

When she stepped into the porter's lodge, I stopped. It was the threshold between Town and Gown.

'We'll wait here,' I said.

'If you're sure.'

I was sure. I'd imagined walking into Somerville hundreds of times, but it was never at the heels of someone like Gwen, and not once had Maude been walking beside me.

'I won't be a minute,' she said.

Twenty minutes later Gwen emerged from Somerville.

'You are officially invited to afternoon tea next Saturday,' she said.

'What are you talking about?'

'It's for the Belgian families staying in Oxford. Somerville is hosting afternoon tea and you're invited.'

'Why? We're not Belgian.'

'That's what I said, but Miss Bruce insisted. She's head of the refugee committee and older sister to our vice-principal, who is also, inconveniently, known as Miss Bruce. The first is Pamela, the second Alice. It really would help if one of them married. Anyway, I told Miss Bruce, Pamela, she of the refugee committee, about you and Maude – that I'd left you waiting in the street – and she said she'd met you at the station.'

Miss Pamela Bruce. Straight and strong and steely. Would she have remembered me if I'd been alone?

'You never told me,' Gwen continued. 'She's an awfully good sort, you know. And an extra pair of hands won't hurt.'

'We're meant to be reading to injured soldiers on Saturday afternoons, Gwen.'

Her hand swished in the air as if she were shooing a fly. 'They'll live.'

My eyes widened.

'Oh, you know what I mean. I'll have a word to Matron when we go this afternoon.'

But I had no intention of walking into Somerville as an extra pair of hands.

~

The following Saturday, Gwen was once again standing outside the Press.

'There you are,' she said. 'I've been waiting.'

We stood on Walton Street: Somerville behind Gwen, the Press behind Maude and me.

'What for?'

'To remind you about this afternoon.'

I frowned and pretended not to know what she was talking about.

'The tea party for the Belgians.' She said it just as Lotte came out of the Press.

Maude waved and Lotte came over. I introduced her to Gwen.

'You must come too,' said Gwen.

'No, thank you,' said Lotte.

'No, thank you,' said Maude.

'Don't you say it, Peg,' Gwen said. 'Miss Bruce will wonder what I've done to offend you.'

An extra pair of hands, I thought. No, thank you, was exactly what

I wanted to say. 'I'm sure there are enough students willing to pass around trays of cake,' I said.

'More than enough. Everyone wants to do their bit, and passing around cake has had more subscribers than anything else Miss Bruce has organised.'

'There you go, then. I'll just be in the way.'

'Nonsense. Just yesterday, Miss Bruce asked after you especially. As a matter of fact, she said, and I quote: *Make sure your friend knows that she will not be required to pour tea.*'

Gwen could see I was out of excuses. Triumphant, she returned to Somerville, and I watched Lotte and Maude walk towards town. Lotte put Maude's arm through her own and I waited for Maude to pull away. When she did, I felt a childish satisfaction. But in the next moment, she took Lotte's hand.

I crossed Walton Street to keep them in view, but they soon became just two women walking hand in hand – close friends, cousins. Sisters, perhaps. Then their ages became indistinct. One tall, one small. They could have been a mother and her daughter. And that's when my eyes stung. When the image blurred.

It was strange coming home to *Calliope* alone. Strange not seeing Maude at the table folding her papers. It wasn't as if it had never happened before, but it was rare and unsettling; I didn't immediately know what to do with myself.

I removed my skirt and sniffed under the arms of my blouse, then removed that too. I slid open the curtain of our small wardrobe to consider my options. I didn't want to look like a bindery girl, but I also didn't want to look like I was trying to be someone else. I had a feeling Miss Bruce would not approve.

I wiped the Press from my face, my hands, my armpits, then put on my Sunday skirt and my white collared shirt. Then I moved into Ma's space. Neither Maude nor I had claimed it. We left it for Tilda – the bed, the little cupboards beneath it and above. The wardrobe, identical to ours with a curtain pulled across. I drew it open – Ma's things and Tilda's, side by side.

Help yourself, Tilda had said, but there was little we could wear. She was as tall as we were short. But she had hats and belts and scarves. And she had two wide ladies' ties.

Chapter Fifteen

'Don't you look the part.' Gwen stepped out of the porter's lodge. My hand went to the tie at my neck; I'd been unsure how to knot it.

Gwen shooed my hand aside. She undid and retied it. She took a step back and inspected. 'You'll fit right in.' Then she took my arm in hers and escorted me into the porter's lodge.

'My friend, Miss Jones,' Gwen said. 'She's my guest for the tea party.'

I watched as the porter wrote my name in the guest book. It wasn't quite how I'd imagined it, but it would do for now.

I tried to take in the buildings, the lawn, the flowerbeds. I noted the plain dress of the women, young and mature – they knew they had more to offer than their figures and faces, I thought. They greeted Gwen, and everyone smiled warmly at me. Did they think I was Belgian? Would it be different if they knew I wasn't?

When we came into the hall we were met by a Somervillian so effusive in her greeting that I had to take a step back. But she was undeterred. Her smile just grew wider and she took my hand in both of hers. Then she spoke, too loudly, and asked if I would like a drink: '*Prendre un verre?*' Before I could reply, she asked if I'd like cake: '*Prendre le gateau?*' Her head nodded up and down and her grasp on my hand tightened slightly. She thought I was a refugee, and she was not going to let me get away from her generosity. It struck me that she might believe her welcome capable of undoing the trauma of a German invasion. I replied, in English, unmistakably Town, that I was all right for the moment, and her face collapsed.

Gwen laughed. 'Miriam, this is Peggy, she works at the Press. One of Vanessa Stoddard's girls.'

'Oh.' Miriam frowned, her enthusiasm completely gone. 'I'll leave you to it, then. Nice to meet you, Penny.' And before either of us could correct her, Miriam was striding towards a family of Belgians with such gusto they all stepped closer to each other to absorb the impact as one.

'Is Mrs Stoddard well known at Somerville?' I asked.

'Among those of us helping Miss Bruce she is. She's very active in the Oxford War Refugees' Committee. Miss Bruce thinks very highly of her – we all do.'

A pretty woman made a beeline for Gwen. 'We need you, Gwen,' she said. 'There are just three of us who speak French, if you don't count Miriam, and half the guests are standing around with no one to interpret.'

'Oh, Vee, this is Peggy Jones. Peggy this is Vera Brittain, a fellow fresher.'

I recognised her. The woman from Mr Hart's office. She'd worn a lavender dress. *Coming up to Somerville to read English*, she'd said.

'Peggy's one of Vanessa's girls, from the Press.'

Vera beamed. 'Really?' She reached her hand towards me. I shook it, like I was used to shaking hands. 'My father makes paper for the Press,' she said.

For a moment I imagined her father stirring rag fibre in a steamy cauldron. But it was just a moment.

'He supplies the India paper for the bibles and dictionaries,' she continued.

The mill owner.

'Do you speak French?' she asked.

'Barely,' I said, recalling my lunchtime French classes at the 'Stute. Mr Hart encouraged us all to keep learning after we joined the Press, and I could read French with some confidence, but I'd never had need to speak it.

'Would you mind, terribly, if I stole Gwen? She's one of our most fluent.'

Yes, I thought. 'Of course not,' I said.

Gwen looked around the hall and I followed the sweep of her gaze. Small groups made up of Belgian couples and English ladies. A lot of hand gestures. Broken English, broken French. The occasional child in a mother's arms or hanging on to her skirts. I knew Lotte wasn't coming, but if Goodie and Veronique were there, I could shelter between them.

'I can't see Miss Bruce anywhere,' Gwen said. 'I know she wants to speak with you; are you comfortable seeking her out yourself?'

'Of course,' I said, terrified at the thought.

'Excellent. Try the gym.' She pointed, vaguely. 'She might be playing games with the children.' Then she left me standing there, looking the part in my Sunday skirt and ladies' tie, but feeling like bad poetry in leather binding.

I wandered out of the hall and found my way to the small, gardened quad. I sat on the nearest bench and buttoned my coat against the cold. I was in no hurry to find Miss Bruce.

I'd been walking past Somerville all my life, imagining what it was like for the women on the other side of the wall. Now, here I was. A little bit of Jericho littering an Oxford quad. I remembered when I first thought of being one of them – I'd been listening when I shouldn't have been. *She'd be well suited to the Oxford High School*, my teacher had said. *I know that*, Ma had replied, *but she won't leave Maude*. My teacher persisted. *I think she's bright enough for college*. Ma sighed, *It's not always enough, though, is it?* I'd thought of the income I could start earning at the Press, the difference it would make. I'd stopped listening.

I rose from the bench and walked across the lawn. I wondered briefly if it was allowed and found myself hoping that it wasn't. *When a privilege is unfairly denied,* Tilda liked to say, *then it must be taken.*

The squeals of children were just audible. I went through an open door and the sound of play echoed down the corridor. I listened for a moment, then walked in the opposite direction.

Most doors were closed, and for a while I was happy just to wander and take it in. Somerville was shabbier than I'd thought it would be. The floorboards were worn and dull and the walls were still stained from gas lighting, despite the new electric bulbs.

I tried a door and it opened. A storeroom with mops and buckets and bags of what was probably laundry. There was a chair in the corner and the strong smell of stale tobacco. A worn basket with a knitted shawl. *No privilege here,* I thought, and I closed the door.

I climbed the stairs to the first floor, pressing myself against the brick wall when I saw two women coming down. They were sure in their step and descended quickly, chatting all the while. 'Sorry, nearly knocked you over,' said one. Then they were gone. No questions. I might have been one of them.

I imagined the buildings would usually be crowded with women going to and from their rooms, their classes, the gym, the dining hall, the student lounge. They would have access to all areas, I thought, while across the road we were restricted to the bindery. The machine rooms, type foundry, store and depot were too dangerous, or too crass. The restriction was for our protection, apparently.

The door at the top of the stairs opened onto a tight corridor wrapped in books. I walked down it, hands dragging along the bookshelves on either side. I desperately wanted to disturb them. Then, another door.

I opened it, stood on the threshold and breathed it in. Wood polish. Paper, leather and ink. Some smells stronger, some weaker than what I was used to. I'd held an image of the Somerville library for the longest time, but I hadn't even come close. It explained the thrift across the rest of the college – it was books they valued, more than anything.

I stepped across the threshold. The desk where the librarian would normally sit was empty, and I walked past it without pausing. Shelf after shelf stretched out in front of me, and I knew they held books with the crest of the Clarendon Press stamped on their front pages. I wondered how long it would take me to find a book with pages I had folded, gathered, sewn. How long it would take me to find a book that I'd been told not to read. Not to ruin by cracking the spine.

I walked forward. The shelves were arranged at regular intervals. They divided the long room into bays, and each bay had a tall window and large desk. A few lamps had been left on, and I realised the weak afternoon light would not be strong enough to read by. I touched everything: a desk, the back of a chair. I flinched from the heat of a lampshade. I ran my fingers along the spines of books. Classics. Shelf after shelf.

I hardly knew what I was doing until I'd done it. It was a thin volume, cloth-covered. Its identity worn away from handling. A privilege, small enough to fit in the pocket of my coat.

~

Arriving at the gym, I understood the empty corridors, the deserted library. It had the character of a school fete. There were quoits and skittles, a long skipping rope with women turning it at each end and girls running in and out. Children were dipping their hands into a bran-tub and pulling out small toys. There was some kind of blindfold game that filled the hall with excited shrieking and caused one or two of the older women to smile and put their hands over their ears. A trestle was set up at one end, with fairy cakes and bread and butter and jugs of lime cordial. I recognised Miss Bruce standing behind it. Mrs Stoddard was beside her. Blessed bloody relief.

'Miss Jones,' said Miss Bruce as I approached. 'So glad you could make it.'

I hated to blush, but I felt it creep up my neck. I wondered what Gwen had told her, and I had a sudden image of them sitting in soft chairs, drinking sherry and musing on Maude and me.

'It was nice of you to invite me, Miss Bruce,' I said. Then, reluctantly, 'How can I help?'

'Well, if you insist, you can help Vanessa and me with refreshments. I'll give the games five more minutes, then ring the bell. You'll find they are a little more assertive than when they arrived at the train station.'

I moved around the trestle to stand beside Mrs Stoddard.

'Vanessa, do you mind sharing her?' said Miss Bruce. 'I have questions I'd like to ask your bindery girl.'

Mrs Stoddard was more than happy to share. She stood back and ushered me to a space between her and Miss Bruce. I wished I was taller. I wished I could look Miss Bruce in the eye. I removed my coat, which was old and dull, and stored it beneath the trestle. Then I straightened and felt for the knot in my tie, Tilda's tie. *It isn't enough to look and sound like your character,* Tilda once said. *You've got to feel like them to be convincing.*

'Can I call you Peggy?' Miss Bruce asked.

Can I call you Pamela? I thought. 'Yes. Of course, Miss Bruce,' I said.

'Tell me about your work at the Press – do you enjoy it?'

Did I enjoy it? No one had ever asked such a question and I'd never considered how I would answer.

'Surely it is not such a hard question?' Miss Bruce prompted.

If I said yes, she would ask what I enjoyed. If I said no, she would ask why not. 'It's not hard to ask, Miss Bruce, but it's quite hard to answer,' I said, regretting it immediately.

She raised her eyebrows; I felt a reprimand. 'Then take your time,' she said.

I searched her face for a hint of mockery but found none. I felt Mrs Stoddard move away a little, just out of earshot.

'I never chose to work at the Press, Miss Bruce. It was always going to happen. It's not like going to a dance.'

'Why isn't it like going to a dance?'

'Well, if you get tired at a dance you can sit down, if you don't like the music or the people you can leave, and if someone invites you to the next dance you can refuse.'

'Go on.'

I was frowning now, wondering if she was goading or genuinely ignorant. 'If I don't enjoy my work, Miss Bruce, I can't refuse to turn up. Working in the bindery is not a pastime, it's food and clothing and coal. It does no good to think about how enjoyable it is.'

'So you don't enjoy your work?'

I felt trapped. A quick glance towards Mrs Stoddard. 'Not always.'

'And why is that?'

'Because it can be boring.'

'Oh, but you are surrounded by books, words, ideas —'

'*Water, water everywhere,* Miss Bruce, *nor any drop to drink.*'

She smiled. 'Coleridge,' she said.

'*The Rime of the Ancient Mariner,*' I said, lobbing the shuttlecock back over the net.

She placed a hand on my shoulder. 'Keep an eye out for the albatross, Miss Jones. And take care not to shoot it.'

Then she rang the bell and the children rushed over.

~

Later, when the tea party was over and I was walking home through Jericho, I took the book I'd taken from the library from the pocket of my coat. I was hoping for Euripides, Ma's favourite Greek. Or maybe Virgil, Ma's favourite Roman. I looked at the spine.

Abbott and Mansfield. Decidedly English. *A Primer of Greek Grammar.*

My heart sank.

~

The next day was Sunday. I was rinsing our breakfast things when Rosie's sturdy high-laced boots walked into the frame of our galley window. Oberon's hobnailed boots followed, and then there was a third pair. Ordinary and familiar. 'Jack,' said Maude. Her voice was matter of fact, but she rushed out to greet him.

I waited until Maude's feet joined the others – she was in old slippers that were no match for the morning damp of the towpath. I sighed, then Jack walked towards her and the slippers left the ground.

Although Cowley was just on the other side of Oxford, Jack's training was intense and we only saw him for a few hours every few weeks. He arrived unannounced, like a postcard, and we gathered round to hear his stories: a shortage of khaki, training with wooden guns, the finer points of digging a trench and making up a cot bed. He told us every time how eager he was to be sent overseas. *Just wait for the lock to fill,* Oberon would say, whenever he was there to hear it.

Oberon retied *Rosie's Return*, then sat mute while Jack told us he'd been picked for special training.

'What does a sniper do?' asked Rosie.

'It's just like shooting rabbits,' Jack said, not quite looking at her.

'But you've never shot a rabbit in your life,' she said.

'Got an eye for it, they reckon. And the training should get me through to my birthday.' He still didn't look at her.

'And then what?' asked Rosie.

There was a beat, then another.

'And then he's old enough to be sent overseas to kill Germans,' Oberon said.

Chapter Sixteen

It rained more days than not through December and into the new year, a steady thrumming that I felt in my body and that hummed in my head even when I was out of *Calliope*. She smelled like a damp blanket, and I'm sure we did too. But Lotte never said a word. She continued to spend time with Maude, one evening a week and a few hours on Saturday, so I could volunteer.

I looked forward to my shifts at the Examination Schools – they were dry and warm and well lit, and conversation was unhindered by the insistent percussion of rain on wood and water. But I was also glad to return to *Calliope*, to walk along the towpath and see the light of the lamp through her windows. To know that Lotte was there and all would be well with Maude. Before stepping on, I would watch them. Usually they were folding, not a word between them, but also no tension. Sometimes Lotte held a book, one of ours. It would be open, but I could stand there for minutes and she wouldn't turn a page. I watched her watching my sister and wondered at the look on her face. A mixture of sorrow and longing.

When I came in, Lotte was quick to close the book and return it to whatever shelf or pile it had come from. While she put on her coat and attached her hat, she'd tell me what they'd done in the manner of a news report. She'd rest a hand on Maude's shoulder and give me a nod. I'd offer to walk her as far as Walton Well Bridge, but she'd always decline. *There's nothing in the dark that can hurt me*, she once said.

~

'Would you like to stay and have tea with us tonight, Lotte, after I get back from the hospital?' We were walking home from the Press, towards the canal. 'Nothing grand, but I'd like to say thank you.'

Lotte didn't answer straightaway.

'Say thank you,' said Maude.

'All right,' Lotte said. 'Thank you.'

'She was just repeating —'

'I know,' said Lotte, the trace of a smile. It was a fragment of who she'd been, I thought. A wry sense of humour and playful, perhaps. I smiled back.

~

When Gwen and I reported for duty, the matron took us aside.

'Normally, I'd not place you with an officer, Miss Jones, but I have been assured you are quite suitable.'

I shot Gwen a look; she was uncharacteristically guileless.

'Quite,' I said.

'So, if it doesn't make you uncomfortable' – she raised her brows, and I shook my head, bit my tongue – 'then I can't see it will do any harm.'

The officers' ward had fewer beds, more light from larger windows, flowers by every bedside. At one end of the room there were armchairs arranged in front of a fireplace. A card table was set up and two patients were playing draughts. Matron handed us over to a stern-looking sister in a heavily starched uniform.

'This is a general surgical ward,' she told us, 'though they vary in the severity of their injuries. Some will recover completely and return to their platoons, while others will be discharged home with fewer limbs than they were born with.' She watched our faces as she spoke and seemed satisfied that we were not the kind of women to suffer faints or excessive emotion.

'We also have two Belgian officers on the ward. Matron tells me you both speak French?'

'We do,' said Gwen, throwing me a glance. *That* was what made me suitable, I realised.

'Let me introduce you, then,' said the sister.

We followed her through the ward.

Gwen went pale. Quiet. She was looking at one of the Belgians. His body was shrouded under a white sheet, a frame protecting one leg from the weight of it. His face and hands were almost completely wrapped in bandages.

The invisible man, I thought, before I imagined what was beneath the dressings. I was relieved to see the contours of a nose and the soft pink of his bottom lip. Only his right eye was uncovered. It was open. He was looking at us.

'*Bonjour*,' I said.

'*Bonjour*.' It was poorly articulated and barely a whisper.

The sister smiled. 'Miss Jones, this is Sergeant Peeters.' She tilted her head towards the chair by his bed. I took my cue and sat.

Gwen was introduced to Sergeant Jansen. He had fewer dressings than Sergeant Peeters, and he immediately offered her his Christian name, Nicolas, and his unbandaged hand. She took the seat beside him and colour returned to her face. Gwen's French was more than up to the task of conversation, and within a moment of the sister taking her leave, she and Nicolas seemed to be talking like old friends. I understood very little of it.

I was trying to fashion a sentence in French when my invisible man began to speak. It was difficult and faint. I leant closer.

'I am Bastiaan,' he said in English.

'Thank goodness,' I said, relieved. 'Not that your name is Bastiaan, though it's a good name, a lovely name. I'm just glad you speak English. My French is actually quite terrible.' I was nervous. I was trying to keep my gaze from slipping away from his one eye. Trying to stop thinking about what might be under his dressings. The words rattled against each other as they tumbled out. He couldn't possibly have understood.

I let my gaze slip to the lap of my skirt and I smoothed the creases. I took a breath and looked back up. His one eye was waiting.

'*Je m'appelle* Peggy,' I said.

He gave the impression of a nod. I tried to think of something else to say but the only French I could recall at that moment was *où est la gare; où est la plage; où est l'hôpital.*

He made a sound that I interpreted as 'Speak English'.

'You are comfortable with English?'

His chest rose and he breathed the words out. 'I am.'

I realised he couldn't move his jaw. 'Does it hurt to talk?'

He nodded and I wondered if that hurt too. 'It is necessary,' he said.

'Is that what the doctors have said?'

He nodded again and his eye closed for a few moments. I had no idea what else to say.

'I'm sorry,' I finally managed.

His eye opened. 'Why?' he breathed.

Because I'm inadequate for this, I thought. 'For what has happened,' I said.

The eye that looked at me was slate-grey, but I knew it would be blue on a summer's day and tend to green if it looked upon a river. The lid closed and I wondered if it was the only part of his body unharmed. We sat in silence until the sister ushered Gwen and me out.

∽

A light snow had begun to fall but I lingered on the towpath and peeked in through the galley window. Maude was folding Ma's good napkins – Granny's napkins from old aunt whatshername – into elaborate table decorations, and Lotte was at the range. I could smell onions frying and for a moment I was annoyed – I'd invited *her* to tea. Then my mouth began to water and I felt relief at not having to cook.

Lotte turned towards me as I came in through the hatch. She wiped her hands on the apron she was wearing; the apron I usually wore. She looked relaxed, her pale cheeks rosy from the heat of the range.

'Maude showed me the Covered Market,' she said. 'We bought *moules*.'

'*Moules*,' said Maude.

'Mussels?' I ventured. They smelled so good.

'Yes,' said Lotte. 'And potatoes. I will make *frites*.'

'Mussels and chips?'

Lotte nodded. 'You speak French?'

'I wish I did,' I said, removing my hat. Hanging my coat. 'I've been asked to sit with a Belgian officer.'

The shake of her head was almost imperceptible. She turned back to the range. 'Supper will be another quarter-hour,' she said. 'You sit.'

'Sit,' said Maude.

I sat.

Lotte turned to the range, her back rigid now that I was home. She looked like nothing could fell her, but I knew there were things that could. I'd been accidentally throwing them across her path since the day we met, forcing her to retreat. I shouldn't have mentioned the Belgian officer.

I stood and went into our bedroom. I rested on our bed, the curtain drawn. I listened to the ordinary sounds of a meal being cooked: a knife against the wooden board, the pan being put on the hot plate, a drawer opening, the clatter of cutlery, the drawer closing. Sliced potatoes being added to fat, the sudden sizzle. There was a smell I didn't recognise.

My mouth watered and I realised that the last time I'd lain on my bed waiting for supper, Ma had been alive and healthy. I took out paper and a pen and began a letter to Tilda.

Why do you never cook when you stay with us, Tilda? Is it because you can't or you choose not to?

Maude pulled the curtain open. 'Supper is ready.' I closed my eyes and wished it was Ma in the galley.

It was odd, being welcomed to our table by Lotte. She and Maude had laid it with Ma's best things. Lotte would have asked where to find the cloth, the bowls and plates, the napkins, and Maude would have told her. But Maude wouldn't have thought to say that we only ever used the ordinary things. That the plates with leaves painted around the edges were a wedding gift – for Granny, not Ma, though sometimes we pretended. They reminded me of the last time Ma had cooked Sunday roast.

In the centre of the table was the pan filled with mussels, still in their shells, steaming and fragrant. To its left was a bowl of chips, thinner than I would make them. On the right was a plate of Brussels sprouts. Instead of being boiled, they'd been fried. We each had a side plate with a thick slice of bread.

Lotte ladled mussels into bowls and placed the bowls on our plates.

'The *frites* you must take for yourself. And the sprouts.' She served herself and sat. 'The bread is for soaking up the broth.' She demonstrated.

Maude took a handful of the chips. Lotte passed her the Brussels sprouts. Maude shook her head.

'Why no?' asked Lotte.

'Eat a sprout then spit it out.' We'd been children the last time she'd said it. She stored phrases like a printer stored plates – the words set and ready to use when needed.

'That is true when the English cook them,' said Lotte, 'but I am not

English.' She picked up the plate of sprouts and served herself a good amount. When she put the plate down it was closer to Maude than it had been, but Lotte did not suggest again that Maude try them.

I watched my sister watch Lotte eat one, then two, then three Brussels sprouts. I noticed Lotte's subtle lick of her lips; I heard the quiet note of satisfaction deep in her throat. She did not look up from her plate.

'They smell so good,' I said.

'Because they have not been boiled,' she said.

Maude leant forward to smell them.

'How do you cook them?' I asked.

'I have fried them with butter and garlic, salt and pepper. It is not hard.'

'Butter and garlic,' said Maude.

'Butter makes everything taste good,' said Lotte. 'Garlic makes everything taste better.' She moved the plate away from Maude and towards me.

I recognised my cue and spooned a small pile of sprouts onto my plate. I was prepared to feign delight, but there was no need. I ate the lot and reached for a second helping.

'Don't be greedy,' said Maude. She slid the plate of sprouts back towards her and took two.

Lotte and I said nothing. We looked to our own meals: eased the mussels out of their shells, tore our bread and dunked it into the broth. Maude ate the sprouts she'd taken, then she took some more.

I lifted my napkin and Maude's folds fell out of it. I wiped my mouth and saw that Lotte was watching my sister eat. Sorrow and longing. The performance was over and her pale face was relaxed. She's done this before, I thought.

Chapter Seventeen

By the end of January 1915, Oxford's hospitals were full with soldiers injured at Ypres, and the paperboys were shouting about Zeppelin raids killing people on the Norfolk coast. Posters asking us to *Remember Belgium* were ripped from walls by the angry and the grieving. But Kitchener's face soon replaced them. He pointed at boys too young and men too old and all those in between who failed to wear a uniform. He stared them down with an attitude of accusation under his huge moustache.

White feathers began to appear around the Press. They were left in doorjambs, on compositor benches and the flatbeds of presses. One was glued to the repair bench where Ebenezer had been working on the binding of an old edition of *The Thousand and One Nights*. I watched from the doorway as he removed the feather with a scalpel, careful not to bend the shaft or tear apart the barbs. He put it in his pocket instead of the bin.

In the bindery, we were reprinting popular Oxford Pamphlets – essays on the war. Explanations. Justifications.

War Against War had come through my hands a few times and the sections were piling up again. I brought the right edge towards the left.

One fold, folio – turn, repeat. Two folds, quarto – turn, repeat. Three folds, octavo – turn, repeat. Four folds. A pamphlet.

I folded the words as Rosie might fold beaten egg whites into a pudding. I was careful, rhythmic, and the words disappeared before I had a chance to read them. This was how it went – if we did our job well there was barely a chance to read. Only when the section was done, in the moment it took to place it on the pile, was there time for a sentence to catch the eye. *A hateful necessity* was one. *In the immediate situation we were guiltless* was another. *We are making war against war, and we can endure all the suffering and horror which war involves.*

Can we endure it? I thought.

And then I was starting again. Making the first fold, the second fold, the third, the fourth. Placing the section on the pile to my left.

We can endure all the suffering and horror.

What did that mean, exactly? Who would have to endure it, how would they endure it?

First fold, second, third, fourth – my movements regular and automatic, a small wrinkle in my forehead the only sign that my brain was actually working. Thinking. Asking questions. What would Mrs Hogg say, I wondered, if she noticed. *It is not your job to think, Miss Jones.* And it never bloody would be, I thought.

◇

On Saturday, Maude asked if we could take the motorbus to Cowley after our morning shift.

'Jack's not there any more, Maudie, you know that.' I'd thought to come home and read for a while before meeting Gwen at the hospital.

Maude shrugged, wanting to go regardless.

After we took our seats, Maude settled in for the ride – her palms flat on the seat so she could feel the grumble of the engine, her gaze ready to watch the streets fly by – and I unfolded a ruined section of another Oxford Pamphlet. *Thoughts on the War*. It was written by an Oxford don, Gilbert Murray. I'd recognised his name from Ma's bookcase. He'd translated *The Trojan Women*. Euripides. Ma's favourite Greek.

I'd kept the section, torn by a slip of the bonefolder (*Careless*, said Maude; *Not at all*, I replied) because his thoughts on war turned to the working man (and I counted myself among them, though it wasn't clear if Professor Murray did). The war, he thought, had softened the feeling between his lot and mine, between Gown and Town, toffs and hoi polloi. It had created a *band of brothers* with a mutual foe. *Thank God we did not hate each other as much as we imagined*, he wrote.

Did we hate each other? I wondered. Did they really have reason to hate us?

Not any more, according to Professor Murray. Because the working man, from Jericho to the slums of India, was willing to stand in line at recruiting offices around the globe just for the chance to bleed for England. *At the back of our minds we loved each other.*

I scoffed. He was an idealist; it was easy when you wore a gown. The war brought it out in everyone. I turned the pages, tried to read between the lines. Working men had no claim to England, no stake in the land, and many would be refused a turn at the ballot box, just like me. But still, they lined up. They bled and died for a country they had no legal rights to, and their wives and daughters went to work making bombs. Perhaps it made the masters, landlords and law-makers uneasy. If they loved us, then *our* deaths would become *their* sacrifice and they could sleep more easily. To love us now might be nothing more than a convenience.

I imagined writing a pamphlet about it.

I scoffed, again, and put *Thoughts on the War* in my bag.

'Sandwich, Maudie?'

She nodded. We ate and watched the streets speed by.

When the motorbus stopped at Cowley Barracks, only a handful of men got off to join the queue. The carnival of the early days had been dampened by the lists of names in every newspaper around the country.

But there were some who'd been waiting six months to come of age. They bounced on the balls of their feet, looking impatiently along the line leading into the recruitment office. The rest were the cautious or the harangued. They'd waited to see what would happen. When the Third Southern General Hospital started to expand beyond the Examination Schools into colleges and the town hall, they answered Kitchener's call, despite their fear and good sense. They joined the queue, but they were in no hurry to reach its head.

'Jack?' said Maude.

'He's training in Salisbury at the moment. He sent a postcard of the cathedral, remember?'

'Sharpest shot of the lot,' she said.

'So he says.'

'They won't know what hit 'em.'

I looked at the queue of men and wondered if it was better to know what was coming or be encouraged by some boyhood image of St George. I thought of my invisible Belgian and what must be hidden beneath his bandages. How many of them would come home like that? How many of them would come home?

A group of men came out of the barracks and ran to get on the motorbus. The recruitment line shuffled forward as the doors of the motorbus closed.

'Ebenezer,' Maude said.

And there he was, at the head of the queue, removing his cap and pushing his glasses up his nose. The bus moved off and I craned my neck to keep him in sight. He looked down at the step, the way he always did, to make sure he didn't trip, then he was swallowed by the recruitment office.

~

Before starting work on Monday, Maude and I walked through the men's side of the bindery and looked into the book repair room. Ebenezer was at his bench. I watched him laying a sheet of gold leaf and lifting his thick glasses so he could peer at the result.

'Blind as a bat,' said Maude.

'Thank God,' I said.

~

1 March 1915

Hello my lovelies,

You'll never guess where I am.

Étaples. France.

My God. It's vast, huge, sprawling like a London slum. ▓▓▓▓▓▓▓▓
▓▓▓▓▓▓▓▓▓▓▓▓▓▓▓▓▓▓▓▓▓▓▓▓▓▓▓▓▓▓▓▓
▓▓▓▓▓▓▓▓▓▓▓▓▓▓▓▓▓▓

It was a shock, I can't deny it. I'm not sure what I expected — something smaller, cleaner, sweeter smelling. It has the stink of your canal on the hottest summer's day. I'm ashamed to say I expected to see the soldiers who smile down at us from posters all over England, but it was like walking into a church where you think there's going to be a wedding and suddenly realising you're at a funeral.

After a while we stopped waving at the lines of men who marched by our lorry. We arrived at the headquarters of the Red Cross looking more like refugees than reinforcements. One poor girl was crying so violently she had to be taken to first aid for a sedative.

A soldier who either had lost a lot of weight or was still growing into his uniform climbed to the top of the lorry to retrieve our belongings. I gave him my best backstage smile, but he didn't smile back or blush or turn away. He just stared at me for a moment. *'Welcome to purgatory,' he said, deadpan. Then he dropped the bag into my arms and called out another woman's name. I don't think it's vanity that makes me wonder about the state of his mind, but I'm pretty hard to resist, as you both know, and he was unmoved. Even as I write this I wonder if he was a ghost.*

Much love,

Tilda xx

I peered at the blacked-out lines. Just two, but they overshadowed the whole letter. I went mad trying to work out what Tilda had written. I scraped at the black with the edge of a knife; I held the page up to the lamp. I finally threw it on the table. 'What don't they want us to know?' I said.

'Truth,' Maude said, without pausing in her folds.

∼

Lotte walked home from the Press with Maude, and I walked straight to the Examination Schools.

The Invisible Man was asleep when I arrived. The frame over his leg had been removed but little else; his features were still a mystery. I sat by the right side of his bed and took out the section I'd brought from the bindery. I would read to myself until he woke. It was another Oxford Pamphlet – we were printing them all the time: *How Can War Ever Be Right?* Gilbert Murray, again. *War,* he wrote, *is the enemy of social progress, friendliness and gentleness, art, literature and learning.* He had always been *an advocate of peace,* he wrote.

The Invisible Man stirred, groaned. His bandaged hands moved against the bed as if trying to dig a way out of it. I put down Gilbert Murray and caught hold of them. I held them gently until the dark dream had passed and the Invisible Man lay quiet.

I continued reading. The first great denunciation of war in European literature was, according to Gilbert Murray, *The Trojan*

Women. *Euripides gives the women a voice,* Ma once said. *Makes them powerful.*

The Invisible Man called out, and his head began to thrash from side to side. The nurse ran in.

'He'll do himself more damage,' she said, going to the other side of the bed and holding her hands on either side of his invisible face. She spoke to him, her voice low and soothing and repetitive. He stopped thrashing and she stood back from the bed.

'He might sleep a little longer,' she said.

'I'll wait.'

I turned back to Gilbert Murray. *Yet I believe firmly that we were right to declare war against Germany.*

Then the Invisible Man opened his eye and spoke.

'*Morte,*' he said. He stared, but not at me. Something in his dream. A memory, perhaps. His eye closed and he slept a little longer. When he woke, he focused on my face.

'Would you like me to write a letter?' I asked.

'To whom?'

'Family?' And as I said it, I realised all the questions it contained.

He turned towards the locker beside his bed. 'In the drawer.'

There was a watch, the face smashed. I wondered why he kept it. A volume of poems small enough to fit in a pocket – *Fusées,* by Baudelaire. A photograph. In it, a woman was seated, dressed for the portrait, her face a little tight. A boy stood on her right – ten, eleven, twelve, maybe. Smiling. A young man stood on her left. Also smiling, and tall, and in uniform. I glanced at the Invisible Man. Back to the photograph. The photographer had coloured their cheeks with pink.

'My mother and brother,' he said. 'His name is Gabriel.'

He was becoming more articulate, but I could see the effort of talking still caused pain.

'And this is you?'

He shook his head. 'Not any more.'

'Where are they?' I asked.

'*Je ne sais pas.*'

~

When I arrived at the book repair room, everything was ready.

It was a one-off. A special job. Everyone at the Press – everyone left at the Press – had contributed. At the very least they'd signed their name on the sheets that were passed through each department, from hand to hand. *THE BINDERY* was printed on the top of the sheet I'd signed. A red border in a simple design. The names of twenty men and nearly fifty women were already there. It was my job to take it to Ebenezer.

'Yours is the last signature, Eb.'

He took the sheet, placed it carefully on the bench and added his name. A memory of him in the queue at Cowley Barracks stung my eyes.

'All right, Peg?'

'It's hard to imagine the Press without Mr Hart,' I said. Without you, I thought.

Very few of us could recall a time when Mr Hart was not the Controller. He'd been strict, but he'd been fair. He'd given us the Clarendon Institute and most of us had used it to better ourselves. No one could say they were his friend, exactly, but we were all grateful.

'He can't bear to hear of another apprentice being killed by a German,' said Eb.

'Still, the Press won't be the same without him,' I said.

'I don't think he'll be the same without the Press.'

> *Address to Horace Hart MA*
> *Controller of the Press*
> *And*

Printer to the University
Presented by the Employees of the Oxford University Press

Eb had already prepared the casing for our farewell address. Blue Morocco leather with gold detail and lettering. It was my job to fold and gather and sew.

The sheets were thicker than I was used to, and it was an excuse to take my time. I wanted to honour Mr Hart with the skills I'd developed since I was twelve, since he'd become my Controller. But it was hard to draw it out. One fold. Folio. That was all they needed.

I gathered the sections and checked their order. I initialled the last page, though there was no need, then I placed the first section on the sewing frame. This was a slower job, my favourite job. I stitched each section to the cords, and to each other. I bound them well and knew my stitching would outlive every person who'd signed their name.

'Finished,' I said.

Eb inspected the stitching. Ran his finger over the spine.

'A pity we have to cover it up,' he said.

Chapter Eighteen

18 March 1915

Hello my lovelies,

I might be in France but this camp is British through and through, right down to the Twinings and McVitie's. I've settled into my hut with seven other VADs, debutantes mostly, though there is one other woman of unremarkable breeding. She's younger than me but looks older. A widow, I suspect. They join the VAD when their husbands are killed. Sad, all of them, but diligent. No one rolls a bandage like a widow. I've been put on a surgical ward. Less interesting than it sounds. I still mostly tidy lockers and clean bedpans. The highlight of my shift is helping men with injured arms or hands to eat and shave. We get to chat, you see. Flirt a bit. It's when I feel most useful.

Tilda x

P.S. Helen used to describe your Mr Hart as stern. But she said he was kind to her, the one time it mattered. I think she would have been glad your names were on his card.

P.P.S. I've made a parcel of all the things I should never have bothered packing — blouses, skirts, the apricot dress your ma loved me in, and a pair of heels (what was I thinking?) and half my make-up. It seems my particular shade of lipstick is favoured by the women of Étaples' number-two brothel, and twice, on my days off, I've been mistaken for a 'girl of joy'! And not even the first-class kind! The parcel should arrive in a week or two — make good use of whatever fits and be sparing with the cherry-red lipstick. You don't want to be mistaken for a 'girl of joy'.

'Girl of joy?' Maude said.

I wasn't quite sure how to explain it.

'A woman who likes to spend time with men, Maudie.'

~

By April, the ward at the Examination Schools was crowded with people. With fathers eager to see and mothers eager to touch their boys. With sweethearts sitting speechless at bedsides, their futures lying ruined under white sheets. We sometimes arrived to find a bed unexpectedly empty. We didn't always ask why. Only the Belgians had nowhere else to go.

Bastiaan's face was still shrouded in white, but the bandages had been removed from his hands and each week they became more expressive. I'd grown used to the lacework of scars and the textured patchwork of skin. He raised his right hand in a kind of wave. His eye smiled.

'You'll be holding a book soon, maybe even a pen. I'll have nothing to do.'

He tried to move his fingers, to curl them into a grip. Except for his thumb, they were stubbornly stiff.

'An improvement on last time,' I said, though I wasn't sure. 'Would you like me to read or write?'

'Write.' He had the paper ready on the bed; he rested his hand on it. 'My mother and brother. They are found, in the Netherlands.'

'Oh, Bastiaan.' My own hand shot forward and covered his.

'Roosendaal,' he said. 'I have an address.'

'You'll have to keep it simple, my ear for French is —'

'Not so good,' he said. 'We will use English. It is better for Gabriel to learn.'

'Let's get started, then,' I said, but his thumb had clasped the tips of my fingers and did not immediately let go.

~

A few days later, Gwen and I walked along familiar corridors, popping into this ward or that to say hello to familiar faces. We asked after parents, sisters and little brothers, farms and family businesses. Gwen delighted in leaning down and asking about lovers. She kept a tally of how many letters she'd penned with proposals and was eager to know the outcome of her efforts. She took considerable credit when a wedding was in the offing, and great offence when she heard of a rejection. 'I don't know how she could have refused,' she said to me once. 'It was a beautiful letter.'

We had become used to things, Gwen and me. The occasional ravings of a patient. The dash of a doctor and the hurried movement of nurses. The unfolding of a privacy screen around someone's bed, then the wail of a mother, quickly stifled. But since the year had turned, I'd begun to notice something subtler – a murmur of dissent. I'd heard it in whispered conversations after the Battle of Ypres the previous autumn, and I saw it in the frowns of people reading newspapers. It followed parents as they left the bedside of a boy whose future would bear no resemblance to the one they had planned, and it was shared with cigarettes among men being sent back to France. When Lotte asked for mussels at the Covered Market, it was in the eye of the fishmonger, and it was in the way some at the Press had begun to turn their backs on the Belgian workers.

On the officers' ward, at least, no one resented the Belgians. These men had seen too many lying dead in the streets of Mons, Dinant and Louvain. Men, women, children. If it could happen on the streets of Belgium, why not on the streets of England? I held the door for Gwen and followed her in. Most of the men knew us, long-termers or short – Gwen had made sure of it. She had a confidence that came from having had doors held open for her, literally and figuratively, all her life. Not all doors, but most. In the officers' ward no one questioned her presence, and so no one questioned mine. Those within earshot of Bastiaan's bed were pleased enough with the poetry I read or the stories I told, and if my patient dozed off, some would ask me to sit beside them for a stanza or two. I thought that maybe what I'd read in the Oxford Pamphlet had been right – we didn't hate each other as much as we'd thought. We just hadn't known each other very well before the war.

On this day, Bastiaan was sitting up in bed, and Nicolas was in the chair I would normally occupy. As we approached, Nicolas hoisted himself up with the aid of a crutch. He motioned for me to sit.

'The seat I keep warm, Miss Jones.'

'How long have we known each other, Nicolas?' I said.

He thought. 'I think, three months.'

'And you still call me Miss Jones.' I folded my arms. 'If you don't start calling me Peggy I might have to stop visiting.'

Bastiaan cleared his throat. 'Call her Peggy, Nicki. I will not forgive you if she stops her visiting.'

He would not forgive him. It caught me off guard.

'The seat I keep warm, Peggy.' Nicolas had moved to hold the back of the chair. I sat, and he pushed it a little closer to the side of Bastiaan's bed.

'You will keep visiting?' Bastiaan asked when Nicolas had moved away towards Gwen.

As long as you want me to, I thought. 'As long as you need a reader,' I said.

'And if I would like to talk?'

'Does it still hurt?'

He shrugged. 'Not so much.'

'Then you can talk as much as you like and I will listen.'

'And if I would like to listen?'

For an hour he talked and I talked and we both listened. I told him about Maude and Ma and *Calliope*. About the Press and Jericho. He told me his mother loved music like my ma had loved books, and their home had hummed with it. Then his father died, and his home went quiet. When it was time for me to go, he had ceased to be invisible.

~

Gwen held her umbrella over the two of us as we left the Examination Schools.

'We're being kicked out,' she said.

'What are you talking about?'

'The War Office has requisitioned Somerville. It's going to be another hospital, and rumour has it that our ward full of officers will be moving in.'

'When?'

'We have to be gone in two weeks. The patients will move in May.'

'Where will you all go?' I asked.

'Oriel College. They've offered us the servants' quarters.'

'You're joking,' I said. 'The men's colleges are half-empty – surely they can offer you something better?'

'Yes, I am joking.' She cocked her head. 'At least, I think I am. It doesn't really matter. The servants' quarters at a men's college are likely to be more comfortable than the student quarters at Somerville.'

~

The nurse gave me a box to pack Bastiaan's things. Too big, I thought, as I opened the drawer of his locker. A watch that didn't tell time. A book of poetry. A photograph. I put them all in.

'You might end up in Gwen's old room,' I said to him.

'I hope not,' said Gwen. 'There's an awful draught.' She picked up the copy of *Punch* that sat on top of the locker. 'Shall we pack this?'

Bastiaan shook his head. 'It does not belong to me.'

'What about this?' A small clock.

'Not mine.'

'This?' she said, hopefully. It was an English translation of Baudelaire's poetry.

'Peggy's,' said Bastiaan.

'Now why doesn't that surprise me?' She looked at me, a teasing smile. 'It's really worth reading him in the French, you know, Peg.' A pause to accommodate the roll of my eyes. 'Perhaps Bastiaan can teach you.'

Bastiaan *was* helping me read it in the French, but before either of us could respond, she bent down and opened the door of the locker.

'Surely this thing belongs to you?' She held up the thing – woollen, green, poorly knitted. Shorter than it should have been. 'What on earth is it?'

'A moofler,' said Bastiaan.

'Muffler,' I corrected.

'Really?' said Gwen. 'It's not long enough, surely. I can't imagine it would keep your neck warm.' She stuck her finger through one of the larger holes.

'Please pack it,' said Bastiaan.

'If you're sure,' she said.

I grabbed it from her and put it in the box. At the very least, it would stop everything else from rattling about.

~

Volunteers were asked to stay away from the new hospital at Somerville until all the patients were settled and nursing routines well established. It was only a few weeks, but the time moved slowly. Nothing I folded or gathered or helped Eb to sew seemed to speed it up, so it was a relief when Mrs Stoddard asked us to join her for a wedding.

'Whose?' asked Aggie.

'Mr Owen's,' said Mrs Stoddard, then she looked to me.

'She said yes,' I said.

'Were you ever in doubt?'

Not for a moment, I thought.

'We are to be a kind of wedding gift from the Press,' Mrs Stoddard continued. 'Mr Hart arranged it, apparently, though he's meant to be retired. He wanted some *sweet voices* to accompany the Press choir in a rendition of "By the Light of the Silvery Moon". You know it, I hope.'

Lotte shook her head. Aggie, Lou and I nodded; Maude began to sing.

'Save your voice, Maude, for when the happy couple come out of the church.' Mrs Stoddard turned to Lotte. 'You're welcome to join us, Lotte. No need to sing, but you will be required to throw rice.'

'No, thank you, Mrs Stoddard. I will stay here.'

We began singing as soon as the doors of St Barnabas were opened, and when the bride and groom came out into the sunlight, we threw rice. Miss Nicoll, he'd called her, but she was Mrs Owen now. She wasn't wearing a veil, and the rice stuck in the curls of her flaming hair. He kissed her then, and as she turned towards him the sun caught on tiny beads sewn into her dress. I felt a pang of something, in my heart and my gut. Not envy, though there was no denying that Mr Owen was handsome in his officer's uniform – Aggie was saying it loud enough for the whole choir to hear. It was something harder to identify. Something about the joy of the moment. It felt so … optimistic.

We followed the wedding party in a happy procession through the streets of Jericho. A great cheer went up from the Bookbinders Arms, old Press workers ready with pints for any of the men who wanted one. People came out of their homes and shops to wish the couple well, and children ran along beside them. When we got to Walton Street we parted ways. The wedding party went towards sandwiches and cake at the Scriptorium on Banbury Road, and the rest of us headed back to the Press.

❧

8 May 1915

Dear Pegs,

It's late, and perhaps I shouldn't write this, but how will you know what it's really like if I don't? I read the same papers as you — they're always out of date — but I pore over the black–and–white details, looking for something that resembles my days.

███

███

█████████ *None of that was there. I suppose my days are of little interest to men in their clubs and women in their parlours. And there's morale to keep up.*

I'm normally all for it — morale — but this boy got to me. He had my brother's ridiculous freckles, and his eyes were the same shade of green. He was younger, which made it worse somehow.

He'd been at ██ ██ *His hands were shattered. His beautiful boy hands, which I imagined were also covered in freckles, like Bill's. But there was no way of knowing. I held the lamp while the doctor washed the blood away. I gagged when the sister passed him the saw. Hours later, the boy woke, confused and looking even younger. I might have been his mother, the way he looked at me. I'm old enough, and in this place I'm often the closest thing. I made him tea — the milk is powdered but the sugar is sweet, and I added an extra spoonful. I sat on the edge of his bed and held his head up from the pillow so I could feed him. He'd finished half his tea before it struck me. This child, who was sent to France to be a man, would always need someone to spoon food into his mouth and hold a cup to his lips.*

But who will do it, Peg? That is what is keeping me awake tonight. He has no sweetheart waiting, and only a father and two younger brothers. The doctor told him he was lucky to be alive. 'Am I?' he asked me. Oh, Peg, what could I say?

And how is your invisible man? Does he talk? Does he laugh? If he laughs, there's hope and your job will be easier. I have nursed my fair share of invisible men and for some it seems that the erasure of their face has silenced whoever they used to be. They seem lost to themselves.

I sometimes wish them dead, Peg. Does that shock you? I've been asked to deliver it, you know. And I've felt the hate of more than one smashed-up boy for withholding it. They turn from me and refuse to eat or drink. It takes longer, but some succeed. The doctor records that they died from their wounds or infection, but some of them have just decided.

Tell Maude that her paper stars have some keen admirers over here in France. I've run out of room around my cot and started hanging them around the windows of the hut. One of the new debutantes asked if they were charms meant to keep us safe. It was clear she wanted me to say yes, so I did. She has settled in quite nicely, and I've noticed that she touches the star I've hung by the door every time she leaves for a shift and every time she returns.

Tilda xx

P.S. Thanks for describing Esme and Gareth's wedding. She obviously loved his gift.

I looked from Tilda's letter to my sister folding her papers. The candle in front of her was guttering, but she didn't seem to notice. I turned up the lamp on the wall.

'Tilda wants you to send more stars, Maudie. They make the nurses feel safe.'

She frowned. 'Tilda is safe?'

I wasn't sure. 'Of course,' I said. 'Not even the Germans would drop bombs on a hospital.'

Chapter Nineteen

I stood on Walton Street with Maude and Lotte, all three of us looking up at the windows of Somerville.

'It's hard to imagine it full of men,' I said, more to myself than to them.

'What is it usually full of?' asked Lotte.

'Women,' I said. 'It's a ladies' college.'

Maude pointed to the room above the porter's lodge. 'Peggy's room,' she said.

Lotte frowned, and Maude tried to clarify.

'Read the books, not bloody bind them.'

How often had she heard me say that? 'Don't swear, Maudie,' I said.

I lowered my eyes to the street and saw people going in and out of the college. Men in military garb or white coats. Nurses and VADs in their Sister Dora caps, matrons in their starched veils. Like nuns, I thought, and an image of Tilda in a virginal white habit made me laugh.

'What is funny?' asked Lotte.

I looked at her and reoriented myself to the conversation. 'Somerville isn't a place for bindery girls, Lotte. In normal times, the only way any woman from Jericho can get through the gate is as a scout with mop, bucket and boot polish.'

'A scout?'

'College servant.'

'But today you will walk in with pen, paper and a book.'

It was the way she said it. She understood what it meant, and I couldn't help the smile that spread over my face. 'Their defences are down,' I said. 'I will storm the gate.' I kissed Maude on the cheek and turned to cross Walton Street.

I stepped into the lodge. The porter wore an army uniform, and I wondered if the old porter had gone to Oriel with all the Somervillians. I gave my name and said who I was visiting, then I held my breath.

'The Belgian, you say?'

I nodded. He looked at his ledger.

'Through the quad to the library building. Someone will direct you from there.'

The Belgian. Bastiaan was the last. Five had died and been buried in the Botley cemetery, and Nicolas had recovered enough to be sent to Elisabethville, the village for Belgian refugees that had been built in Durham.

The main quad had been transformed since the tea party. Enormous tents covered the lawn, and I had to be careful not to trip on the ropes that held them in place. The entrance flaps were open to let in the spring air, and I could see that each tent was filled with cots, and each cot was occupied. The voices were all male, and I was glad to hear them. It was no longer the women's college I couldn't attend. It was a hospital, and I was as welcome as any visitor.

I climbed the steps of the loggia, where a few patients sat in cane chairs playing cards and smoking cigarettes. A sister gave me directions to Bastiaan's ward, but once inside the building, I hesitated. If I went right, the stairs would lead me to the library. I went left.

A VAD pointed to the bed on the right of the fireplace, and I saw a tall man, too thin for his frame.

It was a new version of the man I had come to know at the Examination Schools: the latest draft, I thought. There was still a large dressing over most of the left side of his face, from the ridge of his brow to his newly constructed jaw, but the bandages that had been wrapped around his head had been removed. The right side of his face was visible, and I could see the sharpness of a cheekbone and the seam on his chin where new skin met old. His lips were full and almost unharmed – just the left corner of his mouth looked smudged, as if the artist had wiped his hand over the drying paint of his portrait.

Bastiaan's head turned slightly so he could watch my progress across the room. I sat on his right and found it hard not to stare at his newly revealed features.

'I have heard that we all have a good side,' he said. 'I used to think it was my left.'

His hand hovered near his chin, exploring the new skin where no stubble grew, or perhaps trying to hide it. For months I'd wondered what he looked like. I'd gathered clues through glimpses: olive skin, slightly yellow from months indoors; dark hair on his forearms; the fine bone structure of hands that might have played the piano but would be easily broken. Things that weren't clear from his photograph.

My imagination had not strayed far from the truth. I could see the side of his face that had not been damaged. His eye seemed more blue than grey against the jaundiced tone of his skin, and his nose had been set straight. The large dressing still covered his left eye, cheek and most of his jaw. I imagined neat scars and knitted bone.

'When did they remove the bandages?'

'It has been ten days.'

'They said only family could come while they settled you all in.'

'It has felt long,' he said. His mouth twitched. 'I have missed your reading. My English, it may have suffered from no conversation.'

'That's funny,' I said. 'I was thinking the same thing.'

He frowned, and I had to bite back the quiver in my lip. The dressings had hidden so much. I felt flooded with the detail of him. 'I hate to say it, but your English is better than some of the people I work with.'

The twitch became a smile, of sorts, though the smudge in the corner of his mouth barely moved. His right hand slid across to the edge of the bed and I covered it with mine. His eye closed and his head turned on the pillow. In profile he might have been whole.

'What will you read me today?'

I took out a book of poems and held it up. 'Rupert Brooke,' I said.

He shook his head. 'I have heard these poems. Please, Peggy, I do not want to hear them again.'

'He's very popular.'

'Yes. His war is full of' – he paused – 'a kind of glory. For me, it has not been like that.'

I put Rupert Brooke back in my satchel. Felt the other book, its worn binding, the soft edges of its pages.

'Do you have another?' he said.

I showed him. He read the title.

'*A Primer of Greek Grammar.*' His frown, half-there. 'You are learning Greek?'

'No. Definitely not. I borrowed it. Sort of. From the library here at Somerville.' It was a confession and I tripped over it. I took a breath. 'Actually, I need to return it.'

'Well, then, what delays you?'

'Your hand.'

His smile. Half-there. I blushed. It was a breach of will.

'Do you think this ladies' library will have Rudyard Kipling?' he asked.

'I expect it does.'

'And you could borrow it for me?'

'I don't see why not,' I said, though of course it was probably impossible. He released my hand.

~

'Are you a student here?' the librarian asked.

I wondered if she'd need proof if I said yes. I rounded my vowels. 'I'm volunteering here. Reading books and writing letters.'

'Then I'm afraid the answer must be no. Only Somervillians are allowed access to this library.'

'I don't intend to remove the book from the premises,' I said. 'Just to read it to the Belgian officer. He's a patient downstairs.'

The librarian shifted, her mouth softened. *You can always tell when you have them*, Tilda once said, about an audience.

'Poor thing, he's been in hospital since January,' I continued. 'His injuries are awful.' I held my hand over my mouth, feigned distress. 'He may not —' I broke off, not quite prepared for the lie I'd planned. 'It's enough to break your heart.' My eyes welled; it was quite involuntary. Tilda would have applauded.

The librarian was on the edge of her seat.

'He keeps asking for Rudyard Kipling. But I don't have any Rudyard Kipling. He tries not to be disappointed, but ...'

'Which book?' she asked.

'I beg your pardon?' As if I hadn't been waiting for this exact question. *Give them a chance to show off*, Tilda had coached, *and they're more likely to do your bidding.*

'Which book would he like you to read from?'

'Well, I don't know the name. He said it's a mix of stories and poems. He bought an illustrated copy for his little brother, to help with his English, he said. Before the war. I think it's the poems he might want me to read.'

'We have a few titles, but I think it might be *Rewards and Fairies* he's hoping for. A children's book, but one of the poems has become quite popular among adults.' The challenge of finding the right book had animated her.

I checked my excitement. Looked placidly downward. Held my tongue. *No need to say a word when you have the advantage*, Tilda would say. *Usually best not to.*

'We use a card catalogue,' the librarian said, looking towards the bank of small wooden drawers. 'I assume you are familiar with it?'

I nodded.

'If memory serves, Kipling will be in the second bay of the main room. Bring it back here when you find it and I'll sign it out.'

She watched me walk towards the catalogue. When I found the right card, she smiled; I made my way into the main room and along to the second bay. I expected her to follow my every move. Her desk was perfectly placed to keep an eye on things. I found Kipling and turned to retrace my steps. She was looking at her ledger. I paused, barely a moment. I withdrew *A Primer of Greek Grammar* from under my jacket and placed it on an empty returns trolley.

'I'll need your name.' She held her pencil ready.

'Peggy Jones.'

I watched as she wrote my name in the Somerville library ledger. I stared at it. Evidence. Of something. Not much. But something.

'Are you quite all right, Miss Jones?'

'Quite all right,' I said.

'Well, please have the book back within the hour. I've had a long day pandering to the requests of students and staff, and I would be grateful not to have to track you down.'

'You have my word, Mrs …?'

'*Miss* Garnell.'

'Miss Garnell. You have my word.'

∼

Bastiaan was watching for my return. I held up the book.

'That is the one,' he said, when I sat beside him.

'It's a children's book, you know.'

'I do know.'

'Shall I start at the beginning?'

'No. Read the poem on page one hundred and seventy-five. It is after "Brother Square-Toes".'

'If you know the page number I suspect you could recite the poem by heart.'

'I could. But I like the sound of your voice.'

I read: *'If you can keep your head when all about you / Are losing theirs —'*

Bastiaan began to laugh. It was quiet at first, his body trying to hold it back, but his body wasn't strong enough. A strangled sound made other patients turn, then his laugh came unfettered. It was deep and round and regular like a drum. The effort of it moved his chest and squeezed tears from his eye.

I waited, the book held ready, for the laughter to subside. We all waited, but as his body calmed and the drumming of his mirth became irregular, and his good hand reached up to wipe the tears that ran down his right cheek, the other patients turned back to themselves.

'What's so funny?' I asked.

'It is a metaphor, yes?'

'Yes.'

'But not for me. And I only just understood this. I have barely kept my head,' he said, and again he laughed. 'When all about me, they were losing theirs.'

I couldn't say when the laughter stopped and the mourning started. His chest moved and tears fell, and his sobbing was deep and round and regular like a drum.

No one turned his way. No one acknowledged his pain.

It was how we kept our heads, I thought.

Chapter Twenty

Tilda arrived unexpectedly, on the first Saturday in June.

'There's no point writing to say I'm coming,' she said, as she emptied the contents of her travel bag onto Ma's bed. 'They're always cancelling our leave at the last minute. Better to be surprised than disappointed.' She retrieved a wedge of hard cheese and a bottle of red wine. '*Le dîner*,' she declared.

The next day Tilda insisted we go punting on the Cherwell. I had planned to meet Gwen, so she joined us. She sat beside me and we faced Tilda and Maude, while a boy did the punting.

'Describe a typical day,' said Gwen.

I saw Tilda shift. Her chest rose on a deep breath.

We'd talked for hours the previous night about her last day at Étaples. She'd assisted with ten amputations, one after the other. *Like working in an abattoir*, she'd said. She preferred hands and arms to legs and feet. *Trench foot*, she'd said, her face turning ugly with the thought of it. The stench stayed in her nostrils and polluted her dreams. I didn't say much; she didn't need me to. *Hands and arms, legs and feet?* Maude asked. Tilda understood, laughed, poured another glass of whiskey. *Incinerators*, she said. *They try to light them when the breeze is favourable, but sometimes they have no choice.* She screwed up her nose and shook her head, then she lifted her glass and drank it down in one. I'd imagined the alcohol washing images of those dead limbs into the depths of her gut. Drowning them, for a time.

When she went to bed, she asked me to lie beside her until she fell asleep. She was shy about it. *Just tonight*, she said. *And when you go, leave the curtain between us open. I've become used to sleeping in a hut full of women.*

I lay on my side and Tilda closed her eyes. I stroked wisps of hair from her brow and I remembered Ma doing the same when she'd lain beside her. She still had a beautiful face, but the lines were deeper and the shadows darker. There were strands of silver through her honeyed hair. How old was she now? Thirty-nine? Forty? Older than Ma was when she died.

In the morning, her vulnerability was gone. Thank God.

Sunlight played on the surface of the Cherwell. It lit up Tilda's face and I realised Gwen was smitten. I felt an odd sense of pride – Gwen and I had known each other for eight months and this was the first time I'd been able to offer her something of any value.

'It's like a hive,' said Tilda. 'It buzzes all day and hums all night. Thousands of men pass through from all over the world. They arrive, they train, the enlisted men spend a few precious hours in Étaples village eating pastries and visiting brothels. The officers go across the bridge to Le Touquet. The pastries and brothels are no better, but the beach is beautiful and the sun sets over the ocean – just the ticket for a tryst with a VAD before they're sent to the front.' She blinked once, twice. 'A lot of them are back within days.'

'Where are they from?' asked Gwen.

'Britain, of course. India, Canada, Australia, New Zealand. There are sixteen hospitals, which I thought was excessive.' She paused. 'Word is they'll be full come July. That's why I was given leave now – so I'd be back in time.'

'In time for what?'

'I don't know. Some push, though even the rumour is classified. We usually don't get much notice. Anyway, where was I?' Tilda smiled, theatrical. 'The Indians and Canadians are polite; the Australians are not, but they're fun with it. The New Zealanders are somewhere in between.' She leant forward. 'I'm quite partial to New Zealanders, though God only knows what possesses them to keep coming. They're hardly at risk of invasion. I doubt Kaiser Bill even knows where New Zealand is.'

'I suppose it's one way to see the world?' said Gwen.

'I don't think it ends up being the grand tour they're hoping for,' Tilda replied.

~

'You caught the sun,' I said to Tilda when we were back on *Calliope*. I was in the galley and she was sitting in Ma's armchair, her mouth full of pins. Maude stood before her on a pile of books; Tilda's apricot dress hung loose on her small frame.

Tilda shrugged. She used to care about freckles but now it seemed she didn't.

'Stay still, Maude, or I'll stick you.' The words lost their shape as they negotiated the pins. She used one then another to tighten, to shorten.

'I didn't know you could sew,' I said.

'Bill taught me the fundamentals.'

Her brother. I wondered if I should ask. 'How is he?' Some questions used to be easy.

'He was just fine a week ago.'

'And where is he?'

She sat back, looked Maude over.

'Belgium, I think. Maybe France. His lieutenant takes his job as censor very seriously. Towns, streets, cafes, they're all blacked out. He

163

could be in Brighton for all I know.' She leant forward and adjusted the hem. 'All right, Maudie. Now you can twirl.'

Maude stepped off the books and twirled. Tilda frowned.

'The neckline could be a little lower, I think.'

'It looks fine to me,' I said.

'A little lower,' said Maude.

Tilda winked at her. 'Something to thrill the boys, eh, Maude.'

My sister nodded, blew Tilda a kiss. Tilda blew one back. She stood up and pinned the neckline lower. Then she stepped back.

'You're a picture,' she said. 'Now take it off and I'll run it up on Rosie's machine.'

~

Lotte spent less time on *Calliope* while Tilda was there. She'd walk Maude home when I volunteered, but when Maude stepped onto our foredeck, she wouldn't follow.

'Why don't you insist?' I asked Tilda when I returned one evening after visiting Bastiaan.

'I do. She declines. I can't force her, Peg.'

I took in the scene – Maude was folding at the unlaid table; there was nothing on the range. Tilda was in red silk pyjamas, embroidered and buttoned in the oriental way, a whiskey in her hand.

'I think you make her feel uncomfortable,' I said.

'How so?'

I looked from her slippered feet to the whiskey. I cocked my head.

'Oh, Peg, really? Your Belgian has coped with worse than this.' She gestured the length of her body.

'No doubt, but you can be quite intimidating, you know. *Especially* when you're in silk pyjamas.'

Tilda put her whiskey on the table, then sat beside Maude. She took up a square of paper and began to fold. Her hands had the slightest tremor.

'It's not my pyjamas Lotte is intimidated by,' Tilda said. 'She was happy to come in the first time we met. She sat where you are now and we drank coffee and shared a bun she had bought at the Covered Market. I asked her how she liked working in the bindery and she asked me what kind of work I did.' Tilda stopped folding and took a sip of whiskey. 'Why didn't you tell her I was a VAD in France?'

'I wasn't trying to conceal it.'

'What part of Belgium is she from?'

'Louvain.'

'Ah.' Tilda circled her finger around the rim of the glass, then picked it up and took the last mouthful. For a moment she contemplated the whiskey bottle. I contemplated her. She decided against a refill and put the glass on the table, an arm's length away. The tremor in her hand was gone.

'I think your friend has probably experienced enough of this war to fill her nights for a lifetime. It's my proximity to it that keeps her away, Peg, not my pyjamas. I'd say she's protecting herself from knowing any more about it.' She looked again at the whiskey bottle, then turned to Maude.

'How many stars have you made while we've been chattering on, Maude?'

Maude counted her finished folds as I got up from the table.

'Six,' she said.

I picked up the whiskey bottle and put it on the shelf above the galley bench.

~

Tilda was snoring when I climbed into bed with Maude. We'd been used to it once, but it seemed louder, more ragged. I reached to hold Maude's hand.

'Why didn't you tell her?' she asked.

Maude was never deaf to what went on around her, and I always expected some fragment to be repeated when her mind was freed from the tether of her folding. But I couldn't work out what part of the evening's conversation she was recalling.

'Tilda,' she said, then closed her eyes to search her memory. 'Working in an abattoir.'

She arranged phrases like Dr Frankenstein arranged body parts.

'Maybe I didn't want to share her,' I said.

'Selfish,' my sister replied.

~

'What a tonic,' said Tilda as we came out of the picture theatre and into the foyer of the Electra Palace. '*Alice's Adventures in Wonderland* was my favourite book when I was a girl.'

'Mine too,' said Gwen. 'We have more in common than we might have thought.'

Tilda laughed. 'I doubt that, Gwen. It was also my only book.'

Gwen barely flinched. 'Poor you. Though if you *are* going to have just one book, that is surely the best one.'

'Surely,' said Tilda, a smile still on her face. 'Bill and I were always acting out little scenes from it, so I think it deserves some credit for my mediocre career as an actress.'

'Your Alice would have been formidable,' said Gwen.

'Oh, no,' said Tilda. 'I'd dress Bill up as Alice so I could play the Rabbit, the Cheshire Cat, the Hatter and the Queen of Hearts.'

'Tilda's famous for her range,' I said.

'If only I had been,' she said, then she pushed open the doors of the picture house and we stepped onto Queen Street and back into the real world.

There was khaki everywhere, some uniforms more ragged than others, like the faces of the men who wore them. Sitting against the wall beside the entrance to the picture house was a soldier with his head bowed, his trouser legs neatly folded to just below where his knees should have been.

'I'm afraid I shall drown in my tears,' said Maude, repeating a line from the film.

Tilda took a few coins from her purse and dropped them into his trench cap.

'Thank you, miss,' he said, without showing his face.

'Thank *you*, soldier,' she replied.

I could hear her anger and I added my own coins to his cap. Gwen put in a pound note, thought better of it, and put in another. We walked away and didn't say a word about him.

'Come for lunch on Sunday,' Tilda said to Gwen when we were near the towpath.

Gwen looked at me, as conscious as I was that I'd never invited her to visit *Calliope*.

'Of course,' I said. But what would she make of it? She'd complained about the draughtiness of her room at Somerville, the creaking bedsprings, the food. When I let myself imagine her family home, it had too many rooms and an army of servants to clean it. I never enquired about the detail and was happy keeping my own circumstances vague.

'I'll make a roast with all the trimmings,' said Tilda.

'You hate cooking,' I said, remembering her efforts in the weeks before Ma died and her complete lack of effort since.

'I do, it was always Bill's thing. But I've been staying with you for nearly two weeks and barely lifted a finger.'

'Barely lifted a finger,' repeated Maude.

Tilda laughed. 'You see, Gwen, what a burden I've been? I suppose I'll have to make a pudding as well or the girls might kick me out before my leave is up.'

'Have you ever made a pudding, Tilda?' I asked.

'Why don't I bring the pudding,' said Gwen. 'I'd hate to see Tilda homeless.'

I told Maude to lay the table with Ma's best things. She began folding the napkins into rosebuds.

'Gwen doesn't strike me as the kind of woman who cares much about napkins, Peg,' said Tilda, pushing a lock of hair away from her face and smearing her forehead with lard in the process. 'I don't think she'll judge you.'

'She's the kind of woman who doesn't *need* to care about napkins, Tilda. They're just always there when she sits down to eat.' I smiled. 'I've spent months trying to conceal my true origins and in an instant you've undone all my hard work. She'll take one look at where we live and think we're gypsies.'

Tilda put the potatoes in the oven. 'I'm sure she's seen right through your Sunday hats and exaggerated vowels, Peg. She likes you regardless. As for where you live' – she looked from one end of *Calliope* to the other – 'she'll take one look around and think it's a bloody floating library.'

Half an hour later, Gwen stood just inside the hatch, a cake box in her hands, her mouth hanging open.

'I knew you liked to read, Peg, but this is …' Gwen shook her head, lost for words.

'A bloody floating library,' said Maude.

～

Tilda was flushed and dishevelled when we finally sat down to eat.

'You don't mind if I come as I am, do you?' she said to Gwen. 'Lunch will go cold if I take the time to spruce up.' She looked at all the food on the table and shook her head. 'I didn't think it would be so hard.'

'I can barely boil an egg,' said Gwen. 'I'm sure I'd be far more frazzled if I tried to cook all this.'

I carved the chicken, served up the string beans and potatoes. Then I approached the Yorkshire pudding.

'You'll need to excavate it,' Tilda said. 'I forgot to grease the tin.'

I retreated. 'How about we pass the tin around with the gravy and a spoon?'

Maude had always loved Yorkshire pudding. She held out her hand to receive the tin first. We all watched to see what she would do with it.

She looked at the puddings, each in its own depression, sunken and flat. She frowned and tried to lift one out, but it was stuck fast. A deep breath of resignation, then she lifted Ma's gravy boat. The gravy was slow. When it came, it fell like a cow pat into one of the puddings.

'Plop,' my sister said. Then she looked at Tilda. 'Flop.'

'Thanks for the review, Maude,' said Tilda. 'Now eat up.'

Maude carved out mouthfuls of Yorkshire pudding straight from the tray, then passed the tray and gravy boat along the table. We each took our turn, but it was difficult to eat when we were laughing so much.

'How did you get the potatoes so crisp?' Gwen asked, her face as serious as she could manage.

'Thank you for asking, Gwen,' said Tilda, stabbing a potato with her knife and holding it up to inspect. 'I burnt them.'

'And the beans?' I asked. 'How did you achieve such a rich shade of grey?'

Tilda lifted a limp bean on her fork. 'I boiled the life out of them and withheld the salt.'

Gwen's face was contorted now. 'And the chicken?'

Tilda looked at her sharply. She summoned her Lady Macbeth. 'What's done cannot be undone,' she said. 'All the gravy in the world will not moisten this dry and shrivelled bird.'

For a few moments we were her captive audience, then Maude spoke.

'Dry and shrivelled,' she said in exactly the same tone.

We filled up on laughter.

'It's criminal, really, ruining so much food. I wonder if there's a law against it these days?' Tilda said.

'I bet Rosie could do something with it,' I said. 'Maude, go ask Rosie to come over.'

When Rosie arrived, Tilda grabbed the whiskey bottle and a couple of glasses. 'A lost cause, I'm afraid. Drink?'

'Go on, then,' said Rosie. She poked the leftover food with her finger. 'Cut off the black bits and add a white sauce. Season it and you'll have a tasty chicken pie.' She looked at Tilda. 'Would you be offended if I made it?'

'Of course. But I'm generosity through and through, so I insist you do as you please, Mrs Rowntree.'

'You're so kind, Miss Taylor.' Then she turned to Gwen. 'And you must be the honoured guest from Somerville. Maybe they've saved you supper.'

'I hope not, Mrs Rowntree —'

'Don't "Mrs Rowntree" me. That's the name of my mother-in-law. Tilda knows it rankles. Call me Rosie.'

'Well, Rosie, if you could pass me that knife, I have brought a sponge from Grimbly Hughes.'

La-di-da, said Rosie's expression.

We ate the cake like children, stuffing in more than our mouths could hold and getting cream on our noses and chins. It was hunger and cider and whiskey, but there was something else besides. Gwen cut Maude a second piece of cake. Rosie leant back in her chair, laughed at something Tilda said, and they clinked glasses.

We were celebrating, I thought. But what? I sipped my drink. It was the unguarded moment. The relaxation of vigilance and worry. The unexpected joy of ordinary mishap and easy friendship.

Maude pulled the cake box towards her and pressed the crumbs to her fingertips.

'All gone,' she said, when the box was clean.

'Right, then.' Tilda slapped her hand on the table, harder than she'd intended. We all jumped. 'I have a plan.'

'A plan?' asked Rosie.

'To get around the censors,' said Tilda. 'Peg showed me what they've done to my letters and I'm damned if my words are going to be erased.'

'Jack's too,' Rosie said, 'More lines blacked out than not sometimes. We hold them up to the light but it's useless.' She frowned. 'They're meant for me, those words. It's like I've been robbed.'

'You have,' said Tilda. 'You've been robbed of his experience. And Jack's been robbed of sharing the burden. I've sat by enough beds to know that it helps them to tell. And I've seen boys break when a letter arrives without any acknowledgement of what they've shared.'

Rosie was still. Thinking, no doubt, about her letters to Jack. Not a word acknowledging the pain that might be hidden under the censor's pen. 'What don't they want me to know?' It was a whisper, almost to herself.

'Troop movements, mostly,' said Gwen, and I saw Rosie's relief. 'My brother says they black out the names of towns, bridges, even restaurants, just in case it gives away the next big push.'

'They also black out anything that might make their mothers uncomfortable,' said Tilda, too drunk to realise that Gwen was trying to comfort Rosie. 'Though some are more vigilant about this than others.'

'Like what?' Rosie asked, her body already moving away from whatever Tilda might say.

Tilda turned to me. 'Have you got my last letter, the one with the French postmark?'

It was Maude who responded. She got up and looked through the letters we kept between the books in Ma's bookcase. She handed an envelope to Tilda and Tilda slid it towards Rosie.

'Like this,' she said.

Rosie picked it up. Turned the envelope in her hand. 'Can you read it?' she asked me.

I hesitated. 'Are you sure?'

Rosie opened the envelope. Removed the letter, just one page. She passed it to me to read aloud:

Dear Pegs,

You've been silent on some of the things I've shared, and I was beginning to think you're one of those who would prefer to bury their head in the sand. Then I realised that what I've shared might have been censored. I thought better of you immediately and have asked my friend Iso to send this letter through the French postal system. Iso is an artist from Australia, but she's lived in Étaples with her mother and sister for years (hard to believe this place was an artists' colony before the war; even harder to understand why they stayed, but life would be stark indeed without her). It might not completely avoid the censors, but it will avoid my matron and the censorship office.

He didn't make it, Peg. The boy with the freckles. The one who reminded me of Bill. Ypres was a slaughter, he said. I hear it constantly: the generals don't know what they're doing half the time, they ignore the officers in the trenches and threaten them with court-martial if they don't send their men over the top. Talk about a rock and a hard place — dead if they do, dead if they don't. They'd rather a German bullet than one of ours —

Gwen cleared her throat, interrupting. I followed her glance and saw Rosie's wide eyes, the quiver of fear at the edge of her mouth. Tilda took the letter, folded it. Put it back in the envelope. She was getting tougher, I thought, and I wondered at all the things she'd tried to tell me, and the things she didn't share at all.

'Is your friend a war artist?' asked Gwen.

Tilda scoffed. 'She applied to be, but Australia doesn't allow women to paint war – not officially. Officially, she's only allowed to clean, comfort and care, so she became a VAD. But she paints the war between shifts. Her war, at least. Which is my war. I watch her sometimes – it's beautiful what she does. Not just the picture but the act. She picks up one of her pastels and all the unspeakable things she's seen that day find a way out of her.' Tilda poured the last of the whiskey into her glass. Drank it down. 'When she goes home to her little house in the town, she's answerable to no one, luckily for us.'

'Luckily for us?' Maude said.

'The army has a battalion of busybodies, Maude. Reading all our letters and crossing out anything that gives the game away, but also anything that might upset or offend. Sending it through the local post doesn't guarantee a busybody won't get hold of it, but it does reduce the chances.'

∽

Tilda left a few days later. She was asleep in Ma's bed when we left for work, and when we came home for lunch, she was gone. We knew she would be, but it was still a wrench. The unmade bed was a consolation. I stripped the sheets and smelled her perfume. When I opened one of the cupboards beneath Ma's bed, I found a hanky, hairpins, a pen and four identical blank postcards of Oxford's High Street, green King George V stamps already attached. In the cupboard beside it, Tilda had left an assortment of underthings and accessories, make-up and some jewellery. I took out a long strand of beads and put them on. They reached below my waist.

'Back before you know it.'

I turned. 'Did she say that, Maudie?'

'Back before you know it,' Maude said again. She was reassuring herself, and me. I took her hand and squeezed it.

PART THREE

A Book of
German Verse

June 1915 to August 1916

Chapter Twenty-One

Proof pages. Various texts, with various page sizes: two chapters for *Shakespeare's England*; Marlowe's *Doctor Faustus* with an introduction by Sir Adolphus Ward; a new edition of *The Oxford Book of German Verse*; the next fascicle of the New English Dictionary – *Stead to Stillatim*. I estimated a couple of hours' work. I started with the Dictionary pages, keen to learn a new word.

Stelliferous: Bearing stars.

Calliope is stelliferous, I thought.

I folded the rest then put the sections on a trolley and walked through the bindery to Mrs Stoddard's office. It was closed. The new Controller, Mr Hall, was with her. When the door opened, a wolfhound emerged.

'She won't bite,' said Mr Hall. 'Gentle as they come.'

Even so, I put the trolley between me and the beast. The Controller smiled an easy smile. 'What have we here?'

'Proof pages, sir. All sorts.'

He looked through the sections, nodding at each text. When he came to *The Oxford Book of German Verse*, he shook his head.

'Is something wrong, Mr Hall?'

The smile again, as easy as can be. 'No, Miss …?'

'Jones, sir.'

'Nothing wrong with your work, Miss Jones, just that some of the pages are causing a fuss.' He patted his thigh and walked off. His dog followed.

I called out the titles as Mrs Stoddard registered the proof pages in her ledger.

'*The Oxford Book of German Verse*,' I said.

She put down her pen and looked at the sections I held in my hands. 'Proofs might be as far as that edition gets.'

'Is that why Mr Hall was here?'

'Yes. If they don't go ahead with the printing, it will affect our schedule of work.'

'It's just a reprint – why wouldn't they go ahead?'

'There's concern it shows support for Germany.'

'Are we at war with their poetry?' I asked.

'Quite.' She took up her pen and wrote *The Oxford Book of German Verse* in her ledger. 'Mr Cannan has suggested a title change. Let's hope it's enough.'

Chapter Twenty-Two

Lotte seemed pleased when I invited her to spend the evening with Maude.

'I shall cook?' she asked.

'If you don't mind,' I said. This seemed to please her even more.

As we walked through the quad, she linked arms with my sister and they fell into step.

'I am sorry I did not visit while your friend was here,' she said. 'It was not good manners.'

I remembered what Tilda had said about Lotte. 'Good manners can be tedious, or worse,' I said.

'What is worse than tedious?'

'Dishonest.'

Lotte looked at me, her head tilted. She smiled. 'Dishonest. Yes. Manners are often that.'

I considered them as they walked away. I think I was beginning to understand what Lotte needed, and what Maude gave. I didn't know what this war had done to Lotte, but I knew that she was living in a land that didn't know her, with people who couldn't possibly fathom what she might have endured. She listened to the polite enquiries from bindery girls and Jericho aunts: *Where are you from? Are you settling in? Do you miss Belgian chocolate?* And she heard their real intent: *Tell us what happened. Tell us how brutal it was. Tell us you have lost everything and that our boys are dying for a good cause.*

If it was as bad as the newspapers had said, how could she bear to recall it, let alone retell it?

And then there was Maude. My sister had a simplicity that unnerved people, an honesty that made them uncomfortable. It suited most to think that her words were nothing more than sounds bouncing off the walls of an empty room. It suited them to think she was feeble-minded.

Ma had known different. Maude didn't find it easy to compose an original sentence, but she chose what to repeat. She understood, I think, that most of what people said was meaningless. That people spoke to fill the silence or pass the time; that, despite our mastery of words and our ability to put them together in infinitely varied ways, most of us struggled to say what we really meant. Maude filtered conversation like a prism filters light. She broke it down so that each phrase could be understood as an articulation of something singular. The truth of what she said could be inconvenient; sometimes it made life easier to misunderstand her.

But I realised that what confused most people soothed Lotte. I wasn't sure how, but she had understood Maude from the first, recognised her somehow and felt comfortable. She didn't misunderstand Maude, and Maude was beginning to love her for it.

∾

I crossed Walton Street. Gwen was waiting near the porter's lodge.

'You smell of paper,' she said as she leant in to kiss my cheek. 'I thought it was some exotic perfume when we first met. I almost asked what it was, but it's just paper.' She was pleased with herself.

'It's hardly a good thing,' I said.

'Ah, but it is.' She took my arm and we walked into the college. 'Especially in this town. You smell like a new book – it's positively intoxicating.'

'You're a bit odd, Gwen, do you know that?'

She shrugged, held my arm a little tighter. We walked around the perimeter of the main quad, full of hospital tents, and climbed the steps of the loggia. Gwen barely raised an eye to the buildings, and I realised she was part of Somerville as much as I was part of the bindery. It didn't intimidate or impress her. It barely interested her.

Although I'd been visiting Bastiaan there for months now, I still drank in its details.

~

And Bastiaan drank in mine. I walked in the door of the ward and he watched my every step. He was sitting up in a chair and I pulled another beside it. I leant in and adjusted the blanket that lay across his knees, not because it needed adjusting, but because I liked that it brought me a little closer. I poured water into his glass and offered it. He shook his head. I put it down. I pulled my chair closer still.

His attention did not stray from me, though a nurse had come and gone, and a VAD was flirting with an officer in the bed directly opposite. It was intense and a little unnerving – his one eye, the slight angle of his head.

I let my hand rest on his blanket-covered knee. Hand-knitted squares made by schoolgirls, all sewn together. Doing their bit, I thought. I asked how he was. Again, the leaning in. He put his hand over mine and his fingers curled around my wrist, applied the faintest pressure. My pulse beat against them and I felt him relax.

'Keeping my head,' he said.

~

I left Bastiaan to his evening routines and met Gwen in the loggia.

'Seems a shame to return to Oriel so early when I have a pass to stay out till half-nine.' Gwen looked at me, expectant.

'Join us for tea?' I said. There was something about going back to *Calliope* and sitting down with just Maude and Lotte that I wanted to avoid. I couldn't help feeling I was an inferior copy, surplus to need.

'Will there be enough?'

'With any luck Lotte has found the sausages I bought and made something delicious out of them.'

'The infamous Lotte,' Gwen said. 'What *would* you do without her?'

She didn't expect an answer, but I couldn't help pondering the question as we walked home.

Since Ma died, there'd always been Rosie, but Old Mrs Rowntree needed bathing now, and dressing. Her shakes had become so violent that she could barely feed herself, and Rosie was forever doing laundry – it was draped all over the hedges opposite *Staying Put*, a daily reminder that she had enough to do.

Lotte had stepped in. She wanted to spend time with Maude, and Maude liked spending time with her. Preferred it, sometimes, and maybe that was why I didn't always tell Lotte when I was volunteering, and why I'd started to leave Maude alone – an hour here, two hours there. The anxiety of it a little less each time.

It was the image of Maude and Lotte walking away from me, arm in arm towards the canal or the Covered Market. The familiarity of it. When I saw my sister with Lotte, I was reminded of the easy way Maude and Ma had fitted together. Of all the times I'd walked behind them and how often I'd wished I could change places with Maude. And then, when Ma was gone, how often I wished I'd asked her how she did it. How she loved Maude so completely.

'I hope that smell is coming from your boat and not Rosie's,' said

Gwen, jolting me from my introspection. 'What else did you leave in the pantry besides sausages?'

'Leeks and potatoes,' I said.

Gwen shrugged. 'Not very promising.'

But she changed her mind when we stepped through the hatch. Lotte was bending to the oven and pulling out a dish bubbling with cheese and a white sauce smelling of garlic. The sausages sat in the pan on the hotplate, butterflied and golden crisp. There was just enough to go around.

'Sausages, leeks and potatoes is standard fare for the Somerville cooks,' Gwen said, when her food was eaten, 'but it never tastes that good.'

Lotte smiled, nodded. She was used to compliments, I thought, and I couldn't help wondering who might have given them.

'If you ever get tired of binding books, maybe you could take over the running of the Somerville kitchens.'

'Working in a kitchen is not my ambition,' Lotte said.

'Of course it isn't,' said Gwen, without an ounce of concern that she might have offended. 'You're from Louvain, aren't you? Peggy told me you worked at the university library.' She shook her head. 'Terrible.'

Lotte collected the empty plates. Took them to the galley.

'Your ambition and mine are probably not very different,' Gwen continued.

'And what is your ambition?' asked Lotte. She lifted the kettle off the range and poured hot water into the basin, then added a handful of soap flakes.

'Oh, you know.'

'No, I don't know.'

'To get my degree, I suppose, and engage in the debate, broadly speaking.'

'And what debate is that?' asked Lotte. She cleaned each plate, each fork, each knife. Laid them on a clean cloth to dry.

'It constantly changes, doesn't it? One minute it's the women's question, the next it's the morality of war. Conscription, women's education, workers' rights.'

I laughed. 'What would you know of workers' rights, Gwen?'

'Nothing, really. I've never actually had a job.' She smiled, with not a jot of shame. 'But it shouldn't stop me from engaging in the debate.'

'You are right, Gwen,' said Lotte. She turned to face the table. 'My ambition was to engage in the debate, as you say. I worked in the library. I read the books and formed opinions. I made arguments that should have changed minds, but usually did not. It was important, I thought, to engage in the debate.'

'And now?' I asked.

'Now?' she said, and the flatness of her expression became disturbed, like the surface of a pond in a whipping wind. She looked down, composed her face. When she looked up there was barely a ripple. 'It is all ashes,' she said.

'Ashes,' echoed Maude. Lotte took the few steps from the galley to where my sister sat and kissed the crown of her head. Then she took up her coat and bade us goodnight.

'Oh, dear,' said Gwen. 'I put my foot in it, didn't I?'

'Maybe,' I said. 'But maybe not. That's more than she's said the whole time I've known her.'

'I wonder what she meant?' asked Gwen.

'About what?'

'Ashes. What is *all ashes*?'

'Her library, Gwen. They burnt it to the ground. The books and old manuscripts. All of it. You told me that.'

'It's more than that, Peg. She said *all* ashes – everything. She was more than just a librarian, surely.'

'I know almost nothing about her,' I said. 'I asked a few questions early on, but she's determined to keep her secrets.'

Gwen looked towards my sister. 'What do you know, Maude?'

I suddenly felt uncomfortable. 'I don't think you should ask her,' I said.

'Why not?'

Maude was looking at me, waiting, perhaps, to hear what I said. I tried to form a response that might make sense.

'If Lotte talks to Maude, it's because she trusts her.' I struggled to find the right words with Maude in the room. Gwen was patient; Maude's gaze was unwavering. 'It's hard to explain,' I said, then turned to my sister. 'Can I try?'

She nodded. I turned back to Gwen.

'Maude has no ulterior motives.' Ma's words. 'She doesn't try to please or to hurt, and she doesn't judge. If Lotte has been through hell, Maude might be the only person she feels safe to confide in.' I paused, and reached out to touch my sister's hand. 'Maude doesn't pretend,' I said.

Gwen turned to my sister. 'You're exactly who you seem to be, Maude. It's very refreshing.'

'Refreshing,' said Maude.

∾

I walked with Gwen to Walton Well Bridge.

'Maude's relationship with Lotte makes perfect sense to me,' she said.

'Are you Dr Freud now, Gwen?'

She took my arm and held it tight. 'Don't you want to hear what I think?'

I wasn't sure. 'Do I have a choice?'

'I think that Lotte needs someone to mother,' Gwen said, 'and she thinks Maude needs mothering.'

It felt like a reproach.

Chapter Twenty-Three

August, and Jack came home for his nineteenth birthday. He was broader, taller. His skin had browned and his eyes looked greener. The uniform was a perfect fit.

'I've finally got my orders,' he said.

'Where?' I asked.

'France. My old foreman's platoon. He'll be my lieutenant.'

'Mr Owen?' I said.

'Lieutenant Owen to me now.'

'I take it he had no say in it,' said Oberon.

Jack laughed and I saw the effort it took for Rosie to smile.

We ate supper in Rosie's verge garden. She laid the crate with her best cloth, filled six glasses with cider and served up a fish pie. Jack kept on his tunic and his hat, and we all sat up a little straighter. A little prouder.

We had eaten like this a hundred times, and rarely got more than a nod from those using the towpath to get home from work. But there was Jack in his uniform, and not one person passed without comment: 'Kill a Hun for me, Jack,' 'I'll be joining you soon, Jack,' 'Good luck, Jack.'

'He won't need luck,' said Rosie. 'Look at him, he's fit enough to take on the whole German army.'

'The whole German army,' echoed Maude.

I took the empty plates into Rosie's galley. I washed them, dried them and listened to the low sounds of conversation through her galley window. I made out little but noticed that the silences were longer than usual. What do you say to your son, to your grandson, before they go to war?

Jack said something, then Maude began to sing, *After the ball is over* ... The chairs creaked as the mother, father and grandmother relaxed back into them. This would be the longest and shortest day of their lives.

~

The next morning, we all stood on the towpath. Rosie was in her boatwoman's best, Oberon in clean corduroys and waistcoat. Old Mrs Rowntree offered Jack her tattered copy of Shakespeare's sonnets. Her hand began to shake, and Jack held it.

'What will I do with these?' he said.

'Read them,' said Old Mrs Rowntree, the tremor in her voice now.

'Then bring them home,' said Rosie.

'Bring them home,' said Maude.

A beat. My heart. There were things we didn't say, but the silence rang with them.

'And this is from Maude and me.' I handed him our gift.

Jack had been buoyant the whole time he'd been home, but as I put the parcel in his hand I saw the lie of it, the telltale twitch at the edge of his smile.

'Open it,' I said.

He tore the newspaper wrapping and held up the roll of lavatory paper for all to see. I saw his relief.

'I'll treasure it,' he said. His smile wide, the twitch gone.

'Your nan's Shakespeare is meant to be treasured,' I said. 'This is meant to be used. If you're frugal and avoid beans, it should do you till the end of the war.'

'Avoid beans,' Maude said, and Jack laughed. He embraced her and she let him. Then he hugged me and Old Mrs Rowntree. Finally, he stood before his parents. Oberon removed his neckerchief and gave it to Rosie. Rosie reached up and tied it around Jack's neck. He hugged her. It was a long time before she let him go.

~

10 August 1915

Dear Pegs,

Let me start with the Germans. Don't be alarmed: they are all bed-bound, more or less, except Dr Henning. I can't work out if it is a promotion or a demotion. No one wants to work on the German ward, so perhaps I've offended someone. Then again, I have more freedom and responsibility, so maybe I've proved myself capable. The matron's reputation is legendary — a bitch, by all accounts. I couldn't wait to meet her. She has no sympathy for the filthy Hun, as she calls them, but she'll tend their dressings with the gentlest hand, and straighten the blankets of each and every one before she leaves the ward at night. Matron Livingstone is a bitch of the highest quality. If we have the same evening off, she'll come to the dunes near the camp and help me polish off a bottle of whiskey while Iso draws.

Like every other ward, the floors are always covered in mud and blood, it is boiling hot (I imagine freezing cold in winter) and there are never enough dressings or bedpans. Of course, our patients are prisoners, so the British Army has allocated only one VAD instead of the usual two or three. (A punishment, I suppose, but for whom? It's us who feel flogged at the end of the day.) There are no army nurses besides Matron, and while English doctors saw off German legs and arms, and stuff German guts back into German bellies, Dr Henning (Hugo) attends to everything else. He's also a prisoner, and very capable, according to Matron (though it was clear she resented giving the compliment). It doesn't hurt that he's pleasant to look at and in good working order.

Anyway, Pegs, it seems I'm here for the duration. I've been instructed on 'conduct with and in the vicinity of the enemy', and casually told to always use the army post 'to ensure timely delivery'. I will continue to send a few postcards through the official channels (I don't want them to think I'm friendless), but Iso has given me guidance on how to disguise my letters to look as if they have originated from your old and irrelevant French aunt instead of your beautiful and irrelevant English ... Well, I'm stumped. I've never had to think what I am to you and Maude. I think of you as family, Peg. You and Maude sit right alongside Bill whenever I'm of a mind to pray (which I find I do more often since coming to Étaples, though I doubt anyone's listening).

Tilda x

P.S. If it turns out the French script and postmark are insufficient, I will try to be more creative. I trust you to figure it out.

Chapter Twenty-Four

Bastiaan waited for me to sit before he turned from the open window, but instead of looking at me, he just stared at the ceiling. A breeze stirred dark strands of his hair, and I smelled the soap that had been used to wash it. Petals from the flowers I'd brought a few days earlier had begun to fall. The pink and purple of willowherb and butterfly bush sprinkled the surface of the locker by his bedside. The breeze had tossed their colour to the floor. I reached for the vase.

'Leave it. Please.'

'They're long past their best,' I said. 'I'll bring some fresh tomorrow – the towpath is generous with them this year.'

Bastiaan turned so he could see the flowers. In that moment I saw the other side of him. No dressings, no eye, skin like tripe. I looked away, back to the flowers, the vase, the petals on the floor. I swallowed the vomit that had risen to my mouth.

'They are not *perfect*.' He spat it out. 'But they are not *dead*.'

His head, he was losing it.

I continued to look at the floor.

'They are not *dead*,' he said again, a little louder.

'You're right,' I said, my voice a little quieter. I leant in to smell the blooms that were still intact, hoping for a hint of honey from the butterfly bush. 'And there's still a scent.' Though there wasn't. I began to gather the petals that had fallen, my hands shaking like Old Mrs Rowntree's.

'Look at me.' Low, like a distant storm.

I rubbed the petals between my thumb and fingers. Held them to my nose. Honey, just a hint. Every moment I delayed I hated myself a little more.

'Look at me.' Louder.

But still I didn't.

'I'm begging. Look at me. Look at me. Look at me.' Like a battering of rain or hail. Or gunfire.

I looked. A graft of skin from forehead to jaw, more like vellum than tripe. It had been scraped and stretched and stitched to the good skin around it. But there was no bone to shape it, and where the eye should have been there was just a hole. Every muscle in my face betrayed the nausea in my gut.

Bastiaan turned to face the window again.

'I am tired,' he said.

I was too ashamed to even say sorry.

~

'You are early,' said Lotte when I arrived home. 'I am not finished the cooking.'

'I've done the most terrible thing.'

'I don't think you have.'

I sat on the bench and slumped against the table. 'I looked away, Lotte. I looked away when he wanted me to see.'

Lotte shook her head. 'You English talk in riddles,' she said.

'I didn't know what to do.'

'Didn't know what to say,' said Maude. She passed me the box she had just folded and I recalled the little gifts Ma and I would offer her when children rejected her efforts to make friends. I recalled the excuses we made for them.

I passed it back. 'I don't deserve it, Maudie. I should have known exactly what to do and say.'

'Why?' said Lotte. She turned from the range and looked at me. 'Why should you know, *exactly*?'

I hesitated. 'I've known about his injuries for months, Lotte. I should have been better prepared.'

'Do you think he was prepared? Do you think any of us were?' She turned back to the range. 'Forgive yourself,' she said with distaste. 'What you have done is small. It is nothing. He will get on with living.' She started to shake.

Maude finished her folds. No haste. When she was done, she went to Lotte and held a butterfly on her open palm. Lotte took it, just as she'd taken the paper fan when she'd stepped off the train in Oxford, and once again I watched as she wrapped her arms around my sister and sobbed.

~

I returned to Bastiaan's ward two days later. The flowers were still there, their stems almost bare, the fallen petals accumulating on the top of the locker. I stood beside Bastiaan's bed.

'You let them sweep the floor at least,' I said.

He ignored me. Kept his head turned towards the window.

'I'm sorry, Bastiaan.'

'It could not be helped,' he said.

'I should have tried.'

'It would have been a lie.'

'It's more complicated than that.'

'No, it is simple. You were repulsed.'

'I'm ashamed, Bastiaan. I expected more of myself. I thought that I understood more than I did. But it was a shock. It was beyond my experience and I didn't know what to do or say.'

He said nothing.

'Bastiaan, I faltered. And I wish I hadn't.'

Still he said nothing. I felt myself getting cross.

'Tell me something, Bastiaan. What did you do when the doctor removed your dressings and held the mirror for you to see?'

One side of his face was still perfectly capable of expressing itself, and I saw my question register in the corner of his right eye. I waited, and in his own good time he turned his head halfway and looked up at the ceiling.

'I knocked the mirror from his hand. It smashed on the floor.'

'And have you looked in a mirror since?'

'Yes.'

'And do you throw them all to the floor?'

'Of course not.'

'Why?'

'It does not shock me any more.'

'Well, then,' I said.

'Well, then,' he echoed.

I picked up the vase of flowers and the last of the petals fell. Bastiaan started to protest, but I interrupted.

'Being pretty is all they're good for,' I said. I scanned the contours of his face, the good side and the bad. 'It's a good thing you're not a flower.' And before he could respond I turned and walked towards the nurses' desk near the door. I threw the dead flowers into the bin and left the vase, with its putrid water, on the kitchen trolley. The nurse nodded her approval; she held my hand until the tremor had stopped.

'The graft is good,' she said, 'and he's to be fitted with a glass eye tomorrow.'

When I returned to Bastiaan's bedside, I picked up the chair and moved it to the left side of the bed.

~

A few days later, Bastiaan and I walked the perimeter of the quad, testing his leg, building his strength. He put his arm around my shoulders, for balance.

'My father had a limp,' he said. 'He walked with a cane and it made him look old when he was still young.' I looked up as he spoke but his new eye couldn't see me.

'You don't look old, Bastiaan. You look like you've fought in a war.'

'Even with his limp, I think he would have fought in this war if he'd been alive.'

'What did he do?' I asked.

'He was an architect. And when I return to Belgium, I will finish my own studies and be an architect also. There will be much to rebuild.'

'You were a student?'

'At the Royal Academy, in Brussels.'

I looked at him and tried to imagine the young man he must have been. I'd lied when I said he didn't look old.

'And what of your father, Peggy?' He spoke cautiously. 'You have never said.'

There was almost nothing *to* be said.

'He was a Gown,' I said. Like you, I thought.

Full of words that turned my head, Ma had said, *but most turned out to be meaningless and others became very cruel.* I would push for more and she would say, *He wasn't the man he appeared to be,* and usually that was the end of it. Except once, when I cried, and she understood I needed more. *He was at Christ Church,* she'd said. *Classics. He was writing a treatise on Hipponax, whom he greatly admired, but I didn't know that when we met.* I stopped my crying. *Would it have mattered?*

I'd asked. She'd looked at me and I saw sadness and regret and other things I couldn't name. *Hipponax is my least favourite Greek*, she'd said.

'What does that mean – Gown?' Bastiaan asked.

'He was part of the University,' I said. Then, so there was no confusion, 'Ma was Town. They don't usually mix.'

We kept walking until his leg tired, then we sat on a bench.

'The bookshelves of many grand houses are filled with collections of empty pages bound in leather,' he said.

'Really?'

'Yes, I saw this as a boy, in the library of a man my father had business with. While they talked, I climbed the ladder to see what books were on the upper shelves. They were beautifully bound, and I thought they might be books that boys should not read.' At this, he smiled: his half-smile. 'But when I took one from the shelf, I saw that the pages were blank. I took another and it was the same. Book after book. A handsome cover with nothing interesting inside.'

'You'd like *Calliope*,' I said.

'Why?'

'Full of interesting stories with blighted bindings.'

'But you love them anyway?' he said.

'I do.'

Chapter Twenty-Five

One Sunday in September, I arrived early at Somerville. Nurses were busy with breakfasts and baths and morning dressings, and I was in the way. But the sister in charge of Bastiaan's ward was expecting me.

'He's nervous,' she said.

I would be too, I thought.

'They're not freaks while they're in here,' she said. 'They know it will be different when they leave.'

Bastiaan was sitting in the chair beside his bed. He was fully dressed in civilian clothes. Donated, not quite fitting. His hands were restless in his lap; his good leg was jigging up and down. He was looking out the window – for the last time, I thought. Was he glad, or did he already miss the comfort of it?

I cleared my throat and he turned. A large cloth mask covered his blind eye, his sunken cheek, his vellum skin. But also half his nose and lips and chin. I'd grown used to the landscape of his face and for a moment I felt like a stranger, staring. He looked away.

I sat on the bed and took his restless hands in mine. I waited for him to turn to me. 'It hides most of your face,' I said.

'That is the point.'

There was nowhere to look except his one good eye.

'What is wrong?' he asked.

'I feel like I'm being denied something.'

'You are being *spared* something,' he said.

'What am I being spared?'

'The discomfort of looking at the mess the war has made.'

We both looked down at his hands in mine. My thumbs traced the scars drawn all over his fingers. I looked up, took in the mask again. It was like the censor's pen: it hid what the war had done, was doing. It hid him.

'And it will spare me from pity,' he said.

He was right and he was wrong. I thought about when I first saw his face. I turned away so I could deny the missing eye, the sunken cheek, the unnatural texture of his skin. In that moment, his experience was irrelevant and mine was everything. Pity came later, but it was fleeting – the more I looked upon his face the less strange it became.

I shrugged. 'The mask will make people feel more comfortable, Bastiaan, but I don't think it will stop their pity.'

~

A volunteer was waiting to drive Bastiaan to his lodgings on St Margaret's Road. He held open the door of the motorcar, but Bastiaan didn't get in.

'What do I do now?' he said.

'You get in the motorcar.'

'And it will take me away from you.'

'It won't take you far. St Margaret's Road is just a quarter-hour walk from here.'

He still didn't get in. I put his box of things on the back seat.

'I have become used to your visits,' he said. 'I will miss seeing you.'

I will miss seeing you too, I thought. 'You won't have time to miss me – you'll be too busy at the 'Stute teaching French to Press apprentices.'

''Stute?'

'The Clarendon Institute.'

He nodded at the formal name. 'You will thank your Mrs Stoddard for her arrangements?'

It had been a selfish request, to keep him close. 'I will thank her,' I said.

'We might see each other there?'

That was the plan, I thought. 'We might,' I said.

~

Somerville lost its appeal after Bastiaan was discharged, but for the next few weeks I continued to turn up with Gwen every Thursday evening and Saturday afternoon. We sat with officers in different wards as the sister on duty saw fit. My accent or the state of my cuffs or my talk of work rarely mattered to the men I sat with, and I began to walk the corridors with almost as much confidence as Gwen.

But then for one officer, my situation seemed to matter a lot.

'Sister,' he shouted. Once, twice, three times before she was free to come over. 'Why have I been given her?' His right hand was bandaged but he managed to point in my direction.

The sister looked at me; I shrugged. The letter I'd begun to write lay abandoned on the bed where he'd ordered me to put it.

'She should be attending her own at the Radcliffe Infirmary, not visiting an officers' hospital.'

He'd asked who my father was and I'd told him I had none. *It's just my sister and me – we live on the canal and work at the Press.* He made no effort to hide his disdain.

'My business is none of her business. She shouldn't be here.'

The sister apologised, though to whom, I'm not sure. She looked at the clock. 'It's almost seven,' she said. 'You might as well go home.'

I didn't go back.

'Join the Port Meadow gardening club,' Lou said from the other side of the gathering bench. 'We've finally managed to keep the cows from trampling all over the allotment and the vegetables are thriving. We could do with a few more helpers.'

I passed my sections to Maude; she tapped them on the table.

'It can be muddy work,' chimed in Aggie. 'Not like reading poetry to officers, and Lou will likely put you on manure detail.' She flipped through the sections to check the order, then initialled the last page.

'The secret to our success,' said Lou.

'Manure detail?' asked Maude.

Aggie put the text block on the trolley. 'She'll give you a shovel and a barrow and point you in the direction of the cows,' she said. 'But if you're lucky, the cows will be over near the aerodrome and you might meet a pilot.'

Mrs Hogg arrived then and all conversation stopped.

～

I stood with Gwen outside Somerville.

'You could join me, help grow potatoes.'

'Not on your life,' she said, 'my talent is for love letters, not horticulture. Besides, I'm due home. Mummy has sent a command. I'll be back when Michaelmas term starts. I'll bring you some hand cream.'

～

Rosie tapped on the galley window and waved a letter. I pointed to the foredeck and went to open the hatch. She put the letter in my hand.

'From Tilda?' I was surprised that Tilda would write to her, knowing she'd struggle to read it.

'It's about Jack.'

She looked pale. I took out the letter.

'Why don't you get Old Mrs Rowntree to read it?'

'Says she can't focus.'

And might not want to, I thought.

'What could you make out?' I said, and held my breath.

'Enough to know he's not dead.'

I let my breath go.

'But not enough to know he's not dying.'

Maude stopped folding and came over to where we stood. She took Rosie's elbow and led her to Ma's armchair.

'Sit,' she said.

When Rosie sat, Maude perched on the arm.

'Read,' she said to me.

4 October 1915

Dear Rosie,

Jack will be fine — that's the first thing to say. If I had more time I'd give more details, but Jack is one of hundreds who've arrived from Loos over the past week. Bloody miracle I came across him at all. He's a crutches case and they don't get a look-in until every stretcher case has been triaged. But he kept calling my name. I thought he must be a boomerang, some boy I'd nursed come back for more, but he was covered head to toe in mud and I didn't recognise him. I pretended, of course. 'Couldn't keep away?' I said. Then he smiled — unmistakable. 'It's Jack,' he shouted (still half-deaf from whatever blast filled his thigh with shrapnel). He hugged me then, the rascal, and I've been wearing his muck for the past five hours.

Jack's happy to be alive right now, Rosie, but there were three casualties from his battalion, and one was his lieutenant. It's like losing a parent for some, so I'll keep an eye on him.

Tilda x

Rosie collapsed against Maude. Relief.

Maude's arms wrapped round her.

I focused on the last line, read it again and again, until the information became meaningful. *One was his lieutenant*, Tilda wrote. *Call me Gareth*, he'd said, when he was nothing more than a compositor. He'd typeset the words for the New English Dictionary. And the other dictionary. *Women's Words*. He'd married her. We'd stood outside St Barnabas with Mrs Stoddard and Eb and others from the Press and sang 'By the Light of the Silvery Moon'.

Did she know? I wondered. His name would be checked, the circumstances verified. How many hands would her telegram pass through? She couldn't know yet.

Call me Gareth, he said. I never bloody did. Too familiar, I thought, but now I was crying.

~

There was a day, a few weeks later, when Mr Hart came to talk with Mrs Stoddard. He'd been retired six months, but we still saw him from time to time, walking the corridors with Mr Hall and his wolfhound, trying to hold his tongue.

He wasn't with Mr Hall when he came through the bindery, and when he left, Mrs Stoddard asked to speak with me.

I saw her face and braced myself for news of more death.

'It's Mr Owen,' she said.

It was a relief, in a way, to already know. I just nodded, which is what we did now.

'He kept the formes,' she said. 'For the pages he asked you to help him with.'

I knew this too.

'Mr Hart has asked me to help bind a few more copies.'

'Mr Hart was never supposed to know,' I said.

'He turned a blind eye.'

I felt it then.

'I thought you might like to do it?' Mrs Stoddard said.

I couldn't speak. I just kept nodding. It's how I kept my head.

'Mr Hart is having them printed now.'

~

I folded the sections, as slowly and carefully as I could. I whispered the words and tried to find the voices of the women who'd spoken them. Maude helped. She echoed sentences and repeated names: Mabel O'Shaughnessy; Lizzie Lester; Tilda Taylor.

'Our Tilda,' I told her.

'Our Tilda,' she said.

In print, I thought. I let the bonefolder slip, just a little. Just enough for a small tear. I put the section aside, gathered its sisters and laid them beside it.

'I don't see why not,' Mrs Stoddard said when I asked if I could keep them.

Each night, for five nights, Eb and I stayed late in his book repair room. I bound the words with cord and thread and he gave each volume a simple casing, including the one with the small tear. No leather. No gilding. Only she would have that. When we were done, I sat with my copy, turning each page until I came to the last few, all blank.

Then, on the flyleaf, *Love, Eternal* in Baskerville typeface. He'd chosen it for its clarity and beauty, he'd said.

It didn't seem right for my copy to have it. I took the bonefolder from the bench and used it to tear the words from the page.

I tore the words from every volume – hers needed to be unique, he'd said. Then I left the repair room.

Chapter Twenty-Six

Bastiaan started teaching French at the 'Stute on Mondays and Fridays, and Maude and I would join him for lunch there when his class was over. Lotte joined us once, but when Bastiaan sat down she made an excuse and left quickly.

Then, one day in December, Maude stopped still as we left the Press for lunch, and refused to come with me to the 'Stute.

'Why not?'

Lou came up behind us and took Maude's arm. 'Because there isn't a cloud in the sky, and Maude would rather have a walk with me than sit around the 'Stute waiting for your sweetheart.'

'He is not my sweetheart, Lou.'

Aggie came out of the Press then and took hold of Maude's other arm. 'Of course he is,' she said.

'Of course he is,' said Maude, rolling her eyes exactly as Aggie had.

'Now off you go,' said Aggie. 'We'll have a jolly time with Maude and see you back in the bindery after lunch.'

∼

'It is a beautiful day,' said Bastiaan when his class was over.

'It is.'

'But you are here?'

I turned the pages of the *Oxford Chronicle*, pretending I was concentrating on the headlines.

'And how is the war going?' he asked.

I skimmed an article. 'There's been a rise in men enlisting since the Germans executed Edith Cavell,' I said.

'The English nurse?'

I nodded, then skimmed another article. 'The withdrawal from Anzac Cove and Suvla Bay has been an outstanding success. The Turks had no idea.'

'Why do they fight, do you think?'

'Who?'

'These men from Australia, New Zealand, India. They would be safe if they'd stayed home.'

'They were asked,' I said.

He took up another newspaper and sat down. He unwrapped his sandwich and began to eat. I watched him as he read, and realised my eye no longer caught on the strangeness of his face. It had become *him*. It was the face I looked for every time I entered the 'Stute, and every time I saw it I felt a quickening pulse. When he looked up I didn't look away, and for a moment he didn't speak. But then he cleared his throat and said, 'Will you walk out with me, Peggy?'

'It will be good to strengthen your leg,' I said, to hide my relief and my enthusiasm.

His half-smile. 'It is not for my leg that I ask you.'

~

By February, Bastiaan's leg could carry him as far as Blackwell's bookshop in Broad Street. We stood on the footpath and looked at the window display of *Shakespeare's England*. Bastiaan leant on a walking stick – not *his* walking stick, he was keen to point out. He wouldn't be keeping it. But for now, he needed it. And he needed my arm. We looked like any couple taking in the sights of Trinity College, the Sheldonian, the Old Ashmolean and the Bodley, as Gwen liked to call it. Any couple trying to wrest a day from the war.

'The presses worked around the clock to get it printed in time,' I said.

'In time for what?'

'The three hundredth anniversary of his death is in April.'

'Why do you think he matters so much?' Bastiaan asked.

I laughed. 'A good number of Gowns in this town would be at a loose end without Shakespeare – he keeps them relevant.'

'But they have not made him popular.'

'No, Shakespeare has always been popular, but the Gowns have made him theirs.'

'And what is it about?' Bastiaan pointed the walking stick at the display of books. 'This *Shakespeare's England*?'

'The England his stories sprang from.'

'And where did his stories sprang from?'

'Spring from,' I corrected.

'Come from,' he said.

'Ordinary people, mostly. Even when he was writing about kings and queens, he was writing about us. About what we want.'

He turned away from *Shakespeare's England* and looked at me. 'What *do* we want?'

I remembered the folded pages, the fragments of ideas.

'Love,' I said. 'Power. Freedom.'

'Freedom?'

'From guilt or madness ...'

He nodded.

'Or expectation,' I said.

'Or the dead,' he said.

'What do you mean?'

'We want to raise the dead or silence them,' he said, 'to be free of death's burden.'

There was a time I'd imagined digging Ma out of her grave, but now her voice in my head was sweet company.

'Who would you silence, Bastiaan?'

He turned back to the window display. I waited.

'The people of Louvain,' he said.

~

It was the end of a long day in which the only pages to pass under my bonefolder were covered in mathematical formulae. But it was still light when we left the Press, and Bastiaan was leaning against the fence, waiting – that little trip of my heart. When he saw us, he adjusted his hat and turned a little, so his war face was averted, though not hidden.

'So, you're Bastiaan,' said Aggie, unflinching. 'We've heard *so* much about you.'

'Not that much,' I said.

'No, not *that* much,' said Lou.

'Hello, Bastiaan,' said Maude.

'Hello, Maude,' said Bastiaan, a half-smile. 'I may take Peggy for a walk?'

Maude nodded.

'Yes, take her,' said Aggie. 'Maude, Lou and I have plans and you two will just get in our way.'

~

'Where are we going?' I asked.

'You will see,' he said.

We walked through Jericho, past the Prince of Wales, the Jericho Tavern and Turner's Newsagency. We only stopped when we got to the alley that led to St Sepulchre's Cemetery.

Bastiaan turned in, but I stayed on Walton Street.

'I did not think you believed in hauntings,' he said.

'I don't.'

He came back to where I stood. 'Perhaps you fear the dead?'

A little, I thought. 'Of course not,' I said.

Bastiaan put my arm through his and I let him lead me forward. The lane was overgrown and gloomy, despite the sunny day, and the gatehouse was in darkness. As we passed through I saw the alcove that led into the lodge. I calmed myself with the thought of the cemetery keeper inside, his wife preparing his supper. Bastiaan paused, and I looked beyond the gatehouse into the graveyard.

There was a stone cross and headstones large and small, erupting from the ground like crooked teeth. It seemed haphazard, but I knew there was an order to things, that neighbours in life were neighbours in death. That the dead of Jericho lay together along the north wall and the dead of Balliol, Trinity and St John's lay along the south.

There was the avenue of yews, covered in spring flowers, and the chapel beyond. I remembered it and hesitated again. I knew that if we went past the chapel to the north wall, I'd find the small headstones of my family – great-grandparents, great-aunts and -uncles, children who'd never grown up. *Let me summarise their demise,* Ma liked to say when we came to tend the graves on All Hallows' Eve. *A cough, bad luck, a runny fart. Lust, foul play and a broken heart.* Maude would always repeat it, and Ma would laugh. I'd ask her to explain one death or another, and she would tell me their tales.

It had been five years since Ma was buried. Maude had held my hand that time. We were seventeen, but I'd felt years younger than her. She'd walked half a step ahead of me, accepting all the commiserations with echoes of people's good intent. I didn't want to be there then, but I hadn't meant to stay away so long.

Bastiaan avoided the avenue of yews, and I was grateful he chose not to go too deep into the graveyard. He led me towards the south wall, his step deliberate. He seemed to know every tree root and broken headstone and I wondered how often he came here, and why he would choose to. He stopped at a sarcophagus with a flat stone lid.

'You don't mean to sit on it, do you?' I said.

'Of course – why not?'

'It's a grave, that's why not.'

'So, you *are* afraid of the dead.'

'I'm *respectful* of the dead.'

Bastiaan removed his overcoat and spread it on the stone. 'If I were dead, I would welcome friends to sit on my grave.'

He sat, keeping his bad leg at a comfortable angle. I stayed standing. He took a package from a pocket of his coat and began to unwrap it.

'Chelsea buns,' he said.

I could smell the spice, and my mouth anticipated the sweet, sticky glaze, but I continued to stand.

'A bit squashed, but fresh today, from the Covered Market.' He patted the space beside him. 'Madame Wood died in 1868, Peggy. A long time ago, and her grave is poorly kept. I think she may have gone from the memory of people.'

I stepped towards Bastiaan and his Chelsea buns. 'You know her name?'

'Of course. I have become a regular visitor and she is most accommodating.' He took a bite of his bun.

'You might be the first to say her name in decades,' I said.

He looked up at me, finished chewing. 'I believe that to be true for many people buried here.' Again, he patted the space beside him. 'I have told Madame Wood all about you, Peggy. She has been expecting you.'

When Ma was put in the ground I retched. It was the thought of her buried alive but not able to communicate it. It was illogical, insane, but I hadn't seen her die – I'd refused to – so I didn't see the pain leave her, didn't see her face relax, her limbs come to rest. I didn't experience the quiet that came afterwards. I was plagued by her struggling breath. Tilda held me to her and told me again of Ma's last moments. *They were good*, she said, and Maude echoed. My sister had been braver; she hadn't been angry. Maude had held Ma's hand and said goodbye for both of us. Afterwards, when regret settled in, I hoped Ma had been confused enough to think Maude was me some of the time, but I knew that wouldn't have happened. To Ma, we were nothing alike.

When Tilda was in Jericho, she and Maude would visit Ma's grave together. They'd stopped asking me to join them.

I sat beside Bastiaan on Mrs Wood's sarcophagus. I passed my hand over the uncovered stone and felt the valleys of engraved letters. Someone had chosen the words, a daughter perhaps. Did she visit when you'd gone? I thought.

Bastiaan passed me a bun and watched as I took a bite, as I chewed, as I smiled self-consciously. I licked the sticky sweetness from my mouth and he leant forward, his lips suddenly on mine, tasting the sweetness I had missed. He moved carefully, not knowing, perhaps, how to kiss with his new mouth. Not knowing if I wanted him to try. There was an awkwardness, and I pulled back.

'I am sorry,' he said.

'Don't be.' I rose and moved to stand between his legs. I brought my hands to his face. It was so familiar now but I'd never touched it. I felt the difference in my left hand and my right: the texture of his skin; the contours where bone was and wasn't. I found his mouth again. It would take a little time, I thought, to learn how to kiss him.

~

When the Serbian refugees arrived in April, many of the Belgians left, Goodie and Veronique among them. Mrs Stoddard called us into her office.

'They thought they'd be more comfortable in Elisabethville,' she said.

'What does Elisabethville have that we don't?' said Aggie. She took the news as a personal affront.

'It's a little bit of Belgium in the heart of England,' said Lou. 'I don't blame them. They'll be able to speak their own language, eat their own food. Veronique says they even use their own money. She'll be helping in the primary school – I've never seen her so happy.'

Veronique's happiness was not enough to appease Aggie. 'Well, what am I supposed to do now?'

'Consider Goodie a complete success and find a new project,' said Mrs Stoddard. 'There's no shortage of things you can contribute to, Agatha.'

'No shortage,' said Maude.

'And Lotte?' I asked.

'Luckily for us, Lotte has no interest in living in a little Belgium,' said Mrs Stoddard.

～

A few weeks later, Aggie gave her notice.

'I've got a job at the new munitions factory in Banbury,' she said. 'I start at the end of June.'

Lou was taken aback. 'So you won't be working at the Press any more?'

'Brilliant, Lou,' Aggie teased.

There was barely a day we hadn't all seen each other since starting at St Barnabas when we were four.

'She's not leaving Jericho, Lou. We'll see her at the manure mound on Port Meadow,' I said.

'But what does the munitions factory have that we don't?' said Lou.

'More pay,' said Aggie. 'And I get to wear overalls!'

Chapter Twenty-Seven

Bastiaan was waiting. He sat on the low stone wall in front of St Margaret's Church and looked along Kingston Road. It would be another minute before he was certain the figure coming towards him was me. A minute in which I could take him in.

I could see how deliberately he had arranged himself: the angling of his body, the tilt of his head, the soft cap pulled down a little lower on the left. His war face was turned towards St Margaret's, as if a church would be more forgiving. He looked uncomfortable. I quickened my step.

He saw me and his body relaxed. He turned his head from the refuge of the church, and a child stopped to stare. She was pulled along by her mother without a word, but Bastiaan seemed not to notice. It was me he was concentrating on, my image slowly filling his field of vision, causing him to smile. I was suddenly self-conscious. Shy. I'd been stared at all my life, but only because Maude had been beside me. She wasn't beside me now. Bastiaan's smile, his scrutiny, was for me alone. I, alone, interested him, and each step towards him felt easier than the last. Though it wasn't wholly comfortable. Like a boat coming loose from its mooring, I felt I was drifting from Maude and there was a moment when I thought to look behind me, to check to see if she was within reach. It was my habit. But I desperately wanted whatever this was. I wanted to lose myself, to be lost to her. I put all thoughts of her aside.

'It is you,' he said.

'Yes. It's me.'

The houses on St Margaret's Road were all of a kind. They were tall, gabled, made of a regular red brick that needed no dressing. They were far too grand for Jericho, and, despite the distance from Broad Street and the proximity to the Jericho Tavern, the post delivered to their heavy doors had an Oxford address.

We walked slowly, and I had time to pretend that I belonged on that tree-lined street, that Bastiaan was my husband, that the war was over.

'My ma was a child when these houses were built,' I said. 'It was called Rackham Lane back then, no better than any other lane in these parts. The way she told it, the children of Jericho watched St Margaret's rise up out of the ground.'

'She lived here always?'

I nodded. 'A damp cottage in a narrow lane near the canal. Same damp cottage her father grew up in. Same damp cottage her ma and baby brother died in. The children of Jericho were always coughing, she said. They thought these houses were being built for them.'

'It is easy for children to imagine better.'

'Ma never stopped,' I said.

Bastiaan paused at the gate of one of the houses. It had three storeys, tall windows on every level. So much light, I thought. So much fresh air.

'The family let the basement room to refugees,' Bastiaan said. He opened the gate, but I didn't follow him through it. No one would believe I had the right.

'They have gone to the seaside.' He offered his hand.

'How convenient,' I said, and crossed the threshold without his help.

The basement had its own entrance down some steps at the side of the house. It was a large room with two beds (narrow but sprung), two armchairs (old but well stuffed), a rug over cold flagstones, and a washstand with matching basin and jug. He pulled on a cord and electric light illuminated it all.

'You share it?'

'I did,' said Bastiaan. 'With another Belgian, but he was not at his ease.'

'Not at ease?' I asked. 'You get morning sun and there are *two* armchairs. We can only fit one on *Calliope*. I'd imagined a dungeon.'

'It was not the furniture,' said Bastiaan. He turned his war face in my direction.

'You must be joking?' I said.

'He fled before the Germans came. My face, for him, was a humiliation, I think.'

I sat in one of the armchairs. 'So this is temporary – you'll have another roommate soon?'

'Everything is temporary.'

Bastiaan lowered himself to the rug and leant his back against the solid frame of the chair I was in. He extended his sore leg.

'We should change places,' I said.

'I am comfortable.'

I would have said that his hair was dark brown. But as I sat in that armchair, the electric light above us charged his hair with colour. Chestnut, auburn, a few strands of fiery red. He moved and the colours stirred.

I touched the crown with my fingertips. His hair was clean, no oil. It was silky under my palm. He shifted slightly, so he could rest his war face against my thigh. His injuries disappeared and the war fell away. I saw him as he had been. Before we met.

His head grew heavy and his breathing began to deepen. I sank my fingers into his hair and let them range across his skull. Then I took an inventory: full lips, strong chin, straight jaw, high cheek. Features from a magazine. He would have turned heads in Belgium, received smiles, favours. I will not be the first woman he has made love to, I thought, and a flush and beat of heat moved through me. I traced my finger over the untroubled surfaces of his face: the ridge of his eyebrow, the straight length of his nose. When his lips parted, I felt the warmth of his breath. His jaw, clean-shaven, almost smooth, the only aberration a patch where the razor had not been so close. The lobe of his ear, soft like any other; I held it between my thumb and finger, felt it yield, felt him sigh, felt my own gooseflesh and saw his rise. He was beautiful.

'Do not stop,' he said.

I didn't realise I had.

'My mother, she would do this when I was a boy.'

My fingertips across his cheekbone, around his eye.

'I am not your mother, Bastiaan.'

His eyelid fluttered. I touched it. Calmed it.

'You are something I have no words for,' he said.

'Your friend?'

'Of course. But also, something other.'

The back of my fingers against his cheek. 'Your reader. Your writer.'

'Yes, and yes.'

'Your confidante.'

'That is near, but not quite right. I needed someone to sit beside me, and you came.'

'A bit of luck,' I said.

'I never felt strange with you.'

'You never struck me as strange.'

'You make a joke, but that is my point,' he said. 'For me, everything *was* strange – the language, the smells of the hospital, the sounds of Oxford's bells. The pain.'

A deep breath. His hand rose to hold mine against his cheek.

'It was all absence – I was blind to half the world, I could not feel where my skin had torn or burnt, I could not move as I had. I did not know myself. You made me feel familiar.'

'I am like family, then,' I teased.

'In those first weeks, I did wonder if a sister would have given such comfort.'

'Sister!'

'In those first weeks.'

'And now?'

His lips parted then closed. I touched them. Took the word that played between them.

'Lover,' I said.

A smile beneath my fingers. My trembling fingers.

He lifted his head and looked up at me. 'I want it to be so.'

I held his face in my hands. I leant down and kissed the lip that couldn't smile, I kissed the broken chin, I kissed the jagged jaw and the sunken cheek, and I kissed the eyelid that never closed over the glassy eye that saw nothing. Bastiaan tried to stand but I stopped him. I got up from the chair and drew the curtains.

I stood before him. I removed every garment I was wearing, and I watched him watching. I'd been longing for it. To be seen completely. Uniquely. When he saw the curve of my breasts I saw the rise of his chest. I let my drawers fall and heard him groan. I moved slowly, deliberately. I didn't want to be careless with a single movement. When I was naked I knelt on the rug beside him and helped him undress.

～

We slept. On the rug on the floor in front of the armchair, we slept.

It felt familiar – the weight of my head on his chest, the bulk of him against my body, my leg entangled with his. When I woke, his hand was pressed just above my left breast. I felt each beat of my heart against the pressure of his palm.

I moved. He pulled away.

'I am sorry,' he said.

'Don't be.' I put his hand back where it had been.

'I dreamed you were dead.' So quiet.

My heart beat faster and I wondered how long he'd lain there, needing proof that I was alive.

For me, the proof was everywhere. I could smell our lovemaking – in his armpit and on my skin. I could see it strewn across the floor – my clothes and his, the French letter I'd taken from Tilda's black velvet pouch. I felt it as a tenderness – between my legs and in my heart.

I lifted his hand from my chest to my mouth. He smiled and the shadows of his dead vanished from the room. I shifted my body to straddle his. I took his face in my hands and I kissed the lip that couldn't smile, I kissed the broken chin, I kissed the jagged jaw and the sunken cheek. I kissed the eye that stared but could not see and felt it cold against my lip.

~

I collected every garment I'd been wearing, and Bastiaan watched me dress. I watched him watching. I slowed things down. I went to the mirror and rolled my hair, then I attached my hat. He followed the movements of my hands in the reflection.

'I have to go,' I said.

'I'll walk with you. I would like to see where you live.'

'No, there's still a little light and I'll need to go at a trot.'

~

I'd been gone longer than an hour. Longer than two. The light was fading. When I saw *Calliope*, my thoughts shifted from Bastiaan to Maude. Where my skin had been tingling it now felt dull. I wondered briefly if Rosie had thought to pop her head in. She would have if I'd asked. Why didn't I ask? I was so sick of asking.

There was barely light in the sky when I opened the hatch. I guessed it was half-ten. The lamp was cold, I relit it. I picked up Maude's yellow scarf from the floor, saw her summer jacket on the back of the armchair – she hadn't worn either to work. The table was strewn with papers and six completed stars, a dirty plate and half a glass of milk, skin already forming.

I picked up the dirty plate and the half-glass of milk and took them to the galley. I added vinegar to the milk, put it aside to sour. I put the plate in the basin, already crowded with the morning's dishes. A reflection, in the galley window, the image so distorted that not even I could tell if it was Maude or me. It was dark now, pitch black. I'd left her alone too long.

I pulled back the curtain to our bedroom. She could make herself so small, and anyone else might have thought the bed empty, old and lumpy as the mattress was. But I recognised the shape of her. I touched the curve made by her hip and felt my pulse slow. She held the covers tight under her chin. Her breath escaped in rhythmic puffs through sleep-soft lips, cherry-red. I closed the curtain and returned to the galley.

Cherry-red.

I wasn't ready for bed. I didn't want sleep to take my waking pleasure and consign it to dream, not just yet. I made a weak tea, and instead of taking it to the table I sat in the armchair, Ma's chair, solid and sprung. Upholstered in green velvet but worn down to the weave in so many places. It was far too big for our narrowboat, but Ma had refused to replace it with something smaller.

The chair sat on top of a foot-worn rug. I eased off my shoes and rolled down my stockings to feel the uneven pile. Birds and bowers in faded reds, greens, blues – *an oasis of imagining*, Ma would say as she settled in to read tales from *The Thousand and One Nights*. We would sit at her feet, Maude lost in the patterns of the rug, me lost in the magic spun by Ma's voice. She was my Scheherazade and I hung on every word, played with every idea. When she closed the book she'd lean down, hold my chin. *Don't forget, Peg.* I'd nod, knowing what was coming, anticipating it like a favourite line in a story. *If you shrink yourself to the smallness of your circumstances, you'll soon disappear.*

I rarely sat in Ma's armchair. I didn't avoid it, but there were two of us and the armchair was for one. The table was a better fit.

Had I shrunk myself?

I drank my tea. The lamp guttered. I hauled myself up and took the empty cup to the basin.

I undressed. Each garment, each movement a re-enactment. I closed my eyes to recover an image, a sound, a scent. I undid the buttons of my blouse and slipped out of my shift. When the fabric brushed my breasts, I felt the scarred pads of his fingertips. As the air moved around me, I felt him whisper against my neck. He'd spoken French; I hadn't recognised half the words, but I'd understood.

I lifted the covers and slipped into bed beside my sister. There was a faint smell of tobacco, the kind Tilda sometimes smoked.

~

I anticipated the bells of St Barnabas and woke before they sounded. *Calliope* was dusky with the rising sun and I guessed I had a quarter of an hour before I needed to wake Maude. I pulled back the covers and sat on the edge of the mattress. I slid my feet into slippers and reached for the shawl thrown over the foot of the bed. I'd been dreaming, and as I pulled the shawl around my shoulders I tried to remember what it had been about. Bastiaan, but I couldn't hold it.

Then I saw her stockinged foot.

I peeked beneath the covers. Maude was fully clothed, wearing Tilda's apricot dress.

Her lips – cherry-red. The colour smudged across her cheek.

Dress-ups. It was something we used to do when we were children. I pasted a smile over my frown, covered her up and went into the galley.

'Scrambled eggs,' I said, putting the plate in front of Maude when she sat at the table. She was still wearing the dress. The stockings.

She pushed the plate away.

'But you love scrambled eggs.'

She pulled the plate towards her and began eating.

'That's better.' I sat at the table with my coffee.

'You love scrambled eggs,' said Maude, pointing her fork at the empty space in front of me.

'I'm not that hungry,' I said, and Maude returned to her breakfast. 'You forgot to put your nightdress on last night, Maudie,' I said. 'You went to bed in your new dress.'

'Something to thrill the boys,' she said.

Tilda had said it as Maude twirled in front of her.

'It's a very pretty dress,' I said.

'Pretty dress, for a pretty parrot.'

I couldn't place it. My coffee went cold.

Chapter Twenty-Eight

I couldn't convince Maude to change, so she went to work in the apricot dress. She stood out on the streets of Jericho, where the women were dressed for housework or Press work or a long day behind a counter. Several men doffed their caps, and when a soldier bade her good morning, Maude echoed, 'Good morning,' and gave a twirl.

We stopped at Turner's Newsagency to buy sweets for Aggie.

'That's a pretty dress, Miss Jones,' said Mr Turner.

'It's Aggie's last day,' I added, as if that might explain things.

~

We were arranged around the gathering bench, a little more talkative than we should have been, a little more relaxed. Aggie was louder than usual, but Mrs Hogg knew she had lost her authority and was pretending not to notice.

Lotte and I were gathering the sections. She'd learnt the steps that made it more efficient, and I liked to watch for the moment her face softened as her body found its rhythm. I was sure she was unaware of the change so I never commented; I just made sure my own steps mirrored hers so as not to put her off.

On this day, Lotte moved along the gathering bench like a woman breaking in a new pair of shoes. It was awkward, so I made no attempt to keep time with her. I swept section after section onto my arm and kept my rhythm languid with thoughts of Bastiaan.

Lotte handed Lou her first pile of sections. A few moments later, I handed mine to Maude.

'Slowcoach,' Maude said – not a reprimand, just an observation. She tapped the edges, made them flush, handed them to Aggie to check.

Dear Maude, I thought, and I leant forward to kiss her cheek. At the last moment she turned her head and caught my lips with hers. She studied the shock on my face and laughed. It was an odd sound.

'Not so bad?' she said. A question.

I didn't know how to respond.

'Not so bad,' she said, in answer.

Aggie fanned through the sections Maude had handed her. 'Can't tell what's up or down,' she said. 'What language is this?'

'German,' said Lotte, already handing Lou her second pile. Lou tapped the edges. Made them flush.

'German?' Aggie repeated. 'Why are we printing *German* books?'

I paid more attention on my second run: twenty sections with four folds, thirty-two pages in each. I peeked at the front pages. *A Book of German Verse: From Luther to Liliencron. Edited by HG Fiedler.* I imagined Mr Cannan arguing with the delegates: Remove *Oxford* from the title and no one can accuse us of being sympathetic.

'It's poetry,' I said.

'*German* poetry,' said Aggie.

'Poetry,' said Maude.

Lotte stopped her gathering, so I stopped. She was reading one of the poems, mouthing the words.

'Read it for us, Lotte,' I said.

'O Mutter, Mutter! hin ist hin!
Verloren ist verloren!
Der Tod, der Tod ist mein Gewinn!
O wär' ich nie geboren!'

'What does it mean in English?'

She looked at me across the gathering bench and I felt it as a vast distance. Then she looked back to the poem but said nothing for a long while; I supposed she was having trouble translating it. When she finally spoke, it was a whisper.

'O mother, mother! it is gone!
Lost is lost!
Death, death is my comfort.
O had I never been born!'

She resumed her journey along the gathering bench and so did I, but the easy rhythm in my step had gone.

'You know these poems?' I said.

'In Belgium, we learn the poetry of our neighbours, as we learn their language.'

'I suppose that makes sense,' I said.

'What sense does it make?' Lotte's mask slipped and I thought perhaps she was sneering. I didn't know what to say but I knew she wouldn't look away until I responded.

'Surely it's better to understand your neighbours than not.'

'I used to think so.'

I said nothing. We continued our journey, delivered our sections, began again. 'If my neighbour became my enemy,' I said, unsure if I should be saying anything at all, 'I think I would like to know what they were saying.'

Lotte stopped. I stopped. Her eyes were piercing blue – unshaded by her usually lowered lids. She kept her voice quiet but delivered each word precisely. The effort not to shout was a quiver in her top lip.

'German people are not my enemy, Peggy. But there are some who have used their language like a weapon, to share the evil of their thoughts, the details of what they will do to humiliate you, hurt you. What they have already done.'

She stopped abruptly, and I had the feeling she'd breached some self-imposed secrets act. I watched her contain the spill – shake her head, lower her lids. When she looked up, the blue had dimmed and her voice was steady.

'What is that rhyme you English tell your children about sticks and stones?'

Maude answered before I could.

'*Sticks and stones may break my bones, but words shall never hurt me.*' She knew it well.

Lotte looked over to where my sister sat, and I wondered if something more might spill from her. But she suddenly went slack, as if the capacity to fight had left her.

'It is a lie,' she said, looking back to me. 'Maude knows this.'

'A lie,' said Maude.

'I wish I had been deaf to it all,' Lotte said. She swept the next section onto the pile in her arm; I did the same. We were silent until the bell was rung for morning tea.

~

At the end of the day, one text block had been removed from the others.

'What was wrong with this lot?' I asked.

Aggie inclined her head towards Maude. 'While you and Lotte discussed *poetry*, she made a mess of a middle section.'

'A mess?'

'Yeah, a mess.' Aggie showed me what Maude had done.

'They're nonsense folds,' I said.

Aggie took the ruined section from my hand, turned it this way and that. 'Can't tell what's up from down.'

I looked around the bindery: Mrs Stoddard had her head bent to a ledger, Mrs Hogg was chastising one of the new girls from St Barnabas for chatting.

I took the section back from Aggie and slipped it into the pocket of my apron.

~

We arrived home that evening to the tin-can heat of *Calliope*. We kept the hatch open with *A History of Chess* and I opened the windows, port and starboard. It was a relief to feel air being pulled through.

Maude sat at the table and reached for the biscuit tin of papers. Her hat remained on, as the apricot dress had remained on, all night and all day. I went and stood behind her. I watched for a moment as she began to fold, then I leant forward, wrapped my arms around her shoulders and whispered in her ear.

'Are you planning on going out again tonight, Maudie?'

I wanted confusion – what could I possibly mean by 'again'? But Maude shrugged. She might go out again, or she might not. There was the faint smell of tobacco at the nape of her neck.

A new conversation to be had, and neither Maude nor I had the script. She waited for me to ask more questions, to sit beside her the way Ma would have and help her find the vocabulary she needed.

'Your hat, silly,' was all I said. I applied a smile to my face and removed the hat from her head. I hung it on the peg by the hatch and looked out at the water of the canal. There was scum on the surface, rainbows of cooking oil, and other things. An empty tin floated by, and I wondered how long it would be before it would fill with water and sink to the bottom.

I'd planned to make sausages and mash but decided on toad-in-the-hole. One of Maude's favourites. I beat the batter longer and harder than usual. As it cooked, it rose to swallow the sausages, like Ma's used to. Maude clapped when I put it on the table and our conversation over supper followed its usual pattern.

We had peaches for afters, fresh. Maude put her folding well away from danger as she ate the sticky segments. I watched her lick her fingers clean, wipe them on her dress. I didn't reprimand.

When she resumed her folding, I followed the first few pleats and knew it would be a heart.

'Who is the heart for, Maudie?' I asked.

She shrugged.

I took the section of German verse from my bag and placed it on the table. Maude leant over to see.

'Poetry,' she said.

'*German* poetry,' I mimicked Aggie in tone and facial expression. Maude smiled.

I took a deep breath and fingered the nonsense folds.

'What are these, Maudie?'

Her head shook back and forth, she rocked a little. She couldn't say. She was confused. *Don't insist she say something she has no words for,* Ma used to tell our teachers. *Help her express it another way.*

'Can I straighten it out?' I put my hand on the section.

Her head began to nod, her rocking stopped. 'Straighten it,' she said.

I opened the section and refolded it properly.

'Shall we ask Lotte to translate a bit more?'

'*Sticks and stones,*' said Maude.

'I could ask Bastiaan.'

'*Sticks and stones.*'

'I'll send a couple of poems to Tilda? She could get her German doctor to translate.'

Maude nodded. 'Hugo.'

~

23 June 1916

Dear Pegs,

The poems made Hugo cry. When I asked him to translate, he thought I was talking about something one of the German prisoners had written. He was delighted when he saw it was a poem by Liliencron. He translated the title as 'Death Among the Ears of Corn', then read the first couple of lines aloud off the page. He knew it, Peg, and recited the rest of the stanza by heart. They could have been written yesterday, he said, but they were written decades ago, about another Prussian war with France.

He knows all about Oxford and Calliope. About you and Maude, and Helen, of course. He's not shocked or jealous when I talk about her. This place has reduced our ability to feel either. When I told him you'd pilfered the poems from the bindery, he smiled. They could have refused to print the words of Germans, he said. The fact they didn't makes him hopeful — 'By our poetry you should know us,' he said. 'It is the same as yours.'

It's so romantic, isn't it? But I was incensed. I told him I'd had my fill of poetry that painted ordinary men as saints for dying worse than ordinary deaths or getting injuries that meant they'd live worse than ordinary lives. I told him there was nothing noble about dying in a bloody cornfield — it was just a waste.

Hugo let me rant on and on without heckling once. I need opposition to maintain an indignant rage, so I eventually ran out of steam. When I caught my breath, Hugo kissed the mouth that had harangued him and said, with infuriating logic, 'Poetry is how we endure the unendurable. Sometimes it has to be a lie.'

I understood, then, why Alison (Matron Livingstone) insists on calling our patients 'Filthy Hun'. To think of them otherwise, to think of them as ordinary men, might make this whole experience unendurable.

Tilda x

I read 'Death Among the Ears of Corn'. Then I read 'Wer Weiss Wo'. Hugo had translated it as 'Who Knows Where', and the first line was: *On blood and corpses, rubble and smoke.* There was no glory in it, and when I reached the end, I wondered if the truth of it had pleased Tilda. I didn't think so, but it wouldn't have enraged her either. It would just have made her terribly sad.

Chapter Twenty-Nine

It was still light when Bastiaan and I came out of the picture theatre. Oxford was crowded with people, and if not for the uniforms it might have been any summer's night. Groups of young officers spilled from the same pubs they'd spilled from as students. Young women moved through the streets in twos and threes. Couples walked arm in arm, stopping at this college or that church to admire the architecture. Oxford still attracted tourists, despite the war. And, despite the war, a warm summer's night could still make you feel at peace.

I'd been avoiding the towpath when I returned home from Oxford of an evening, but it was still dusk and I had Bastiaan with me. It felt more romantic than the street.

Just beyond the Hythe Bridge we noticed the men. Some wore uniforms, some wore collared white shirts. Some wore overalls and clearly had not been home since their labouring had ceased for the day; they stumbled along the towpath with their guts full of beer.

'He will end up in the stream, I think,' Bastiaan said.

'It might be just what he needs.'

Bastiaan laughed, and I turned to look at him – a laugh could transform his face, and I was still gathering all the reasons why.

Then, a voice. Unfamiliar. 'Well, hello again.'

I can't say where he came from, but a man stood in front of us on the towpath, just near the Isis lock. He was in uniform, but there was nothing orderly about him. He looked me up and down, the way some men like to do, and the confidence I'd had when I put on the dress earlier that evening disappeared. I felt the breeze from the canal play across my shoulders, my collarbones, my chest. I thought maybe the neckline was too loose, the fabric too sheer. It was one of Tilda's cut-downs. I took my hand from Bastiaan's but moved closer to him. He put his arm around my shoulders, and I felt the muscles in his chest tense.

'I said *hello.*' The man swayed a little, smiled a little. Looked at Bastiaan, then back at me. 'Now it's your turn to say it back.'

We stepped past him.

'Don't be like that, my pretty parrot.'

I swung around.

'What did you call me?'

A twitch across his brow. Confusion. He leant in.

'My pretty parrot.' He attempted a smile. He smelled of tobacco.

'Why?'

'You like it.' Again, the twitch. And then it dawned on him, as it dawned on me. He stumbled back, glanced at Bastiaan. Flinched.

'What did you do?' I hissed.

'He is drunk,' said Bastiaan, holding me tighter, to reassure or restrain, I wasn't sure.

'What did you do to her?' I shouted.

The man looked me over again, as if checking for errors, the slightest misprint. Only when he came to my eyes was he convinced. He shook his head.

'Your *pretty parrot*?' I spat.

'I did nothing,' he said.

'You did something.'

230

A quick glance at Bastiaan. 'Nothing she didn't want me to do.'

I pushed him, both hands to his puny chest, just like I used to push the St Barnabas bullies when they made fun of Maude. I shrugged Bastiaan off. I ran.

～

'Maude! Maude!'

The armchair was empty. The galley was empty. There was no one sitting at the table.

'She's asleep. It is late.' Lotte came from behind the curtain of our bedroom.

I ignored the unspoken direction to leave my sister be, and as Lotte came back into the galley I pushed past her and pulled back the curtain of our bedroom.

Maude was curled around a pillow, her eyelids fluttering with dreams. I touched her cheek. She was warm, safe. I kissed her forehead. She didn't stir. On the end of our bed lay the apricot dress.

Lotte watched as I closed the curtain. She followed my progress to the table. When I sat, she stared at me, waiting for me to say something. I didn't know what to say. I put my head in my hands.

'Something has happened,' she said.

I snapped my head up. The look on Lotte's face shamed me. She wasn't asking a question. She was telling me. Telling me something I should already know. 'What has happened?' I asked.

At that moment, Bastiaan arrived. It wasn't how I'd planned to introduce him to *Calliope*. He tripped on *A History of Chess* and hit his head coming through the hatch. He was pale from the effort of running after me, and Lotte went to help him to the armchair.

She went back into the galley and made a point of not looking at me. She took up the jug and poured a glass of water, then took it back to where Bastiaan sat.

'Lotte,' I said, too loud for the small space. 'What do you know?'

She looked at me then, her face hard with scorn. 'I don't *know* anything,' she said. 'But I can guess.'

'What have you guessed?' I said, my voice quieter. The anger that had propelled me along the towpath, now dampened by guilt. The apricot dress was laid out and ready. She was planning to go out again. Be someone's pretty parrot.

'She wears Tilda's dress, paints her lips red,' said Lotte. 'She has a new vocabulary. You have heard it. Did you not wonder where it came from, what it meant? Or have you been too busy to pay attention?'

'What is that supposed to mean?'

'Did you leave her?' Lotte asked. A quick glance at Bastiaan.

'When?'

'Ever! Did you leave her alone? Did you think she would be all right without you?'

I couldn't answer. Of course I'd left her every now and then. I always had. But not for long, not without telling Rosie. Though lately ... Maybe. Once or twice. But Maude knew she wasn't to cook. She was happy to be left with her papers, her folding. Had I lost track of time? Maybe. Once or twice. Once or twice when I'd felt all the carelessness of being singular I might have lost track of time. Once or twice. Lotte was glaring at me.

'Who calls her a *pretty parrot*?' she said. 'What does it mean when she says, "Not so bad, not so bad", when she tries to kiss you the way she did in the bindery the other day?'

I said nothing and Lotte's voice rose.

'You choose to misunderstand her,' she shouted. 'You, of all the people, should know what can happen. But still, you leave her.'

'I, of all people —' but Lotte hadn't finished with me, and I faltered.

'You think because you have told her to stay that she will. But she is curious, they are all curious.'

And then she was pacing, pushing her fingers through her hair, and I was trying to find my voice.

'She's *my* sister, Lotte. I think I know when she can be left and when she can't.'

Lotte stopped and turned on me, her pale face blotched with a rage I couldn't comprehend.

'She is a child!' she screamed. 'A child with a mouth full of rhyme. Nonsense to them. A reason to hurt. And you left him. Why? Why did you leave him? *Pourquoi? Pourquoi?*' The word continued, over and over, fragmenting on great sobs that racked her body. And then Bastiaan was by her side, and the sobbing became gasps for breath, but the question kept coming, '*Pourquoi?*', in ever quieter tones. Then his arms were around her, the arms he'd wrapped around me, and she collapsed into them.

Bastiaan spoke to her – I caught fragments of French. He helped her towards the armchair. Only when she was sitting did I notice Maude. She was standing motionless, expressionless. Framed by the curtain that kept our bedroom dark but did nothing to keep out sound. I wondered what she'd heard and what she'd seen. I wondered how she understood it. I moved to go to her, but she put a finger to her lips. *Don't disturb them*, she was saying. She understood. She always understood. I waited.

Bastiaan asked where Lotte lived, and I told him how to find Mrs Stoddard's. He helped Lotte off *Calliope* and I followed. I stood on the towpath and watched their silhouettes walk towards Walton Well Bridge. They were the same height.

They spoke the same language. I imagined them speaking in French. It would be easy, I thought, and a relief, for both of them, to be fully understood.

Maude had gone back to bed. I climbed in, fitted my knees into hers and pressed my belly against her back. I let my hand rest on her hip and for a moment breathed in the scent of her hair. I shivered with the memory of Bastiaan's touch, his breath on my neck. I imagined how my sister's body might respond if my hand was a man's. I thought of the soldier on the towpath and my skin crawled.

My skin crawled. But had hers?

The apricot dress had been all laid out.

'You look beautiful in that dress, Maudie,' I said.

It wasn't enough.

'Maybe you could wear it to the fundraiser coming up at the 'Stute? There'll be dancing.'

'Boys and old men,' she whispered.

'And airmen from the aerodrome at Port Meadow,' I said. 'By special invitation.'

She softened and I imagined her being held at the waist and moved around the dance floor. I imagined the possibility of a kiss at the end and knew how good it might feel.

'I don't think you should go alone to the Hythe Bridge any more, Maudie. The man you met, he's not the right kind of man.'

She was quiet a long time – thinking, not sleeping, and I wondered what she wanted to say. *Be patient*, Ma would have said. I closed my eyes and let my head sink into the pillow.

'The right kind of man?' Her question pulled me from a doze and I almost said *Bastiaan*.

'I'm not sure,' I said, and I felt her disappointment. I imagined Ma shaking her head: *Try harder and be clear.*

'He'll be someone who wants to understand you, Maudie. Someone you will want to understand.' Like a book, I thought. 'Like a beautifully complicated fold,' I said.

∼

During my lunch hour the following day, Bastiaan found me in my usual spot at the 'Stute, reading the papers. He unwrapped his sandwich. I turned a page.

'What did you talk about with Lotte when you walked her home?' I asked.

'Nothing,' he said.

'Surely, something,' I said.

'Nothing,' he said again.

I stopped turning pages and looked at him, incredulous. 'Bastiaan, you must have spoken about something. What was wrong with her last night?'

'She is …' He was searching for the right words. 'She is not right, I think. Damaged. She has not buried her dead,' he said, 'and I think she has no desire to.'

'I'm sorry,' I said, ashamed of my tone.

'No.' He took my hand. 'I don't think Lotte cares about very much any more, except for Maude. Last night, she became scared.'

'Why Maude, do you think?'

He didn't answer, but his discomfort grew.

'What did she tell you, Bastiaan?'

I searched his face for a clue. He'd stopped eating and I saw his jaw was clenched. I wondered how much it might hurt. I was patient.

'Maude, I think, is like her boy,' he said. His eye was on the table, not on me. 'Like her boy *was*,' he said.

I recalled fragments of words, gestures from the night before. Lotte slumped like a broken doll. *Why did you leave him? Pourquoi? Pourquoi?* Bits of a story falling into place.

He looked up. 'René. Her boy's name, it was René. He was twelve.'

There were things I wanted to know. Things I didn't want to know. They were the same.

'How is Maude like him?'

'René barely spoke. Just a few words, some favourite phrases from nursery rhymes and songs. Hand signs.'

'He was deaf?'

'Not deaf, but different. One of a kind, she said, like an illuminated book. Her life is barely possible without him.'

'Lotte told you this?'

'She told me over and over. It was not a conversation.'

'What was it?'

He shook his head. 'She told these things in French, then Flemish, German, then English. She began as soon as we left *Calliope* and did not stop until we came to Mrs Stoddard's door. There was a rhythm to each telling, and gestures.'

'Gestures?'

'She used hand signs – René's hand signs, I think. I am not sure what they all meant but they came at the same time in each language. It was as if she was reciting lines from a play; she has rehearsed them, I think, so they will not be forgotten. So *he* will not be forgotten.' He said nothing for a few moments. 'There were tears at the end, but she did not seem to know they were falling.'

'She's never said a thing to us. Why did she tell you, do you think?'

'Because it was convenient. Because I can understand the words. Because I was there when her mind broke.' He took a moment. 'She needs a witness, I think.'

'A witness? To what?'

He looked troubled. 'She wants her son remembered.'

'Of course she wants to remember him! And it must be a relief to finally talk. I wish she'd talk to me.' But even as the words left my mouth, I wasn't sure they were true. It would be easier not to know Lotte's pain. Easier to sit beside her at the folding bench, to walk with her back to *Calliope* and talk about what she might cook for supper. If I knew nothing about her boy, it would be easier to see her with Maude.

'I do not think Lotte desires relief. I think she wants someone *else* to remember René.' He paused. 'I think she was passing her memories on …' The rest just hung between us, but I knew what he was thinking.

We sat in silence for a while and I thought of Maude, the rhymes I would repeat, the words I would use to describe her: unique, one of a kind, a perfectly bound book of the strangest poetry. Bastiaan, I knew, was still thinking of Lotte. Of René.

'He was shot, I think.' He said it so quietly.

René was twelve. Spoke in rhymes. 'She told you this?'

He shook his head. 'I was there, in Louvain, soon after. I saw where they took the men and boys. The wall with their blood. Their bodies. Some so young they must have been carried there by their fathers.'

His dead were her dead. I knew, then, why Lotte had recited her pain to Bastiaan.

'They executed them,' he said. 'All of them.'

Even the boys who needed to be carried. Even the boy who spoke in rhymes. Unique. One of a kind.

'Then they burnt the university library.'

'Lotte was a librarian,' I said.

'*I was saving the books when they herded them to the wall.*' Bastiaan sighed. 'She said it in every language. *Illuminated manuscripts*, she said. *Irreplaceable.*'

'Did she save them?'

'What?'

'The manuscripts,' I said, because it was easier than any other question, not because it mattered.

He looked confused. Disappointed, perhaps.

'She saved nothing, Peggy. None of us did.'

All ashes.

My gut twisted. His name was René. He barely spoke. He was unique, like an illuminated book. I thought of Lotte in the bindery – folding and gathering the manuscripts, and every night the memory of them burning. Like some kind of Promethean punishment.

I felt sick.

'How can she bear it?' I looked at Bastiaan. 'My God, how can you?' I kept my voice low, not wanting to attract attention, but I felt like shouting it. 'How?'

He looked at me as a parent looks at a child, a doctor a patient. I'd had no idea and now I did. I was disturbed, angry, upset. As I should be. He could guide me through the maze of emotion, but he would not spare me the truth of it.

'Maude,' he said. 'Maude helps her bear it. And you, Peggy. You help *me* bear it.'

'But I know nothing of any of it.'

'You know enough.'

I shook my head. 'There's a war, Bastiaan. All this trauma, yours and Lotte's, and all I ever talk about is books and the bindery and —'

'And that is how I bear it,' he said.

Chapter Thirty

On a warm evening at the end of June, I helped Maude into her apricot dress and she helped me into a frock with very little to recommend it. She surveyed me and screwed up her nose.

'It's comfortable,' I said.

I twisted my hair into a bun at the nape of my neck, the way I did every morning. Then I styled Maude's hair into a loose chignon, the way Tilda had shown us, and I pinned in a few sprigs of flowering meadowsweet.

'You're a picture,' I said, and she twirled.

We walked along Walton Street: past the Jericho Tavern and the Prince of Wales, where drinkers doffed their hats; past the grounds of the Radcliffe Infirmary; past the Press and Somerville. I saw Gwen and Bastiaan standing outside the 'Stute with Aggie and Lou, all in their finest. As we approached, Gwen exclaimed.

'Maude!'

'A picture,' my sister said.

'You are, indeed,' said Gwen, then she turned to me. 'And you're ...' She smiled. 'Well, let's just say, there's little chance you'll be confused for Maude tonight.'

'Good thing your dance card is already full, Peg,' said Aggie.

Bastiaan took my arm, and we all walked into the 'Stute together.

Maude danced with half the airmen invited to the 'Stute fundraiser, and in the weeks that followed, she insisted we *do our bit* at Port Meadow more often than we'd signed up for. Lotte would sometimes join us, and together we dug up potatoes and lugged manure and prepared new beds for carrots and spinach. By August we'd become strong and suntanned and generally exhausted. But our aching limbs lifted our spirits and once or twice I caught Lotte smiling at the end of a day spent in the Press patch.

One evening, we sat on the foredeck of *Calliope*, and Maude entertained us with her own version of charades. It had always been a favourite, but Maude's version was more concerned with what she saw around her than with books and songs. In the last light of the day, she re-enacted the tussle Lotte and I had had in the galley over who would get supper on, and my easy defeat. That moment was uncanny, not because Maude and I had the same features, but because she manipulated our features so convincingly. I squirmed as she mimed my false insistence that Lotte *relax, put her feet up, give me back my kitchen*. I'd meant none of it. I hated cooking and we all knew it. I turned to see Lotte's reaction and was struck by her delight: she leant towards my sister, her hands clapped together under her chin, her face transformed.

Her before face, I thought.

Then Bastiaan arrived. Lotte saw him first, and the smile that had lit her up waned reluctantly, as if the feel of it on her face, like the sun, would be missed. I glanced at Bastiaan, then looked back at Lotte. Her hand played at the edges of her mouth. Her smile was completely gone. It was as if she were ashamed of it. Had no right to it.

Bastiaan's hand was on my shoulder. 'May I take Peggy for a walk?' he said, to Lotte or Maude, I wasn't sure.

'I will stay,' Lotte answered. Which was what Bastiaan needed to know, because it was what I needed to know.

'I will walk you home, Lotte, when we return,' he said.

Of course he would, I thought, and I recalled how suited they'd seemed, walking away from me towards the bridge. But then I saw the uninterested way Lotte nodded, and I realised she didn't care, one way or another.

∿

'I have a new roommate,' said Bastiaan, as we walked into Jericho. 'One of the Serbian refugees.'

I barely even tried to hide my disappointment. Bastiaan smiled.

'I, too, will miss having the room for myself.'

'I thought all the Serbian refugees in Oxford were boys,' I said.

'Also a few of their teachers.'

'He's a teacher, then?'

'His name is Milan.'

'And he came alone?'

Bastiaan hesitated, and I realised the answer was not straightforward. The Serbs had fled over the Albanian mountains to get to the Adriatic coast in the dead of winter.

'Only half of his group arrived,' Bastiaan said.

The papers said hundreds had frozen or starved or been shot.

'Milan's father became sick. He couldn't walk. They found a barn for him to rest, but then he could not get up. His mother refused to leave him. She gave Milan her shawl, her warm hat, her husband's woollen vest.'

'She knew she would freeze.'

Bastiaan nodded. 'She told Milan it would be quicker.' He took a breath. 'By the time he reached the Adriatic, Milan had lost his wife, his parents and five toes.'

'And how does *he* bear it?'

'The boys,' said Bastiaan. 'Milan says they are the future of Serbia. The war, he says, cannot go on forever, and their education in Oxford will help them to heal their country when they return.' He smiled. 'And I will help. Today, Milan asked me to tutor the younger boys in English and French.'

When we arrived at the cemetery, Bastiaan laid his jacket on Mrs Wood's sarcophagus. Then he produced two bottles of cider from his satchel.

'Why do you really come here?' I asked.

He said nothing while he opened one of the bottles. He handed it to me.

'Because, unlike you, I *am* afraid of the dead,' he finally said.

I sipped. 'What do you mean?'

He opened the other bottle and held it by the neck. When he took a sip, his fingers touched the smudged edge of his mouth. It was practised and subtle; they'd feel a spill when his lips couldn't.

'Do you really want the truth?' he said.

'Of course.'

'Sometimes it is easier not to know,' he warned.

I thought about the truth he and Lotte had shared and all the experiences neither of them would talk about, but which bound them in some way.

'Sometimes it is harder not to know,' I said.

He looked out towards the gravestones. 'I dream of the dead,' he said. 'Every night. Dead Belgians. Men, women, children. They are shot or beaten or burnt. And they are everywhere they shouldn't be: in the street, at their pew in the church, around the kitchen table, in the school room.' He took a deep breath. I didn't move. 'The stairs leading to the library of the university are always covered with bodies, so many bodies I can't make my way through them. They lie broken where they should be standing. In some dreams, the library is as it was before the Germans came; in others, it burns.'

He looked at me then and his face was grotesque, in a way it hadn't been since the day I first saw it. In that moment, it was a mirror to all he had seen. I reached up and touched it, his war face. If these were the scars war left on the skin, what must it leave on the soul? I kissed his awkward lips; we'd found a way.

'I come here because this is where the dead belong, where they can be at peace. I want to bury them, Peggy.'

'Is it working?'

He shrugged. 'Not yet, but this is the only place I can be sure they will not torment me in my waking hours.'

I looked around the cemetery, moonlit now and full of shadows, but not ghosts.

'I know the people in my dreams,' Bastiaan continued. 'Not their names, but their faces – I cannot forget them. Always the same three women, the same man. The same boys beside the wall. I closed their eyes, covered them if I could. I tried to pray for them, though there was no God watching over Louvain, and the prayers I'd thought I knew wouldn't come.' He shook his head, as if trying to rid it of something. 'But I have had an idea. To find each a grave, here in St Sepulchre's, and lay them in it.'

'Lay them in it?'

'You are worried I am mad.' He smiled. 'I do not mean it literally. It is my imagination that makes these dead restless. And so I think it must be possible for my imagination to lay them to rest.' He laid his hands on the stone we were sitting on. 'Madame Wood has kindly agreed to welcome one of the women into her grave. It has taken me a while to convince her, but I think, maybe, I will not dream of that woman any more.'

I put my hand on the bare stone of Mrs Wood's sarcophagus and felt the cool of night. But where Bastiaan and I had been, where we had kissed and talked of his dead, the stone had warmed.

If the spiritualists were right, I thought, and it were possible to have consciousness beyond death, then I would welcome lovers to sit on my grave one day, and I would gladly lie with the restless dead if it meant the living could be in peace.

~

27 August 1916

Dear Pegs,

German soldiers also dream of the dead, their own and ours. They confess to me and I don't understand a word. Hugo interprets sometimes. We had one whose dead were as real as me. Boys, mostly. Bloody corpses lying all over the floor and slumped over cots. He felt the weight of one on his chest and genuinely struggled to breathe. He tried to choke himself with his drip line.

Your Bastiaan sounds like a sensible man.

Tilda x

PART FOUR

Homeri Opera Tomvs III: Odysseae Libros I–XII Continens

August 1916 to May 1918

Chapter Thirty-One

Proof pages for me. This and that.

'Anything interesting?' Lou asked.

I looked at the section I was folding.

Homeri

Opera

Thomas W Allen

Tomvs III

Odysseae Libros I–XII Continens

Books one to twelve. Just half the story. I tried to remember what happens in the middle of *The Odyssey* – Circe, the Sirens, Calypso, Scylla. The women who aid, tempt, seduce, devour. Ma loved the middle. We loved the middle – the way Ma told it, at least.

I finished the section and started on the next. Solid blocks of Ancient Greek, footnotes in Latin. Indecipherable. I didn't envy the reader who had to check the pages.

'It's all Greek to me, Lou,' I said.

Chapter Thirty-Two

By the end of August 1916, the only conversation anyone seemed to be having was about *The Battle of the Somme*. It was playing in picture theatres all over Oxford, and everyone I knew had seen it at least once. Some saw it over and over until it was no longer a documentary but an entertainment. They recalled the worst scenes (the best scenes, they'd say) like beats in a play. I waited until Gwen had returned from her summer break to see it. Lotte spent the evening with Maude, and I met Gwen at the Electra Palace in Queen Street. We sat near the front, our necks craning, and the film took us into the trenches and showed us all the mud. It gave us what we needed in order to imagine something worse. 'Poor Jack,' I whispered into the dark. 'Poor Tilda,' Gwen whispered back. When the casualty lists swelled and Haig reported the fighting as 'singularly economical' and our losses as 'small', I did not believe him.

Jack was to get leave in October, so Oberon organised for *Rosie's Return* to have her hull repaired and blacked. Five days with his family; the longest since the war began. Oberon arrived by foot along the towpath, and Rosie met him with a letter – Jack's leave had been cancelled. Oberon stayed.

He checked *Calliope*'s ropes and seals and cleaned our flue. One evening we sat in Rosie's verge garden around an old drum with burning coals. Oberon read Jack's latest letter – he couldn't say where he was or what he was doing, and he didn't say what he felt about anything. When Oberon was done reading, he passed me the pages. Not a single line had been censored. I felt a strange sense of grief.

The day before Oberon had to leave, Rosie fried up bacon and eggs for breakfast and I was charged with the coffee. It was all drizzle and wind, so we sat in the cabin of *Staying Put* and Oberon read from the *Oxford Chronicle*. He skipped the local roll of honour and read from the 'Personal and Social' column.

'*The new MP for Berkshire has taken his seat in the House of Commons; Worple Flit and Other Poems, by the Prime Minister's nephew, the honourable Wyndham Tennant, will be published immediately after his death in France; Professor Gilbert Murray has had a sharp attack of influenza, which has compelled him to cancel all his public engagements.*'

'Poor Professor Gilbert,' said Maude.

We expected Oberon to continue reading, but he didn't.

'What is it?' asked Rosie.

He was frowning. 'You never said.'

'Said what?'

'Your controller, Mr Hart.'

He must have seen our blank faces. He read the headline.

'*Tragic Death of Mr Horace Hart.*'

There was a photograph. Mr Hart in the black gown of the University. His life and death took up two and a half columns, and Oberon read every word. But all I could recall when he stopped was the fact that Mr Hart had folded his gloves and laid them on the ground beside Youlbury Lake. It would have been cold – *freezing*, according to the paper – but he walked in regardless.

He won't be the same without the Press, Eb had said. But it was more than that. Dead apprentices, compositors, printers, foundry men – the news of each had been wounding.

Another casualty of this bloody war, I thought.

But I knew it wouldn't be counted.

~

Tilda's postcards came irregularly. Sometimes we'd wait weeks, and then Mr Turner would hand over three in a single day: one with an army postmark, two with the French. Some weren't even *to* us or *from* her, they were just fragments. One day I arranged them on the table, hoping to make some sense of what they said.

3 August

Too many died tonight. A bunch of new recruits, just graduated from the Bullring — the camp training ground. Hell's waiting room, they call it. They were at the front for less than a week before they were brought back here on stretchers. Every poem and poster would have you think that their march towards death is a willing sacrifice. But it's not like that. It's nothing like that. They're all the same, and nameless, like the men in those stories your ma liked so much. The men who died and died and died so Odysseus could be a hero. Haig is our Odysseus now, and the Somme offensive is his bloody journey to glory. Have you seen the film? It's just the half of it.

10 August

Too exhausted to sleep. Helping at St John's on top of my usual shifts. It's been weeks since I had a day off. Trains arrive all day and night from the Somme. Stretcher cases, most of them. Some so bad they die on the ground where they're offloaded. Out there six hours yesterday after a full night on the sauerkraut ward. VADs picking over the bodies of men, finding their wounds, cleaning them up just enough, moving on to the next bit of carrion. Feels like the work of vultures. They're covered in war. Mud and blood and other things that stink. Shit is the least of it. It's everywhere. The first thing to leave them, and the last.

6 September

At night I nurse men who British soldiers have tried to kill. In the day it is the opposite. And it goes on and on.

7 September

I chat to the Germans who are dying as if we are customers waiting in line at the bakery. I ask if they've seen Bill in their travels. I describe him in detail. I tell them how unsuited he is to soldiering. He should have been put to work as a cook, or a gardener or a seamstress — there is no end of repairs needed on uniforms. Is seamstress the right word for a man? Maybe it's seamsman. Why do I do this? The Germans don't understand a word.

10 September

I saw Alison weep over the body of the filthiest of Huns. A boy, his voice still squeaking. He'd taken to calling her 'Mutter'. It sounds so much like 'Mother'. And 'wasser' sounds like 'water', and 'freund' sounds like 'friend'. Would it surprise you to know that their blood is red, and when they are in pain they groan? When they know they will never see their home again they cry?

28 September

Do you know it is an offence for me to love Hugo?

It offends all the British mothers who have lost their British sons.

And it could get me arrested.

They were more like journal entries than messages and I felt the discomfort of prying. But it wasn't the content that concerned me, it was the growing understanding that Tilda was coming apart and I could do nothing to stop it. I could not take her place, I could not offer advice, I could not spin a single lie that would convince her the carnage was noble and just.

'I'm worried about her, Maudie.'

Maude looked up from the star she was folding. 'I'm worried,' she said.

Then she remembered the afternoon post, still in her pocket from when Mr Turner had given it to her.

'Tilda,' she said, handing me the envelope.

My chest tightened. I looked at the others lying exposed on the table and wanted to leave this next envelope sealed, avoid whatever it contained.

I ripped it open in shame.

15 October 1916

Hello my lovelies,

The injuries are getting worse, and seasoned VADs (moi) are expected to do the work of nursing sisters. For the past month or so I've been existing on just three or four hours' sleep whenever I can grab them. Not a single day off. When I'm done on the sauerkraut ward I've been assisting at St John's or with surgeries at No. 24 General. This is my tally from yesterday (or was it today? I really have no idea): two arms amputated at the shoulder, one below the elbow; four legs above the knee, two below; three feet; eleven fingers and six toes. Digits are my favourites — the boy wakes to see his hand or foot in bandages and he fears the worst. I tell him it's just his pinkie finger or big toe and watch as the truth of it sinks in (they pray for this, every time they go over the top). 'I'll be going home?' they ask. Yes. 'And they won't send me back?' No. Every one of them will reach for my hand, even if theirs is a wad of dressings. They kiss it like I'm the Virgin bloody Mary.

Tilda x

Delivering them from evil, I thought.

'Good news?' asked Maude.

I realised I was smiling, the tightness in my chest gone. I looked at the page in my hand – *Hello my lovelies*. Neat script, her name signed at the end.

'She seems a little better,' I said, then I read it aloud.

Moments of appreciation were what Tilda needed. A little limelight, an audience of one or of many – it didn't matter. The boys who woke up, who decided to live, who kissed her hand – they were her stage-door admirers. Her show would go on as long as there was adequate applause.

I searched through Maude's biscuit tin for a blank sheet of paper. I would clap as loud as I could.

~

Jack was due to come home for two weeks' leave in November, then December, then January. It was cancelled each time. *Too good at what I do*, Jack wrote, in apology. We never talked about what he did.

Then one day in February 1917, we saw a soldier come along the towpath.

'He looks completely knackered,' I said.

'Knackered,' said Maude.

'Poor lad,' quavered Old Mrs Rowntree. She had to take our word for it; he was just a blur to her.

But Rosie said nothing. And then she stood. And then she ran. She wrapped her arms around the stranger, and he collapsed into her. I couldn't hear his sobs, but I could see how they racked his body and how Rosie had to brace hers to absorb them.

Jack was exhausted. Maude took him to sit in Ma's armchair while Rosie and I transformed their table back into a bed. It had been their daily routine when Jack was home, and Rosie was quick. When I lifted the bedding from beneath the bench seat, *Staying Put* filled with the smell of lavender.

Maude helped Rosie undress her son while I boiled water. He seemed not to notice or care that we were there. When I brought the basin and flannels, he let Maude wash his face and neck, his arms and chest, while his mother attended to all else. He was thin, taut. His feet were blistered and peeling, the skin pale and puckered like they were a hundred years old. On that first day his head was too hot to touch.

Jack's fever lasted six days. He was congested and aching and needed help spooning broth into his mouth. Rosie now had two invalids to care for, and by the end of each day she was worn as thin as India paper. Maude took over in the evenings while I cooked for us all. No one cared how it tasted. On the seventh day, Oberon came home and sent me for a doctor.

When the doctor arrived, Oberon had to step out to make room for him. I offered, but he insisted. He struggled to look on his lad without emotion, and I realised he wanted to spare Jack that, or himself. Keep his head.

Jack's feet were healing well, the doctor said. Rosie's salvia dressings had done their job. A mild case of trench foot. No infection. He might feel a tingling for a while, but it wasn't bad enough to be released from service. We hadn't even considered it but were suddenly crushed that discharge wasn't possible.

'The fever is just flu,' the doctor continued. 'A lot of boys sent home from France have it. They're exhausted; it's hitting them harder than it should.'

The doctor looked around *Staying Put*, and I saw it as he must have. Tiny and impoverished, but clean and warm. Everything in its place, no more than was required, but also no less.

'You're doing all the right things,' he said.

Rosie took an old tobacco tin from the back of the cutlery drawer and asked his fee.

The doctor shook his head. 'It's his service that's made him sick. It wouldn't be right to charge you. But if he takes a turn for the worse, you might think about the Radcliffe Infirmary.'

Jack's fever broke a few days later.

'Two weeks,' the doctor said when he stopped by to check on his patient, 'and he'll be fit to return to France.' Then he turned his attention to Maude. She still held the cloth she'd been using to tend Jack's feet before the doctor arrived. She was flushed. He put his hand to her head. 'Better get this one to bed.'

~

A light tread on the foredeck. A gentle knock. I expected Rosie to just open the hatch and come in, so I kept washing the dishes. Another knock.

I dried my hands and went to open the hatch.

'You were not at work.' It was Lotte. The colour was high in her cheeks: the cold night, perhaps. Her eyes shot past me into the cabin. She was looking for Maude.

'She has Jack's flu,' I said. 'I've put her to bed.'

Her hands twisted around themselves, and I realised they were bare, probably cold.

'She is sick?' Her darting eyes, wide and icy blue, settled on me. It felt like an accusation.

The cobweb moisture of a heavy mist clung to her hat and the shoulders of her coat. I should have invited her in, made her a hot drink. It would have warmed her hands. Calmed her.

'She has a bit of a fever,' I said. 'But she'll be fine. I'm looking after her.'

It was tiny, the movement in her face, the narrowing of her eyes. *Are you?* it said.

'I will help,' she declared.

If it had been a question, I might have agreed. I looked beyond her, into the night. A drizzle had started. 'I can't ask you in, Lotte.' Maude was my sister, my responsibility. 'You might get sick yourself.'

She tried to insist but I was stronger.

Two days later, Maude was up and playing chess with Jack. The day after that, she was back in the bindery. When she took her seat at the bench beside Lotte, I saw the Belgian's body yield.

At the end of the day, Lotte hovered in the cloakroom.

I should have let her help, I thought. 'I'm seeing Bastiaan tonight,' I said.

She waited for the invitation.

'If you feel like visiting? I think Maude might have missed you.'

'Missed you,' said Maude.

The truth of it echoed in my head. A reprimand.

Chapter Thirty-Three

Bastiaan and I had had little time alone during the long winter, and by March 1917 we longed for the solitude of St Sepulchre's. The dregs of a late snowfall still sat in the shelter of the graves, but we had prepared for the cold. Bastiaan placed a blanket on Mrs Wood's sarcophagus, and when we were seated, he laid another across our knees. I poured two mugs of tea and we held them tight in gloved hands.

'What book were you binding today?' he asked.

'We're folding the pages for *Homeri Opera*.'

He tilted his head. 'Homer?'

'*The Odyssey*. Books one to twelve, to be precise. In the original Greek.'

'In school we were made to read Homer,' he said.

'You make it sound like a chore.'

'It was a chore.' He laughed. 'We had to translate lines from those pages you are folding, into French. The story was not the intention.' He sipped his tea.

'You learnt Ancient Greek?'

'A little. But I did not excel.'

'Did you ever read the whole story?'

'Yes. In French. And you?'

It was my turn to laugh. 'I'm from Jericho, Bastiaan, not Oxford. I left school at twelve, and Homer was not on the curriculum at St Barnabas – not in English and certainly not in Ancient Greek.'

'But why not in English?'

'There was no point. Our destinies were too ordinary to bother the gods, and our journeys would take us no further than the Press.'

'The same Press that prints Homer in English *and* Ancient Greek?'

I raised my eyebrows and did my best impression of Mrs Hogg. 'Your job, Miss *Jones*, is to bind the books, not read them.'

'But you do read them.'

'Some of them,' I admitted, though in truth I read a lot. 'Bits and pieces. But I never had the first clue how to decipher Greek.'

'But you know the stories of Homer. You must have had a translation.'

'A bookshelf of translations,' I said. 'Ma brought books home from work, poorly bound. Too grandiose to read aloud, she said, but she'd tell us the tales as she understood them, adding details from other versions of the Greek myths. She'd spend five minutes summarising the Trojan war and an hour explaining why it wasn't Helen's fault.'

Bastiaan smiled. 'She read more than Homer?'

'Anything she could get her hands on. Her favourite was Euripides. She read *The Trojan Women* so often it's fallen apart.' Ma had sewn it; Eb had covered it. He'd botched the knocking-back just enough so it would still get its boards but not pass inspection. His inspection. Dear Scrooge, I thought.

'Euripides?'

'He gave the women something to say.'

'You are like your ma, I think.'

I shrugged. Ma was a bindery girl till the day she died. 'It was Ma who named our narrowboat,' I said. 'She was almost beyond repair when Oberon salvaged her. No name, so Ma called her *Calliope*, the muse of poetry. Homer's muse, some say.'

I stopped talking. *It won't change a thing,* Mrs Hogg had scoffed when Ma told her who Calliope was. *Knowing something like that makes you no better than the rest of us.*

But Bastiaan didn't scoff. He sensed there was more and waited for me to continue.

'I asked Ma once why Calliope didn't just write her own stories.'

'What did she say?'

'That Calliope was a woman.'

'That is all?'

'Does there need to be more?' I raised an eyebrow. 'I understood what she meant.'

'And what did she mean?'

'That it was a woman's place to *inspire* stories, not to *write* them.'

Bastiaan studied me. 'I think you did not believe that, even then,' he said.

I sighed. 'The problem is that I *did* believe it, mostly. But then there was *Jane Eyre* and *Pride and Prejudice* and *Middlemarch.*'

'And this proof, it changed your mind?'

'Just enough to make me want something I can't really have. The Brontës and Jane Austen were far from rich, apparently, but they still lived in houses where one woman cooked their meals and another made their beds and set their fires.'

'If you did not have to work in the bindery, you would write?'

A conversation I had no script for. Again, he waited.

'Almost everything I fold and gather and bind is written by a man, Bastiaan. When Ma told me George Eliot was really a woman, I changed my name to Edward. For a whole week I answered to nothing else.'

I think he understood there was nothing more to say.

'Is she buried here, your ma?'

It was my fault. Talking about Ma had conjured her, and I wondered if I'd done it on purpose. But Bastiaan's question still took me by surprise, and I couldn't answer.

'I am sorry. I thought, because you lived so close ...'

And then I felt ashamed. 'I've never visited her grave,' I blurted.

He said nothing.

'I never saw her dead,' I said. 'And I couldn't watch her casket go in the ground. In my waking and sleeping dreams Ma is alive and healthy. I can hear her, and I'm scared her grave might change that.'

We sat in silence, drinking our tea. I played with the steam that came out of my mouth, trying to make rings out of it.

'You are cold,' Bastiaan said.

'Freezing.'

'Then we will leave.'

We stood and I watched as he folded the blankets and put them in his satchel. I watched as his hand touched the stone where we had sat, a gesture of thanks to Madame Wood.

'I'd like you to meet her,' I said.

I walked ahead through the avenue of yews and past the chapel, as if I did it every day.

Bastiaan didn't take my arm or guide my step. He fell behind, and I was grateful. I needed to arrive alone, I needed to apologise. I'd been angry more than sad, and it had been easier to stay angry if I thought of Ma as a living, breathing woman capable of coming back and taking charge.

The north wall was crowded, just like the streets of Jericho. I hesitated. I thought I'd know exactly where to go, but I was lost. It had been nearly six years, and other mothers had died. Fathers and grandparents, a child from the St Barnabas parish school. I'd known them all, a little or a lot. Half of them had worked at the Press. There was a machine minder, a tea lady and the eldest son of a compositor. When I die, I thought, I will still be a bindery girl.

St Sepulchre's had no room for Jericho's war dead, but a few families had inscribed the names of sons and brothers on the graves of their parents or grandparents. These were men who would never come home. They were lost, or buried in France or Greece or some other place too far away. I slowed to read their names. *William Cudd, aged 24, died in Flanders.* I remembered him from St Barnabas. I also remembered *Thomas John Drew, aged 23, died in France.* He was so tall we called him Tom Thumb. I had to bend to read the next inscription – the gravestone was small, but the lettering was beautiful. It belonged to *Derryth Owen, beloved mother.* And the inscription below was for her son, *Gareth Owen, aged thirty-seven, died in France.*

My breath caught. The compositor. Jack's lieutenant. I'd known when his sweetheart hadn't. His wife. I'd been there when they came out of the church. *Beloved Husband* was inscribed below his name and below that, *Love, Eternal.* All in Baskerville typeface. Clear and beautiful.

Bastiaan must have thought I'd found Ma's grave. He moved close, rested his hand on my back while I crouched.

'Someone I knew,' I said.

'I am sorry. Take your time.'

I looked around and saw the copper beech. I'd stood beneath it with Tilda and Maude. I'd studied its bark, its foliage, the pattern made by the sunlight that shone between its leaves. I'd leant against its trunk and rubbed the backs of my fingers over its roughness. I hadn't wanted to hear a word being said around that hole. I hadn't wanted to imagine the box inside it. When the vicar started talking, all I'd heard was the dull scraping sound of my knuckles moving back and forth over bark. Only when Maude had moved towards the grave had I realised the vicar was quiet. I'd reached out to stop her, but she'd shrugged me off as she went to the edge of the hole, took a handful of dirt from the pile beside it and threw it in. By then, my knuckles were bleeding. I'd stared at them, but it hadn't stopped me from hearing the dirt land on the box.

The beech had grown and the low afternoon light stretched its bare limbs and thickened its knotty crown so it loomed. It had been a refuge then, a distraction. I moved towards the shadows beneath it. I stood in the same place. I leant against its trunk. I felt the rough bark against my knuckles.

Then I followed my memory of Maude.

The headstone was small and almost hidden. Tilda had maintained the grave, but the war was keeping her away and weeds grew all around it. I had to push them back to see the inscription.

Helen Penelope Jones
Beloved mother
Beloved friend
Who died 25 April 1911
Aged 36 years

Below the words, an engraving of an open book.

I'd expected her name and age, and I'd prepared for *Beloved mother*. I remembered Tilda asking if she could add *Beloved friend* and me saying I didn't care. But I'd understood the nature of their relationship, and there it was, inscribed in stone – Tilda had put herself where a husband should be.

It was the book that made me sob. The book that overwhelmed me. Bastiaan was right – I was like her. Six years of grief poured from my eyes and my nose. It shook my shoulders and bent my back and it forced me to the cold ground where my mother lay.

~

I don't know how long I stayed murmuring into the dirt, asking her to forgive. My anger. My absence. All the times I'd left Maude with a stranger. All the times I'd thought of a life without my sister in it.

I felt the weight of a blanket. Bastiaan was lifting me up, and blood was rushing into my legs. Pins and needles prickled my feet, and Bastiaan had to hold me until they bore my weight. I was shivering.

'She takes up so little room,' I said.

He sighed. 'In the end, we all do.'

Chapter Thirty-Four

Homeri Opera. Odysseae.

Thomas W Allen had used Latin to write his bloody *Praefatio*, so whatever insights the preface held were lost on me.

Another locked door, I thought, as I made the first fold, the second fold. The Latin teased – *Homeri, academia, exemplar, antiquae, Athenis, linguae, vocabulorum traditionem* – echoes of a language I knew. But the Greek …

Another sheet; the Greek swept across my vision with each fold. No rhyme, no reason. This way or that it made no difference, no sense. It was dizzying, nauseating. One fold, two folds, three. My head swam with it. Swam with it.

…

…

'Miss Jones!' A sting to my cheek. The freckly frog.

'Give her some air,' I heard her say. 'Go back to your benches.'

I was on the floor. Mrs Hogg kneeling, her eyes wide. Worried?

'You gave us a fright,' she said. It was soft, no bark in it. Yes, worried.

'I …'

I didn't know how to speak. *Vocabulorum traditionem*, I thought.

'I ...'

'Don't fuss, Miss Jones. You've fainted, that's all. You'll be fine in a minute.'

Her hand on my forehead, my cheek. I was so hot.

Maude moved a paper fan in front of my face. Cooling. Mrs Hogg helped me sit up. Helped me back into my chair. She was gentle.

Maude gave me the paper fan. One fold, two folds, three, four, five ... ten at least. The Greek concertinaed into something useful.

~

Gwen took the thermometer from my mouth and frowned. 'It's still high,' she said, giving it an efficient shake. She put her other hand on my forehead, then against my cheek. 'I'm not sure you have anything to smile about.'

It had been a long time since I'd been looked after, and I couldn't help being a little grateful for my fever. For Gwen.

'You should join the VAD, become a nurse,' I said.

'I've thought about it.'

My smile faded. 'Please don't.'

'I'm not the sort, Peg. If I was, I would have done it years ago.' She returned the thermometer to the cup by my bed, then pulled the covers up to my neck. We both cocked an ear when we heard Maude step onto the foredeck. She brought the post and the cool March evening onto *Calliope*.

Gwen secured the hatch, then Maude passed her the letters so she could remove her coat and hat. Gwen sorted through them as she came back towards my bed.

'Two with an army postmark, and one with a regular French postmark from Madame Taylor.'

'Tilda,' I said, and Gwen put the last letter into my outstretched hand.

It was hardly a letter, just a short note written on the back of a small card – one of Iso's pictures. It might have been a postcard except the subject was a hospital ward. The colours were subdued. A row of beds with just enough brushstrokes to conjure a man in each; white covers, greyed by night; a bright dab of yellow from the torch held by a nurse. She had her back turned, but I could see honey hair falling in a thick plait from under her nurse's cap. I recognised her figure, so tall and straight. The nurse was the focus of the picture, not the men, and I imagined Iso sitting out of the frame, watching Tilda as she went about her work. She'd captured something I could never articulate in words. Some truth about Tilda that was borne in her body.

I turned to the words.

20 February 1917

Hello Pegs,

Glad to hear Maude is back on her feet, but it's quite unlike you to moan about a cold so I can only assume you are quite sick. Normally I wouldn't worry, but my ward is filling up with boys who can barely breathe (and we're down a third of our nursing staff). The French call it 'la grippe', but Dr Hammond believes it's a new kind of bronchitis. Very contagious. Jack's your culprit, I reckon. Brought it home as a souvenir. My advice is to drink plenty of water and let Maude look after you. She's good at it, you know.

Much love,

Tilda x

She didn't mention the drawing, and I wondered if she was aware of how Iso saw her.

I looked beyond our bedroom curtain and saw Gwen searching Ma's bookcase. She took a novel from the top row. As she opened the cover, I realised Ma's hand would have been the last to touch the pages. I watched as Gwen's eyes scanned the first few lines. I couldn't see the detail of the cover and didn't know what she was reading, but she smiled in the way that you do when you come across something familiar, something you once enjoyed but had forgotten. She closed the book with such care, then turned it in her hand. She stroked the jacket. Ma would have liked Gwen, I thought.

'Have you read all of these books, Peg?'

'Most.' But I wasn't sure she heard. My throat felt like cheap paper – fragile, easily torn.

Then she bent to the bottom shelf. The Greeks.

'Have you read this?'

Green cloth, *The Trojan Women* printed in gold on the front. Translated by Gilbert Murray.

I nodded. 'Ma's favourite Greek.'

'Really?' she said, opening the book. Glancing, not reading. 'I sometimes think Euripides hated women. He makes them so cruel.'

I'd said the same to Ma.

'Some women *are* cruel,' I said to Gwen. *Especially if they've been treated cruelly,* Ma had said. *Like most women in Ancient Greece.* 'I think he makes women important. Powerful,' I echoed Ma and my throat burnt. 'He lets them speak.'

I expected Gwen to argue her point. But she nodded. Just nodded. She returned *The Trojan Women* to their place in Ma's bookcase then crouched to the pile of unbound manuscripts and loose sections on the floor in front of it. She took up the section on top.

'What's this?'

'Part of a book.'

'Why on earth have you got just part of a book?'

'There must have been something that interested me.'

The section was uncut. She turned it to look at the last page. 'It ends mid-sentence, Peg.'

'There's always a chance I can pick up more pages.'

Gwen laughed. 'Pick up! You make it sound as simple as popping out for bread. If it interests you that much, why don't you just borrow it?'

Gwen had hit a minor nerve. The sections she'd found were mostly from large books, expensive or rare. They all hinted at something worth knowing, and I hated not being able to find it out. 'Sometimes I try to find the book at the 'Stute or the Oxford Public Library. They don't always have it.'

'You should try the Bodley; they have every book ever published in England. You can't borrow them, of course, no one can, but you're certain to find whatever you're interested in.'

'And how would *I* get into the *Bodleian*?'

'Now that I think about it ...' She began to look sheepish. It didn't suit her.

'I can't get in? What a surprise,' I said.

'You need a proper introduction. No less than a college principal if you're a woman. I shouldn't have suggested it.'

'And if you're a man?'

'As long as you wear a gown, long or short, no introduction is required. And if they want to *borrow* a book, they go to the Oxford Union Society Library. It has every book you could possibly need to pass college exams.'

I began to laugh, which started me coughing.

'Oh, Peg, you're so cynical.' Gwen came over, dipped a spoon in the pot of honey beside my bed and passed it to me to suck on.

'It's not as if it's impossible for a woman to access the library at the Oxford Union Society,' she said.

'And how would that happen, exactly?'

'Well, she'd have to flatter some chap from Oriel until he agrees to be her chaperone, and then she'd need to accommodate his timetable, no matter when her paper is due, and of course he will expect a degree of fawning, and she may have to endure afternoon tea. It's only fair, since he will be borrowing the books on her behalf, and the risk to him is significant.'

'What risk?'

'She's likely to read it in the bath, isn't she? And it may slip from her tiny hands. But she'll submit to it all for the chance to read the right books and gain the right knowledge. And one day she'll get a first, and her chaperone from Oriel will get a second, and she will go on to chair a committee with little renumeration, and he will go on to run a company or a country and eventually become a lord. Any other questions?'

I sucked the last of the honey from the spoon. 'No questions, just a point of fact. No chap from Oriel would take the risk for a bindery girl.'

She nodded. 'You're probably right,' she said. Then she sat on the bed and unfolded the section she was holding. 'It's all upside down and back to front.' She turned it this way and that, then settled on a page and read aloud:

'*He came. Life is so constructed, that the event does not, cannot, will not, match the expectation. That whole day he never accosted me.* Thwarted affection,' she said. 'It must be a novel. But which one?' She looked more closely at the section. 'Page four hundred and fifteen. A long one.'

'*Villette*,' I said. 'The printed sheets have just arrived in the bindery.'

'A brand new book? How wonderful!'

'Not new, Gwen. It's an Oxford World's Classic – we print it every few years. Surely you've heard of it?'

'Should I have?'

'Charlotte Brontë?'

'Of course I've heard of *her*, Peg, I'm not a philistine. I'm sure *Jane Eyre* is one of my favourite novels.'

'You're sure?'

'Well, I'm sure it *should* be.'

'What books do you actually read at Somerville, Gwen?'

'I read what my tutor tells me to read. Though sometimes I skim.' She refolded the section, then held it up for me to see. 'What happens when you've picked up the whole set?'

'I bind them. The sewing frame is on the table.'

She walked out of sight, and I heard pages moving through her fingers.

'*English Prose: Narrative, Descriptive, Dramatic.* Good God, Peg, why would you bother?'

'I prefer not to skim,' I said.

She came back into view. 'Each to their own. My particular academic strength is mimicking the analytical style and arguments of my tutors.' She smiled, as if sharing a secret. 'Despite being so poorly read, I sometimes do quite well.'

'Of course you do – you're flattering them.'

'That's right. Flattery works a treat, no matter the circumstance.'

'Surely they challenge you.'

'The old stalwarts do. But my current tutor is a bit green. If I agree with her, she doesn't have to defend her own ideas. It suits us both very well.'

'But what's the point?'

'The point of what?'

'Why are you at Somerville if you don't want to learn?' My voice had risen just enough to start me coughing again. Gwen patted my back.

'Miss Penrose, our principal, asked me the very same question a few weeks ago.'

'What did you tell her?'

'That I would try harder.'

'And will you?'

Again, that teasing smile. 'Of course not. I'll just be more careful to disguise my complacency. I'll do well enough.'

'Well enough for what?'

'Interesting conversations with men at dinner parties and women on committees.'

'You drive me mad, Gwen. I'm too sick for this.'

She soothed me, an exaggerated 'there, there' as if I were a child having a sulk. I brushed her hand away.

She studied me a moment.

'And how would *you* approach it, Peg?'

'You mean if I were a Somervillian?'

'Yes. What would your strategy be to get through it?'

'I wouldn't be there to *get through it.*'

The mirth that had been playing across her face retreated. She became serious, and I grew uncomfortable. I closed my eyes. When I felt her hand on my forehead, I realised I was holding myself rigid.

'Still warm,' she said, 'but I think it's coming down.'

I relaxed, opened my eyes. 'Tilda thinks I have *la grippe.*'

'La what?'

'It's what Jack had. Half the boys being sent home from Étaples have it.'

'Lucky things. Better to be sent home with a French cold than a missing limb, or, worse, missing marbles.'

Chapter Thirty-Five

Bastiaan stopped in one evening to see how I was feeling. Maude took his coat and then his hand. She sat him in Ma's armchair.

'Stay for supper,' she said, then she returned to the galley to mash boiled carrots and potatoes with milk.

It was something Lotte called *stoemp*. Maude could also make *frites* and *tartines,* which were really just sandwiches without the bread on top, but she made them perfectly, without distraction or disaster. Lotte had taught her, and each meal had its own song, like a nursery rhyme, that kept Maude focused. I watched her reach for the pan of fried leeks and cabbage, never pausing in her song. She added them to the mash, and I felt a wave of gratitude for Lotte, for her patience and ingenuity. I'd been eating *stoemp* almost every night since my appetite returned, and I longed to eat something else, but if *stoemp* was all Maude wanted to cook, I would keep consuming it.

I heard Gwen's footsteps on the deck. Maude paused in her song. We waited for Gwen's familiar *rat-a-tat-tat* and another rush of air when the hatch opened.

'Cosy,' said Gwen when she'd closed the hatch. 'How's the leg, Bastiaan?'

'I have returned the stick,' he said.

'Jolly good.'

Maude returned to her song, her stirring. I watched Gwen watching my sister. Maude added nutmeg, salt, pepper. '*One plate, then two,*' she sang as she reached up to the plate rack. '*A dollop for me and a dollop for you.*'

She passed me a plate of food.

'Thank you, Maudie, I'm starving.'

'Starving,' she said, then she took a plate of food to Bastiaan so he didn't have to move from Ma's armchair. Finally, she sat at the table with her own meal.

'I'll help myself, shall I?' said Gwen. She went to the kitchen and filled a plate with *stoemp,* then she joined us at the table. 'Thank you, Maudie,' she said. 'I, too, am starving.'

Maude looked at her.

'Well, not starving, exactly. I've just had dinner. But it was all a bit brown and it smelled too much like liver. This smells much better. Worth the risk of sneaking out of grounds.'

'Much better,' said Maude. 'Now, eat up.' It might have been Ma speaking, and it had the desired effect. Gwen took up her fork and began to eat.

Afterwards, Gwen collected our plates and took them to the galley. She put the kettle over the hot plate and leant against the bench while the water heated.

'I had tea with Miss Bruce the other day,' she said.

There was a time when I couldn't get enough of Gwen's talk of Somerville. I'd inserted myself into her anecdotes and let a fantasy take root. But my fever had cured me of delusion.

'Vice-Principal Bruce or Pamela?' I asked, with barely disguised irritation.

'Pamela, she of the refugee committee. She said something quite interesting.'

Steam started to rise from the kettle. I hoped it would boil and distract her. I stayed silent.

'Don't you want to know what she said?'

Not really, I thought. 'Of course,' I said.

'She asked if you'd ever thought to further your education.'

I sat very still, unsure what it was I felt. Gwen noted the impact of her words and turned to attend to the kettle, though it still hadn't boiled. She was playing with me.

'Gwen,' I said, perhaps too loud, 'why would Miss Bruce ask you that?'

Gwen took the kettle from the hot plate and poured hot water into the basin. She added soap flakes and swished them around with her hand as if she'd been doing it her whole life.

'Gwen!'

She turned. Leant against the bench again, her face full of mischief. 'She thinks you're made of good Somerville material.'

I wanted to throw something at her, and I knew it must have shown on my face, but she continued.

'I had to agree,' she said. Then she looked to Bastiaan. 'You'd agree, wouldn't you?'

'I do not know what Somerville material is,' he said. 'Are *you* Somerville material?'

'Well, it depends on who you ask. I'm rather less committed than some. In fact, I told Miss Bruce that Peg was probably better suited to Somerville than I am.'

'And what did Miss Bruce say to that?' I said, teeth gritted.

Gwen laughed. 'Oh, she quickly concurred and then she poured me another cup of tea.'

I looked at Gwen as if I'd never met her before. Was it possible she had walked through our friendship with her eyes half-closed to the life I lived?

'I don't like being talked about, Gwen.'

'Rubbish. We all like being talked about. Miss Bruce thinks you have a scholar's mind.'

'Peggy likes to read,' Maude said, as Ma had when people asked why she collected so many books.

'Exactly,' Gwen said.

'Should I be flattered?'

'Of course. No one has ever said that about me.'

'And yet there you are, in a room of your own at Somerville College.'

'Oriel, actually.' She was infuriating. 'For now, anyway.'

'I know I have a scholar's mind, Gwen. I have always known. But while it may be a desirable trait for a Somervillian – necessary, I would have thought, though apparently not – for a bindery girl it's a character flaw. A hazard. Unattractive.'

'A bloody waste,' said Maude.

'Poor Pegs,' said Gwen.

'Don't "Poor Pegs" me. Bloody hell, Gwen, you have no idea! You've had everything handed to you, even things you don't really care to have, like an education.'

'Not everything,' Gwen said. 'I'd care to have the vote, but nobody's handed me that.'

'Only a matter of time,' said Maude. She'd heard Tilda say it, and Mrs Stoddard. She'd even heard Ma say it. Always the same phrase, I thought. Meaningless when time could stretch with such ease.

'We could be dead before we get the vote,' I said.

'Oh, surely not, I've heard rumours it's closer than ever,' said Gwen.

I slumped back in my chair, unable to hold the tension in my body any longer. I didn't have the energy to raise my voice.

'Closer for you, perhaps, Gwen, but *we*' – I pointed to Maude and myself – 'won't be included. *We* have no land, no education, and *therefore*, it goes without saying, no experience or opinion worth considering.' I looked her in the eye. 'Can we stop this now? This conversation is of no interest to Bastiaan and I'm still sick. I haven't the energy to call you a spoiled brat and sound like I mean it.'

'It is of interest,' Bastiaan said.

'Of course it is,' said Gwen. 'Miss Bruce – Pamela – thinks you are the perfect candidate for a Somerville scholarship.'

She's bright enough, my teacher had said. *It's not always enough,* Ma had replied.

'I checked, and we have two full scholarships for women with the desire but not the means. In other words, for Poor Pegs like you.'

She might have taken a bow, but I wasn't looking at Gwen, I was looking at Maude. She'd taken up some loose sheets, India paper, pages from the New English Dictionary. I remembered how difficult they were to work with, how patient Ma had been when she showed us how to handle the thin paper. Maude was folding them into designs of her own making. Nothing I could identify, but balanced and beautiful. The softness of the pages gave Maude's creations a sense of movement, as if each one was petalled or winged. I tried to catch a word as the paper moved through my sister's hands.

Trist (obsolete): Confident, sure. When Maude had finished the fold I picked it up and read from the topside of a wing. A quote from 1400: *Of him ye might be trist.*

Maude's hands had slowed, and I realised she was listening to what Gwen was saying.

'Miss Bruce suggested I talk to you about it,' Gwen said. 'She wants me to gauge your appetite for an education.' She became oratorical: 'Your stamina for the rigours of study.'

A scholarship. For Poor Pegs like you.

'The perfect candidate,' said Maude. I kept my eyes on the dictionary pages. I'd never known the bindery without them. Neither had Ma. She once said that you needed stamina to define the English language.

Why? I'd asked. *Because there are so many words,* she said. *But we don't need to know what they all are,* I argued. *We'll never use them.* She put her hand on my cheek, the way she did with Maude when she wanted her attention. *Some people will use them, Peg. It doesn't hurt to know what they're saying.*

'How would I study?'

'Read the books,' said Maude.

Gwen drifted from the table to Ma's armchair. She ran her finger along Ma's bookcase, then bent to the piles of manuscripts and sections on the floor. She walked the length of *Calliope*, fore to aft.

'My God,' she called, 'there are pages in your chamber-pot. Please tell me you don't—'

'Wipe your arse with them,' Maude called back. Tilda loved to say it.

Bastiaan laughed. Gwen laughed. She came back into the galley.

'I dare say you have most of the books you need for the Somerville exam – in part if not in full.' She looked at Maude. 'I wonder what fine words have ended up in the …' She turned to me. 'I know it's indelicate, but where does your business end up?'

'Gwen!' I looked towards Bastiaan. He couldn't keep his before face straight.

'Canal,' said Maude.

As uncomfortable as the previous conversation had been it was better than where we had found ourselves.

'What would I do about the books I don't have?' I said. 'The chapters I haven't managed to pilfer – how would I access those?'

'I have a library card for the Oxford Public Library,' said Bastiaan.

'Their collection isn't very up to date,' I said, and my mind began to race. 'And the Somerville entrance exam is just the start. What would I do for Responsions?'

'My goodness,' Gwen said. 'You know quite a lot about Oxford University exams for a bindery girl. I had a whole tutorial planned about the style of questions in the Somerville entrance and the content of Responsions.'

'I know all of that,' I said.

'Responsions?' said Maude.

'To respond,' I said. 'It's another exam, and I have to pass it if I want to do a degree course.'

'Not that the University will *give* you the degree once you've done all the work,' Gwen said. 'How on earth do you know all of this?'

'I've been folding and collating the exam papers for years,' I said.

'Well, I think you've answered the question of *appetite*. Miss Bruce will be thrilled.'

Appetite, I thought. I'd been hungry my whole life. 'Does Miss Bruce know I left school at twelve?'

'That's not unusual for a Somervillian,' said Gwen. 'I never went to school at all.'

'But you had tutors,' I said.

She shrugged. An inconvenient truth that didn't help her argument. She drifted back towards Ma's armchair, picked up a book – an unbound volume, a bunch of sections. 'I think you'll be just fine for the Somerville entrance – general knowledge, a bit of French translation.' She looked at Bastiaan. 'You can help with that. And a few questions on your chosen subject.'

'Will she need to *speak* French?' he asked.

'No, thank goodness. She'd never pass.'

'And Responsions?' I said.

'Your old school primers will do to get you started.'

'What kind of school do you think I went to, Gwen? We learnt the mathematics of shopkeepers and the only Latin I know is *Te Deum Laudamus* – "God, we praise you" – because it's in the stained glass in St Barnabas church. As for Ancient Greek, what use would that be to a child attending St Barnabas?'

She was stricken for a moment but gathered her wits. 'Ancient Greek is little use to anyone, Peg.'

'And yet you need it to get into Oxford University. Could it be, Gwen, that Ancient Greek is just another hurdle designed to keep people like me out of Oxford?'

The more I argued, the happier Gwen seemed to be. 'I hope you do get in, Peg. You could join the debating club. You'd be quite formidable.'

'I hope you do get in,' said Maude.

I was suddenly ashamed. After years of wanting my life to be different, here I was looking for reasons not to change. I'd always thought I was more than a bindery girl. Now, I was making excuses not to be. Fear must have shown all over my face, because when Gwen sat beside me again, her sparring tone had softened.

'The University insists all Somervillians know their *eta* from their *theta* if they want to take a degree course. So you will do what other Somervillians before you have done – commit just enough to memory to scrape through, and then forget it entirely.'

I took a deep breath and accepted Gwen's hand. 'That doesn't sound too hard,' I said.

'As long as you don't intend reading Classics, you'll be fine.'

I pulled back. 'But of course I want to read Classics.'

'Really?' Gwen looked shocked.

'Not really.' I laughed.

'What, then? I'm sure you've thought about it.'

'English,' I said.

Chapter Thirty-Six

Gwen was right: *Calliope* was lined with pages, loose or bound, that might prepare me for the Somerville entrance. Of course it was. Every few years, the Press reprinted the texts required for all the College entrance exams so there would be ample supply for young men and, increasingly, young women who wanted to come up to Oxford. Inevitably, there were mishaps – misalignments, poor folds, inadequate knocking back of a spine. They might be bound too tight or too loose, and sometimes the glue would dry on a good leather binding. They were not worthy of the Clarendon Press seal. *See what you've got*, Gwen had said before leaving Oxford for her term break. Then she'd handed me a list of subjects and books I should study.

Maude and I began to rearrange. We sorted through the mess of books, manuscripts and sections from fore to aft, and made piles of texts that might be useful for the exams. I bent to the task every evening – before supper and after. Sometimes I just sat in front of the bookshelves and ate bread and Marmite. So many of my habits changed. I still saw Bastiaan at the 'Stute on Mondays and Fridays, but I read history instead of the papers and we rarely walked out in the evening so there was less need for Lotte to spend time with Maude. On

Sundays I barely got my hands dirty at Port Meadow before making my excuses and rushing home to the books.

There were some I'd forgotten about – books that Eb had given to Ma or that Ma had brought home before I cared enough to notice. I came across an old copy of Elizabeth Barrett Browning's *Aurora Leigh*, its pages dog-eared but its binding still sound. She'd paid for this, I thought, or someone had. And she'd loved it. I read from a page with its corner folded:

> *The first book first. And how I felt it beat*
> *Under my pillow, in the morning's dark,*
> *An hour before the sun would let me read!*

I put it on my study pile, still so small – it was a slower process than I had imagined.

I gave Maude the task of searching for the books that Gwen had said were on the recommended reading list: History, Classics, English Literature and Literary Criticism, mainly. A text on Philosophy, and an essay on Economic Theory (*Nothing too taxing,* Gwen had said. *What would be the point?*) – the Press had printed them all. She found a few and my study pile grew, then one day she handed me a thin volume, board-bound and familiar. I remembered letting Ma's bonefolder slip, the small tear. It was big enough to make the volume mine, but small enough not to ruin it.

Women's Words and Their Meanings, edited by Esme Nicoll.

I turned the pages, each one full of words that had been overlooked, the names of women who had been overlooked. She'd collected them on scraps of paper, Mr Owen had said.

I looked around *Calliope*, at the piles of sections and parts of book looked at the manuscripts that had been sewn but not boun with binder's tape but no boards. We weren't so I gathered scraps of books – ruined page the Press or the University. But they were worth something to me, and the books had been worth something to Ma. I wondered if Ma had ever wanted to do anything more than read them. Then I remembered her reading to me, explaining things, asking me questions. So many memories, all folded together. *Do you think the Trojan War was Helen's fault? It would have been quite easy for Jane Eyre to marry St John. Why do you think she didn't? Can you understand why Mrs Graham ran away to Wildfell Hall?* It was important to her that I understood.

One day she said, *It might be a dangerous thing for Mr Darwin's theories to be applied to people.* When I asked why, she looked at Maude. *How should we judge who is fit and who isn't, Peg? Should it be how clever you are, or how rich? Or should it be how kind you are, the unique way you see the world, or maybe how often you make others smile?* She tickled me then, and I thought nothing more of it.

I looked again at *Women's Words and Their Meanings.* Words that no one valued, spoken by women that no one would have remembered if she hadn't written their names on slips of paper. I put it in my reading pile.

∽

We went on like this for two weeks, maybe three. Then Lotte asked if Maude was sick.

We were taking off our aprons, hanging them on hooks, gathering our things to leave the Press for the day.

'She is getting thin,' Lotte said.

I looked at my sister. She was in front of the small mirror by the door, attaching her hat. We've always been thin, I thought, and I nearly said it. But then I caught Maude's face in the mirror and noticed the sharpness of her jaw. I ran my thumb around the waistband of my skirt and realised there was more room than there had been.

'You are both thinner,' Lotte said. 'You are not eating well.'

She walked over to where Maude stood and put her hand on Maude's shoulder and spoke to her reflection. I couldn't hear what she said, but I could see how gently she said it and I wanted to tell her to stop, move away, leave Maude alone. *She's mine,* I wanted to say.

Maude turned from the mirror, her hat on crooked. 'Lotte will cook lunch tomorrow.'

'Lovely,' I said.

~

The next day was Saturday. Lotte made us lunch while I sorted through a pile of sections, trying to work out what books they might have come from and if any of them could be useful. When we sat down to eat, Lotte asked how we were getting on with the sorting.

'A bloody mess,' said Maude, without my vitriol.

Lotte nodded. It was obvious.

'We're getting there,' I said.

'I think you are not,' Lotte replied. 'And you should be studying the books, not sorting them.'

We ate the rest of the meal in silence, and it was a relief to finish and clear the plates. As I washed them, I heard Lotte explain to Maude how she could catalogue what we had. How she could account for everything – the sections and loose papers, as well as the bound books and unbound manuscripts.

'They are all important, yes?'

'All important,' I heard Maude say.

'Then they must all be catalogued.'

She'd brought a ledger, and I watched her put it between her and Maude. I listened as she explained how to use it. How to divide it into categories and record each book, the author, the date.

'Most important, the location,' said Lotte. Then she suggested a shorthand code for every shelf, nook and cranny where a book might dwell. She curated *Calliope* as if the narrowboat were a library.

A library.

Of course.

Lotte had been a librarian. The ledger, the lesson. She'd thought about this. I heard Maude echo, one thing, then another – committing the process to memory.

Lotte set up the ledger that day. She catalogued a handful of books and sections already in one of my study piles, then she watched as Maude catalogued more.

'She is precise,' Lotte said when I walked with her onto the towpath. The day was already dusky, and I wondered if she would be home before it was dark. 'She should make a survey of all your texts.' She nodded towards *Calliope*. 'You should know what you have.'

'A lot of it is rubbish,' I said.

She shook her head. 'That is not what you think.'

∼

'*The Immigrant* is still showing at the George Street Cinema,' Bastiaan said one day, over a sandwich at the 'Stute. 'Lotte can maybe visit with Maude and we could see the six o'clock?'

An image of Maude and Lotte alone on *Calliope*, bent over the ledger and surrounded by our books. Ma's books. My books and papers. If I had my way, I thought, I'd sit among them all day and night. There'd be no bindery to go to, no sister to care for, no sweetheart to keep happy. I'd just read and learn and …

Bastiaan took a deep breath, and I noticed he'd turned his war face my way. All the better to hide what he was feeling.

'Why don't you have supper with us,' I said. 'Lotte will be cooking – she always makes too much. And then you can walk her home.'

He shifted in his chair so I could see his smile.

Over the next few weeks, Bastiaan joined us whenever Lotte did.

We settled into a routine, and after a while I was grateful not to be sitting alone. I worked my way around the books and piles of papers lining the walls of *Calliope*. I checked each against a list of texts and topics that Gwen had given me, and if I thought something was useful, I'd give it to Bastiaan. He sat in Ma's chair, his bad leg outstretched, and ordered the piles of books into subjects. If a section had nothing to identify the book it came from, he would put it aside to be labelled.

Lotte kept us fed, and after supper she helped Maude catalogue our library. That's what she called it: *Calliope's Library*. She wrote it on the front of the ledger in beautiful script.

Ma had collected more books than I remembered, but she had been deliberate in her acquisitions, so many of her books were on Gwen's list. My own collecting had been haphazard and opportunistic. I'd created a kind of chaos where once there was order, but Maude managed to find a place for everything. When the sorting was over and the ledger was full, she became vigilant about keeping *Calliope's* library organised.

I began to read whenever I had the chance. Over coffee in the morning and after supper. I lost hours of the evening in pages I had forgotten and others I'd never known. Some of the pages were on Gwen's list, some weren't – I read them anyway, thinking that Ma might have. I'd been acquainted with the books on *Calliope* my whole life, but now I wanted to know them from cover to cover. When I was done with a book or section, I left it on the table. Maude forbade me to return anything to a shelf, knowing I might put it in the wrong place.

∾

Oberon stopped by, his flyboat full of bricks instead of coal, which was disappointing. He was to stay the night, so Rosie made him fashion a few extra seats out of overturned buckets, enough for seven, and arrange them in her verge garden so we could all eat supper together. She wore her boatwoman's bonnet, because seven was an occasion, and passed each of us a bowl of stew.

When the food was eaten, she took a letter from her pocket. It was from Jack, unopened. She gave it to Oberon, and he read aloud:

'*We're still in Flanders, but exactly where I better not say or the censor will muck it all up.*'

Lotte got up, cleared the plates. Took them into *Staying Put*. I hoped Oberon's voice would not carry.

'*For three days we were billeted in a little town, and I reckon the locals were glad to have us. Kept bringing us fresh pastries – my favourite are like little pies with curd inside. A nice change from bully beef and dry biscuits.*'

A half-smile. '*Mattentaarten,*' Bastiaan said. 'They are good.'

'*But then we got our orders,*' Oberon continued reading. '*The Huns hold a ridge near here, and we're aiming to take it. But half the battle on the first day was getting through the mud and flooded shell holes. It's bloody wet here, bloody muddy – excuse my swearing, Nan. Both sides have made a mess of the place.*'

A noise came out of Bastiaan. He bowed his head and Oberon stopped reading, but his eyes darted over the words.

'Go on,' said Old Mrs Rowntree. Oberon looked over to Bastiaan.

'Go on,' he said, without looking up.

'*Them poor Belgians won't have much to come back to. It's like something from that book you gave me, Nan,* The War of the Worlds. *I reckon the Huns might have a heat-ray. Whatever was here – trees, buildings, carts, horses – they're nothing but blackened skeletons now. Dead trees reach into the grey sky, and any minute I expect to see a Martian tripod coming out of the gloom.*'

Oberon read the rest, but I was only half-listening. I was watching Bastiaan. The clenching of his jaw. His head stayed lowered until Oberon had read the last word, then he stood up and started walking along the towpath.

I went to follow, but Oberon put a hand on my arm.

'Let him be, Peg. Just for a minute.'

I sat.

'And this,' Oberon said, 'seems to be for you, Miss Maude.' He handed her a single sheet of paper, folded in half, *Miss Maude* written on it in Jack's best hand.

Maude nodded. Took it. I expected her to open it. Instead, she stood up and went into *Calliope*.

I caught up with Bastiaan near Walton Well Bridge.

'It is not right,' he said.

I knew what he was thinking and had no answer to it.

'Jack should be here,' he said, 'and I should be in Belgium.'

∽

6 April 1917

Dear Pegs,

Your news came as a wonderful surprise, yet it also feels inevitable. Helen would be so ... well, it's something she used to dream of.

Speaking of wonderful inevitabilities. We are all beside ourselves with news of the Americans. Better late than never, I suppose. Surely their arrival will be the beginning of the end of this damned war.

Tilda x

∽

When the Gowns returned to Oxford for Trinity term, Gwen was among them.

'*Calliope's Library*,' she read aloud. She held the ledger in her hand; her eyebrows were raised. She made it sound like a school project.

'What?' I asked. 'Is our home not grand enough for a library?'

Gwen laughed and looked around. 'I'm afraid it might sink under the weight of all these books.'

Then it was my turn to laugh. '*Calliope* was a working vessel, Gwen. Designed to carry coal and bricks. A few books will hardly test her.'

'A *few* books?' She opened the ledger and turned page after page. 'Hundreds of books, more like it. Did Maude do all this?'

'Lotte showed her how.' I moved to stand beside Gwen and was impressed, all over again, by Maude's work. *Precise*, Lotte had said.

'I had no idea,' said Gwen.

I brought the teapot to the table and began to pour. Gwen looked up from the ledger.

'It's quite extensive, your *library*. Does your controller know how much you've brought home?'

'Not everything is from the bindery,' I said, though most of it was. 'Some are from bookshops – Blackwell's, mostly. Ma loved it there. She'd browse the shelves until Maude or I started to complain, then she'd find the latest from Everyman's Library or World's Classics and take it to the counter.' I paused: the memory of Ma opening her purse, handing over the coins, smiling as the book was carefully wrapped in brown paper. 'I think Ma liked to see the care that was given to the book,' I said. 'The respect.'

'My mother never took me to a bookshop,' said Gwen. I felt a moment of pity, then had an image of Gwen and her mother walking into a dress shop, a jewellery shop, one of those hotel tearooms that serve tiny cakes on silver trays.

'Poor Gwen,' I said.

She smiled, put down her mug. 'So you know what texts you've got. You know where to find them. What do you do now?'

'I study.'

She shook her head. 'Mugging up is the last thing you should be doing.'

I frowned.

'You're new to this, Peg. If you dive straight into the books after all the work you've clearly done to sort them out, you will collapse before you're halfway there. Take my word for it, a bit of fun now will make the task ahead more manageable.'

When Lotte and Maude returned from the Covered Market, I asked Lotte to stay into the evening. 'I'm going to the pictures with Bastiaan,' I said.

~

I woke early. So early it was still dark. But my head was clear. Clear as a bell, I thought. Sharp as a tack. 'Time to start studying,' I said into Maude's ear.

'Mugging up,' she slurred, as she rolled away from me. She'd sleep for hours yet. I kissed her cheek and slipped from the room as quietly as I could.

I lit the lamp. A misshapen book waited on the table, left out from the night before. I'd started reading it after Bastiaan walked me home from the pictures. 'Not yet,' I whispered. I went to the galley to make coffee. I knelt to the range and rekindled the embers. The morning was chilly, but *Calliope* would be warm in no time. An advantage of the small space, I thought. I closed the range door.

When the coffee had brewed, I poured it hot and black into a mug and held it in both hands, warming them. I looked out the window at the inky canal and the darkly shadowed sky and saw the belltower of St Barnabas rising up, a darker shadow against the rest.

I'd had my fun, and now I asked for some kind of blessing. It was awkward because I didn't know what words to use, or whether I should address it to God or some patron saint of learning – I didn't know who that might be – but I asked that my appetite for knowledge not wane and my stamina for study be up to the task. Then I took a sip of my coffee as if to seal the bargain.

I sat down with the book and a new routine was begun. I barely noticed the passing of spring into summer.

Chapter Thirty-Seven

Bastiaan was waiting when we came out of the Press, his jacket slung over his satchel, his shirtsleeves rolled up.

'A walk?' he asked.

I thought of the book I'd left open on the table that morning. He noticed the hesitation. '*Calliope* will be too warm for study.'

'Go,' said Lotte. She put Maude's arm through hers and it was decided.

It took no time at all to forget about the open book. Bastiaan's arm felt strong beneath mine, and his limp was only slight. It felt good to be out walking with him, and I wondered why I didn't say yes more often.

We turned off Walton Street and into the lane that led to the cemetery. Bastiaan's dead were spending less time in his dreams, and St Sepulchre's had become a place of peace, its inhabitants familiar. Jericho's war dead were not buried there, and so could not ambush him.

'How are your studies?' Bastiaan asked as he spread his jacket on old Mrs Wood's grave.

'I've made a start on Ancient Greek.'

We sat and Bastiaan passed me a sandwich. 'I thought you wanted to study English literature?'

'I do, but Ancient Greek is the monster I must slay to get into Somerville.'

'And will you have help from the gods?' Bastiaan asked.

I smiled. 'You know the gods, Bastiaan. They favour highborn mortals. I am far from highborn.'

'Then you must work twice as hard,' he said.

We sat close and ate the sandwiches. Bastiaan took a bottle of ginger beer from his satchel.

'I don't mind the idea of learning Ancient Greek,' I said.

'As it is necessary, that is good.'

'I'd quite like to read Homer and Euripides in the original, interpret them for myself.'

He passed me the bottle and I took a sip of the ginger beer. Then I felt his hand on my knee, I heard the rush of fabric as he gathered up my skirt, I felt his fingers, cool, on my stockinged thigh. I anticipated him moving further, finding the top of my stocking, but he was still for the longest time. I could barely think what we'd been talking about.

'Homer,' I said.

'What about him?'

'I'd like to read him in the original.'

'You have said.' His hand travelled higher and I put the bottle down. I leant back a little. Bastiaan shifted, made himself more comfortable. There was a thought I couldn't articulate, then his fingers found the top of my stocking, the edge of my drawers, my bare skin.

I turned my head to look at him directly. 'I have always wondered if Helen was seduced or kidnapped by Paris.'

'We like to think she was seduced,' he said, and his fingers found the softest part of me. I drew a breath. 'We prefer it to be a love story,' he said, challenging me to keep the conversation going.

I kept my eyes open against their will. I gathered words.

'As long as it's a love story,' I breathed, 'she can be blamed for the war.'

He said no more and I felt myself move beneath his fingertips. It was a dance we'd practised, and my eyes closed, but I knew he was watching my face, registering change, adjusting the rhythm. Proof of life, I thought.

My breath grew heavy and I heard the low groan that had embarrassed me once but no longer did. I arched my back and in the silence of the graveyard my cry became a vixen's call.

I began to unbutton his fly, but Bastiaan covered my hand and lifted it to his mouth. He kissed it.

'Are you sure?' I said.

He smiled. 'It is one of those things that has suffered in translation.'

'What is?'

'The idea that fucking is the most important thing.'

I loved that he said fucking. *My favourite English word*, he'd told me. 'But isn't it the most important thing?'

He shook his head. 'I used to think so.'

'What changed?'

'Your pleasure. It is something I can see, and feel on my skin. I can smell it and taste it and hear it.'

'You might not be the only one.'

But he didn't laugh at the joke.

'Your cry of pleasure, it is also a cry of pain, Peggy. That first time, it was so familiar and I thought …'

That first time, he'd frozen and started to shake.

'You cried,' I said.

'And after that, you were silent.'

I had held my lip between my teeth to keep his dead at bay.

'And that was worse,' he said. 'But now, to give you pleasure, it feels like I am filling your lungs with air, warming your blood, making your heart beat.'

'Proof of life.'

'It is selfish,' he said.

I smiled. 'Very.'

Bastiaan folded the blanket, then emptied the dregs of our ginger beer onto the bare ground of a child's grave. *William Proctor – Beloved son – 1843 to 1854*. Cholera, most likely. If anyone had seen Bastiaan's gesture they would have been shocked, but I'd come to know it as kindness. He cared more for the souls beneath our feet than anyone had for half a century, and it was always to this child that he gave the ginger beer, like a libation. I wondered if he'd found a resting place for all the boys who haunted him.

∾

6 August 1917

Hello Pegs,

We've been discovered and I'm being replaced. Not sent home — Alison made sure of that — just moved away from the Filthy Hun. Hugo's already been sent away — I don't know where. Keep those poems, will you? The ones he translated?

Tilda x

P.S. My replacement on the German ward is a Somervillian. Her name is Vera. She has the bunk opposite me. Alison says she's very serious, very competent. I can't imagine we'll ever be friends, but I like to watch her write in her journal. You'd think her life depended on it. (Perhaps it does. She writes like I sometimes drink. She doesn't stop until her mind is empty of every thought and image that might keep her from sleeping.) She's one of the widows. Fiancé killed. Rumour has it she was dressed in her finest and ready to walk down the aisle when she got the news.

P.P.S. How's the study going? God, I can't think of anything worse.

Vera. I wondered if it was the same Vera I'd overheard telling Mr Hart she was coming up to Oxford to read English. The woman I'd been introduced to at the Somerville tea party.

I'd envied her then.

I stole time from sleep and studied before dawn and well into the night. Maude was spared my morning vigil, and even benefited from it – autumn brought cold mornings but *Calliope* was always warm and the coffee always brewed when she woke. I'd rise with the five o'clock bells and study until they chimed seven. Then I'd make some hasty note about whatever I'd been reading, mark my spot and close the book. I'd wake Maude, and our morning would be like any other.

One morning I didn't hear the seven o'clock bells. Maude didn't wake, and I didn't close my books until close to eight, when Rosie rapped on the door to check that we were well. We were late to work that day, and the next. The day after that, I failed to hear the five o'clock bells, and we both slept through until Rosie woke us. Mrs Hogg enjoyed that dressing-down, and Mrs Stoddard was forced to give a warning.

'I know you're studying, Peggy, but I can't keep turning a blind eye.'

The next day, she gave me an alarm clock.

'I don't know how you've managed all these years without one,' she said.

'The bells,' I said.

'And a lifetime of habit, I suspect. But your habits have recently changed.' She looked at me with concern. 'You need to pace yourself, Peggy. If you keep on like this you'll fall before the finish.'

'I've so much to make up.'

She nodded. 'Perhaps, but you won't make it up by burning the candle at both ends.' She took the alarm clock and turned the mechanism.

'I'm setting this for half-six. That is a decent time to wake, and it will give you a half-hour to read over your notes from the previous night before rousing Maude. Just your notes, mind you.' She held my eye. 'Do not open a book or take up a pen. You will retain more this way.' She handed me the alarm clock. 'Do we have an understanding?'

'Yes, Mrs Stoddard,' I said, grateful for her intervention.

We were never late for work after that, though I lost my morning solitude. Maude insisted on getting up when the alarm rang out, and I couldn't convince her not to.

'Let her make the breakfast,' Lotte said, when I complained. *Care for her, Peg.* Ma's words, strained and desperate. Practised in my mind.

'But that's *my* job,' I said.

Lotte sighed. 'She is not a child.' But she looked away, remembering, perhaps, when that was exactly what she thought Maude was. After a moment, she looked back. 'She can learn to make breakfast, and I think she will like very much to look after you.'

Lotte taught Maude to make porridge in the same way she'd taught her to make *stoemp*. The process had a rhyme, and for three nights we had porridge for supper while Maude learnt it by heart.

And so our roles reversed. Maude became my morning keeper – she set the alarm to wake, to dress, and then set it again to go to work. How I wanted to throw that bloody alarm clock in the canal.

My evenings were alarm-free, though not all my own. After we'd eaten and washed the dishes, Maude would fold as she always had, or else she would take the *Calliope's Library* ledger and return the books I'd finished reading to their various shelves and ordered piles. She was happy to go to bed without me, and I would stay up studying until the midnight bells.

∼

It was a Sunday and I heard Bastiaan's uneven tread on our foredeck.

A moment of frustration, then a wave of guilt. I marked my place.

'You did not come,' he said. He stayed standing, slightly stooped. He was too tall for *Calliope*. I was supposed to have met him at St Sepulchre's.

'I —'

'Lost track of time,' he said.

'Lost track of time,' Maude repeated.

I'd said it so often. It wasn't always true, but this time it was. I closed the book.

Bastiaan shook his head. 'You prefer to study.'

'Not *prefer*.'

A small shrug. He came over to where Maude and I sat at the table. He opened his satchel and took out two bottles of ginger beer and two Chelsea buns. He looked at Maude.

'Make her pause for afternoon tea,' he said.

She nodded and he left.

~

'I am a distraction,' Bastiaan said, a week later.

My fingers found the groove of letters carved into stone: *Sarah, beloved wife of Henry Wood*. I did not contradict him.

~

One day in late September, Tilda was sitting at the table when Maude and I got home from the Press. My books were closed and piled up out of her way.

'Ten days' leave,' she said. The smile on her face quivered with the effort. 'To recover my nerve.'

To sober up, I thought. I watched her pour whiskey into a coffee mug and convinced myself that a week would make no difference to my study. Her hand shook almost as much as Old Mrs Rowntree's. She was thin. For the first time, I thought she looked middle-aged. She put her whiskey on the edge of the pile of books. It teetered. It spilled. I said nothing. Maude handed me a cloth; I wiped the books, then Maude took them from me and found their proper places. She wrote in her ledger, then went to tell Rosie that Tilda needed a good meal.

~

Rosie fed her. Maude and I listened.

'It's a kind of hell, Étaples …

'A week in the Bullring and they long for the front …

'It's the Red Caps and Canaries … on our side, they say. Worse than the Hun … They shot him … Australian. Poor lad joined up in New Zealand. Jack. His name was Jack.'

Did she hear my intake of breath?

'Not our Jack. Not our Jack. It happened last year, but it was the start.'

Her head shook from side to side. More whiskey.

'They shot him. Not our Jack. Australian Jack. Australian Jack from the New Zealand Army. Poor lad. We can't shoot Australians, apparently. But we can shoot New Zealanders. Even when they've volunteered.

'They turned the water off. He had soap in his eyes and had a go at an officer. They do, you know. Have a go. Australians. All the time. Stupid buggers.'

She laughed and laughed.

'Keep seeing him with a towel too small to cover his balls. They turned the water off. Did I say? They beat him. But I dressed the wounds; a bit of iodine, they weren't too bad. I washed the soap out of his eyes. Then he was shot.'

She cried and cried.

She vomited up everything she'd been trying to hold down. Words and whiskey both. But each day, there were fewer words. And each day she drank less.

Rosie fed her. Maude and I listened.

~

The day before she was due to go back to France, Tilda made us supper. Chicken pie. Rosie's help was obvious in the flakiness of the pastry, the tenderness of the chicken, but neither of us said so.

'I'm going to tell you something,' she said.

There was no whiskey bottle on the table. No whiskey on her breath.

'And I'm not supposed to.'

I wondered if she was aware of what she'd already said.

'There was a kind of mutiny at Étaples. New Zealanders, Australians, South Africans, Canadians, Tommies. It all started when a New Zealander was arrested coming back from the beach at Le Touquet. It's a beautiful beach. An officers' beach – he wasn't an officer. Actually, it probably started before that. With an Australian. Called Jack.'

She repeated what she'd told us. We let her talk.

'They locked us up. For days. VADs, nurses. All the women. For our protection, they said. But I don't think we were at risk. I think they didn't want witnesses. They brought us food and let us out to do our shifts, but we were chaperoned there and chaperoned back. Some of us had to nurse the men they beat. So some of us found out what was happening.'

Her hands shook and she looked to the shelf above the galley bench. There was nothing there.

'We were told not to repeat any rumours we may have heard. We were told not to say we'd been locked up. We were told that if we said anything, at any time, we'd be breaking the *Official Secrets Act* and we'd go to gaol.'

'So why are you telling us?'

A smile spread across her face.

'It's not the first time I've been told to keep my mouth shut or risk gaol.'

And there she was. Ten years younger. The suffragette we'd fallen in love with.

~

Tilda packed three tins of Horlicks for her return to Étaples.

'I'll try not to drink if you try not to repeat the terrible rumours I've been spreading,' she said to us both. 'I don't think gaol would suit either of you.'

'Try,' said Maude.

But of course, it slipped out.

They shot him.

Not our Jack.

Poor bugger.

My very own Cassandra.

No one took any notice.

Chapter Thirty-Eight

We bumped into Eb on the way out of the bindery.

'For you,' he said.

It was a book. *Who's Who in Dickens.* 'How did you know I needed it?'

'Vanessa,' he said. Then he was distracted by something behind me.

I turned to see the freckly frog. I clasped the book to my chest, but Mrs Hogg barely looked at me. Eb moved towards her. A hand on her arm, a few words, so quiet that *sorry* was all I heard. She looked at him like she didn't understand. Wanted not to. Then she kept on her way, out of the Press.

'Freddie's missing,' Eb said to me.

Freddie. Mr Hogg. He'd enlisted when Eb couldn't. Ma had liked Freddie Hogg. They'd been neighbours when they were children, she'd said. He'd helped Eb and Oberon fix up *Calliope*. He never shunned Ma for having us. *Is that why Mrs Hogg doesn't like you?* I'd asked. Ma just shrugged.

'But she came to work,' I said to Eb.

'Might have been the best thing,' he said. 'She's got no one at home.'

~

Maude and I came out through the arch of the Press and saw Gwen leaning against the iron fence, reading a book. We were just two of hundreds of Press workers leaving for the evening, so she didn't notice when we stood in front of her. I put my hand over the page.

'Peg. Thank God, I don't know how anyone is supposed to remember them all.' She closed the book and handed it to me.

I read the title: '*Who's Who in Dickens*.'

'In his own words, apparently,' said Gwen. 'Full of excellent insights into how his characters reflect humanity. Just the kind of question they are likely to ask on the Somerville entrance.'

I decided against telling her I now owned a copy. 'Thanks, Gwen.'

'No need for thanks. The librarian was quite impressed that I was reading beyond my subject, especially as I hardly read within my subject. I think I may have risen in her estimation.'

'Maybe,' I said.

'Surely. The last pile of books she had delivered to Oriel included an invitation to tea. Quite the privilege. I was never a frequent visitor, but I miss our library. There's something about being told you can't have access that makes you long for a place, don't you think?'

Where would I start with an answer?

'Maybe she just wants to interrogate you about your sudden studiousness,' I said.

We started walking home and Gwen fell into step. At each corner I expected her to take her leave of us, but she didn't.

'We can only offer bread and margarine tonight, Gwen.' I held the book and felt a wave of guilt for not being able to thank her with something more appetising.

'Not even butter?'

'Not even butter,' Maude said.

'I'll just have tea.'

The table was strewn with Maude's folding papers and scavenged sections of books from the reading list Gwen had given me: *The Complete Poetical Works of William Wordsworth* (parts thereof), *A Century of Parody and Imitation* (parts thereof), *The Oxford Thackeray* (parts thereof), *Poetical Works of Dryden* (in full and cloth-bound), *The Complete Works of William Shakespeare* (sewn but naked).

Our porridge bowls were in the basin with dishes from the night before – I'd been too tired to fetch water. My coffee cup was perched on top of a section.

I hung my coat by the door and put my bag beneath it, then I hurried to tidy the table, as if I could hide the worst of it before Gwen came through the hatch.

'A bloody mess,' declared Maude, an echo of my rant that morning.

I picked up my coffee mug and traced the ring it left around one of Wordsworth's poems. 'The Solitary Reaper'. *Alone she cuts and binds the grain ...*

'You're not wrong, Maude,' said Gwen. 'A bloody mess indeed.'

I put the coffee cup in the basin and covered the whole unwashed pile with a tea towel. Then I went back to the table and began to gather up the books and sections and my loose pages of notes. I failed to put them in the right order and began trying to sort them, reading the last line of this page, the first line of that. 'Damn,' I said, under my breath.

Gwen was fingering what still littered the table. 'How's the mugging-up coming along?'

'How does it look like it's coming along, Gwen?'

'Chaotically,' she said.

'Chaotically,' said Maude.

Gwen turned to her. 'Shouldn't you be helping? I thought it was your job to keep it all in good order.'

Maude picked up a book.

'Leave it,' I snapped.

Maude turned to Gwen and shrugged her shoulders. Then she put the book back among the mess, sat beside her biscuit tin of papers and began to fold.

Gwen read the cover. '*Appreciations and Criticisms of the Works of Charles Dickens.*' She turned to me. 'Do you need any other books?'

'Look at this pile of flotsam, Gwen. It's all just scraps and leftovers. I always need other books.' My voice was louder than I intended. Maude began rocking, ever so slightly, to the rhythm of her folds.

I took a deep breath, put the books and sections and loose papers back on the table, and slumped into a chair. 'I'm sorry, Gwen, but one topic leads to another and I don't have the books to follow the trail. They're rarely at the 'Stute and I can never get to the Public Library before it closes. I love you for borrowing this book for me, but I feel like I'm assembling a jigsaw without all the pieces.' I looked at my sister. 'Poor Maude, she's sick of hearing it.'

'Sick of hearing it,' Maude confirmed, and the rocking stopped. She nodded, to make it crystal clear she wasn't echoing.

Gwen smiled, and I braced for one of her *Poor Pegs* quips. Instead, she stepped into the galley, stoked the coals in the range and put the kettle on the hotplate. When steam began to escape, she removed the tea towel I'd thrown over the basin of dirty dishes and poured warm water over the lot. She rinsed my dirty mug, dried it and took two others from the shelf.

'I had tea with our librarian at Somerville yesterday,' she said.

'English breakfast or Darjeeling?' I sniped.

'Darjeeling,' said Gwen, ignoring my tone. 'Served it in her best china, too.' She picked up one of our mugs and held it against the feeble light coming through the galley window. 'It was so fine I could see right through it.'

'And what was the point of this little tete-a-tete?' I asked.

'Now, let me see ...'

'The point,' Maude said.

Gwen turned to her. 'Miss Garnell was curious about my sudden studiousness. I've borrowed more books this term than in the previous three years.'

'Three years,' said Maude. An echo, but Gwen thought otherwise.

'I know, and I'll probably be there another three at the rate I'm going.'

'How nice to be able to dillydally,' I said.

'It is, rather,' she teased.

'The point,' Maude said, again.

'Your sister was the point.'

'Me?'

'At great risk to myself, I told her all about you. Rather than reprimanding me for lending Somerville books to hoi polloi, she asked if you had access to all the other books you might need.'

'*Calliope* is hardly the bloody Bodley,' said Maude. She knew my complaints.

Gwen looked around. 'Though it does try,' she said. 'Somerville is hardly the Bodley either, but Miss Garnell says we have the best college library in Oxford. She also said that if Peg wished to avail herself of it, she is sure she could arrange it with Miss Bruce. Which is to say Vice-Principal *Alice* Bruce, not her sister Pamela, though Pamela does have sway, and I'm sure she would have mentioned you to the vice-principal.' She shook her head. 'All these unmarried sisters – it's very confusing.'

The kettle boiled and Gwen made tea. She handed us both a mug, her infuriating smile as wide as could be. The game was over, and she was delighted with her performance. 'What do you say? You can start *availing* yourself when the new term starts in January.'

I said nothing. I was being offered access to the books and a place to read them.

I looked at the mess on the table, then I looked at Maude. She held my gaze, nodded. Then she turned to Gwen. 'Yes,' she said.

'Yes,' I echoed.

∼

Bastiaan's dead were still being settled in their Jericho graves. Some were content, he said, but others were restless. I knew when they were restless: nightmares and his hand above my heart when I lay still for too long. We paid each a visit whenever we were at St Sepulchre's. And then we sat with Mrs Wood.

Bastiaan opened a ginger beer and I brought out the poems Hugo had translated so long ago. I'd been reluctant, not sure how Bastiaan would feel, but I wanted to share them now.

'"Death Among the Ears of Corn",' he read. 'This one I know.'

'I hope it isn't painful for you to read it, but the way Tilda spoke of Hugo ...' I hesitated. 'He didn't seem like the Germans we've read about. The Germans who were in Louvain.'

Bastiaan read the poem.

'It *is* painful,' he said. 'Because the German who wrote this poem knew what it was to live with the dead, and the German who translated it would rather heal than kill. They are not the same men as those in Louvain, but it is sometimes hard not to hate them.'

Silence, for a moment. Then Bastiaan took a long swig of the ginger beer and his mood lifted.

'Madame Wood does not like me speaking like this,' he said, and he handed back the poem. 'It is better, by the way, in German.'

'Everything is better in the original,' I said, taking the bottle from him.

He shrugged. 'Only in the original can you really know what was meant.'

'I regret not knowing any German, not speaking better French,' I said.

'Maybe your children will speak German and French,' Bastiaan said.

I said nothing.

'Maybe they will speak Flemish,' he continued.

'Flemish?'

He took back the ginger beer. Sipped. 'I thought that, maybe, it was possible?' he said.

'Possible that I'll have children, or that they'll speak Flemish?'

He took a deep breath. 'I am hoping both.'

I understood, and, without meaning to, I looked away.

'Let's get back,' I said.

We walked to Walton Well Bridge in silence. When we were on the towpath, Bastiaan spoke.

'I am sorry,' he said. 'It was not right. Not romantic.'

I wanted him to stop speaking. Instead, he stopped walking.

I looked along the towpath. It was barely lit by the waning moon, and our narrowboats would have been no more than shadows if not for the yellow light slipping illegally from *Calliope*. Maude had forgotten to cover the windows and we risked a fine. It was reason to hurry, though I knew there was no one to notice.

'I want to marry you, Peggy.'

I turned to face him.

'Bastiaan, please —'

'I want to get down on my knee,' he looked at his stiff leg, 'but I cannot.'

I smiled despite myself.

'I want to put a ring on your finger, but I do not have the means.'

'Bastiaan —'

'I want us to have children who speak English and French and German.'

'And Flemish,' I said, tears already falling.

'Yes,' he said. 'And Flemish.'

We stood there on the towpath, but neither of us spoke for the longest time.

'What do you want?' Bastiaan finally asked.

'I didn't expect this.'

'But what do you want?'

'I want to pass the entrance exam.' It seemed so trivial, but it felt so big.

'After you have passed the exam. After the war. For your life, Peggy. What do you want?'

I had an answer; it came to me in an instant. I was wearing a gown, I was reading books.

'I don't know,' I said.

'You do know,' he said.

I had always thought it was *my* heart that would be vulnerable in love. That as a woman I would be ruled by it. It was what I'd read in novels and poems, time and time again. But in that small lie it was Bastiaan's heart that broke. I saw it happen and I felt his pain in my chest.

'I want you, Bastiaan. But ...'

'It is not enough.'

'I want to write the books, Bastiaan. I want my ideas to be printed, I want my experience to count. I want to share something —'

'But not with me.'

'Of course with you, but I can't be a wife and mother and a scholar as well. It just isn't possible, and I can't deny you those things that you want.' My voice faltered. I'd never said it aloud, never even articulated it in thought. 'The life you offer is too much.'

'You think you have to choose?'

'Oh, Bastiaan, I know I have to choose.'

The truth. I could not take it back and he could not deny it. But he waited for me to make some small edit, to rephrase or clarify in our favour. I stayed silent.

'I could stay,' he said.

I put my hand to his cheek and wiped his tears with my thumb. He wanted to be an architect, he'd told me once, like his father. When the time came, he'd said, he would go home and help to rebuild Belgium. It was before he loved me, before I loved him. It had animated him, this idea of repair, and I knew as he spoke of it that he would need it to fully recover.

'I'm not sure that staying in England is what you want,' I said.

'You are saying no.'

'I am saying no.'

Chapter Thirty-Nine

I presented myself at the porter's lodge on Walton Street on the first day of the Hilary term, January 1918. The porter still wore a uniform, but this one was younger, and his left arm was missing.

'Are you here to volunteer?' He probably wore a gown before the war; I could hear it in his voice.

It had been more than two years. At the time I thought I'd never be back.

'I'm here to use the library,' I said.

He looked at me more closely.

'I'm sorry, miss, but Somerville students aren't permitted to visit the library.' He was as polite as can be. 'You'll have to make a written request and the librarian will arrange for the books to be delivered to Oriel.'

'I'm not a student,' I said.

He frowned. 'What are you, then?'

'I work across the road.'

'At the Press?'

'In the bindery.'

He raised his eyebrows. 'And why does a bindery girl need to visit the Somerville library?'

'To study Ancient Greek.'

'You're pulling my leg.'

'I wish I was,' I said. 'But it turns out that if I ever want to *stop* being a bindery girl, I need to know Ancient Greek, which of course I don't, and so here I am with a note from Miss Alice Bruce, Vice-Principal of Somerville College, giving me permission to visit the Somerville library.'

I held out the note. The porter took it, read it, shook his head slightly, then handed it back.

'Good luck,' he said. 'I've been learning Ancient Greek since I was twelve – still can't say I understand much of it.'

I walked into the grounds and a familiar anticipation prickled my skin, a memory of my invisible man. He'd offered me everything he had and I'd said no. Keep your head, I thought.

I followed the path around the small quad of lawn where officers sat in wheeled chairs, blankets tucked tight around laps, getting a few minutes of winter sun after a week of poor weather.

When I got to the main quad, I picked my way around the hospital tents. I tripped twice on the ropes anchoring them to the ground, but I didn't fall. As I approached the loggia, my desire to turn back struggled with my desire to move forward. I'd done this dozens of times, but my purpose had been different, selfless, part of the war effort. Now the loggia felt intimidating. It was raised above the quad and framed by stone columns and arches. In its shade were men in heavy woollen dressing-gowns – an arm in a sling, a patch over an eye, a leg in plaster or missing. Those without bandages wore their uniforms and greatcoats against the cold. They sat on the steps or leant against pillars. They were all officers. No missing limbs, no eye patches or masks to hide a war-damaged face. They talked and smiled and smoked cigarettes. It won't be long before they are back in France, I thought. Or Italy or Palestine. I'd read somewhere that officers were more likely to die than enlisted soldiers. I found these men the hardest to look at.

I put my head down and climbed the stairs.

'Can I help you?' It was a woman. I hadn't quite made it to the top step and had to crane my neck to look up into her face. She wore the grey dress, scarlet cape and long white cap of a military nursing sister. I didn't recognise her. 'Are you here to volunteer?'

'No, Sister, I'm here to use the library.' I passed up the note from Miss Bruce.

'It says here that your name is Peggy Jones.'

'That's right.'

'It says here that you are from Jericho.'

I nodded. She looked down – at me or on me I wasn't quite sure, until she spoke again.

'And what does a girl from *Jericho* want with the *Somerville* library?' Her enunciation was perfect.

She moved forward slightly and I retreated down a step.

The loggia, I realised, had gone quiet. The officers were listening, waiting. Most were university students or graduates. They could walk into a college library without question, and this fact alone had marked them as officer material, as if reading about Odysseus could make you a leader of men.

I tried to fashion a response.

'Sister …' I began, my voice quiet, tentative, but audible in the now silent loggia.

She folded her arms, pretended patience. We were two women in a crowd of men and I suddenly realised she wanted nothing more than to humiliate me, remind me of my place. I was asking for something I shouldn't be, and she thought she had the right to deny it.

It was a game to her. And she expected me to concede.

Sisters, I thought, remembering the word the compositor had set in type. The word his sweetheart had defined. I took back the step I had lost. The irony of this woman's title made me smirk. She faltered, and I recalled the definition as best I could. *Women bonded by a shared desire for change.* I was not alone, I realised, in wanting something I was not born to have.

I took the top step, forcing the sister to shuffle back so as not to knock the chair of one of her patients.

'It's the oddest thing,' I said, 'but I want to read the books.'

I saw her hesitate. I watched the muscles in her face twitch as she thought through the value of reprimanding me for my sarcasm, how it might look to the officers if I ignored her. I held out my hand.

'My note, if you don't mind, Sister. Unfortunately, you're not the last person I'll have to explain myself to.'

I felt the eyes of the officers follow me into the building and I walked as tall as I could. I turned right and moved along the corridor as if nothing had happened, but when I got to the stairs leading up to the library, I found I had no breath to climb them. My heart beat hard against my chest and my mouth was dry. Proof of life, I thought, and I leant against the cool brick of the stairwell until I was sure I had the strength to do it all again.

∾

The librarian was seated at a desk crowded with small stacks of books, the details of which she was transcribing into a ledger. I stood before her and read the titles, the authors, the names of the students who had presumably requested them.

She put down her pen and I held out my note. It had got me into the library, but she did not have to honour it, and I realised the librarian had a power that the nursing sister did not. I began to compose an argument that I hoped would convince her to let me use the library, but as she scanned the note, I saw a smile forming. When she looked up, she took a moment to scan my face, then her smile widened.

'Welcome back,' she said.

She thought I was someone else. I felt the prickle of panic.

'Of course you don't recognise me.' She touched her hair. 'I've gone completely grey since we last met. Gosh, it must be two years, three? For some reason I let you borrow a book.'

She'd taken no offence, and my panic was replaced by the memory of Bastiaan before I knew his face, and the rhythm of Rudyard Kipling. I remembered her now.

'Miss Garnell. Sophia Garnell,' she quickly said.

'Rudyard Kipling,' I blurted, and the librarian laughed.

'The book, I assume, not your name. I might just call you Peggy, if that is all right?'

Miss Garnell came from behind the desk. She smoothed her skirt and adjusted her glasses, then she held out her hand and wrapped it around mine. I noticed her ink-stained fingers, but the strength of her grip surprised me. I responded in kind and she smiled.

'You can always tell something of a person by the way they shake your hand,' she said, without letting mine go. 'You're adaptable.'

As if I have a choice, I thought, trying to keep my face passive.

'But not malleable.' She waited a beat, hoping for a response I had no intention of giving, then she smiled. 'And a little stubborn, I suspect.'

She let my hand go and picked up a small pile of books from her desk. 'You don't mind, do you?' She began walking towards the shelves and I walked with her.

'I have to confess that I was looking forward to meeting you again,' she said.

'Really?'

'You are Gwen's favourite subject.'

'I thought History was supposed to be her favourite subject.'

Miss Garnell laughed. 'She says you should be reading books, not binding them.'

'Does she?'

'She has a way with words.'

Other people's, I thought.

'And she's quite the crusader for a good cause.'

My step faltered. Miss Garnell stopped.

'Oh, dear, you're offended.'

A good cause? Of course I was offended. But I shook my head.

'Of course you are. But don't be. You are just one in a long line of good causes. I dare say you have a good cause of your own.' She waited for a response and saw it flicker across my face. 'I thought so. There are few in this world who do not benefit from being a good cause for someone else. Your friend Gwen has more advantages than most; it is right that she shares them.' She continued along the aisle, paused to shelve one of the books in her arm. Moved on.

'And whose good cause is Gwen?'

Miss Garnell smiled, the way Gwen sometimes smiled when my questions gave her permission to expand on a point.

'Gwen would not be here without the advocacy of a well-connected aunt.' Miss Garnell leant in and lowered her voice. 'Academically, Gwen is better suited to one of the other women's colleges. She lacks ...'

'Commitment?'

She inclined her head. 'But her temperament suits Somerville perfectly.'

'And the aunt – whose good cause is she?'

Miss Garnell shelved another book. 'Her husband's, of course. But not for the reasons you might think. She is the one with money and she has a vastly superior intellect by all accounts, but he is the one with a vote in Parliament. His good cause is women's suffrage – his wife's suffrage in particular – and he has made it clear he will support any bill that provides it.'

She ended with a nod, and I imagined her at one of the college debates Gwen talked about. 'Were you a Somervillian, Miss Garnell?'

'Oh, yes,' she said. 'And always will be.'

Miss Garnell shelved the last book, then led me to the bay in the middle of the library.

'English literature,' she said. 'Or part thereof.'

As with all the bays, there was a large desk, big enough for six students, and the tall casement windows provided ample light.

'This is my favourite bay,' Miss Garnell said. 'It gets the afternoon light, and you have Miss Austen and the Brontë sisters as constant companions.' She looked at me. 'It is the one consolation of our current arrangements – with the students absent, I can come here with my ledger and teapot and spend a pleasant hour.'

'However, not all the desks are as comfortable as this one.' Miss Garnell reached towards one of the lamps at the centre of the desk and turned it on, then she pulled up a small easel that had been hidden in the desk's top. 'To rest your book,' she said, turning to me with delight. Finally, she pulled out one of the heavy chairs and motioned with her hand. 'Sit,' she said.

I sat.

When I'd imagined Somerville, I'd been lazy. I'd fashioned rooms and bookshelves and leather-bound volumes, and I'd gone so far as to take those volumes from the shelves and imagine the weight of them, fully bound. But I'd failed to sit at the desks or see the light from the windows or register the smell of books that had not been recently glued, books that had had time to settle.

I sat on the chair and Miss Garnell helped tuck me in closer to the desk. She went to the shelves and let her fingers search the spines for a title. She could have chosen any book to demonstrate the utility of the desk, but she took her time. Finally, she levered a small volume from its place and handed it to me.

Jane Eyre.

It was an Oxford World's Classics edition. Similar to the one we owned and similarly worn from constant handling. There was a difference between a book that was regularly opened and a book that was not. The smell, the resistance of the spine, the ease with which the pages turned. This book felt a little like ours, but I knew it would fall open on a different scene, and that the pages with creased corners or worn edges would not be the same pages Ma had read over and over.

When we bound these books, I thought, they were identical. But I realised they couldn't stay that way. As soon as someone cracks the spine, a book develops a character all its own. What impresses or concerns one reader is never the same as what impresses or concerns all others. So, each book, once read, will fall open at a different place. Each book, once read, I realised, will have told a slightly different story.

I let the book open where it willed and put it on the easel. Miss Garnell scanned the page then read aloud.

'*I had the means of an excellent education placed within my reach.*' She put a hand on my shoulder. 'I think you should be quite comfortable here,' she said. 'Feel free to stay as long as you like. I stay quite late.'

~

I had only intended to introduce myself, not to stay, but I found myself reading to the end of the chapter.

When I looked up from the page and beyond the lamp, the bay was in shadow. It was time to get back to Maude. I closed *Jane Eyre* and thought to find its place on the shelves, then changed my mind.

Miss Garnell was back at her desk, her head bent to the ledger. She finished her entry before looking up.

'So soon? From what Gwen said, I thought I might have to hurry you along when I was ready to leave.' She looked at the piles of books on her desk. 'Another couple of hours, at least.'

'My good cause,' I said. 'I need to get home.'

She nodded, and I supposed Gwen had told her all about Maude.

'Well, tell me what books you need and I'll make sure they're ready for the next time you visit,' she said.

I searched my satchel and brought out the list. Miss Garnell glanced at it.

'It's what I anticipated, mostly.' She looked up. 'Though you're missing the works of Wordsworth, Dryden and Shakespeare.'

'I already have them,' I said.

'Really?'

'We have copies at home,' I said. 'Mostly unbound, but mostly intact.'

'Clarendon Press publications, I assume?'

I nodded.

'Resourceful.'

'If a book doesn't look right, it becomes waste. If I can, I bring them home.'

'Waste?' She raised her eyebrows.

'It's a matter of perspective.'

She re-read the list. 'There shouldn't be a problem with any of these.' Then she looked up. 'How's your Ancient Greek?'

'Non-existent.'

'A little, often, is my advice. I'll add a Greek primer to your pile.'

'I can't take them home?'

I asked the question before thinking and wished I could swallow it back.

'I'm sorry, Peggy ...' She was embarrassed. 'You need to be a Somervillian ...'

I felt my own cheeks flush.

'Your sister is welcome to come here too, if she'd like,' Miss Garnell offered.

'Maude's not really interested in reading,' I said.

'I'm sure I could find something for her to do.'

Chapter Forty

Maude liked the idea of visiting the library, so the following Saturday, when our morning shift was ended, she put her arm through mine and we crossed from the Press to Somerville.

'Jericho to Oxford,' she said as we negotiated a busy Walton Street.

We entered the lodge and the porter looked from me to Maude, then back to me. 'Miss Jones?'

'Well done,' I said. He entered *Miss Jones x 2* into the ledger.

We made our way around the small quad, past officers enjoying the noontime sun.

'Double trouble, lads.'

'I think I might be hallucinating.'

'Twice the fun, if you ask me.'

Maude greeted them all. I lowered my head and pulled her along. When we climbed the steps of the loggia, an officer in a cane chair put out his walking stick to block the way.

'Nurse,' he said, his gaze moving back and forth between Maude and me, 'I'm seeing double.'

His neighbour chimed in: 'Enjoy it while it lasts.'

The nurse was smiling. I glared at her until she wasn't.

'Gentlemen,' she said, finally. 'Manners.'

But it was too late.

'Double trouble, double trouble, twice the fun but trouble doubles.' Maude started up the familiar refrain, repeating it in a singsong voice, and I felt every eye follow our progress through the armchairs and daybeds under the loggia. If only they knew how ordinary their comments were, how predictable. When we were inside the building I put my hand on Maude's arm.

'Time to stop, Maudie.'

She held her bottom lip between her teeth until the urge was gone.

Miss Garnell was just as she'd been a few days earlier – half-hidden behind piles of books. She looked up as we came closer, looked from me to Maude, hesitated, decided on me.

'Miss Jones, so lovely to see you again. This must be your sister.' She stood, wiped her inky fingers on an inky handkerchief.

'Maude, this is Miss Garnell.'

Miss Garnell held out her hand, and Maude took it.

'Please, call me Sophia, then I can call you Maude and your sister Peggy. And we can avoid the confusion of having two Miss Joneses in the library.'

Maude smiled. 'Sophia.'

'We're used to confusing,' I said.

'I'm sure. But I'm also sure you tire of it.'

I smiled, shrugged.

She nodded. 'Twin brothers. Not even our parents could tell them apart. Appalling really, but they were at boarding school most of the time, so there you are. Now, I'm sure you're keen to get on.'

I nodded. She turned to Maude.

'You're welcome to sit with Peggy, but if you get bored I can always use a hand sorting returns.'

Maude considered her options. 'Sit with Peggy.'

My heart fell a little, but I led the way through the library to the study bay.

'The Brontë bay,' I said to Maude.

We stood on the threshold, and I looked at the space afresh. I was trying to imagine it through Maude's eyes: the tall windows, the shelves full of bound books, the light playing across the desk. The desk was two, maybe three times larger than our table on *Calliope*. Miss Garnell had already turned on the lamp, and there was a book resting on the easel. Other books sat beside it in a neat pile, waiting their turn.

I felt Maude squeeze my hand, and I turned to see *my* joy on *her* face. I took her to the shelf where the Brontë sisters sat side by side. Like us, I thought. Forever together. Maude took *Jane Eyre* from its place.

'Ma's,' she said.

'Almost identical,' I said.

I took *The Tenant of Wildfell Hall*. Anne Brontë. Ma preferred it to *Jane Eyre*, but she could never explain why. I opened the volume at a page I knew, a page Ma liked to pause on. I found something to read to my sister.

'*If she were more perfect, she would be less interesting.*'

Maude nodded. 'Yes,' she said.

We returned the Brontë sisters to their shelf and went to the desk. Maude sat opposite me, so far away I had to slide her folding papers across the desk. They were the latest set of coloured papers from Tilda, smooth and uniform, and they spread apart like a trickster's pack of cards. Maude considered them but made no move to gather them up, so I considered them too – I'd never be able to concentrate until her hands were moving in the familiar way.

'Kaleidoscope,' I said.

Maude smiled. She swept her hand through the papers again, then again, pausing each time to admire the effect. Eventually, she gathered them up and began to fold. I turned to the book on the easel. Abbott and Mansfield, *A Primer of Greek Grammar*. A little, often, the librarian had said.

❦

I was startled by Maude's chair being pushed back across the floorboards. I straightened my back, moved my neck from side to side, rubbed the muscle between my thumb and forefinger. I flipped through my notebook and was surprised to find that I'd filled five pages. I tried to recall something I'd actually learnt, but couldn't.

Maude stood up, a blue paper box in her hands. 'Sort the returns,' she said.

'Do you need me to come with you?' I wanted her to say yes. I wanted an excuse to close the book on Ancient Greek.

'No,' she said, then she nodded at the easel. 'Read the book.'

I did as I was told. I read pages I could barely comprehend and scrawled notes I could hardly read. When my hand cramped, I rubbed it and shook it. I straightened my back and looked around the bay and reminded myself how precarious this arrangement was. There were so many things that could disrupt it: Maude could refuse to come, Lotte could be unavailable, someone might complain and the note from Miss Bruce might be rescinded. I rested my hand on the pile of books Miss Garnell had placed on the desk. I needed them, but I had no right to them. I was here by the grace of others. I closed my eyes and tried to recall something about Greek syntax – agreement, cases, something about mood. I gave up, turned to a clean page and attempted to write the Greek alphabet from *alpha* to *omega*. I was four letters short and mixed up *pi* and *phi*, *xi* and *psi*. I slapped my notebook shut but resisted the urge to throw Abbott and Mansfield across the bay. Instead, I flicked through the pages and felt my anxiety grow. I'd barely managed to learn French; how would I ever learn a language that no one spoke any more? How did anyone? Tutors, I thought, and for a moment I wondered about their hourly rate. More than I could afford, I decided.

I was about to close the book when I saw a note written in the white space at the end of the chapter. It was in pencil, a scrawl I had to decipher: *It's all Greek to me*, it said. Beneath it, another hand had written, *Me too*. Beneath that, a third hand: *What's the point?*

~

I made my way slowly along the bays, back towards the librarian's desk. It was almost cleared of books, the piles transferred to a trolley, ready to be returned to the shelves. I put my own small pile in front of Maude, and she immediately opened the cover of the top book to reveal the borrowing details. She slid it in front of Miss Garnell.

'Peggy's books haven't left the library, Maude. No need to record them.'

Maude took the book back, closed the cover. Miss Garnell turned to me.

'If your sister wasn't already gainfully employed, I'd offer her a job.'

'Offer her a job,' Maude said, or echoed – I wasn't sure.

'Would you prefer to sort the books or bind them, Maude?' I asked.

She shrugged. Either, neither, she wasn't sure. She turned to the trolley, the Greek primer in hand, and searched for the right spot to put it.

'Will you be back tomorrow, Peggy?' asked Miss Garnell.

'I hope so,' I said.

'In that case' – she turned to Maude – 'we'll keep the books Peggy needs off the shelf.'

'Off the shelf,' said Maude, and she retrieved the books she'd just placed on the trolley.

'Thank you, Maude,' said Miss Garnell.

'Thank you, Maude,' I said.

~

Maude enjoyed coming to the library whenever Lotte was unavailable to spend time with her, but she never sat with me after that first visit. She helped Miss Garnell and Miss Garnell appreciated it. *She has an eye for order*, she once said.

I began to spend more time there: Saturday afternoons, Sunday afternoons, some evenings. Eventually my lunch hour every Monday and Friday. I couldn't help thinking of Bastiaan teaching his French classes at the 'Stute, and I needed something to quell my desire to meet him there. To talk with him.

~

I was tired when I arrived at the library, and hungry. Our Saturday shift had gone into overtime and I hadn't been home for lunch. There were just a few weeks until the Somerville entrance, and I didn't want to waste a moment. A weak February light came through the window of the Brontë bay, so I turned on the desk lamp. A pull of a little cord and the page was illuminated. So easy, I thought, recalling the failing light of our oil lamp the night before; my strained eyes. I was grateful all over again for being given permission to sit in the Somerville library.

I didn't know Gwen was there until she plonked herself down in the chair on the other side of the desk.

'When was the last time Bastiaan took you to the pictures?' she asked.

I coloured. 'Somerville students aren't supposed to visit the library, Gwen. You shouldn't be here.'

'I'm not visiting the library, I'm visiting a patient.' She peered at me. 'Well?'

'Bastiaan and I don't go to the pictures any more.' It silenced her, but not for long enough.

'Well, then, it is up to me to rescue you from the books.'

'I don't need rescuing.'

'I think you do, so come along.'

I was tempted. 'Where?' I asked.

'Martyrs' Memorial. The women are gathering to celebrate.'

The vote, I realised. The bill had passed a few days earlier. My interest waned.

'It's not my celebration, Gwen.'

'Oh, don't be like that. It's a huge step in the right direction. For all women.'

'It's easy to see it that way when you're doing the stepping. A little harder when you're the stepping stone.'

She gave me her *Poor Pegs* look.

'Why you, Gwen? Why do you get the vote when I don't?'

'I don't have it yet – I'm not thirty.'

'But you will get it, won't you? Even if you fail to ever get a degree, you'll have property.'

'As far as I'm concerned,' she said, 'it's all for one and one for all. This is momentous. It's the beginning of something. And I'm going to sing about it.'

'You go right ahead,' I said. 'I'm going to stay and study.'

'Good idea.' She stood up. 'If you get a degree, this bill will mean as much to you as it does to me.'

Miss Garnell pushed her trolley into the bay.

'I'd leave now, Gwen, before Peggy throws that book at you.'

Gwen looked at the book under my hand. 'No chance of that, Miss Garnell. Peg would never risk injuring a book so beautifully bound.'

Then she blew me a kiss and turned on her heel.

Chapter Forty-One

I took a desk at the back. They were all the same, I noticed. Identical. Each had three pencils, a rubber, the exam paper facedown, a notebook beside it. Each had a young woman and each of those young women, no matter how relaxed she had seemed before entering the hall, was nervous. They arranged pencils, tapped fingers against thighs, crossed and uncrossed their ankles.

'Ten minutes' reading time,' the don said. 'Feel free to make notes and plan your answers, but do not mark your exam paper until I tell you it is time to start. You will have three hours.'

A rustling. A turning of pages. The exam was so familiar. The font, the feel of the paper, the size of the pages. Each examination booklet would fit on a single sheet: eight pages, four leaves, two folds – quarto. A quick trim and it was ready. Since I was twelve, I'd folded thousands like it. Though not this year – Mrs Stoddard had made sure of that. She'd even made me sign something saying I would *not seek to access the exam papers directly, or indirectly by soliciting information from others at the Press.*

It's like the Official Secrets Act, I'd joked. *Does everyone have to sign this when they take an exam?*

Mrs Stoddard had smiled. *You're the first,* she'd said. *It will protect you, and if anyone compromises your opportunity, they will be dealt with as if they'd shared exam questions with a Gown.*

No one had compromised my opportunity.

I read the general questions.

I read the passage in French for the unprepared translation. I thought of Bastiaan, then put him out of my head.

I read the questions for my chosen subject. *English literature. Not more than FOUR questions to be attempted.* There were twenty to choose from – discuss, compare, give instances, explain. There was Shakespeare, Milton, Wordsworth, Spenser, Dickens, Thackeray, Dryden. I searched for Eliot, Austen, one of the Brontës, but they weren't there. Not a single woman. I looked at the clock – one minute before we could start. *Repeat what you've read and don't get creative,* Gwen had said. I chose my questions:

Discuss the different ways in which the sonnet is handled by Shakespeare and Spenser.
Give instances of Wordsworth's close observations of nature.
'Neither Dickens nor Thackeray could make a "good" character interesting.' Discuss.
'The playing of women's parts by boys may have limited Shakespeare's art.' Discuss.

I recognised their form. I'd thought about these kinds of questions for years; Ma had asked them, in one way or another, and I'd read the works, and now I'd read the criticism.

'You may begin.'

I began.

The general questions. The French translation. My pencil ran across the page.

The first of my chosen questions, the second. I paraphrased and quoted and wove this argument with that. It wasn't so hard, but then, suddenly, it was.

I put down my pencil and rubbed the muscle between my thumb and forefinger. I reviewed what I'd written. Exactly what they would expect, but not quite what I thought.

I looked at the clock; more than an hour had passed. I read my responses again – echoes of things I'd read. Modern men's critiques of dead men's writing. Ideas that were reprinted every year, in texts that were scattered around *Calliope* as loose sections or naked manuscripts. I could recite them in my sleep, but I hadn't always agreed. *You don't always have to*, Ma had said.

I struck a line through my answer to question one, and what I'd started to write for question two.

I began again.

~

The exam papers were collected, and the door to the hall was opened.

'How did you go?'

A stranger in a fine wool jacket. A fellow candidate. The difference between us was not so great as it had been three hours earlier.

'I couldn't say,' I replied, honestly, 'but I like what I wrote.'

'That's a funny way to put it.'

'Is it?'

She tilted her head. 'My tutor says it's all about evidence – acknowledge the prevailing views and show how one is superior to the others using evidence from the right people to justify your position.'

'Is that what you did?' I asked.

She smiled. 'I think so. Though I memorised so many quotations it's possible I confused a few.' A horn sounded. 'Oh, that's me.' She turned and waved at the young man driving. He was in officer garb, and I wondered if he was her brother or lover. She didn't say, but she took up my hand and shook it. 'I do hope we come up to Somerville together.' She didn't wait for a reply, but as the motorcar drove off, she waved as if we were already friends.

I walked slowly back to Jericho with the exam questions and my responses circling around each other in my head. *Don't get creative,* Gwen had said.

~

'Went well, then,' said Gwen. She was sitting with Miss Garnell, a pot of tea between them.

'How can you tell?' I asked.

'A hundred little telltale signs,' said Miss Garnell.

'And you clearly haven't been crying,' said Gwen.

Miss Garnell nodded towards a chair and poured tea into a third cup. 'Tell us all about it,' she said. 'What were the questions?'

I told her.

'Did you repeat what you've read?' asked Gwen.

'Mostly.' I raised the cup to my mouth.

Her face clouded. 'What do you mean, *mostly*?'

I swallowed, took another sip. Her discomfort was strangely pleasing. 'I can think for myself, Gwen. I don't always agree with what I've read.'

'Oh, God,' she said. 'Independent thought.'

Miss Garnell put her hand on Gwen's arm to quiet her, but Gwen's concerns only heightened my sense of achievement. The truth was, I couldn't shake the thrill of the experience. My opinion had been sought – no, my *educated* opinion had been sought – and I had brought *everything* to my answer. Not just the ideas of others, but my own. Gwen was thinking that I had jeopardised my chances, and maybe I had. But someone would read what I wrote, and whether they thought it Somervillian or not was, at that moment, irrelevant. They would read it, they would consider it.

'What was your approach, Peggy?' asked Miss Garnell.

'I acknowledged the prevailing views and showed where they might be flawed.'

Gwen groaned.

'Don't fret, Gwen. I quoted the usual suspects. I just pointed out how remarkably similar their perspectives were and why alternative perspectives might be enlightening.'

They let me talk and we drained the pot.

'You'll know one way or the other in a few weeks' time,' said Miss Garnell. 'What will you do with yourself in the meantime?'

'I expect I'll keep studying for Responsions.'

She smiled. 'Some wait to find out if they've been offered a place before they begin that marathon. At the very least, it's not a bad excuse to relax and replenish your intellectual resources.'

'I'm not sure relaxing will replenish my stores of Greek,' I said. 'They are still very low. I have to assume I'll be offered a place or I'll lose all momentum.'

'Very well. Just promise to look up from the books occasionally. I've always thought the blossoms of spring as stimulating for the intellect as any text.'

Chapter Forty-Two

I did as Miss Garnell and Gwen suggested. In the evenings I spent less time in the library and more time with Maude and Lotte. I made sense of Latin and studied Greek verbs but I also saw *The Cure* and *The Golden Idiot* at the George Street Cinema with Aggie and Lou, and I went punting on the Cherwell with Gwen. One Saturday afternoon, I took the motorbus with Maude out to Cowley. The fields near the barracks were no longer littered with men wanting to enlist, but I was struck by an image of the men we'd seen then, littering other fields in other lands and never coming home.

When the horse chestnuts started flowering, I picked a candle of white blossoms and presented it to Miss Garnell.

She took it and smiled. 'And do you feel relaxed and replenished?'

'I do.'

'And have you heard?'

I tried to look unconcerned. 'Not yet.'

~

I was reading as we walked to work; I knew the route well enough not to trip. On Walton Street, Maude skipped ahead to Turner's

Newsagency. I heard the bell over the door and put the book in my bag.

'Post, Mr Turner?' I heard her say as I opened the door and entered behind her.

'I trust you are well, Miss Jones.'

I browsed the headlines on Mr Turner's paper rack.

British, French, Australian reinforcements halt German offensive at Ypres.

'Yes, Mr Turner,' Maude said. 'Offer from Somerville?'

Red Baron buried with honour by British squadron.

'I could hardly tell you, Miss Jones. It's not my place to look.'

Something in his voice. I turned to see him leaning on the counter, smiling at the envelope Maude had separated from the rest of the bundle.

'What you've been waiting for, I hope.' He had turned to me.

It was a plain envelope, with my name and the address of Mr Turner's newsagency typed on the front, Somerville College in the top right corner. I opened it.

I read it.

I re-read it.

'Offer from Somerville?' Maude asked.

I handed her the pages so she could read the letter herself.

~

'And a full scholarship,' I told Miss Garnell.

She came out from behind the piles of returns and embraced me.

I'd grown used to the gesture. Maude had broadcast the Somerville offer across the bindery, and Lou, Mrs Stoddard and even Lotte had responded with a hug. Mrs Stoddard had become glassy-eyed. 'Your ma ...' she'd said, but she could go no further. When Eb heard about it, from Mrs Stoddard, I assumed, he'd braved the girls' side to come and congratulate me. He'd stopped short of hugging, but I leant forward and gave him no choice. 'Your ma ...' he'd said. But Ma got the better of him as well.

'Your sister must be so proud,' Miss Garnell said.

'She really is.'

'You sound surprised.'

I was surprised, but mostly I was relieved. 'I thought she might be upset,' I said.

'Why would she be?'

'Things will change.'

Miss Garnell smiled. 'Things *will* change, but Maude seems quite capable of adapting.'

Miss Garnell returned to the other side of her desk. 'Your books are already on the desk in your bay,' she said. 'It would seem your decision to continue studying was a good one.'

And then it hit me. I could only take up the Somerville offer if I passed Responsions. Miss Garnell must have seen it spread across my face.

'The final hurdle awaits,' she said. 'Now is not the time to shy away.'

~

3 May 1918

Oh, Pegs,

Somerville! A bloody scholarship! I'm sure everyone who knew Helen would have already told you how proud your ma would be. Of course, it's true that she would have been proud, but I'm going to tell you what they can't. So, brace yourself—you know how rubbish I am at gently, gently.

If your ma was alive, the first thing she'd do is draw you into her beautiful embrace and whisper in your ear that she'd always known you were capable of this. The second thing she'd do is worry. And I can tell you what she'd worry about because she worried about it when she was alive and I have heard it expressed in a hundred different ways. Here's one version: 'Peg spends so much time looking back to see where Maude is, I'm afraid she'll never move forward.' And here's another: 'Peg spends so much time looking back to see where Maude is, I'm afraid she'll never let Maude move forward.'

Helen never forgave herself for not insisting you stay at school. The truth is, your attachment to Maude made her life easier. She didn't like the idea that one day you might leave, but it also terrified her to think that you wouldn't.

You will thrive on the other side of Walton Street, Peg, but I worry you might find a reason not to — please don't let it be Maude.

Tilda x

~

Jack was home on leave. For the first week, he slept a lot and said very little. When he was awake, he sat in the galley of *Staying Put* and read Shakespeare's sonnets to Old Mrs Rowntree. Sometimes Maude would join them. She'd take a pile of papers to fold and leave Jack with a handful of stars.

In the second week, Oberon came home. He stayed seven nights instead of his usual one, and he got Jack working. They crawled all over *Staying Put* and *Calliope*, tending to rust and leaks and mould. They cleaned water barrels, checked the bilge pumps and repaired window seals. Jack fixed the hook on the hatch door so we didn't need *A History of Chess* to keep it open. He greased our brass, and when all that was done, he sat with a few pots of paint and touched up the flowers on *Staying Put*.

Then I heard Jack laugh. It wasn't as loud or long as I remembered, but it was familiar. It was Jack. Oberon readied to leave the next morning.

Rosie in her boatwoman's bonnet stood at the helm. Jack stood beside her.

'Hop on, Miss Maude,' he called to my sister. He took her hand and she settled between them.

I watched as *Rosie's Return* steamed away, but I didn't wait to see Maude coming home along the towpath. It was enough to imagine it. Rosie and Jack. Maude in the middle.

It was enough.

~

I sat at my desk in the Brontë bay and arranged the pages from *Odysseae*. Then I took Ma's translation from my satchel. It was so familiar. The leather warm, as if she'd just been holding it. I leafed past the introduction and splayed it open on the first page of Book One. I wanted to compare it to the Ancient Greek, to make some sense of it, but it was bewildering.

Miss Garnell walked past the bay and noticed what I was trying to do. 'It's not always possible to make a direct translation,' she said, coming to stand beside me. She looked to the page in Ma's book. 'And to be honest, the only way to know what Homer wrote is to learn the language that Homer wrote in, otherwise you are at the mercy of the translator, their times, their perspective. Their gender,' she said. 'Take these first lines from your Butcher and Lang translation.' She read aloud:

'*Tell me, Muse, of that man, so ready at need, who wandered far and wide.*'

Ma always started with that line, no matter what part of the story she went on to tell us. *The Muse*, she'd say, *is Calliope, though she is never named.*

'That's all well and good,' said Miss Garnell, 'but is it what Homer wrote? Others have interpreted the Greek differently.'

She went to another bay and came back with an armload of books. She sat beside me, then opened one of the books and read: '*The hero*

335

of craft-renown, O Song-goddess, chant me this fame.' Then she opened another. *'The man for wisdom's various arts renown'd, Long exercised in woes, O Muse! Resound.'*

Miss Garnell took a deep breath. 'Sometimes, Peggy, it doesn't matter how a story is told,' she said, 'but sometimes I think it matters a lot.' This time she picked up a copy of the original text. She turned towards the end and read the ancient script. I watched her lips as they formed the Greek sounds, and I heard the words with a mixture of awe and envy.

'Now, let's see how our modern scholars have interpreted it.'

She found the relevant page in each of the translations, including Ma's, and laid them beside each other. 'So, remember, Odysseus has returned to Penelope after twenty years, found his house full of suitors and slain them. But he doesn't stop there,' she said, and her finger jabbed at each line in turn. 'He tells his son to kill the women who lay with the suitors. And no matter what translation you read, we are told that they are strung up by their necks so their deaths are an agony, and their feet twitch until there is no more life in them.' She straightened. Took a deep breath. Looked at me. 'What are we to think of these women?'

I felt like the dimmest girl in class. I wasn't sure. Ma had always skipped this part of the story.

Miss Garnell leant over the books again. She moved her eyes, her jabbing finger, from one translation to another.

'Your mother's Butcher and Lang translation refers to the women as maidens. AS Way called them handmaids – he's likened them to servants. Alexander Pope called them prostitutes.'

'Why does it matter what they're called?' I asked.

She smiled. 'The words used to describe us define our value to society and determine our capacity to contribute. They also' – and again she poked at the translations – 'tell others how to feel about us, how to judge us.'

'So what *should* the women be called?'

Miss Garnell picked up the Ancient Greek version and re-read it. 'I think the most direct translation is *females*. But it is not, in my mind, the best translation for our times. These women were slaves, Peggy. So common a condition in Ancient Greece that their storytellers did not need to explain it. But for the story to be properly understood today, in England, I think we need to use words that make the position of these women clear. They weren't just maidens —'

'They were bondmaids,' I said. *Slave girl. Bonded servant. Bound to serve till death.* It had been in *Women's Words*.

'Exactly. They couldn't *refuse* to go with the suitors any more than they could *refuse* to do the laundry. But the reader might think less of a prostitute who has been paid, or a maiden who has gone with the suitors of her own free will. And they will not judge Odysseus so harshly for the punishment that he oversees.'

'And so he remains a hero.'

'Quite,' said Miss Garnell, and she closed each book. 'In my opinion, the men who translate Homer have not always served the women well.'

'An opinion you have formed because you can read the Greek,' I said.

'Well, yes.'

I picked up the pages I'd brought from the bindery. The text was so strange. It felt like a wall I couldn't scale, a locked door I had no key to. It was the Bodleian, it was Oxford University, it was the ballot box. I couldn't imagine ever being equipped to penetrate it.

'I hate that I can't form my own opinion,' I said. 'That I can't think the way you think, talk the way you talk.'

'You'd better keep studying, then. Learn the Greek.'

∾

'It is a danger to read while walking.'

It was his voice. My heart beat harder, a reminder that it did not always agree with the choices of my head. I looked up and saw his war face, his before face, his half-smile. How I'd missed him.

'You are studying,' he said, 'even as you walk.'

'Ancient Greek,' I said, unable to say anything else.

'Of course.'

His half-smile, I wanted to kiss it. It had taken a while to learn how.

'And so, you passed?'

I nodded. And I knew he wanted me to say something more, but my mind was struggling with gravestones and ginger beer and his hand on my thigh.

'I am glad,' he finally said.

I watched him walk towards his lodgings and had to fight the urge to follow.

PART FIVE

The Anatomy
of Melancholy

May 1918 to November 1918

Chapter Forty-Three

It was an old book. I could tell by the discolouration around the edges of its leaves, the musty-vanilla smell, its odd size – quarto, strangely narrow. Ebenezer had already cut it from its ancient leather covers and was releasing it from its binding. I watched him sharpen his knife, then run the blade over the threads holding the sections to the cord. I felt a twinge of regret for the woman I imagined had bound the book. She would be long dead, but seeing her work undone so swiftly made me stop in the doorway.

He released the final cord, and it was as if the book took a breath.

I entered the repair room. 'Mrs Stoddard says I'm yours for the afternoon.'

Eb pushed his glasses up on his nose. 'Glad for the help,' he said. 'My apprentice signed up last week.'

I already knew. Eb had had five apprentices since the war began and he'd lost each one to the army.

'I don't blame him,' Eb said. 'The repair room is probably the least exciting part of the Press for a lad. No machines.'

'I think the girls' side might take that prize,' I said. 'Lately, we spend almost as much time knitting as we do folding.'

Eb stepped back from the bench and ushered me towards the naked book. 'It's slow everywhere,' he said. 'A lack of men and a lack of paper, and now this flu.'

He passed me a knife so I could remove glue from the folded edge of each section before lifting it away from its sisters. I'd bind them again when Eb had guarded any folds that were damaged.

'Go carefully, Peg, she's elderly.'

'What is it?' I asked.

Eb retrieved the old covers, showed me.

Burton's Anatomy was faintly visible at the head of the spine. The place and date of its binding, *London 1676*, was imprinted on the tail.

'*The Anatomy of Melancholy*?' I said.

'The very same.' He put the covers aside.

'Aren't we reprinting it this year?'

'As we speak. Should keep us all busy for a little while – it will run to more than twelve hundred pages in the new format.'

'Just when I was getting the hang of knitting.'

He nodded at the text. 'Take a look.'

The pages were thick and sepia-coloured, the top edges stained dark. I turned a few until I came to the frontispiece – detailed engravings of men in various attitudes, each representing a cause of melancholy as Robert Burton saw them nearly three hundred years earlier.

'What are they?' I asked.

Eb looked over my shoulder and gave his interpretation of the Latin below each engraving. 'Roughly speaking: religion, love, jealousy, solitude, ill health and despair.'

'That seems to cover it,' I said.

Eb came closer. 'I think he left out war.'

Chapter Forty-Four

30 May 1918

You were right to be worried, Peg. It was terrible. Unbelievable. The red cross on the roof is meant to keep us safe but it might as well have been a bloody target. The 1st Canadian General Hospital is mostly rubble now. Three nurses are dead. I knew Katherine and Margaret, but the other nurse — Gladys, her name was — only arrived at Étaples a few days before the air raid. Now she'll never leave.

    Tilda x

Rain fell steadily against the window of the Brontë bay, and I tried to imagine the thrumming of it as something more sinister, more deadly. But I couldn't. It was just rain. And I felt a long way from Tilda.

'You seem distracted today,' said Miss Garnell. She had her trolley loaded with books. 'Perhaps you need a break. Walk with me while I reshelve.'

We walked into the next bay, and I passed Miss Garnell the books that belonged on its shelves. Then we walked into the next bay, then the next. Eventually we came to the bay with all the texts on medicine.

There was just one book to return to its shelves. I picked it up and checked the spine.

'*The Anatomy of Melancholy*,' I read aloud.

'One of our oldest books,' said Miss Garnell.

I thought of the book Eb and I had repaired. This was a different size, and the casing was cloth-covered and in need of repair. I opened the front cover and felt the old rag paper – strong, a little rough to my practised hand, still supple and barely discoloured. I turned the pages.

'What's wrong?'

'The frontispiece is missing,' I said.

She frowned. 'You know this book?'

'The Press is reprinting it. I'm folding the pages.' I passed her the volume. 'The frontispiece is quite beautiful – it's the main causes and cures of melancholy as a series of engravings.'

Her face was alight. 'A new edition, and you're binding it? How wonderful.'

'I'm only part of the binding process – I fold, gather, sew. Everything that's visible is done on the men's side. They cover it, decorate it.'

'Men's side?'

'We're quite separate,' I said. 'Even now. Only a couple of women have been allowed to work the men's machines. We'd grind to a halt if they didn't, but it still doesn't sit well with some.'

She nodded. 'A shift in the normal order of things. It can be uncomfortable for some but an opportunity for others. It seems appalling to think there might be a silver lining.'

I remembered hoping there would be.

'I was lucky enough to add the frontispiece,' I said. 'It happens once the rest of the book is compiled, and if I do my job well enough, no one will notice where I've glued it in.' I nodded to the book in her hand. 'Yours is missing the best part – I think someone's removed it.'

She opened the book and turned the pages, as if seeing them for the first time. She shook her head. 'I'd never thought about how a book was bound,' she said. Then she looked at me, in the same way she had just looked at the book. Anew. It was a few moments before she spoke again.

'I'm afraid this copy has been very poorly treated.' She showed me a page where someone had written in the margins. 'The people who read the books do not always think about the effort that has gone into binding them, or the expense of replacing them.' She caressed the cover, and I recognised the gesture. It was the same movement I made every time I held a section or manuscript or poorly bound volume before placing it among all the rest that lined the walls of *Calliope*. 'Have you read it?' she asked.

I thought of the sections I'd taken from the bindery and how I'd read them over and over. 'We're discouraged from reading on the job,' I said.

'Surely that doesn't stop you.'

I smiled. 'Even if we can make sense of parts of the text, some books, like this one, take weeks to bind, and a single bindery girl might only fold a few chapters.'

'And of those you've folded, have you a favourite?'

'Right now, it's *Love of learning, or overmuch study, with a digression on the misery of scholars, and why the muses are melancholy*,' I recited.

She laughed. 'Why use three words when you can use twenty! No wonder it is such a long tome.'

'Apparently it grew every time he edited it,' I said.

'And have you found it useful?'

'I've found it interesting.'

'Interesting is infinitely better than useful,' she said. 'What does Burton say that interests you?'

'That too much learning will make me lonely, send me mad and keep me poor.'

'And yet you persist.'

'Study is a curse but it might also be a cure, according to Burton.' I thought of Bastiaan. 'I'm damned if I do, and damned if I don't.'

∽

In the bindery the next day, I paid closer attention to the frontispiece and to the strange verses the author had written to explain it. Seven causes of melancholy had each been given a rhyme, and I imagined the scratching of Burton's quill and his solitary struggle with the ideas and the words. It puzzled me, this book. It was unlike anything I had read or seen in print. It was unique and illuminating.

I read the verses again and paused on *inamorato*. Eb had called it love and I had thought of Bastiaan. But now I wondered if it was meant as a love of self, of one's own ambitions and accomplishments. *A love of learning and overmuch study* was a particular source of woe, Burton said, if it was uncompromising. He knew a thing or two about it, I thought.

∽

'If you're not ready now, you never will be.'

I looked up. Gwen was standing in front of the Brontë window, casting a shadow over *A Primer of Greek Grammar*.

'What are you doing here?' I said.

'I'm kidnapping you.'

'No, you're not.'

'You think I'm kidding, but it's all arranged. Maude and Louise are waiting for us at the Cherwell boathouse. Your friend Aggie was going to come, but she's down with this awful flu. And Lotte declined, of course, though she was kind enough to put a picnic supper together, making a feast of our pooled rations. It seems she approves of others' fun, just not her own.'

'Gwen, I can't. Responsions is in two days.'

'You said Mrs Stoddard was giving you tomorrow off – you'll have the whole day to study.'

'Not a whole day. There's the principal's address to candidates.'

'If Miss Penrose could address you right now, she would tell you to go punting with your friends.'

'She would not.'

Gwen put her hand over the text I'd been studying. 'Tell me, if you will, what you have just been reading.'

'Don't be annoying.'

'Tell me,' she said.

I sighed. I thought. I panicked. It was gone. I had no idea what I'd been reading. I tried to remove her hand from the page but she held it tight.

'Quite,' she said. Then she lifted the book from the desk and looked at the page. 'I'll give you a hint – verbs.'

I thought. I shook my head.

'How many moods do Ancient Greek verbs have?'

I thought again. There were moods, voices, persons, numbers. So much to remember, and just then I couldn't remember a thing.

'Exactly,' said Gwen. 'Your brain has gone on strike. It requires a little recreation.' She closed the book and gathered my things. She put them in my satchel.

How many moods? I thought. How many bloody moods?

'Are you coming?' said Gwen.

She was standing beyond the bay, my satchel over her shoulder, the book in her hand. She turned and started walking. I followed.

'Gwen,' I said, desperate. 'How many are there?'

'Four,' she called over her shoulder. 'There are four moods, three voices, three persons and three numbers. Don't ask me what they're all called. I knew once, but not now. Though I always liked the idea of verbs having moods. God knows studying them always put me in the foulest kind.'

She passed Miss Garnell, deposited the book on her desk and strode out of the library.

'Take this with you,' Miss Garnell said as I hurried to catch up with Gwen. She handed me the primer. 'I won't tell if you don't.'

~

Lou was getting ices when we arrived at the river.

'What flavour, Peg?'

I had no idea.

'Whatever you're having, Louise,' said Gwen. She handed me over to Maude. 'Don't let her fall in,' she said.

Maude took my hand and led me to the punt. I looked at her as if she were a stranger – familiar, obviously, but strangely so. Maude looked to Gwen.

'I wouldn't worry,' she said. 'It's within the realms of normal. She's been studying too hard and thinks she's forgotten everything. She hasn't, of course, but she will only be restored to herself when we are on the Cherwell eating ices.'

Lou arrived on cue with four cups of flavoured ice and we all got on the boat.

'I'll punt, shall I?' Gwen took up the pole before anyone could answer and steered us confidently along the river. We ate our ices and said very little, but the movement relaxed me.

After half an hour we pulled into the bank and Maude took out the picnic Lotte had packed. Gwen poured us each a glass of lemonade. The sun was an hour from setting and the day was still warm. As my belly filled, I suddenly remembered.

'Indicative, imperative, subjunctive and optative,' I said out loud.

'What's wrong with her now?' said Lou.

'Absolutely nothing,' said Gwen.

'Restored to herself,' said Maude.

My own mood lifted.

∼

The next day, I walked with Maude to the Press, then continued on to Oriel, where Principal Penrose was making her address to Somerville's Responsions candidates.

The hall was full and something about that annoyed me. It seemed so easy for so many. I looked around, hoping to see another Town among the Gowns, but how would I know?

'I wondered if you'd be here.'

I turned. It was the woman I'd spoken with after the exam. She'd passed, I realised. *I hope we come up together*, she'd said.

She pointed to a couple of seats, and I followed her. We sat between women already wearing the short black gowns of a student.

'Freshers,' my companion said. 'They need Responsions before they can be accepted into a degree course. Not everyone bothers. They're happy to complete the usual courses and leave with better prospects than when they arrived.'

The look on my face must have disturbed her.

'Well, you know, a bit of English, a bit of History, passable French. That's all most of us need to make a good marriage and not be an embarrassment.'

Was she mocking? It was hard to tell. 'You can't think like that, or you wouldn't be here,' I said.

'I *do* think like that, actually. I doubt I'll pass Responsions, but even if I do, what's the point? No amount of brilliance will get me a degree from *this* university.'

'Why are you here, then?'

She leant in. 'I have to put in a showing. Mother is a bluestocking and a suffragist. It's unbearable.'

The din in the hall faltered, and my companion turned to the stage. Miss Penrose was waiting for silence.

She stood tall, her white hair mostly contained by the three-cornered cap, her figure and clothes obscured by a full black gown. She was the first woman at Oxford to achieve first-class honours in Classics, Miss Garnell had told me. 'Better than most of the men,' she'd said. 'But not even *she* was given her degree.'

And yet she'd seen a point, I thought – a reason to pass Responsions and take the degree course. There she stood. Principal of Somerville. Unmarried but an embarrassment to no one. She looked us over: students and hopefuls, each wanting what she'd wanted (with some exceptions, I now realised). It pleased her, I think, to see the hall full.

'Welcome,' she said.

I took a few blank pages and a sharp pencil from my bag.

'The importance of education,' she said, and I wrote it down.

'... the obligation to fulfil potential and to put it in service to community and country,'

'... the scholar's life ...'

'... the current state of the world ...'

My pencil broke. I looked around and realised no one else was taking notes.

'And once again, the War Office asks for our brightest and most gifted to work as waitresses, cooks, clerks. To roll bandages and clean bedpans. Essential work, all of it, and I am aware that some of you would consider it right to trade your education, and your potential, for such war work as could be done by anyone.'

There was movement, and a whisper rustled among some who wore short gowns. Miss Penrose sighed, as if she knew her speech was already meaningless to them.

'Please, take the long view,' she said. 'Those of you in the middle of your courses, consider how you can serve the state in a year or two, when you are fully trained. Those of you about to begin, consider how well you may serve your country when your talents are fully realised. Some of you have been offered bursaries, a few full scholarships. You are the future of this country, and it is vital that the most highly gifted women commit to scholarship – an Oxford training cannot be improvised.'

I shifted in my seat. Blushed. A full scholarship. Most highly gifted.

'Should you fail to pass Responsions,' she continued, 'then of course answer the call of the War Office. It will be hard to justify another year waiting for a place at a university.'

~

On the day of the Responsions exam, I dressed slowly, carefully. Maude in attendance. Both of us mute.

Should you fail to pass Responsions ...

I pinned my hair in place, my hat.

It will be hard to justify another year waiting ...

Maude rummaged around in the cupboard above our bed and found Tilda's lipstick. 'A smudge for confidence,' she said.

'More for a good time.' I smiled.

I took it. Applied it. Kissed the handkerchief Maude passed me. She whistled, the way Tilda whistled when she dressed us up and made us twirl.

'I'm not going to a dance, Maudie.'

She came closer, took the handkerchief and dabbed at my lips. She stood back. 'Perfect.'

~

'Break a leg,' Maude said, when we were standing on Walton Street.

'It's not a play, Maude. If I forget my lines I can't do it again tomorrow.' My anxiety was making me mean. Tilda had explained the phrase to Maude and she struggled to think of something else to say. I hugged her. Tight. 'Thank you, Maudie,' I whispered in her ear. 'For letting me do this.'

She held me as I held her. 'Break a leg,' she said again. Then she let go and walked into the Press.

I watched her. Wondered if she was beginning to feel unmoored. I wanted her to turn.

She never did.

~

Mathematics, Latin, Ancient Greek. Ancient bloody Greek.

'Pencils down, please, ladies.'

My eyes darted to the clock – surely not. But pencils were being put down. The don waited, just a moment, before saying it again. I put my pencil down.

~

I don't know how long I leant against the wall outside the Somerville Lodge. They were waiting, I knew – Gwen and Miss Garnell. They'd have a pot of tea and three cups ready. A plate of biscuits. But I couldn't move. I had walked from the exam room at Oriel, through the streets of Oxford, grateful for everyone's ignorance, grateful not to be asked how it had gone. Wanting, desperately, never to have to say.

~

Gwen poured the tea. It was black from steeping and as bitter as I felt.

'Sugar?' she ventured.

I shook my head; the bitterness seemed right.

She took a sip and made a face. 'God, it needs it.' She added a lump of sugar to her own cup, tasted it, then added another.

Miss Garnell pushed a clean handkerchief into my hand.

'I failed,' I said. I blew my nose.

'Which part?' asked Gwen.

'The part I was always going to fail.'

'Ancient bloody Greek,' she said.

Chapter Forty-Five

We turned into Walton Street and Maude walked ahead.

I heard the bell above the newsagency's door, and I heard Maude call out, 'Post, Mr Turner?' I didn't hurry after her.

'Is this what you've been waiting for, Miss Jones?' said Mr Turner to Maude, as I entered the shop.

'The final hurdle,' said Maude.

The final hurdle, I thought.

Maude held out the letter for me to take.

I stared at it. I had an urge to grab it and tear it up. If I never opened it, I'd never know. An echo: women said it all the time, women with absent sons or husbands. I flushed. I had no right. I took the letter.

'Open it,' Maude said.

'Not now, Maudie. We're running late.' I put it in the pocket of my skirt.

                                   ~

'This will not do, Miss Jones,' said Mrs Hogg, and she held up a section to draw attention to its edges, poorly aligned.

Oh, Maude, I thought.

'Miss Jones, are you listening to me?'

I let my hand drift again to the pocket of my skirt. The corners of the envelope had softened under my constant touch.

'Miss Jones!'

Then I realised – it wasn't Maude Mrs Hogg was chastising, it was me. Miss Margaret Jones, C/- Turner's Newsagency.

'I'm sorry, Mrs Hogg.' I held out my free hand. 'I'll refold them.'

She continued to hold them. 'You might think you're too good for this place but you're not gone yet.'

'Too good for this place,' said Maude, her hands not pausing.

'Enough of that,' barked Mrs Hogg. Since her husband had been missing in action, she barked all the time.

I saw Maude bite her lip.

'She can't help it, Mrs Hogg.' It was Lou who said it, because I didn't. 'You know she can't.'

'I'm not so sure,' said Mrs Hogg.

'Not so sure,' echoed Maude. Her lip had escaped. She added another perfect section to her pile, and I prayed that Mrs Hogg would stop talking.

'Like I said, Mrs Hogg, I'm sorry. I'll refold them straight away.'

Then Mrs Stoddard was there, standing tall behind our freckly frog.

'Thank you, Mrs Hogg. An eagle eye.' She took the section from her floor supervisor and examined the text. 'I'm sure Tolstoy will be grateful.' Then she moved closer to our bench and placed the poorly folded section in front of me. 'When you've fixed this, Miss Jones, could you come and see me?'

Mrs Hogg was satisfied. She forgot about Maude and continued along the benches.

I unfolded the section and used Ma's bonefolder to smooth the wayward creases. Pages from *Anna Karenina, Vol 1*. They were upside down and out of order. I refolded, careful to align the printer's marks.

I put the section on the pile; I wasn't the least bit tempted to take it home. I knew how her story ended.

~

Mrs Stoddard was recording something in her ledger. So like Miss Garnell, I thought, the way her head turned to the title page of the sample manuscript, then to the ledger. Her fingers stained with ink from a leaking pen, her handkerchief ready to wipe them. I watched her write the name and author, the number of gathered copies, the amount of waste. I wondered how often they failed to reconcile, and I stood a little straighter. When she'd completed the entry, she looked up.

'Are you quite all right, Peggy?' she asked.

'Quite all right, Mrs Stoddard,' I said.

She studied my face and frowned. I knew it was like a blank page. Maudified, I thought, and the effort was killing me. I was desperate for her to let me go.

'Have you heard?' she said.

It was no good. My lip quivered, I felt it and hated it. I wanted to bite down on it, like Maude might. I wanted to make it bleed.

'Oh, Peggy,' she said. But she had misunderstood, and I did not, yet, deserve her sympathy.

I retrieved the letter from the pocket of my skirt. Its corners were dog-eared. I handed it to her.

'You haven't opened it!' Her face looked more hopeful.

'It arrived this morning. I couldn't. I couldn't come to work if …'

She smiled. 'Would you like me to hold it for you? Just till the end of the day, so you can get on with your work.'

I took a deep breath, relieved she didn't suggest I open it then and there.

'Yes. Please. I can't stop touching it and I've made more mistakes today than in the past six years.'

'You're exaggerating, Peggy.' She smiled. 'Though not by much.' When she saw me relax, she dropped her voice. 'We don't want to give Mrs Hogg any more cause for concern.'

~

Mrs Hogg rang the bell for the end of the day, and the bindery erupted in a scraping of chairs and chatter.

I ignored it and took another printed sheet. I made the first fold, the second fold, the third.

'Peggy.' It was Mrs Stoddard. The bindery was quiet now. The girls all gone.

I looked over to Maude's bench and felt the familiar prickle of panic when I didn't see her sitting there. It was unnecessary, but habit forced a quick scan of the room. She was sitting at the desk in the forewoman's office, her hands busy with folds of her own design.

It's time, I thought. But I was still in no hurry. I tidied my bench, tidied Maude's. I tucked in our chairs and walked towards the letter.

'It's time,' said Mrs Stoddard.

'Offer from Oxford,' said Maude.

'Oh, Maudie,' I said. 'What if it isn't? What if I failed?'

She shrugged. 'What if,' she said.

Mrs Stoddard put the envelope into my hand. 'Lord knows you deserve it, Peggy, and you've already been offered a scholarship. You're obviously good enough. Why so anxious?'

'Ancient Greek,' I said, taking the envelope.

'Ancient bloody Greek,' said Maude.

I put the envelope in my pocket and left the bindery. Maude followed.

~

Maude walked me through the quad and onto Walton Street. I stopped and she tried to steer me left – towards the canal. *Calliope.* Home.

357

Towards everything that was familiar and ordinary. Everything I dared to imagine I might miss. But I couldn't be steered.

Somerville stood, as it always had, on the other side of the road. It was so close now, closer than it had ever been, but as I stared, it seemed to recede. I felt Maude pull on my arm. I resented her for it and shook her off.

'Coming?' she said.

I turned. 'You go, Maudie, I'll be home soon.'

But she didn't go. She had something to say, and her face twitched with the effort. 'You're obviously good enough.' Mrs Stoddard's words. The tone almost identical. Her face relaxed and she nodded, satisfied she'd said what she wanted to. Then she turned towards home.

~

I'd never been to the cemetery without Bastiaan and I half-expected him to be there. I stood by the gatehouse and looked towards Mrs Wood's sarcophagus. Bastiaan wasn't there, but I went that way regardless. I sat with Mrs Wood until my buttocks felt the cool of her stone. *Move along*, I imagined her saying. *It's not me you need.*

So I moved on, meandering through the gravestones, pausing at each of Bastiaan's dead. They were familiar now – the Belgians and their English hosts. I came to the grave of young William Proctor and wished I'd brought a ginger beer. I apologised. *Move on*, the boy said.

Through the avenue of yews and past the chapel.

To the north wall crowded with Jericho's dead.

Light and shade danced over names and dates. There was a breeze and the trees whispered overhead.

Helen Penelope Jones

An engraving of an open book.

I knelt, cleared the leaves and pulled weeds from the ground beside her grave. I ran my fingers over her name and felt the shape of each letter. Why did we have to wait until we were dead to have our names inscribed on something? I wondered.

I took the envelope from my pocket.

'Did you ever dream of more?' I asked.

I eased my nail beneath the flap. I didn't want to tear it. Didn't want to ruin it. I could see the letter inside – folded, just once. I slid it out halfway. *Dear Miss Jones*. I slid it back. Despite her voice constantly in my head, I hadn't spoken to Ma for six years.

'I hated you for leaving.' It was a relief to say it.

I looked into the canopy above her grave. Full of breath and movement and shifting light.

'Why didn't you make me stay at school?' But even as I said it, I remembered her trying.

'You should have tried harder. I didn't know who I'd be without Maude and I was scared. I imagined you sitting beside her in the bindery and I felt ...'

What had I felt?

'Left out. Pushed out. Superfluous.' Maude was extraordinary, Ma had always said.

I took a breath. Calmed myself. I'd felt like a copy, an echo. Too fragile to be alone. I'd anticipated the loneliness of it and fought Ma until she gave in.

'I regretted it, Ma. A little more every year. And then you died, and everything became impossible.'

I slid the letter out. All the way.

'Did you know?' I asked, and I realised in that moment that she must have. 'Is that why you brought home so many books?'

I unfolded it.

Dear Miss Jones, it said.

There were more words than I could commit to memory but I felt the impression of those that mattered.

Failed.

Not permitted to take up scholarship at this time.

Shade and light were soon replaced by shadow. The cemetery grew cold. I returned the letter to its envelope and pressed down the flap. It didn't seal, of course. None of it could be undone. I laid it on the ground in front of Ma's gravestone and secured it with a rock.

~

The house on St Margaret's Road rose three storeys from the ground. Tall windows on every level. I remembered pretending it was ours.

I opened the gate and went to the side of the house and down the steps to the basement entrance. I knocked.

No one answered.

I knocked again, then sat on a step and waited.

Milan came home first.

'He is not far,' he said. 'He helps prepare our boys for English exam, but they will have to stop for dinner.' He held the door open.

'I shouldn't have come,' I said.

He smiled. 'He will want you to wait.'

I sat in one of the armchairs and watched Milan fill a kettle with water and put it on their small kerosene stove.

'You will like tea, yes?'

'Please.'

An uneven step on the stairs and I had to stop myself from getting up from the armchair and running. Towards him or away, I wasn't sure.

Milan opened the door before Bastiaan could open it himself. I saw him put a hand on Bastiaan's shoulder, squeeze it. Then he stood aside and Bastiaan came in.

'She will like tea, my friend,' said Milan. 'Make it sweet, she is upset, I think.' I realised he'd never removed his coat or hat. 'I will eat with the boys at Wycliffe Hall.'

And we were alone.

Bastiaan looked me over, head to toe, a frown worrying his brow. I remembered all the times his hand had rested above my heart.

'I'm not hurt,' I said.

He relaxed, but turned away, towards the little stove. I saw his hand shaking as he reached to lift the kettle. When he handed me the tea, it was steady.

A little too hot. A little too sweet. But I drank it down, aware the whole time of Bastiaan's gaze.

'I failed,' I said.

'How is that possible?'

He had never doubted me.

I got up from the armchair and took a step towards him, but when he didn't move to meet me I stopped, suddenly embarrassed.

'I don't know why I'm here,' I said.

Bastiaan said nothing. He didn't move an inch.

'I should leave,' I said.

Still, nothing.

'Bastiaan, I don't know what to do, I don't know what you want.'

'I can't tell you what to do, Peggy, but you do know what I want.'

And I did. I could see it in his skin and hear it on his breath. I had not forgotten.

Neither had he. I had said *no*.

'It is up to you, Peggy.'

~

We lay on his bed, our breathing yet to slow. His hand already resting above my heart.

'Will you stay in England?' I asked. 'When it's all over?'

A beat. 'If you want me to,' he said.

'There'll always be Maude.'

'I know.'

~

6 August 1918

Dear Peggy and Maude,

My name is Iso Rae. I believe Tilda has talked to you about me and that some of my drawings have made their way to your narrowboat in Oxford. I feel I know you, and I hope this letter is not out of place.

Tilda has had some awful news. Her brother, Bill, has died. He was injured at Marne and brought to Étaples to be treated for wounds to his stomach. I'm not sure if you can imagine how big this place is. There are more people here than in Oxford — we have nearly twenty hospitals and thousands of men are being treated at any one time. Tilda did not know Bill had been brought here until after his death. He was in St John's hospital, not far from the isolation ward where Tilda is currently working. It seems so cruel.

She's not herself (or perhaps she's more herself, if that makes sense to you — every vice is exaggerated). I am not sure if she has written to you, but I suspect not.

If you knew her brother, please accept my condolences.

For my part, this camp is an intolerable place. Tilda makes it less so. I will keep an eye on her.

Sincerely,

Iso Rae

More herself. It made perfect sense.

Chapter Forty-Six

Mrs Hogg leant over my shoulder so only I could hear what she had to say.

'You won't soon forget your place again, will you, Miss Jones?'

She wasn't the only one. As I came and went from the bindery, others looked at me as though I hadn't spent my whole life in Jericho; as if I hadn't gone to St Barnabas with them or their daughters or their granddaughters; as if my mother was never a bindery girl, nor my grandmother; as if my grandfather had not been a typefounder. For some, my presence in the bindery was a trespass. I felt it as much as they did.

I was the girl caught reading when she should have been folding; who wanted to be Gown instead of Town. If I'd passed, they would have wished me well. But I'd failed. I'd thought myself better when I wasn't. They wouldn't forgive me for that, and they'd only forget when I had. Few were as straightforward as Mrs Hogg, but more than one asked if I was there to stay, and I saw the smirk play on their lips. *Let that be a lesson to you,* they were saying. *You're no better than the rest of us.*

Was that what I'd thought?

But they soon lost interest. News of the Battle of Amiens brought hope and grief. Then reports of people dying from Spanish flu became more and more sensational. The driver of a motorbus stopped in the middle of the road, then stumbled to the footpath and collapsed, dead. A soldier home on leave, right as rain in the morning, dead in the evening. Everyone knew someone who was terribly sick or in the Radcliffe Infirmary. And every day more of us knew someone who had died. My thwarted ambitions became irrelevant.

I was back to being a bindery girl. I folded the same pages over and over. I didn't bother to read them. Instead, I let the sounds of paper fill my mind: the rustle of printed sheets being pulled from quires, the turn of pages, the swift stroke of Ma's bonefolder making the creases sharp. They drowned out the *alpha, beta, gamma* of Ancient Greek; the perfect, pluperfect and imperfect verbs.

Of course I remembered them now.

When Mrs Stoddard rang her bell, the sounds of paper hushed.

'Ladies. Once again, I must ask those of you who can to work additional time over the next little while.' She looked around the bindery and we saw what she saw: benches half-occupied, piles of sheets unfolded. 'We've lost another four to munitions and a dozen are down with flu. If you are willing and able, could you please see me before you leave today.'

It was not an unusual request; the bindery had been losing women to the munitions factory ever since Aggie. But I'd been unwilling to do the extra time for months. When I had offered to stay back to help with *The Anatomy of Melancholy*, it had been to avoid Ancient Greek rather than to assist the Press. Mrs Stoddard had refused. 'You have better things to do,' she'd said, her eyes lit with the possibility.

This time her eyes, like mine, were dull. 'Thank you, Peggy,' she said. 'I will roster you on with Maude and Lotte.' Then she looked to the next woman before either of us could become emotional.

The following week, two more women left for the munitions factory and more were down with influenza. Mrs Stoddard rang her bell again, but it wasn't a request for overtime. It was a request from the Red Cross.

'Volunteers,' Mrs Stoddard said. 'Single women, and married women without children.'

War work, I thought, remembering Miss Penrose's speech. There was no reason for me to take the long view now. I was not *the future*, et cetera. I was not *the most highly gifted*, et cetera. *Should you fail to pass Responsions*, she'd said, *then of course, answer the call of the War Office. It will be hard to justify another year waiting for a place at a university.* Et cetera, et cetera, et cetera.

I joined Lotte and Maude at the information session and paid attention as a nurse told us what we should and shouldn't do. I signed my name and said I was available three evenings a week as well as Saturday afternoons. I took the identity card and the cloth mask and assured her that I could sew well enough to make another.

'Thank you for answering the call,' she said.

∽

Bastiaan joined me on my visits, and Maude went with Lotte. We mostly made people comfortable, swept floors, tidied rooms, heated up soup left by neighbours. That first week, we were sent to help a woman with four children and a husband in France. She could barely move from lack of breath, and she asked us to wash the children and get them off to bed. One cried at the sight of Bastiaan's face, and the others quickly followed. He left them to me and busied himself with the dishes that had piled up in the sink.

After that we gave our families to Lotte and Maude in exchange for their elderly. And a new routine was established.

Maude and I woke, put in a full day at the bindery, then Bastiaan and Lotte would walk with us to *Calliope* for tea before heading out to the homes on our Red Cross lists. We did more than we signed up for: three evenings became four, and not every Sunday was our own. But things were getting worse. Boys were coming home from France, Italy, Macedonia. They'd survived the war only to be embraced by the Spanish lady. How unfair, I thought, when I saw my first soldier dead from flu. We arrived before the ambulance, and his mother asked us to put him in his uniform. His limbs were still soft, and Bastiaan kept checking for a pulse. I had to pull his hand from the boy's wrist.

'He got it in France,' the mother said. 'Will he be counted among the war dead?'

'Of course,' I said. But I later learnt the answer was no.

Thank God for Rosie. She could only answer to Old Mrs Rowntree's needs, but she did her bit by feeding us. And Oberon managed to keep our coal bin half-full when others were going without. The long summer days also helped. They weren't always dry, or even warm, but the light made everything more bearable. Very few homes in Jericho had electricity, and oil had become expensive. The long days meant we could stay later if we were needed. And we always seemed to be needed.

∽

On Saturdays, we tried to finish our visits before tea so we could have the long evening for ourselves. Bastiaan sometimes took me to the cinema, and if Milan was out we'd take cheese and pickles and a half-loaf to their basement room. We'd make love, then eat. We let the crumbs fall among the sheets of his bed and I welcomed their scratch and tickle. It proved my nakedness, and his. It was evidence that our bodies could do more than work and bleed and struggle for breath. We'd pretend the room was ours. That the war was over and Milan had returned with his boys to Serbia. I'd imagine Maude living a life of her own.

'But you might return to Belgium,' I said once, slicing cheese, spreading it with pickle, as if I didn't care how he responded.

He shrugged. I pretended not to see.

'I might have to,' he said. 'Your government wants to send us all home when the war is over.'

'If we marry, you could stay,' I said. He hadn't asked me again, but I'd been thinking about it.

'If we marry, you might come with me,' he said.

'To Belgium?'

'There will be much to rebuild.'

'There's Maude.'

'She can come.'

I shrugged. He pretended not to see.

It was a game, like chess, and it always ended in stalemate.

Chapter Forty-Seven

The summer of 1918 limped towards its end, then three Jericho women died; volunteers who'd been visiting the sick. I overheard it waiting at the fishmonger's, during a tea break at work, from Mrs Townsend, the woman Bastiaan and I were visiting. She couldn't stop weeping because she'd given the last pretty girl her cold. Mrs Townsend's skin hung from her bones, having lost its flesh too fast, and I wondered where she got the energy for tears. I sat beside her with a bowl of broth; she turned her head away from me. 'You should go,' she rasped. 'Or I'll kill you too.'

Three women who'd answered the call. I wondered if any of them had failed Responsions or ignored Miss Penrose and her long view. The Red Cross was looking for single women and married women without children, Mrs Stoddard had said. They knew this would happen; of course they did. They didn't want orphans.

Three women. I searched the local papers but there was no roll of honour. *Their lives are barely recorded,* Ma had said once, when I asked what happened to the women of Troy. *So their deaths aren't worth writing about.*

So say the poets, I thought. The men who hold the pen.

Our new routine left us so exhausted that we didn't have the wherewithal to deal with the piles of books and manuscripts and sections that still littered *Calliope*. Between the bindery and our volunteering, Maude didn't have the time to consult her ledger, and I didn't have the heart to put them away for good. For a few weeks we stepped over and around, we moved this book here and that book there, we rested our mugs on them and used them to swat the mosquitoes that plagued us through that wet and humid summer. But neither of us spoke of them. Neither of us could.

Then, one Sunday in late September, Maude took out her ledger and began shelving what lay around. She didn't ask for help and I didn't offer.

I stood with my empty coffee mug and watched my sister. She was assured, she was happy. If the weather had been better, I might have gone with Bastiaan to walk along the Cherwell and not given a second thought to leaving her alone.

I'd thought it would be me the war would change, but I was beginning to realise it was Maude.

I cleaned up our breakfast things, made another pot of coffee and put a steaming mug in front of my sister. I looked over her shoulder at the neat columns. She really could be a librarian, I thought.

I moved away. I made the bed, then sat in Ma's armchair and pulled a book from her shelf. *The Tenant of Wildfell Hall*. Anne Brontë. I thought about my library bay. No longer mine. I put the book back, stood up, looked from fore to aft. *Calliope* was so small that I felt like I was suffocating. And there was Maude. She knelt and found a place for one book, then another. The books, sections and manuscripts. They made *Calliope* even smaller, even tighter. *They will expand your world,* Ma had said. But if I hadn't read them, I wouldn't know how small my world was.

'We should get rid of them,' I said.

'No,' said Maude.

She went back to the pile of books on the table. She picked one up and searched for it in her ledger. She wrote something, then stood and came towards me.

'*The Anatomy of Melancholy*,' she said. 'From Eb.'

I'd hinted. And when the folding and gathering and sewing was done, and the books had been cased and finished and sent to the warehouse, Eb had presented it to me. *The spine was poorly knocked back,* he said. *It will lose its shape.* But right then, it looked perfect.

'From Eb,' she said again, and she glanced around *Calliope*, at the shelves packed with books and sections and manuscripts. They were all gifts, she was saying to me. Gifts or hard-won. And they were not mine to get rid of. They were ours.

I opened *Melancholy* to the first few pages. A poem, from the author to his book – *Go forth, my book, into the open day.* It ran for two pages. Then the rhymes describing the frontispiece. Then the frontispiece itself. I fanned through the rest of the pages until I came to the loose plate. I'd told Eb the engravings were missing from the Somerville copy and he'd given me a plate to replace it.

I held *Melancholy* to my chest. 'All right,' I said.

When Maude had returned all the books and manuscripts to their shelves, all the loose sections and pages to their nooks and crannies, only one book remained on the table.

A Primer of Greek Grammar by Abbott and Mansfield.

I won't tell if you don't, Miss Garnell had said when she'd handed it to me.

Maude was looking at me, frowning. 'Return it.'

~

Bastiaan came with me to Somerville.

The quad, the hospital tents, the loggia with officers recuperating in beds or cane chairs. Only the faces were different. But the sister was the same woman I'd shown my note to nine months earlier. *What does a Jericho girl want with the Somerville library?* she'd asked. Nothing, I thought now. Not a bloody thing.

Miss Garnell was at her desk, hidden behind piles of books, her head bent to the loans ledger. I'd missed her.

'Peg!' Delight turned quickly to concern. 'Oh, Peg.'

She came from behind her desk and wrapped her arms around me. I wished she hadn't. I would have been fine if she hadn't.

She gave me a hanky, and Bastiaan stood a little closer. Ready to catch me, perhaps, but I felt like I'd already fallen.

'This is Bastiaan,' I said. Glad to shift the focus from my failure.

'Rudyard Kipling,' said Miss Garnell.

He smiled his half-smile and bowed a little. 'It is a pleasure to meet you, Miss Garnell. You have been important to Peggy.'

'I hope I may be again.'

I took the Greek primer from my satchel. 'Thank you for letting me borrow it.'

There was a moment when the book was held by her hand and mine, neither of us ready to do what needed to be done.

'Are you sure?' she said. 'You could hang on to it, try again.'

'It's an uphill battle,' I said.

'Where would we be if we shied from the uphill battle?' she said.

'I am sure,' I said. I let go of the book.

She returned to her desk and flipped the pages of her loans ledger. She ran her finger down the left-hand column until she found it. Then she put a ruler beneath the entry, and my eye moved along to the right-hand column. *Peggy Jones* was written in her lovely script. *Peggy Jones*, in the Somerville library loans ledger. She drew a line through it.

'What now?' she asked.

'Back to the normal order of things,' I said.

'Things *are* changing, Peg.'

'Are they?'

'There's the vote.'

I smiled. 'Not for me.'

'Another uphill battle, but it's only a matter of time.'

Ma used to say it. For years she said it. Then her time ran out.

'I have something for you,' I said, changing the subject.

Miss Garnell held the frontispiece for *The Anatomy of Melancholy* as if it were a sheet of gold leaf that might fold in on itself and be ruined.

'Colour,' she said. 'Beautiful.' Emotion made her inarticulate.

Work in the bindery slowed as printers and compositors and machine minders fell ill.

When we came through the quad, people went out of their way to keep their distance. Word had gone around about who was volunteering for the Red Cross, and as more people in Jericho fell ill, more efforts were made to avoid us. Mrs Hogg suggested to Mrs Stoddard that volunteers be restricted to one side of the bindery. There were nine of us, all single, all childless. Mrs Stoddard didn't exactly comply, but she did spread us out a bit more, and if anyone requested to move to another bench, she agreed.

A space was created between them and us, and before long we were all calling it 'No Man's Land'. Mrs Stoddard lost her temper more than once when perfectly good folds or collated pages were the casualty of *the stupid dance of avoidance* that took place when one of *them* came too close to one of *us*.

'What's wrong with you all?' she shouted once.

I'd never, in all my years, heard her raise her voice.

'If you had littluns, you'd be the same,' said one of them.

It reverberated like a slap and Mrs Stoddard looked stunned. She went back to her desk without another word.

But No Man's Land didn't stay empty for long. Women who'd been ill recovered. They came back to the bindery and they occupied No Man's Land with a kind of gloating freedom. They laughed more often and spoke louder than either *us* or *them*, and they moved through the bindery without ever dropping their pages. They'd been sick, and I'd sat by enough beds to know that each one would have been scared, even if their fever had broken quickly and their lungs hadn't filled with phlegm. They'd read the papers, nursed brothers sent back from France, known someone who'd known someone who woke up feeling well and was dead before the sun set. They'd feared this influenza more than they feared the Hun, but now they'd had it, they felt invincible.

More women fell ill and returned, two women died, three never really got better.

We stopped calling it No Man's Land.

∼

19 September 1918

Hello Pegs,

It was clever of you to report my poor behaviour to Iso in your note. She has little tolerance for self-pity and is a stickler for obligation — you are my obligation, apparently. I don't know where she got that idea.

When she found out I'd left all your letters unanswered she took me to task, handed me a few sheets of her best writing paper and told me not to waste it. I'm not sure what she thought I'd do. Blow my nose with it, perhaps. Tear it up and throw it in her face (I wanted to but, like I said, her best writing paper). She waited for me to pick up a pen before she agreed to leave me alone, and now she's sitting outside my hut. She doesn't trust me to send whatever I write.

Iso might want me to apologise and tell you that everything will be all right. But that would be a waste of her best writing paper. Lies and propaganda. I think we know, now, what this war is and what it does to people. I won't insult you.

The truth is, too many of the boys who come through here look like Bill. I attend to all of them as if they were him, and when they die I could be reading that telegram all over again. It's better if I can stroke the terror from their faces or hold their hands or whisper fantasies of heaven into their ears. Each time, I imagine some pretty nurse doing the same for Bill, and each time I am released for a moment from the grief. The anger.

Oh, Peg, I feel like I've been occupied by an enemy force, and the only way to rid myself of it is to destroy myself. My weapon, it will not surprise you, has been alcohol, but it's now been a week since I had a drink. A week since Iso found me sleeping in my own vomit. I might have died, she said, choked. 'Death by misadventure' she said they'd call it, to spare my family the humiliation. 'What family?' I sneered at her. 'Whoever lives at the address you've provided to the War Office,' she sneered back.

It's you, by the way. Though the address is Turner's Newsagency, your name will be on the envelope.

Tilda x

P.S. They're dropping like flies over here. Before they even get to point a gun at a Hun they're taking up a hospital bed. It's far worse than last year, so take care when you go visiting your sick. Wear your mask.

P.P.S. I think Helen would have liked your Miss Garnell — are you sure you're sure?

∽

The bell rang for lunch hour and I finished my fold. Lotte finished her fold; we waited for Maude to finish hers.

'Can I see you, Peggy, before you go for lunch?' It was Mrs Stoddard, standing with her hands on the back of Maude's chair, looking down at me.

I turned to Maude.

'I might see you at home,' I said. 'Or I might grab a sandwich and eat in the quad.'

'Eat in the quad,' she said.

I looked at Lotte; she nodded. I stood and kissed Maude's forehead.

The bindery was empty when I finally stood in front of Mrs Stoddard's desk.

'I have recommended you to Mr Hall for a new position.'

'What new position?'

She smiled. 'Junior reader.'

It took a moment to understand.

'There is a vacancy,' she said. 'More than one, actually. I spoke to the Controller about you a little while ago and he asked me to organise it.'

'A vacancy?'

'I thought I might have a bit more time, but there you go. Between the war and the flu we're struggling to fill orders. Mr Hall is quite insistent that you start sooner rather than later.' She was flustered. 'If you want the job, he'd quite like you to start this afternoon.'

'This afternoon?'

'I know it's short notice.'

'I'll need to get Maude used to the idea,' I said.

Mrs Stoddard frowned, put her hand on my arm. 'Peggy, Maude doesn't need you to hold her hand.'

I didn't say anything.

'I sometimes think she'd quite like a little …'

'What?'

'Well, independence.'

'Wouldn't we all,' I snapped back.

We were silent. It was uncomfortable.

'She's grown a lot in the past few years,' Mrs Stoddard continued.

'Since Lotte arrived,' I said, without any generosity. Like a sulky child. I pinched myself. Quite hard.

'Maybe,' Mrs Stoddard said. 'Or maybe Maude has just taken advantage of the opportunities that have arisen. Lotte was one, but there have been others.'

Maude cataloguing *Calliope*'s library. Making stars for Tilda, helping Miss Garnell, cooking *stoemp* and porridge. The apricot dress and cherry-red lipstick. Tending to Jack, to me.

'She's quite capable, Peggy.'

I shook my head. Mrs Stoddard looked stricken.

'You won't take the job?'

'No, I mean, yes.' She was asking me to read the books, not bind them. I wanted to laugh. I wanted to cry.

'What's worrying you?' Mrs Stoddard asked.

'Did you always think I might fail?'

It took her a moment to answer.

'I hoped you wouldn't,' she said. 'And when you got the scholarship …' She looked down at her ledger.

'Why did you encourage me?' I was suddenly angry with her. Angry with Gwen and Miss Garnell. They'd all needed a good cause but it hardly mattered to them when the good cause failed.

'Because it was what you wanted,' she said. 'I knew how difficult it would be, but I also knew you'd regret not trying.'

'How could you know that?'

Her face went slack, and it suddenly made sense.

'Did you ever try for Oxford, Mrs Stoddard?'

'No, I never did.'

'Did you want to?'

How to describe her smile? If I drew it, I'd call it melancholy.

'More than anything,' she said.

～

The Controller gave me a copy of *Hart's Rules*.

'Any questions about style, start here,' he said. Then he escorted me to the Reading department – a series of small offices on the next floor.

'A broom cupboard, I'm afraid,' he said.

'I'm used to small spaces.' But when he opened the door, I realised it wasn't a euphemism. An old laundry trough was being used to store reference books.

'You're the last in a long line of readers,' he said. 'You'll get a sample of copy just before it's printed in bulk to go to the bindery. You just need to check it for obvious printing errors.'

'I won't be proofreading?'

Mr Hall smiled. 'The copy you get should be well past the stage of proofreading.'

'Then why give me this?' I held up *Hart's Rules*.

'We give it to all our readers.'

~

As a reader, my days were free from the dictates of the tea bell and the lunch bell and the freckly frog. The tea lady came around twice a day, and I had time to linger over the printed sheets in a way I never had in the bindery. But I missed the girls' side, and in that first week I found an excuse to visit every day.

'How is Maude getting on?' I'd ask Mrs Stoddard each time.

'She hasn't missed a beat,' she said the first time.

Then, 'Quite well.'

And finally, 'If I'm honest, Peggy, I think you might miss Maude more than Maude misses you.'

I barely visited after that, and I began to look forward to the end of the day, when I'd meet Maude in the quad and she'd take my arm.

'I missed you, Maudie,' I sometimes said. She didn't always echo.

Chapter Forty-Eight

It was the first day of Michaelmas term; the last day of September. The towpath was littered with leaf fall – yellow, orange, burnished reds – but most of the colour still clung to the trees, and squirrels scampered among them. They were busy collecting what they could before the weather turned cold. It's what they did, every autumn. A routine that not even war could change.

We walked through the streets of Jericho, the same route we'd walked almost every day since we began in the bindery thirteen years earlier. The same route we would walk until our hands shook and our sight failed. As we came along Walton Street I was grateful that Somerville was still a hospital and not a college, that the people going in and out were mostly men in white coats or khaki. Since becoming a reader, I barely thought about Miss Garnell, except to imagine her, occasionally, in the Brontë bay. I was glad that the excitement of Michaelmas would be absent from Jericho.

But then Maude held my arm a little tighter. 'Gowns,' she said.

I didn't look. I thought about the manuscript I was reading. The errors that had nothing to do with the printing: sloppy grammar, lazy ideas. I would pass it for binding and let it be criticised by others.

But I could hear them. A group of young women all talking at once. A cultured voice rising here and there. They were excited but trying to be restrained. In their bloody breeding, I thought.

Maude put a hand to my cheek, looked into my eyes. With me it was so easy, and I'd always wondered if it was because she saw herself, not a stranger. She held my gaze and the voices of the new students felt less insulting. She held my gaze and I felt calmer. She held my gaze and I was less alone. I looked for my reflection in her eyes, and there I was, in miniature, where I'd always been. But when I adjusted my focus to look – not at myself, but at Maude – I was reminded that her eyes had never mirrored mine. They'd never reflected my anger or my disappointment. They'd never shown a longing for something denied or a frustration with those who kept it from her.

If anything, Maude's eyes were Ma's eyes. Maude was gazing at me with the same tenderness, the same concern, and at that moment it was Ma I remembered. What had she said, all those years ago? *This is your one opportunity, Peg. Please, please take it.*

Still Maude soothed, and I remembered the pity in Ma's eyes when I'd refused to return to school. *Why?* she'd asked. *The money,* I'd lied. *We'll find the money.* She'd smiled, as if she'd won the argument. *Maude,* I'd shouted, and Ma had flinched, then slowly shook her head. *Maude does not need you, Peg.*

But I knew she was lying.

And Maude knew she wasn't. And now I saw Ma's pity in Maude's eyes. *Maude does not need you,* my sister had echoed when we left St Barnabas on our last day of school, then again when we entered the bindery, and once more when we sat on either side of Ma. Before she began to show us the first folds, Ma leant towards my sister and whispered, *Enough now, Maudie. Be kind. Peg needs you to be kind.*

Standing there, between the Press and Somerville, I understood us differently. Maude had never confused me for her – that was my error, my anxiety and burden. Maude was singular: *one of a kind*, Ma had always said. Like an illuminated manuscript, I thought. I was the one who took refuge in our pairing. She was my excuse. She'd always been my excuse.

Maude gently turned my face towards the other side of Walton Street, forcing me to look at what I was missing out on. There they were, the new Somervillians in their short black gowns, hovering around the porter's lodge, trying to see something of the college that would be theirs when the war was done with it. The fact they weren't allowed in was my only consolation.

'They look like a murder of crows,' I said to Maude.

'Crows.' Maude smiled. And as if on cue, an officer strode out of the Somerville Lodge, disturbing the group. They fluttered back to let him pass, fluttered forward. Finally, they realised they were getting in the way and dispersed in twos and threes back towards Oxford and their temporary digs at Oriel.

I should have turned my back on Somerville and walked through the archway of the Press. Instead, I watched the women until the curve of Walton Street hid them. I shuddered, despite the blasted sunshine. My chest tightened, and the sounds of Jericho became muffled. I gasped for the air that my grief required, and felt Maude move in closer. Her belly was against my back, a perfect fit for the curve of my spine. Her arms were around my chest; her chin came to rest on my shoulder.

'As good as any of them,' she said in my ear.

Ma had said the same to Maude, a thousand times. The memory of it filled my lungs with a trembling breath because Maude had always believed her.

But I never had.

～

Rosie came round with a pot of mutton stew.

'Old Mrs Rowntree is on the mend,' she said, putting it on the table and going to the galley to fetch bowls.

'Mrs Townsend, also,' said Bastiaan.

'What's their secret, do you think?' I lifted the lid of Rosie's stew and *Calliope* filled with the smell of allspice.

Rosie shrugged. 'Will Maude and Lotte be home soon?'

'Soon,' I said. 'They're with Mrs Hillbrook.'

'How is she?'

'Not worse, thank God, but sleeping most of the time. She needs help with her boy, mostly. Full of beans, according to Maude.'

'Code for a handful,' said Rosie, and I knew she was thinking of Jack – always a handful.

'Any news?' I said.

'A letter came, barely a page,' she said. 'Maude read it to me.' She shook her head. 'Anyone could have written it.' She filled our bowls and passed me mine. 'But there was a note for Maude, as usual. And as usual, she squirrelled it away.' Rosie passed a bowl to Bastiaan. 'Does she let you read them?' she asked.

I wanted to give her a line or a joke or an observation that she would recognise as Jack's, but Maude never did share his notes.

The stew was good, and we'd had our fill when we heard someone running along the towpath.

Maude burst through the hatch, breathless. She locked eyes with me, nodding, the way she sometimes did when she had no words and hoped I knew what she was thinking. I had no idea.

'What is it, Maudie?'

Great breaths, shuddering through her. More than just running.

'It is Lotte?' said Bastiaan. We were both standing. Sentries on either side of her.

Maude turned to him; he was close. She looked to me for help.

'Mrs Hillbrook? Is she worse?'

The words were locked behind a wall of emotion. She stamped her feet.

'Her boy,' I said. 'Is it her boy?'

Relief. She nodded, *yes*. 'Her boy,' she said.

'He is hurt?' asked Bastiaan.

'Sick,' said Maude. 'Sick.'

'Does he need an ambulance, Maudie?'

She nodded and Bastiaan took up our coats, helped me into mine, put on his own. 'I will go to St Barnabas and telephone.'

~

Maude ran along the towpath, up and over the bridge. By the time we got to Walton Street we were gasping. We slowed, caught our breath, put on our masks. We turned into Cranham Street, and I felt the squeeze of the terrace houses – narrow, bare-bricked and coal-stained.

Two women talking on their doorsteps retreated into their homes. An old man touched his cap but crossed to the other side of the street. It was our haste, our masks. We were already contaminated.

Maude pushed on a door that looked like all the others and bounded up the steep stairs to the bedrooms. I should have bounded up the stairs behind her, but the smell … slightly sweet, slightly acidic, something else I couldn't identify. I didn't have the stomach for it and I began to retch. I ran to the kitchen. The window barely opened, just a few inches, but the cold air rushed in and I gulped it. I went back to the stairs and began to climb.

Bastiaan and I had been visiting old people. Their homes smelled of stale tobacco smoke, old frying oil, sometimes urine. *Your job,* the Red Cross nurse had said, *is to feed the cat, insist they take a little broth, help them get back on their feet.* And they had all got back on their feet, even Mrs Townsend, who didn't particularly want to. But no home had smelled like this.

My hand gripped the banister too tightly. My legs felt like lead. When I reached the landing, the smell was worse, and I wished I'd sprayed my mask with disinfectant. *More for the stench than any hope it will stop you catching something,* Tilda had written.

I could see into both rooms. Mrs Hillbrook was in one, her fair hair damp on her pillow, her breath a rattle in her chest. There was a bucket beside the bed, and vomit had dried on the sheet that hung down from the mattress.

I wondered why they hadn't changed it, why they hadn't emptied the bucket, why Lotte wasn't wiping her brow with a cool cloth. I wondered all these things. Then I knew.

The other room.

I turned towards it. A metallic smell, like monthlies, a soaking rag left too long. It was awful. Fetid. It stained his nightshirt. It stained the edge of his mouth. I heard it bubbling up and saw it frothing from his nose.

The boy. Fair like his mother. His face the colour of lavender.

Lotte held him. She sat on the floor against the side of the bed and held him like he was a much smaller child. *Ten*, Maude had said. *Full of beans.* His thin legs spilled over Lotte's lap and she held his body against hers, his head tucked into the curve of her neck. Mucus, frothing pink from his nose, his mouth. Her cheek was slick with it, her chin, her lips. Where was her mask? She rocked back and forth and spoke a stream of words into the crown of his head. French, I realised. Her words only stopped when she kissed him.

I stepped into the room. Maude was backed up against a wall, eyes wide, staring at Lotte and the boy. He should be in bed, I thought. Propped up, I thought. So he can breathe, I thought.

I moved towards them.

'*Nein!*' she spat, eyes wild, as her foot kicked out and caught my shin.

I began to understand.

'She doesn't recognise us,' I said.

'Scared,' said Maude.

Terrified, I thought. Lotte was terrified.

That was how Bastiaan found us. He stood in the doorway and watched Lotte rocking the boy. He listened to what she was saying, then sat on the floor, well back. He spoke to her, his voice low and soft. He spoke in French and Lotte began to listen.

I don't know what he said, but there was a rhythm to it. *Because I was there,* he'd told me. He spoke like a parent soothing a child. It calmed Lotte and it calmed Maude and it calmed me. When Lotte stopped rocking, Bastiaan crawled towards her, his bad leg dragging. She held the boy tighter and Bastiaan stopped, but he kept speaking, his French soft and lulling.

A shuddering breath and she looked around the room. Her eyes had lost their wildness. She knew who we were, where she was. She looked at the boy lying in her arms and her face collapsed with grief. Bastiaan was beside her, had his arms around her and the boy.

It might have taken a minute, it might have taken an hour, I don't know. But when Bastiaan took the boy from Lotte's arms and laid him on the bed, he was dead.

Chapter Forty-Nine

Mrs Stoddard said that Lotte slept for two days.

In that time, Mrs Hillbrook's fever broke and her chest began to clear. Maude sat with her while she wept, and I busied myself with the copper and dirty linen. We didn't expect Lotte to return to Cranham Street, but she did. The last of the towels were barely dry when she came through the front door and told me I wasn't needed. She nodded at the tea and toast I'd just put on a tray.

'I will take it up,' she said. She seemed her old self, and it made me nervous.

'Should you be here, Lotte?' I asked.

'Of course – why not?'

I didn't dare say. I picked up the tray and she held out her hands. We stood for a moment, both holding our ground. She would not yield, I knew that, so I gave her the tray, then gathered my coat and bag.

Lotte walked with me towards the door and stood with the tray at the bottom of the stairs. She was not going to let me climb them.

'It is all right, Peggy,' she said. 'I am all right.'

I called up to my sister: 'Maudie.'

She came to the landing and looked down.

'Lotte's here. I'll head home and get tea on,' I said.

She nodded, unconcerned.

I walked home without her, worried. But an hour later, Maude was sitting at our table, folding, while I boiled two eggs.

'Stars,' she said, when I asked.

'Who for?'

'Mrs Hillbrook.'

Maude had folded very little since we began our Red Cross visits, but in the week that followed Lotte's return to Mrs Hillbrook's, she went back to her old habit. She folded while I made coffee in the morning and tea in the evening. When I asked her to cook, she did, singing the process as Lotte had taught her, but as soon as she'd eaten she would push her plate away and pull her papers close. She made stars, only stars, and she wouldn't stop until it was time to go visiting or go to bed. If the coal was low, we'd go to bed early and, even then, Maude would bring the papers with her to make the most of the light I tried to read by.

I closed my book, not bothering to mark the page. Three stars adorned our bedcover and Maude had almost completed a fourth. Stelliferous, I thought, recalling a word I'd seen on the pages of the New English Dictionary. I imagined them hung all around the terrace house in Cranham Street. 'How is Mrs Hillbrook, Maudie?'

'Better.'

'But you still need to go?'

'Sad.' She finished the star.

Sorrow, I thought. The mother and daughter of melancholy. 'She'll always be sad,' I said. 'Is that for her?'

Maude shook her head. 'Lotte,' she said.

It was dark when I heard them on the gangplank. Fat had congealed around the sausages, so I put them back on the hot plate, reboiled the beans and heated the potatoes. Lotte will struggle to eat this, I thought, imagining the turn of her lip. I took down three plates.

Maude pulled out a chair and guided Lotte into it while I arranged the food on plates. The beans were khaki, and I couldn't help my own lip curling. I braced myself and put one of the plates in front of Lotte. She looked at it without a flicker of disgust. Without recognition, I thought.

'*Merci*,' she said, flat and low. French, again.

I sat. I watched Maude cut into a sausage – once, twice, three times. Four equal portions. An old ritual, returned. Then I watched her repeat the process with the other sausage.

I ate all my beans, to get them out of the way. My stomach turned.

'How is Mrs Hillbrook?' I asked, cutting into a potato.

Lotte looked at me but didn't answer. The potato was overcooked. Watery.

'Mrs Hillbrook?' I said again, putting the potato in my mouth. Trying not to spit it out. *It's good food, Peg, don't waste it*, Ma always said. 'How is she?'

'*Disparu*,' she said.

I had to think. *Disparu*. Gone. I swallowed. It didn't taste right. 'Gone to hospital?' I said.

Lotte shook her head but her face added nothing; her eyes were dull. I realised she wasn't actually looking at me at all. I turned to Maude.

'But she was getting better,' I said, pretending calm.

Maude nodded. 'Better.' She looked frightened. She arranged the sausage segments on her plate.

I turned back to Lotte. 'What happened, Lotte? I thought her fever had broken.'

Lotte shook her head. '*Pas possible.*'

'What do you mean, not possible?'

Lotte focused for a moment, and it was like she had just woken. 'She could not,' she said, the English difficult.

'Could not what?'

'*Vivre.*'

'*Vivre?*'

'Live,' whispered Maude, hands busy, busy. Rearranging the sausage.

'Did you send for an ambulance?'

Nothing.

'Maude. Did you go for an ambulance?'

She nodded.

'And they couldn't help?'

She shook her head and put one bit of sausage in her mouth, then arranged the rest to fill the gap on the plate. I watched her eat each bit, fixing the pattern each time.

She left the beans and the potatoes. 'Not good,' she said.

'I know,' I said, and gathered the plates. Lotte had eaten nothing, drunk nothing. She made no effort to help clear the table. When the dishes were washed and dried, she sat just as we'd left her, staring but not looking at anything. She was pale. Paler than usual. I put my hand to her forehead.

'Hot?' asked Maude, fear still haunting her face.

'No,' I said. 'But she's not quite right, is she, Maudie?'

'Not right,' she said.

It was too late, too dark, and Bastiaan wasn't there to walk her home, so we helped Lotte to Ma's room. We removed her skirt, her blouse, her corset. We sat her on the bed and took off her shoes, rolled down her stockings. Maude on the left, me on the right. When Maude sat behind her and started removing the pins from her bun, Lotte stayed perfectly still. I found Ma's brush and gave it to my sister. Then I stepped back to where the curtain separated Ma's bed from ours. I watched as Maude removed the tangles from the ends of Lotte's hair. Lotte was so fair and Ma had been so dark, but the image was the same. Brushing Ma's hair had always been Maude's job. When she began to brush Lotte's, I pulled the curtain closed.

~

Maude came to bed, and I fitted myself into the shape of her. For a while we listened to Lotte snore.

'Almost as loud as Tilda,' I said, trying to make light when it was impossible.

Maude said nothing, and I wished Tilda were there. I moved in closer, my belly against her back. I found her hand holding the blanket tight under her chin and I took it in mine.

'How can I live?' my sister whispered.

'What does that mean, Maudie?'

'Without him.'

Her boy. *Full of beans,* Maude had said. His skin like lavender.

'Did you hear Mrs Hillbrook say this, Maudie?'

A nod.

'Did Lotte?'

Another nod.

I tightened my hand around hers and I thought that perhaps there *were* things we should leave well alone. Questions we shouldn't ask because the truth is so difficult to hear. But I felt Maude's body tense and I knew she was waiting for what I would ask next. The truth weighed too much for her.

'Did Mrs Hillbrook hurt herself, Maudie?'

The slow movement of her head. *No.* We lay still. We listened to Lotte snore.

'What did Lotte say, Maudie, to Mrs Hillbrook?'

A deep breath. I felt her whole body expand.

'*Pas possible, pas possible,*' said Maude.

'Over and over?'

'Over and over.'

'And what did Lotte *do*, Maudie?'

The breath blew out of her; her muscles began to relax. Warm, I thought. I was asking the right questions.

'Something,' she said. 'Not. Right.'

'Were you there, Maudie, when Lotte did something not right?'

She shook her head, and I felt her tears between our fingers. I remembered the boy's hair, fair like his mother's. Almost as fair as Lotte's. As fair as the hair of another boy. *Pas possible,* Lotte had said. Life had been impossible for her.

'She sent you for the ambulance, didn't she, Maudie?'

Maude nodded.

'Even though Mrs Hillbrook was getting better,' I said.

Maude nodded.

'And when you got back?'

'*Disparu,*' Maude said, as Lotte would have said it to her.

'Gone,' I said.

'She could not live,' Maude whispered.

'Lotte told you that?'

'Over and over.'

∼

When we woke the next morning, Lotte had a fever we could not cool.

∼

On the third day, Mrs Stoddard came with a doctor. He bumped his head as he came through the hatch, then he paused to look around *Calliope.* 'Clean, at least,' he said, to no one, and I wondered if it was pity or disdain hidden behind his mask. He heard Lotte's crackling breath and went straight to her.

'Just one of you,' the doctor said, when he was at the bedside, and Mrs Stoddard went to leave. 'Stay, Mrs Stoddard, if you would, but one of these girls is more than enough.'

Maude was already sitting on the bed, wiping sweat from Lotte's face and singing 'Frère Jacques'. I moved out of the way.

I watched Mrs Stoddard and Maude sit Lotte up so the doctor could listen to her chest. I saw him move the stethoscope from one side of her back to another. They laid her down and he checked her eyes, her ears, her mouth. He picked up her hands and examined her fingers, then he lifted the bedclothes and checked her toes. Lavender.

'Influenza,' I heard him say, as if we didn't already know. Then he looked at Maude. 'She's been like this for three days?'

Maude nodded.

'She's oxygen-starved,' he said to Mrs Stoddard. 'A refugee, you said?'

Mrs Stoddard nodded.

'I'll do what I can to find a hospital bed.' He turned to Maude. 'You've done a good job, young lady. She's as comfortable here as she would be anywhere.'

Mrs Stoddard walked with him onto the towpath and I watched them through the galley window. She asked him something and he shook his head. He looked tired, I thought. So very tired.

⁓

Maude sang to Lotte until her last breath, if breath is what you'd call it. And she kept singing until the nursery rhyme was at its end. It was French. They had all been French. Lotte must have sung them to Maude when it was just the two of them.

I stood aside and watched as Mrs Stoddard took away the pillows that had been propping Lotte up and, with Maude's help, eased her body to lay flat on the bed. Maude kissed Lotte's fingertips and laid her hands across her chest.

I'd been there before. On the other side of the curtain. It had been Tilda that time, not Mrs Stoddard, but Maude was the same. She could sit with death. She did not recall the past or imagine the future in that moment. She had no compulsion to rage against it, to scream and beat life back into the body she loved. She cared for Lotte as she had cared for Ma, and I watched until I could bear it no longer.

The doctor must have told Mrs Stoddard that Lotte wouldn't last the day. That's why she'd stayed. And she would stay longer. She would help Maude lay out the body as Maude had helped Tilda. They would wash Lotte and dress her, and when that was done, Mrs Stoddard would go again for the doctor, or maybe just the undertaker. What use would the doctor be now? And Maude would sit with Lotte, unafraid. As she had sat with Ma.

I left them to their work.

~

I arrived at Bastiaan's, damp and shivering. Milan opened the door.

'He is better.'

I hadn't known he'd been ill.

'I will leave you.' He took his coat from the hook by the door and left.

My shivering increased and my legs refused to move me forward. I stared at the foot of his bed and imagined a bluish hue on the tips of his toes.

And then he was getting out of bed. He was taking my coat and wrapping a blanket around me. He was talking close to my ear, his breath coming smoothly between the words. His breath warm on my neck.

His breath. The rhythm of his breath. Proof of life, I thought.

I sank to the floor and he sank with me; I told him about Lotte.

'She could not return,' he said.

'What do you mean?'

'To Belgium. She told me that if she was sent back, she would not have the strength to bear it. For her, she said, there was nothing left to rebuild.'

Chapter Fifty

7 November 1918

Hello my lovelies,

What a horrible time you have had. I'm so, so sorry to hear about Lotte. But I'm glad to hear that Jack is home and has survived the war with all his fingers and toes and most of his senses. I doubt he'll return to the Jack you knew in 1914. How can any of us return to who we were then? It's good to hear he's back at the Press — the old routines might help. My advice in the meantime is to keep him away from loud noises and get to know him anew.

Now, speaking of war's end, everyone who's anyone is saying it will happen any day. The Huns will keep shooting right up until the armistice, of course, and we will insist on shooting back. So the end of your war will not be the end of mine. I will stay until I'm not needed — six months at least.

Tilda x

P.S. Bill's wife declined my offer to help with the boys — she's made other arrangements and is to marry a man who lost an arm at the Somme.

How could any of us return to who we were then? I wondered. I folded the letter and put it with all her others.

We tried to celebrate. We joined the crowds and drank whatever was offered, and Bastiaan was offered a lot. His face was a badge of honour now the war was won; nothing to fear now they'd had a skinful. 'You did it,' an old man said, slapping him on the back. Others shook his hand. A girl ran up and kissed his sunken cheek, the vellum skin, then returned to her friends, giggling and wiping her mouth.

'Was it worth it?' someone said.

I turned and saw a woman, her glance fleeing from Bastiaan's face, her body bent, though not with age or infirmity. Her question was directed at no one. Everyone. I had the feeling she'd been asking it for a while, that the curve of her shoulders was from the weight of loss.

'Let us find somewhere quiet,' Bastiaan said, his voice raised against the noise of the revellers, his accent strong.

'We fought your bloody war, now bugger off home.' It was spat out by one man, applauded by others. Without discussion, we made our way along the High, pressing ourselves into the shopfronts to avoid being jostled.

Calliope was dark, but a warm yellow light spilled from *Staying Put*. I bent to peer inside.

Maude and Jack playing chess, Rosie knitting, Old Mrs Rowntree asleep in her chair.

Bastiaan nodded, and I knew how the rest of the evening would play out: I would knock, Rosie would answer, Maude would join us on the towpath and we'd walk the few feet from *Staying Put* to *Calliope*. Bastiaan would make sure we were safely in, then he'd say goodbye. I'd climb into bed with Maude and wish she was him.

In the past twelve hours everything had changed, but not this scene. I knocked. Rosie answered. Maude gathered her things.

'It's over,' Maude said as she joined Bastiaan and me on the towpath.

Inside *Calliope*, Bastiaan stood by the open hatch, his head bent a little to the curve of the boat. His coat still on. He took my hand and raised it to his lips.

'It is over,' he said.

He should have been going, waving from the towpath, confirming when we would meet the following day, or the day after. That was our routine, the pattern of life we had established. It kept us going while we waited, as everyone waited, for the end. But the end had come, and instead of going he held my hand to his cheek.

He stood there, not moving, my hand growing warmer against his skin, his thoughts all his own behind a closed eye. There was something in the silence between Bastiaan and me. Melancholy. No one living is free of it, I remembered.

'Stay,' I said, loud enough for Maude to hear.

He opened his eye.

'Please, stay.'

Bastiaan looked beyond me, to where Maude sat at the table. It was never just about me.

'Stay,' she said.

I raised my head.

'You are sure?' said Bastiaan. It may have been for her or it may have been for me. We both answered.

'Stay.'

∼

We lay in Ma's bed, face to face and naked. I reached my hand to cup the curve of his shoulder, I followed the line of his arm and wondered at the growth of hair – sparse on the upper arm, thick and black on the forearm. I continued to his wrist and the hand that rested on his thigh. I traced each finger, felt each knuckle, noticed ridges on his thumbnail.

There was still so much of him to know, I thought. I wove my fingers between his and lifted his hand to my face. I wanted to feel the texture of it, the variations between palm and fingertips on my cheek. I kept my eyes open, not wanting to hide a thing. His fingertips were rough, patterned with scars. I moved them towards my mouth, the scars more vivid against my lips. My tongue sought out the shape of them as if they might leave their print and tell their story. The whole time, I held his gaze, but then it wavered and his eyelid closed. I felt the deep intake of breath and the rise of his chest.

'Look at me,' I said.

He did. He let the breath leave him. Let it return to its steady rhythm. Then he moved his hand towards my jaw and his fingers played around the lobe of my ear, tangled themselves in my hair. Gooseflesh, as if a breeze had crossed my skin. But I barely blinked. I would miss nothing.

I returned my hand to his body and my fingers brushed the hair of his armpit, thick and damp. I could smell the excitement of armistice – the joy and the anxiety, the sweat from the quick walk along the canal. I could smell the alcohol coming off him, and beneath it all I could smell his desire. I tasted it, licked it from my fingertips. Salty. A little sweet. I moved my hand over the rise of a sinewy band of muscle and the impression of every rib. He was pocked with scars made by metal, fire, stone, the surgeon's knife. I took my time. I counted, I measured. They were small, they would fade, they'd smooth over, I thought. But they'd always be there. Then I was stroking the valley of his waist and the small rise over his hip, and I was surprised by how smooth the skin felt. How vulnerable.

'Your skin, here, is like a woman's,' I whispered. Then my hand swept up to his chest, where the hair grew sparse. I circled one nipple, then the other, the areolae were so soft the pads of my fingers felt rough against them. 'And here, it is like a girl's.'

From his chest to his bellybutton to the hair of his pubis. It was coarser than the hair of his armpits, the curl tighter. I felt him stir.

He took his hand from where it had been at the nape of my neck and stopped me going further. 'Now, it is my turn,' he said.

It was the work of cartographers. We were mapping each other's bodies so that we might return.

~

I woke, disoriented. A dull throbbing in my head, my mouth dry. The light was all wrong, and for a few moments I forgot where I was. Then I remembered we were in Ma's bed.

Stay, we had said, and he'd stayed.

I moved my hand and felt the dip of the mattress, the heat in the sheets. I touched his skin – the valley of his waist, the small rise over his hip. I closed my eyes and recalled the contours I'd traced. The map of him that I'd drawn. It had been slow, something beyond the desire we usually had when there was a chance to satisfy it. We'd held that at bay for hours. Yes, it was hours; I could feel it in the sandy scrape of eyeballs against lids. We'd held them open until it was almost impossible. Only when we knew every curve and scar and blemish, had felt every surface and smelled the nature of our longing and anxiety, had we closed them. And only when they were closed had we made love.

His breath puffed out through the soft side of his lips. Rhythmic, unchanged. My hand against his waist had not stirred him, and I was in no hurry for him to wake. When he does, I thought, the business of living will resume. That was what people were celebrating. A return to things as they had been. As if that were possible.

Or desirable.

I lay there and thought of other women in their beds, waking with a throbbing head and dry mouth. Remembering the night before, when they'd danced at this hall or that until the beer ran out, embracing strangers and letting themselves be kissed. Or when they'd stood on the back of a truck driving along the High, waving and shouting, 'It's over! It's over!'

Did they wake, like me, with 'It's over' ringing in their ears and wonder what it really meant? Did they think about the job they might lose when all those brothers and lovers and husbands came home? Did they think of the freedoms they would have to relinquish, or fight to keep? The girl who'd kissed Bastiaan's cheek had done it as a dare, and I imagined other women looking on, wondering if they could love the man who would walk back through their door in a week or a month or a year. Did they wake with the conviction that they would love him, despite the ruined face or useless legs or the clinging dead that refused to be buried?

It's over, they might think. But it wasn't.

Melancholy, I thought. It would smell of Bastiaan and taste of salt. I would never be free of it.

The sound of the kettle going on the hot plate. Lotte had taught Maude a rhyme for that too. I lay still and listened for it, but Maude was silent. She sang it in her head now, though sometimes a line would slip out.

I heard a mug being taken from its hook and placed on the bench. Then another. Then a third, bless her. The rolling boil of water – I heard it being poured into the pot, swirled, poured out. The lid of the tea tin. *One for each cup and one for the pot, pour in the water, then keep it all hot.* Would she remember the tea cosy? She sometimes didn't.

I slipped out of bed and into the dressing-gown hanging on the side of Ma's wardrobe. Then I heard a tinkling. *When the tea is done, the bell is rung,* I thought. I looked to the bed, but Bastiaan slept on.

Maude's eyes were bright with a good night's sleep. She smiled, then looked me up and down. 'Tilda's,' she said. I held my arms out and did a twirl. 'Too long,' said Maude.

I held the hem off the ground so I wouldn't trip and joined Maude at the table. She poured for me, for her. She added sugar – two each, an indulgence. She looked towards Ma's bedroom.

'Shall we let him sleep?' I said.

She nodded and left the third cup empty.

'It's over,' said Maude.

I barely knew how to respond.

'The Belgians will go home?' She was repeating what she'd heard, but I knew it was a question.

'Some might have a reason to stay,' I said.

She looked to Ma's bedroom again, then she looked at me. She held her mug in both hands, warming them. She was waiting for an answer.

I sipped at my tea, hot and sweet, and thought about everything Bastiaan and I had done the night before, and all the things we hadn't said. When the cup was drained, I looked at my sister.

'I don't know, Maudie. I really don't know.'

She poured me another cup. Added sugar. 'A reason to stay?' she said.

He had a reason to stay, and a reason to leave. We both did.

'I love him, Maudie. I feel …' I was going to say, *Like myself. Completely myself whenever I'm with him.* But it wasn't quite true. 'I feel torn,' I said.

She nodded, and the brightness in her eyes dimmed with the slight bow of her head.

'It's not you, Maudie.'

She raised her head.

'You don't need me to hold your hand.'

It was my first attempt to articulate things, and I was afraid of how the words might come out, about how accurate they might be.

'I think it's Somerville.'

I stopped. Maude lifted her mug and sipped until it was empty. She poured herself another, then lifted the lid of the teapot and peered inside. She hadn't remembered the cosy, then I remembered Lotte saying she'd had trouble finding a word that would rhyme. I'd offered nosy and posy. *They make no sense*, she'd said, *and in the end, the cosy is not so important.* I was offended. But she was right. The cosy was not so important. Maude left the table and put the kettle back on the hot plate.

'Is there enough water?' I said.

She lifted the kettle, judged its weight and nodded. Then she returned to the table.

I added sugar to the tea in her mug, just one. I stirred.

'Somerville,' she said.

Somerville, I thought. Bloody Somerville. I shook my head and Maude put her hand over mine, a gesture of understanding she'd seen a hundred times. 'I keep dreaming of Somerville, Maudie. I'm still studying and the exams haven't happened,' I said.

The rolling boil of water. Bastiaan pulled Ma's bedroom curtain aside.

He stood, dressed in the clothes he'd worn the day before, waiting, I think, for an invitation to join us at the table. I didn't offer it. I was searching his face. We'd come to no conclusions. Made no plans. Did he have a good enough reason to stay, or did he need to return, to rebuild, to heal? I could barely read him, and I knew he could barely read me. It was as if we had again wrapped ourselves in all the layers we'd removed the night before. To hide or protect, I wasn't sure.

Maude brought the fresh pot to the table, and Bastiaan watched her pour his tea, then he sat at the table, opposite me. Without asking, Maude added two sugars – I didn't say he took none. She put the mug in front of him and sat. We watched him drink and he was careful, I thought, not to react to the sweetness.

Bastiaan put his empty mug on the table. 'Thank you, Maude. A good cup of tea.'

She tilted her head and looked at him. It was a little too long for comfort, and Bastiaan shifted to turn his ruined face away from her. But he'd misunderstood.

'It's over,' she said at last.

'It is,' he replied.

She kept looking at him, and I realised the conversation she wanted to have. I had an impulse to intervene, to change the subject and spare him. Instead, I rose from the table and went to the room I shared with Maude. I closed the curtain behind me.

'It's over,' I heard her say again. 'The Belgians will go home.'

Bastiaan was silent, but Maude was more patient than most. I held my breath and thought again of the night before. I knew every inch of his body now, but we had failed to talk. Chosen not to. I did not know his mind.

'Many will,' he said.

'Some might have a reason to stay?' she said. An echo, but also a question.

'They will have every reason,' Bastiaan said, and my breath caught. 'But they may not have a choice.'

I turned to our wardrobe and took out a clean skirt, a clean blouse. It was not an answer, I thought.

And then she was talking again. The words and phrases stilted as she strung them together.

'Peggy,' she said.

'I love her,' said Bastiaan, but I knew that wasn't what she wanted to know.

'A reason to stay,' said Maude.

'I know this,' he said.

I dressed. Rolled my hair into a bun and pinned it. Then I moved into Ma's room to retrieve my stockings and shoes.

Bastiaan had made the bed.

It was as if we'd never slept there. I looked around the floor – nothing of his remained. *Stay,* Maude had said.

Stay, I'd said.

Chapter Fifty-One

The day after Armistice was a workday for the likes of Maude and me, but the Press was not immune to the effects of the previous day's celebrations and sorrows. The words *Peace* and *God Save the King*, were spelled out in gaslights above the entrance to the Press, and the bindery was missing a third of its staff.

'Have you come to lend a hand?' said Mrs Stoddard when I came to visit at morning tea time.

I shook my head. 'Just saying hello,' I said. 'We're short of readers as well, which suits me. I've been given real proofs to check for real errors, not just printing mishaps.'

'It's about time,' said Mrs Stoddard.

'A pity it won't last.'

'Why do you say that?'

She knew as well as I did. 'I'm just filling in, Mrs Stoddard. They'll all be home soon and I'll be back at that bench, folding pages with Maude. Exactly where I was four years ago.'

She couldn't deny it.

Proofs for *The Concise Oxford Dictionary of Current English* were waiting for me in the broom cupboard. I only had to check the preface pages, and since it was the seventh impression, they were likely to be error-free. I placed Ma's bonefolder and slid it down the page, scanning each line. I found a space where there shouldn't have been one, but nothing else. I fanned through the other pages looking for printing problems. None. Job done.

But I didn't put it aside. I searched for the word that seemed to sum up the past four years.

Loss.

The Concise Dictionary simply defined it as: *Detriment, disadvantage. See lose,* the entry said. I turned back a few pages. *Lose: Be deprived of, cease by negligence, misadventure, separation, death.*

It didn't quite explain the feeling I had. Since giving up on Somerville, I'd felt I'd lost a part of myself, the person I might have been. When I thought of my future, there was a space where there shouldn't have been.

I stood and stretched my back. Mrs Stoddard's calisthenics had become a part of my reader's routine as they had been a part of my folding routine, my gathering routine. Whether I thought the definition was adequate or not was irrelevant. My job was to ensure the words were printed clearly. *Your job is to read the books, not think about them,* Mrs Hogg might have said.

I delivered the pages, then went to see Maude in the bindery – not because she needed checking on, but because I missed her.

Mrs Hogg was walking behind the folding benches. She used to stalk, I thought, looking for weakness. But she wasn't stalking. She was barely looking over the shoulders of the few bindery girls who'd turned up for work. Her husband's name had been in the paper: *Killed in Action, Corporal FJ Hogg.* He was no longer missing and her anxiety was over, but her grief had just begun.

It occurred to me, then, that she might have her own opinion about the meaning of loss. But I knew what she'd say, if I asked her: *My opinion is irrelevant, Miss Jones.*

~

I was in time for the lunch bell.

'Mr Hall has allowed an extra half-hour on account of the Armistice,' Mrs Stoddard called above the scraping back of chairs.

I walked with Maude into the quad, where Jack was waiting by the pond.

He was a little stooped, a little fidgety, but when he saw us he stood tall. He waved his hand and gave us the best version of his smile. We came out onto Walton Street to find that Jericho had started celebrating again. Jack shied from the noise. The best version of his smile wavered.

'Coming, Jack?' someone shouted. It was an apprentice compositor, too young to have served. There was a group of them, and they waited for Jack to respond. He might have been their supervisor if he hadn't lost four years.

I saw his fingers start their worrying. He wanted nothing more than the quiet of the canal, I thought.

'Jack,' I said. 'Can Maude have lunch with you and Rosie? I told Gwen I'd meet her.'

'Course,' he said, his face relaxing. 'Duty calls,' he shouted back to the lad waiting for a reply, and with a flare of gallantry he held out his arm. 'May I escort you, Miss Maude?'

An echo of the old Jack. Maude took his arm.

'Tell Rosie I'll pick up something nice from the Covered Market,' I said, 'something to share after supper.'

'Something nice,' said Maude, and she held Jack to her.

'Something nice,' he repeated, looking at her, then at me. 'I'll have her back in the bindery at half-one.'

Oxford was full of people who'd been given the day, or taken it. Half of them were still drunk, and I wondered if Gwen would remember our date. She'd shouted the invitation from the back of a motorcar as it drove down the High the night before. It had been full of students – women from Somerville, men from Oriel. I'd wondered if Miss Penrose knew, or Miss Bruce. Surely they'd have turned a blind eye.

Gwen was sitting on the steps of the Martyrs' Memorial. When she saw me, she stood, swayed a little.

'Oh, dear,' she said. 'I'm still dizzy with champagne.' She took my arm. 'Or perhaps I have a hangover. Either way, I need a pot of strong tea.'

We walked to Cornmarket Street, and Gwen stopped outside the Clarendon Hotel.

'Really?' I said. It would be expensive.

'Why not?' she said. 'We're celebrating.' It was a given she would pay.

The doorman nodded at Gwen with some familiarity, and I followed her through the lobby to the coffee room. She asked for a table near the window. 'So we can watch the joy on people's faces,' she said.

The waiter assisted Gwen with her chair. I sat before he could attempt the same with me. 'They're not all covered with joy,' I said.

The waiter poured water into our glasses and placed two small menus on the table in front of us. Gwen nodded in his direction, and he understood he'd been dismissed for the time being.

'Most of them are,' she said to me, 'and they're the faces I choose to look at.'

I raised my eyebrows.

'Oh, don't. There's been so much misery for so long, surely we're allowed to indulge in a little frivolous joy for a few days.'

I lowered my eyebrows, smiled. 'Of course we are.'

Gwen looked at her menu. I did the same but all I could focus on was the prices. She put her menu aside, decided.

'And it *will* be just a few days, Peg. After that we have to push our advantage.'

'And what advantage is that?'

The waiter returned. He wore a starched white shirt, bowtie and jacket. Thinning hair was greased in place, and his shoes reflected the light of the bloody chandelier. Gwen didn't seem to notice any of it, and so it was Gwen he deferred to.

'A large pot of breakfast tea, strong. And a plate of scones with jam, cream *and* butter, if you have any,' she said.

He forced a smile, and I wondered how he would be celebrating when he had the chance.

'Where was I?' said Gwen.

'Pushing your advantage,' I said.

'Oh, yes. It's like emerging from a chrysalis. The past four years have been an incubation, and we women can only emerge brighter, stronger.' She frowned. 'No, that's not it at all.'

I decided yes, she was still a little drunk.

'Incubation makes it sound like we've been hidden away,' she continued, 'waiting for change. But that's rubbish. We've been tested and we've proved ourselves, don't you think, to those who needed convincing? We've done their bloody jobs, made their bombs, driven their buses ...'

'When did you do any of those things?'

She ignored me and continued. 'We've mopped their brows, and when they asked us to march towards death, we did – nothing but a face mask between us and the enemy.'

I drew a breath. Sharp.

'Oh, Peg, I'm so sorry.'

I couldn't name what I felt. There was sadness, but there were other things, to do with regret. I wanted Gwen to keep talking so I could stop remembering, but Lotte hung there between us. Lotte *had* marched towards death, willingly, her face uncovered so that death would know her.

'There should be a memorial for women like Lotte,' Gwen finally said, her voice lower, her words slower. When the refreshments came, Gwen poured milk into her teacup and put a slice of lemon into mine. She checked to see how steeped the tea was. 'Every town will have a memorial for the men,' she said, lifting the pot to pour. 'But I don't think there will be one for the women.'

I watched my cup fill with tea. Noticed the slice of lemon rise to the top and sit like a raft on the surface. The steam rose and I sent a gentle breath towards it.

'Their sacrifice was not glorious or noble,' Gwen continued. 'It was women's work and it was just expected.' She sipped her tea, then relaxed back into her chair. She was happy with her observation, but she did not understand what happened to Lotte and I didn't have the heart to explain.

'Anyway,' said Gwen, after a minute's silence, 'some exciting news. I have it on good authority that a general election is going to be called. Any day now, according to my aunt.'

'How wonderful for your aunt,' I said.

'What's that supposed to mean?'

'Do you think she'll cast her vote with my interests in mind? With Rosie's or Tilda's?'

'I thought we'd moved past this argument,' Gwen said. 'It will happen, Peg. Before you know it, we'll be walking arm in arm to the ballot box.'

'How will it happen, Gwen? You might not get to vote in the next election, but once you turn thirty your right is guaranteed. Mine is not. My God, you're absolutely right that women have earned it, and the papers are saying it too. But how many of the women who've made bombs and driven buses have property or a degree? They've earned it, all right, but only your lot will get to cast a ballot.'

'Why are you so angry, Peg?'

How could she not know? 'I want what you take for granted, and for a few moments I thought I might get it, but I didn't. I couldn't jump all the bloody hurdles, and now I realise it isn't just Somerville I'm locked out of, it's everything.'

She reached her hand towards mine and tried to compose her face into something resembling sympathy. I pulled away.

'Your little project has failed and it's clearly of no consequence to you, but I'm no better off than I was, Gwen, and I'm bloody furious.'

'My little project?'

'It was cruel,' I said.

'Oh, you were perfectly content before I put the idea in your head – is that what you're saying? You'd never given Somerville a second thought? I suppose you lined your boat with books because it kept you warmer in winter, not because you liked to read, or gave a jot about the ideas that were in them.'

I hated her then, her privilege and advantage, her debater's tongue.

'They do keep it warmer,' I said, my tone unyielding.

'I know,' she said. 'I wouldn't have said it otherwise.'

We stared at each other. Stony-faced, both of us. Each with a hand on our teacup, ready to lift it to our lips, to sip. But the gesture would concede something. The first to move would lose the argument.

Her lips twitched. Mine didn't.

'You win,' she said, the twitch turning to a broad smile. She brought her teacup to her lips, sipped. 'Drink up, Peg, or it will go cold.'

I didn't feel like I'd won. I watched as Gwen poured another cup. I watched her break a scone and was annoyed by the butter and the cream. The expense. The fact she would leave the remnants on the china plate when she'd had her fill. I remembered the first time I'd seen her at the Examination Schools. She'd walked ahead, opening doors without knocking. I'd followed, glad for the shield of her confidence. A little resentful, but that passed. She made sure of it, and the war made it easy – we were all in the same boat, everyone kept saying, and it did feel that way, most of the time. But now the war was over and the likes of Gwen would no longer be expected to muck in with the likes of me. The likes of Gwen would line up to cast their vote because the likes of me had proven we could do the work of men.

Thank God we did not hate each other as much as we imagined, Gilbert Murray wrote in his Oxford Pamphlet. Thank God, I'd thought.

But I hated Gwen now.

I let my tea go cold. 'I have to go,' I said, pushing my chair back and standing.

'You haven't eaten your scone.'

I looked at the scone, high and generous, and imagined how good it would taste with the butter, with the cream and jam. In that moment, all I wanted to do was sit back down and laugh, watch the anxiety fall from Gwen's face and let her top up my cup with hot tea. All I wanted was to eat that scone and forgive Gwen for everything.

But I couldn't. I put on my coat and scarf, and I checked my hat. 'I need to get to the Covered Market before I go back to the Press,' I said.

She looked at her wristwatch. 'Do you really have to go back?'

'It's my job, Gwen. Not a bloody hobby.'

$\sim$

I let the tears fall freely as I walked towards the Covered Market. I didn't wipe them away or look down when people noticed. I was sick of pretending to be content. I wanted so much more and I felt like I'd been swindled.

'Are you all right, dear?' An old woman, chapped hands holding a full basket with bruised fruit on top. I imagined the cheap cuts of meat and day-old bread below.

'I want more,' I said.

She shook her head a little and put her free hand on my arm. 'Thank God for that,' she said. 'I thought you'd just found out you'd lost someone. Some have, you know. Terrible timing. Makes it worse, somehow.' She gave me a sad smile and kept walking.

I peered in at the Covered Market. It was decorated in flags and bunting, and I could hear a booming voice hawking victory buns. I wondered if grief would be worse when the papers were full of peace. I was overcome with shame.

I wiped my face and followed the booming voice through the Covered Market. I bought six victory buns, then walked back towards the teahouse.

I wished I'd stayed with Gwen to eat the scones; the cost alone should have glued me to my seat. *What do you want?* she might have asked. I would have shrugged, and she might have told me to stop sulking. But she would have persisted; she would have found a way to get the truth out of me. If I'd stayed to eat the scones, I thought, I would have let her. I hurried a little, in case she'd waited.

I was out of breath when I got there. The chandelier lit up the interior like a stage, and I saw two old women sitting where Gwen and I had sat. The scones had been cleared – the jam, the cream, the butter. There were sandwiches in their place. I walked the rest of the way to Jericho, my head lowered and my mind on the answers I might have given Gwen if I'd stayed, if she'd waited. But the truth of what I wanted changed with every turn in the road. By the time I reached the Press, all I knew for sure was that I wanted much more than I could possibly have.

'Who doesn't?' I said aloud.

~

At the end of the day, we gathered on *Staying Put*. Rosie fed us supper, and when the meal was over I brought out the buns.

'Hot cross buns,' said Maude, frowning slightly.

'Victory buns,' I said.

Rosie picked one up and broke it open. 'Smells like a hot cross bun.'

She helped Old Mrs Rowntree put a bit in her mouth. 'What do you think, Ma?'

We waited, as we had to now, for Old Mrs Rowntree to find the words. When they came they were barely audible. 'Tastes like a hot cross bun,' she said.

Maude picked up her own bun and broke it open. She offered one half to Jack.

'It's over,' she said.

Jack said nothing, but he looked into her eyes and she let him. After a while she nodded, very slowly. 'It's over,' she said again. He seemed unable to look away from her, and unable to agree.

'There's one bun each,' I said.

We ate and drank our tea. We gossiped about people from the Press.

'Aggie's coming back next week,' I told Rosie.

'That will be nice,' she said.

'She's not happy about it.'

'No more overalls and less bloody pay,' said Maude with Aggie's attitude. She reached for the last bun and I pulled the plate away.

'Is Bastiaan joining us?' asked Rosie.

He wasn't. We'd agreed. We both needed a few days to think. I shook my head.

'Who?' asked Maude.

'Gwen. Maybe. I don't know.' But it was dark and drizzling and she'd have to bribe the porter to let her out at this time. She wouldn't come now.

We finished our buns and drained the teapot. The last bun sat there, conspicuous. When we returned to *Calliope*, I wrapped it in a napkin and put it in the bread bin.

~

I woke early the next day and let Maude sleep while I made our morning coffee. I heard steps on the gangplank, heavy and sure. Unmistakably Gwen's. I took the victory bun from the bread bin, sprinkled it with a little water and put it in the range.

Her cheeks were rosy with cold. Behind her, the day was barely lit and I realised she must have left Oriel in the dark.

'Gwen,' I said. 'I'm sorry.'

'I know you are,' she said. 'And that's why I'm here, so you can apologise.' She saw my expression and quickly added, 'I'm sorry too. Now, let that be the end of it.'

I ushered her in, took her coat and hung it over mine. I watched her remove her gloves and hat and put them on the end of the table. I think she knew I was watching her, and so she dragged out each action. So like Tilda, I thought. It was one good reason not to hate her.

'You know, Peg,' she said, looking around *Calliope*, her brow in a serious furrow, 'I think you should get more books.'

'More books! Why on earth would I need more books?'

She looked at me and I saw a smile straining against the serious set of her face.

'Because it's bloody freezing in here.'

∿

The bun had warmed and filled *Calliope* with its spicy smell. I placed it on one of Ma's good plates and put it in front of Gwen.

'Is it Easter?'

'It's a victory bun. I bought it yesterday.'

'Especially for me?' She was being falsely coy.

'Yes, actually. I shouldn't have left you at the Clarendon.'

'You shouldn't have left the scones – they were delicious.'

'That is the biggest of many regrets.'

'I hate regrets.' She took something from her bag and put it on the table. I recognised the napkin. It fell away to reveal a scone. 'Pop it in the oven,' she said.

I did. 'Pity you didn't steal a little butter.'

Gwen placed a paper box on the table between us. It was something Maude might have made, and I remembered Gwen asking how it was done.

'I'm not so privileged that I don't appreciate the value of butter,' she said.

I opened the box. Two small rounds of butter. 'Oh, Gwen.'

She waved her hand. 'Pour me some coffee.'

Then an echo. 'Pour me some coffee.'

Maude was there, wrapped in the blanket we slept under. I poured three mugs of coffee, and she joined us at the table. I passed Gwen her mug, and Maude passed her the victory bun. Then Maude reached for the scone. I let her have it, and when she reached for the butter, I let her have that too. All of it.

~

Gwen walked with us to the Press.

'Halls are empty today,' she said. 'Half the girls have gone home, some to plan homecomings, some to mourn all over again. Classes are cancelled for the rest of the week.'

'Will you go home?' I asked.

'We have nothing to plan and nothing to mourn, which means,' she took my arm, 'we can eat scones for lunch every day.'

'Scones for lunch,' said Maude.

'You must join us, Maude,' said Gwen, and she squeezed my arm as if she knew I might want to object. 'Though you mustn't abandon Jack – I have it on good authority that he looks forward to his lunch hour with you.'

It was true. Rosie had told me, and I'd told Gwen, and now she was telling Maude. I watched my sister for any sign that it mattered, but she didn't blush or smile or slow her step. Though she did nod.

'I don't think Mr Hall will let us take any more extended lunch hours,' I said.

'Oh, we won't go to the Clarendon Hotel. It's so expensive. We'll stay in Jericho, perhaps the teahouse on Little Clarendon Street. Now the war is over, they'll have to get used to us Somervillians again. We'll be the advance guard.'

'*Us* Somervillians?'

'Why not?'

'Because I failed, Gwen.'

Gwen shrugged.

'Dreaming of Somerville,' said Maude.

'I thought she might be,' said Gwen.

I pulled my arm from Gwen's. 'Will you please stop talking about me as if I'm not here?'

Gwen stopped walking.

'Is it true, Peg? Do you still want to go to Somerville?'

Maude stopped walking. 'True,' she said.

I stopped walking. 'I did more than dream, if you recall. And after doing more than dream, I failed.'

'Once,' said Gwen.

'What?'

'You've failed *once*. I failed *twice*.'

'What?'

'Now you sound like Maude.' She turned to Maude. 'Sorry, Maude.' She turned back to me. 'Surely I've told you that.'

'No, Gwen. You never did.'

'I must have wanted you to think I was cleverer than I am.'

'I never thought you were cleverer than you are.'

Arched brows. Mock shock. She took my arm and we fell into step.

Chapter Fifty-Two

Christmas gifts.

Mine to him was wrapped in a section of text, uncut and unfolded.

'Uninteresting,' I said, when he started to read it. 'Just open it.'

He pulled on the string and the section fell away.

His half-smile. 'A muffler?'

'Isn't it obvious?'

He held it up. The yarn was cornflower blue, and the tension was almost perfect. Lou had made me unravel it three times. *Failure is good for you, Peg,* she'd said when I showed her my final effort.

'Put it on,' I told him.

He passed the muffler to me. 'I would like you to put it on me.'

He bent his head so I could reach over. One loop around his neck and a knot in front. It was the perfect length. I pulled him close.

His gift to me was wrapped in newsprint, but it was obviously a book. I tried to guess.

'Rudyard Kipling?'

He shook his head.

'Baudelaire?'

'Your French is not good enough,' he said.

'But you will keep teaching me.'

A tilt of his head. 'Open it.'

It was old, the red cloth was faded to brown and worn at the corners. The words on the spine were barely visible.

HOMERI

OPERA

ODYSSEAE

I–XII

The original Greek. I had an urge to throw it across the room, so instead I held it to my chest. But I couldn't soften the edge in my voice.

'I can't read it,' I said.

'You will learn,' he said.

For a few moments I was dumb, angry, confused. *Try again*, Miss Garnell had said when I returned the Greek primer. *No. An uphill battle.* Then I'd watched her draw a line through my name in the Somerville loans ledger.

I touched the muffler around Bastiaan's neck. It looked good on him.

'I would have preferred Baudelaire,' I said. My voice was softer, sadder.

'Baudelaire would have been a consolation,' he said.

After

5 *October 1920*

My dear Peggy,

The Americans have conquered us all! Ninety-five medals, forty-one of them gold. They have grown faster and stronger since the war, and the rest of us struggled to keep up. But in this struggle, we do not mind the loss. The Games have been a great tonic for Belgium. In the last days they allowed students into the stadium for free. I travelled to Antwerp and watched Paavo Nurmi win the ten-thousand-metre race. They call him the Flying Finn. I am not ashamed to tell you that I cried. I saw men from all over the world line up together and run side by side. They did not all finish as well as the Flying Finn, and some were so exhausted they stumbled and fell as they crossed the finish line. One of these men fell close to where I stood, and I could hear him gasping for air. Then another bent to help him off the ground, and I watched them embrace. It was hard not to think of other men doing the same just a few years ago. I tried to keep my head, Peggy, but I could not.

The papers have called them the Peace Games, and that is how it felt, but there were no Germans in that race, no Hungarians or Austrians or Turks. I wonder when we will forgive them.

My final exam went well. I took your advice and hired a boat on the canal the day before. I convinced two student friends to come with me, and we rowed around for an hour, getting in the way of working boats and almost tipping ourselves into the water. We agreed we would make better architects than sailors, and we made a game of testing each other for our last exam. We knew more than we thought and have all received our diplomas!

It is a good time to be an architect — some Belgian cities still look like a child's toy box: they are full of half-built structures and scattered blocks. But there are arguments about how to rebuild, and so the building is slow. Some want each building to be an exact copy of what was destroyed. Others want to forget the past and make a new Belgium. It is a struggle, I think, between remembrance and hope. I do not think they need to compete.

Which brings my letter back to the Americans. They are helping to rebuild the library of the university in Louvain. Lotte's library. An American architect has made the designs, and it will be larger and even more beautiful than before. There are many jobs for new graduates, and my professors encouraged me to apply. But for a while I could not.

It was my dead, Peggy. This opportunity in Louvain disturbed them. I could not think of the new library without imagining the blackened and bloodstained rubble of the old. Not all my dead returned (most seem quite settled at St Sepulchre's), but there is a boy who visits most nights. And there is a woman. She sometimes has the face of Lotte. I decided it was my reluctance that made them restless. Louvain has not healed, and the university library is perhaps its biggest wound.

So I applied for a position and have just received notice I am successful — the letter is in front of me as I write mine to you. It says I will be part of the team responsible for detailed drafting of the belltower. I do not expect it to be enough to quiet my dead completely, but it is a start.

The library will take many years, Peggy, but I have already begun imagining it full of books — they are in Flemish and French and German, and there will be many in English. Your universities have donated them. I hope, when it is built, it will be another reason for you to come.

Remember me to Gwen and pass on my congratulations. It is, as you said in your last letter, about bloody time.

Yours,

Bastiaan

P.S. The next time you visit our friends at St Sepulchre's, please give my regards to Mme Wood, and make an offering of ginger beer to the boys. It may help, it may not, but I like to think of you there.

~

I folded the letter with care. It had arrived the week before and already the creases were wearing, and the words caught within them were beginning to fade. I returned it to the envelope and slipped it between the pages of my copy of Homer's *Odysseae*. The book was worn from handling and swollen with letters. Some in English, others in French – Bastiaan continued to tutor me. I returned *Odysseae* to its place beside my bed and went to stand by the window.

People hurried beneath the arch of the Press building on Walton Street as they had for nearly a hundred years. Men and women of Jericho, boys and girls who'd sat in classrooms at St Barnabas just months before. Fathers and sons, mothers and daughters; three generations from some Jericho families. They were printers, compositors, typefounders and bindery girls.

I'd chosen a plain navy skirt and a white blouse with a ribbon of burgundy sewn along the square neckline. No collar, no embroidery. Black brogues sat at the end of my bed. The smell of shoe polish filled the room. I stood in my stockinged feet. I was waiting for Maude.

She appeared on the street wearing the apricot dress, the hem a little shorter, the neckline refashioned into a curve that showed off her collarbones. She walked ahead of Rosie and Tilda but held tight to Jack. A handsome couple.

She stopped where I'd always stopped. She looked up to the windows on the first floor of Somerville College. I waved, but she didn't wave back – I was invisible behind the glass, behind the reflection of the morning light, of Walton Street, of Jericho. But she continued to look towards my window, and when her lips moved I breathed the words with her: 'Read the books, not bind them.'

Some things have to be voiced over and over, they have to be shared and understood, they have to echo through time until they become truth and not just fancy.

Tilda and Rosie caught up. They followed Maude's gaze and Tilda smiled. It was a pre-war smile, a smile Ma would have recognised. It had been a long time, and I'd forgotten how beautiful she was. I turned from the window and sat on the end of the bed. The springs protested, and I had an image of other women sitting here to put on their shoes. I tied the laces, stood and went to the door. As I reached for the gown that hung on the hook, my heart leapt. It was a scholar's gown – longer and fuller than the commoner's gown worn by most undergraduates. I'd earned it. I'd learnt the Greek, and for a second time I'd been given a scholarship. *You've read your way from Jericho to Oxford*, Gwen had teased. *From one side of Walton Street to the other*, I'd replied. From bindery girl to scholar, I thought. I draped the gown over my town clothes.

It had been a week since I'd been given the gown. A week since the porter had opened the door to this room and apologised that the bed was a little soft and the fireplace slow to draw. It could be a little noisy, he'd said, being right on Walton Street. The Press workers gave no heed to the needs of students.

The only mirror in the room was above the fireplace. It was just big enough to see my face and the pleats at the shoulder of my gown. I smoothed my hair – it was still a surprise. I'd had it cut in the new style, just below my ears. It suited me, everyone said. *You look completely different*, Tilda had commented.

I turned back to the window. They were still there, Maude still looking up, her mouth repeating the same phrase over and over. Making a song of it. Tilda and Rosie moved as one to encourage Maude and Jack across the road. I turned and left my room.

'They've waited a long time for this day,' said the old porter as I came into the lodge.

'Decades, some of them,' I said.

'They were pretty young things like you when I first met them, and I barely recognised some of the matrons who popped in to say hello this morning. Three of them were grandmothers!'

'Grandmothers,' I repeated. The meaning of it sinking in.

'You must be grateful you won't have to wait that long, Miss Jones.'

I wasn't sure *grateful* was the right word.

~

The women were gathering.

'A murder of crows,' said Maude.

'No offence to our very own crow,' said Tilda, wrapping her arm around my billowing black wings.

They moved closer to me as we walked towards the Sheldonian Theatre, as if my gown might afford them entry. They had passed it often enough, but rarely had any of them had reason to walk beneath the busts of the bearded philosophers. Those stony men were the gatekeepers, and the gates had been closed to the likes of us.

'Gwen,' said Maude.

And there she was, being ushered into formation by Vice-Principal Alice Bruce. Gwen wore a long black gown with a white-trimmed hood and the four-cornered soft cap of a graduate. When she saw us, she broke ranks.

'Isn't it just wonderful?' She wrapped her wings around mine.

'A murder of crows,' said Maude, again. 'Just wonderful.'

'Which reminds me,' said Gwen, 'I've changed my mind about a good marriage and all that. I'm going into politics instead.'

'When did this happen?' I asked.

'Minutes ago, when Miss Bruce told us to get into line.' She took hold of my hands. 'You were right, Peg. It's my bloody duty – to you lot.' She looked at Rosie, Tilda, Maude. 'What makes my vote more important than yours?'

'Miss Lumley!' shouted Vice-Principal Bruce. 'Do you think we have not waited long enough?'

Gwen let go of my hands and took a step back. She looked me up and down. 'Town in a gown,' she said. 'You'll be marching into the Sheldonian before you know it, Peg.'

Gwen found her place among the women of Somerville, St Hilda's, St Hugh's and Lady Margaret Hall. There must have been more than a hundred women standing between the Bodleian Library and the Sheldonian Theatre. Principal Penrose found her place, as did Vice-Principal Bruce, Miss Garnell and the principal of St Hilda's. They all stood in line – students, professors, principals, all eager to receive their degrees.

The courtyard between the two ancient buildings suddenly reminded me of the quadrangle of the Press. The milling of women, like the milling of men six years earlier.

I looked around at the women arranged in their lines. Some were grey-haired, their faces lined with life. Others were young, the memory of their final exams still fresh. How many had grieved for fathers and brothers and lovers? How many had grieved for sons? Which of these women had been nursed back to health? Which had buried a mother, a sister, a friend? How many were missing?

They are the survivors, I thought, of war and influenza. And now they have triumphed over tradition. They are smiling; excited for a future they have earned, and know they deserve.

From somewhere down the line, an instruction was given. The women turned as one towards the open doors of the Sheldonian. They fell silent. They stood tall. I watched them march into the theatre to receive their degrees.

Author's Note

The idea for this story came to me in the archives of Oxford University Press (OUP). I was searching for details that would lend truth to another novel I was writing: *The Dictionary of Lost Words*, about the Oxford English Dictionary. I found detail aplenty, in photographs and news clippings, administrative records, and in the *Clarendonian*, a wonderful in-house publication begun in 1919 and designed to give workers at the Press an opportunity to reconnect with their Press family and the broader Jericho community after four years of war.

Within the pages of the *Clarendonian,* Press staff remembered the fallen, and they were encouraged to reflect on their own experiences of the war, though very few did – in 1919, it seemed, most people wanted to put the experience behind them. Instead, there were advertisements for performances by the Press's dramatic society, band and choir; reports about the success of their sporting teams; a notice about the upcoming flower and vegetable show, which would showcase produce grown at Port Meadow; and updates on the preparation of a war memorial for the forty-five Press men who had fought and died for their country. But most pages in the *Clarendonian* were dedicated to biographies of Press staff, past and present. Apprentices and foremen from the composing room to the foundry penned funny, articulate and compassionate anecdotes about themselves and others. This is what I love about archives – the voices of people whose names will never end up in a book of history, telling me what history felt like. I hit the jackpot with the *Clarendonian*, but something was missing; something is always missing.

I knew that dozens of women had worked on the 'girls' side' of the bindery during the Great War, but they were neither authors nor subjects of biographies in the *Clarendonian*. When I searched through the rest of the archives for their voices, I found very little. There were a couple of black-and-white images of women and girls sitting in neat rows along long benches, folding large sheets of printed pages. There was a silent film made in 1925 by the Federation of British Industries, about the making of a book at Oxford University Press – in it, a woman gathers sections with such rhythm and grace it seems like she's dancing. And there was a farewell address to the Press Controller, Mr Hart, on the occasion of his retirement. When I turned the pages of this farewell address, I came across the bindery girls – forty-seven of them, from Kathleen Ford to Hannah Dawson. They had signed their names, each in her own characteristic script. It was proof they existed.

That was all I had, but it was enough. I started to imagine a woman dancing along the gathering bench. I wondered what book she was gathering onto her arm, and then I wondered if she'd stopped to read any of it. Suddenly, I had a character.

This story is fiction, and all its main characters have sprung from my imagination, but the places they live, work, volunteer and study are real. Oxford University Press and Somerville College still stand where they stood during the Great War, and some of the people important to those institutions are depicted in my story. In particular, Mr Charles Cannan, Mr Horace Hart and Mr Frederick Hall of OUP; and Miss Pamela Bruce, Vice-Principal Alice Bruce and Principal Emily Penrose of Somerville College. The principal's address that Peggy hears in the novel is taken almost directly from the speech given by Principal Penrose at the time. The Somerville entrance exam questions are taken from an actual exam set a few years after the war.

The army base camp at Étaples, in France, was also a real place. It housed up to 100,000 men and could treat 22,000 men across almost twenty hospitals. It had a reputation for brutality, and the harsh punishment of enlisted men led to a mutiny in September 1917. One inciting incident was the court-martialling of four soldiers following an altercation, which began when the water was cut off while one of the soldiers was showering. In the novel, I have combined details of this incident with some others, but a soldier *was* executed for his role in that incident. His name was Private Jack Braithwaite, an Australian serving with the NZEF's 2nd Battalion Otago Regiment. Today, the only sign of the Étaples Army Base Camp is the military cemetery, with its haunting cenotaph and 11,504 white headstones laid in neat avenues across manicured lawns; 10,773 of these graves are from World War I, and the vast majority belong to men from Commonwealth forces, including the United Kingdom, Canada, Australia, New Zealand, South Africa and India. But Étaples is also the final resting place for twenty women killed in air raids or by disease, including Canadian nurses Katherine Maud Mary MacDonald, Gladys Maude Wake and Margaret Lowe. Another 658 of these headstones commemorate German soldiers, many of whom were nursed in the German ward as prisoners of war.

A note on the use of women's literature and visual art. The vast majority of contemporaneous commentary, literature and artistic representations of World War I was produced by men and inevitably focused on the experiences of those who had fought and died. When the gaze moved to women, it tended to settle on those who waited and grieved. In writing this story, I wanted to focus instead on women who worked and women who were forced to flee their homes. As well as turning to archives and histories, I sought out the commentary, literature and art of women who lived through the war. These works were almost always produced by well-educated women from middle- or upper-class backgrounds – those with the time and means to write and paint. Despite the inherent bias of this body of work towards women of privilege, much of it was enormously useful.

A few of these works deserve particular acknowledgement: Vera Brittain's memoir *Testament of Youth* provided insight into the experience of VADs (Voluntary Aid Detachment members) at the army base in Étaples, as did Penny Starns's *Sisters of the Somme: True Stories from a First World War Field Hospital*. Catherine Reilly's anthology of poetry written by women during World War I, *Scars upon My Heart*, revealed women's diverse and often complex experiences of war – experiences largely ignored by general poetry anthologies of World War I. *The Diary of Virginia Woolf, Volume 1: 1915–1919* was fundamental to my understanding that war, once established, is accommodated by those who are not fighting or fleeing or grieving – it is there in the background, but life goes on. Finally, the paintings of Australian artist Isobel Rae conveyed an emotional experience of the army base at Étaples that I found irresistible. Many of Rae's drawings are now held in the archives of the Australian War Memorial. They whisper rather than shout, capturing a perspective that only a woman behind the lines and at the bedside might have had – a perspective considered irrelevant when Rae applied for a role as a war artist and was rejected on account of her sex. One of her drawings depicts the mutiny at Étaples. This mutiny is also referred to in Vera Brittain's memoir, but went unreported at the time and was subject to the *Official Secrets Act*. Both Iso Rae and Vera Brittain seem to have contravened the act. I suspect Iso Rae would have enjoyed the company of my character Tilda Taylor, and so I have made them friends – an artistic decision I hope Iso Rae would be happy with.

A note on the books mentioned in this story. They were not sought or chosen with any great care. Rather, they presented themselves in the course of my work, just as they present themselves to Peggy in the course of hers. As I turned the pages of the historical archives, these books made themselves known. In each case, there was something that piqued my interest, something that was echoed within the story I had begun to tell.

The books play themselves. Whether cameo or main part, they can all be found on a shelf in the Bodleian Library. The University of Oxford has had the right to print books since 1586, and while complete records do not exist for all books printed and bound at OUP since that time, I have found sufficient reference to those depicted here in various sources, including *The History of Oxford University Press* by Gadd, Eliot and Louis (eds) (2014) and the *Oxford University Press General Catalogue* issued by Humphrey Milford (1916) though actually compiled by May Wedderburn Cannan, poet and second daughter of Charles Cannan. Despite her considerable efforts, she is not acknowledged for the outcome. In short, if Peg folds the pages, then the pages were folded at Oxford University Press more or less at that time in history.

There are five books that deserve particular attention. They give their titles to each part of the story and were there from the beginning. As I wrote, I imagined Peggy folding their pages, gathering their sections or sewing the whole together. Then I imagined her reading them.

Like Peggy, I came to these books completely ignorant. But by engaging with them – with their form and content, and what they might have meant at that time and in that place – I could not help but be influenced by them, and therefore, neither could Peg. In this way, Peggy's story is folded around them. If you, too, want to know them a little better, here is a brief biography of each.

Shakespeare's England: An Account of the Life & Manners of His Age

Published in two volumes in 1916 to coincide with the three hundredth anniversary of Shakespeare's death. *Shakespeare's England* is a collection of essays written by male scholars from diverse disciplines including law, medicine, science, religion, the arts, folklore, agriculture and the book industry. In each case, the author reflects on Shakespeare's writings in the context of life as it was lived in Elizabethan England. *Shakespeare's England* was first conceived in 1905 by Sir Walter Raleigh. Production then fell to Sir Sidney Lee and finally to Charles Onions (then co-editor of the Oxford English Dictionary). Concerns about its progress were ever-present and many doubted it would be published in time for the Bard's tercentenary.

The Oxford Pamphlets on World Affairs

During 1914 and 1915 Oxford University Press published a series of eighty-six pamphlets designed to inform, stimulate and influence debate around the war. Politicians, academics and public intellectuals (all men, as far as I can tell) wrote about all manner of topics in relation to the war, including the causes of war; the right and wrong of conflict; geopolitical influences and outcomes; issues around trade; theology and war; European obligations to Belgium; German motivations for war; and poetry. Peggy engages with four of these pamphlets: 'War Against War' by AD Lindsay (1914), 'Thoughts on War' by Gilbert Murray (1914), 'How Can War Ever Be Right?' by Gilbert Murray (1914), and 'Might Is Right' by Sir Walter Raleigh (1914).

A Book of German Verse

Oxford University Press regularly publishes books of verse from England and internationally. In 1916, a new edition of *The Oxford Book of German Verse* became controversial. How could a British press publish the poetry of Germany when so many British men were being killed by German guns? Some may have seen it as unethical, unpatriotic and in poor taste. Oxford University Press stood by its decision to publish the work but removed 'Oxford' from the title. *A Book of German Verse: From Luther to Liliencron*, edited by HG Fiedler, was the result.

Homeri, Opera Tomvs III: Odysseae Libros I–XII Continens

Oxford University Press has been publishing the Oxford Classical Texts series since the late 1890s. This series contains Ancient Greek and Latin literature in its original languages. The books are published primarily for students of the classics, and prefaces and footnotes are traditionally presented in Latin with no English commentary or translations. In this story, Peggy folds the pages of the second edition of *Homeri, Opera Tomvs III: Odysseae Libros I–XII Continens*, edited by Thomas W Allen and published in 1917. We might translate this title as *Homer's Odyssey, Books 1–12*.

The Anatomy of Melancholy

Written by Robert Burton and first published in 1621, *The Anatomy of Melancholy* is a book of extraordinary eccentricity. The full title is *The Anatomy of Melancholy, What it is: with all the Kinds, Causes, Symptoms, Prognostickes, and Several Cures of it. In three Main Partitions with their Several Sections, Members, and Subsections. Philosophically, Medicinally, Historically, Opened and Cut Up*.

It is a book about melancholy but it is also about literature, philosophy, theology, psychology and myth. The length of the title tells us something about the author. Burton, a fellow of Oxford University, poured himself and his reading into this book over a lifetime – 'I write of Melancholy, by being busy to avoid Melancholy,' he writes in his introduction. In his efforts to manage his own melancholy, Burton revised his book five times, always adding, never taking anything out, so that the version published by Oxford University Press in 1918 ran to nearly 1500 pages. At the heart of this book is the belief that melancholy is part of being human: 'No man living is free,' Burton wrote. And no woman either.

Acknowledgements

I acknowledge the Kaurna and Peramangk peoples on whose traditional and unceded lands this book was written. They were the first storytellers in this place I call home, and their stories echo through the long history of this country. We need only listen, in order to hear.

To the people who make my sentences better, gratitude is barely adequate. At Affirm Press, thank you, Ruby Ashby-Orr, for your emotional intelligence, your calm and steady hand and your sheer brilliance as an editor. Thank you, Martin Hughes, for understanding the story I was trying to tell. Thank you, Vanessa Pellatt, for your clear eyes and precision; Helen Cumberbatch, for double-checking the facts; and Emma Schwartz, Julian Welch and Armelle Davies, for proof-reading. I am enormously grateful for the editorial input of Clara Farmer and Amanda Waters at Chatto & Windus in the UK, and Susanna Porter and Sydney Shiffman at Ballantine Books in the US. Your generous and insightful feedback is woven all through this story.

Thank you to all the people who have ushered this book into the world and made it look good – including Keiran Rogers, Laura

McNicol Smith, Bonnie van Dorp, Stephanie Bishop-Hall and everyone from Affirm Press, as well as cover artists Andy Warren (Australia), Kris Potter (UK) and Belina Huey (US).

I am particularly grateful to the people who have held me to account for the way I write about particular lived experiences, including autism and echolalia, and the experience of being an identical twin. Thank you, Carol Peschke, Eli Cohn and Olivia Nicoll.

Enormous gratitude to early readers of this book, especially to Tegan Bennett Daylight – your insights regarding the writer as well as the writing are something to behold. Thank you, Shannon McCune, for caring but never sparing the necessary critique. A huge e-hug to my lockdown Writing Cluster – Alison Rooke, Tee O'Neill, Amanda Skelton, Gabrielle Coslovich and Sally Bothroyd. And to all the good people at Affirm Press who have peeked at the unpolished pages of my manuscript and provided perfect gems of feedback – Grace Breen, Susie Kennewell, Wendy Sutherland and Laura Franks – thank you all.

A special thanks to Linda Kaplan, from Kaplan/DeFiore Rights, for championing my work on the international stage.

It would not have been possible to write this book without the knowledge and generosity of the following people. To Peter Zajicek, bookbinder and Senior Conservator at the State Library of South Australia – thank you for sharing your memories and expertise, for showing me the processes involved in binding a book the old-fashioned way and for patiently teaching me how to fold the pages. Thank you for finding a pdf copy of *Women in the Bookbinding Trade* by Mary Van Kleeck (1913). The fact it was researched and authored by women makes it extraordinary for its time. The fact you bound it with board and cloth to make it easier for me to read makes it a gift. Also, to Lee Hayes, curator of the brilliant University of Adelaide online exhibition *Cover to Cover: Exposing the Bookbinder's*

Ancient Craft – thank you for bringing it all together and then explaining it all over again in person. To Dr Martin Maw, Archivist at Oxford University Press – this is the second time you have helped me to get the history right. Thank you for always answering my emails, for welcoming me (again) into the archives of that grand building on Walton Street, for your chapter contributions to *The History of Oxford University Press*, and for recommending I read Mick Belson's wonderful book *On the Press*, and May Wedderburn Cannan's book *Grey Ghosts and Voices*. Thank you also for sitting with me and talking through the history of OUP and its people, and for the context you wove around it – Jericho, the war, and all the detail that makes history come alive. Finally, to Kate O'Donnell, archivist at Somerville College, University of Oxford – thank you for your wonderful online resources detailing the history of Somerville College during World War I and for inviting me to visit the college. It was the greatest pleasure to walk with you around the grounds and through the library, and I am incredibly grateful for the efforts you made to locate exam papers, speeches, letters and maps.

While I cannot tell you who they are, there are other archivists, librarians, curators and enthusiasts whose passion and knowledge have enriched this story, and there are institutions and streams of funding that make their quiet but important work possible. Thank you to Oxford University Press; Somerville College; the Bodleian Library; the Oxfordshire History Centre; the Jericho Centre online (jerichocentre.org.uk); the Historic Narrowboat Club (hnbc.org.uk); the London Canal Museum; the Imperial War Museum, London; the Military Cemetery in Étaples; the State Library of South Australia; the Australian War Memorial; and the Barr Smith Library at the University of Adelaide.

An extra-special thanks to Donna Adkinson (much loved cousin and interpreter extraordinaire) for making sure I didn't get lost in France and interpreting menus and tourist information boards relating to the British army base in Étaples. Thanks also to Carly Adkinson for help with general research (punting in Oxford being a particular highlight).

For the kindness of strangers, I am indebted to the narrowboat owners on the Oxford canal who were happy to speak to a nosy stranger about their life afloat. A special thanks to Lorraine and to Maffi for so generously inviting me onto their narrowboats and allowing me to take notes and pictures. Thanks also to Julian Dutton for his wonderful book *Water Gypsies: A History of Life on Britain's Rivers and Canals.*

The following people and places have supported the writing of this book by providing a space to write, refuge during research trips, discussion, validation, celebration and distraction: Varuna, the National Writers' House; all the good people who keep the coffee coming at Sazón and Lady Luck; Nicola Williams; Jo and Don Brooks; Lisa Harrison; Ali Elder; Suzanne Verrall; Andrea and Krista Brydges; Anne Beath; Lou-Belle Barrett; Vanessa Iles; Jane Lawson; Rebekah Clarkson; David Washington; Jolie and Mark Thomas; Margie and Greg Sarre; Suzie Riley; Karen and Doug in Port Elliot.

To my parents, Peggy and Islwyn Williams, thank you for always believing I could do this. To my marvellous mother-outlaw, Mary McCune, thank you for listening to all the ideas and for sage advice. To Aidan and Riley, thank you for taking the writing stuff for granted and keeping life real – I love you both to bits.

And to Shannon, my trusted reader, personal assistant, driver, therapist, grower of flowers that delight and food that nourishes, my deepest love and biggest fan. I could probably do this without you, but I wouldn't want to.

Finally, to the women and girls who have folded, gathered and sewn the books. I honour you.

THE BINDERY

Image of signatures from bindery staff on the occasion of Mr Horace Hart's retirement in 1915. Reprinted by permission of the Secretary to the Delegates of Oxford University Press

About the Author

Pip Williams was born in London, grew up in Sydney and now calls the Adelaide Hills home. She is the author of the international number one bestseller *The Dictionary of Lost Words*, described by *The Times* as 'an extraordinary, charming novel'. It was also a *New York Times* bestseller, a Reese Witherspoon Book Club pick and has been translated into over thirty languages to worldwide acclaim. Pip's second novel, *The Bookbinder of Jericho*, sprang from her discovery of archival footage of women who worked in the bindery of Oxford University Press during the early twentieth century. When she tried to find out more about them, there was almost nothing. Despite their important role in the production of books, barely a word has been written about them until now.